THE BELIAL FALL
A BELIAL SERIES NOVEL

R.D. BRADY

SCOTTISH SEOUL PUBLISHING, LLC

BOOKS BY R.D. BRADY

The Belial Series (in order)
The Belial Stone
The Belial Library
The Belial Ring
Recruit: A Belial Series Novella
The Belial Children
The Belial Origins
The Belial Search
The Belial Guard
The Belial Warrior
The Belial Plan
The Belial Witches
The Belial War
The Belial Fall
The Belial Sacrifice

Stand-Alone Books
Runs Deep

Hominid

The A.L.I.V.E. Series
B.E.G.I.N.
A.L.I.V.E.
D.E.A.D.

Be sure to sign up for R.D.'s mailing list to be the first to hear when she has a new release and receive a free short story!

"Hatred is gained as much by good works as by evil."
-Niccolo Macchiavelli, The Prince

"Everyone has his own idea of good and evil and must choose to follow the good and fight evil as he conceives them. That would be enough to make the world a better place."
- Pope Francis, 2013, Interview by La Repubblica's founder, Eugenio Scalfari

PROLOGUE

ROME, ITALY,

1099 A.D.

The meeting was not going well. Pope John Anglicus had known it was going to be a difficult one. Change did not come easily to most people. With the Roman Catholic Church, it seemed even more difficult. But the Pope was dedicated to making at least some small inroads.

"The issue of indulgences must be addressed. Jesus saw no reason for money to determine a person's worth. He saw the opposite. In His name, we should follow His example. The indulgences should be disallowed."

The Bishop of Padua stood. He was a short, round man with only a fringe of hair. He usually wore a brown frock, giving him the appearance of a monk, while performing his Church duties. But John had it on good authority that he had a second wardrobe that would rival a crown prince's. The Pope nodded to him, allowing him to speak.

"Your Holiness, what you say is true. However, the indulgences do bring in money that allows us to continue our good works. Many of us fear that without that money, our charitable abilities will be greatly restricted."

The Pope stared at the Bishop, then pointedly looked at his right hand, where four rings encrusted with jewels adorned his chubby fingers. The Bishop's cheeks flamed red. He quickly sat down. The Bishop was well known for his "charitable" works, his favorite charity being himself. But the Bishop was also powerful within the Church. And the Pope, while omnipotent in the eyes of his followers, was not viewed as such by the other high-ranking members of the Church's hierarchy. Still, changes needed to be made.

Pain shot through the Pope's midsection. John grunted, his hand flying to his stomach.

"Your Holiness?" Ignatius, the Pope's lead guard, stepped forward, a frown on his face.

John waved him back. "I'm fine. Breakfast does not seem to have agreed with me."

"Perhaps this would be a good time to adjourn. Your procession will begin within the hour," Ignatius said.

John nodded. "Very well. I ask that you all think upon my words. We will meet again next week to discuss the issue of indulgences further."

The cardinals bowed in John's direction before quickly taking their leave. John stayed where he was until the room was cleared of all but Ignatius and Lucia, his servant.

Ignatius closed the door after the last priest had left. He stood in front of it, his arms crossed over his chest. "We are clear."

Lucia hurried over to John's side. "You are doing too much," she chastised, reaching for John's arm to help him out of his chair.

John sighed, letting Lucia pull him up. The action caused the pillow he held in his lap to fall away, revealing his large, or more accurately, *her* large stomach.

"You will not be able to hide the child much longer. You are taking too many risks."

John nodded as she clutched her friend's arm. She and Lucia had grown up together. Lucia had been the daughter of her parents' servant. And the Pope's given name was indeed John. Her father had been so angered that his wife had given him a daughter that he had refused to change the name he had chosen.

But the name had served John well. She had kept her hair short and enrolled in school, an act forbidden to her gender. Lucia had been her accomplice, binding her breasts and tailoring clothes to fit her other persona.

Years of study and toil had paid off when she had reached the dream she had had since she was a child: to become Pope.

She had no illusion of making the Church an egalitarian bastion. But she knew in this position she could begin the changes that one day would recognize the importance of women in the eyes of God.

John grunted as pain rippled across her stomach. She folded over, taking a deep breath.

"What is it? Is it the babe?" Lucia asked.

Ignatius strode across the room, making as if to sweep John off her feet. She straightened, stepping back. "No. The two of you are worrying like old hens. It is the eggs that did not agree with me. The babe is fine and not due for two months."

"But still, you need to take care," Ignatius said.

John looked up into his eyes. When she had met Ignatius ten years ago, she thought he would be her undoing. He would reveal her secret, undo all her carefully laid plans. But he had been the opposite. He had been another pillar. With Lucia and Ignatius by her side, she had fulfilled her dreams. Now she was bringing Ignatius's child into the world. She did not regret that. Not for a moment.

But he was right. She needed to take care.

"After today, I will go into seclusion until the baby is born. We can say I have the flu, or perhaps something contagious that will keep the Church away."

Lucia clasped her hands together. "Yes. We can go to the summer cottage."

John smiled at the idea. The summer cottage. It was their home, nestled into the banks of Lake Como. John had purchased it for the three of them seven years ago. When they could, they escaped there to allow themselves to truly be themselves. It was beautiful. The sun shone against the blue waters as it rose in the morning. Flocks of heron and swans sailed its surface. Wildflowers surrounded it. John loved to sit out on the porch in the early morning, just enjoying the peace. Yes, the summer cottage was the perfect spot for their child to be born.

"All right. We will leave for the cottage first thing tomorrow morning, after I have finished up some paperwork."

"As you wish." Ignatius took her hand to his lips.

John smiled. It would be good to get away. The pressures of the papacy had been getting to her more and more, the Church teachings leaning further and further away from their origins. She needed to get the Church back to Jesus's message and to his original intention for the Church. "How long until we leave for the procession?"

"An hour," Ignatius said.

"Let us get you changed and perhaps you have time for a short nap," said Lucia.

John stared at her friend. "I am not a child, Lucia."

Lucia didn't bristle at her tone and merely stared her down, her hands on her hips. "No, but you *are* creating one. Rest when you can, my friend."

John wanted to be mad at her. But unlike others who felt the need to tell her what to do, Lucia was coming at her statements from a place of love. "Very well. I will rest."

Lucia's shoulders sagged. "Good, good."

Pain rippled across John's abdomen, but she was careful to

keep any sign of it from her face. One more day, and then she would rest. She could make it through one more day.

∽

THE NAP HAD NOT DONE much to restore John's energy. In fact, she felt even worse after it. The pain and cramping seemed to be increasing. Lucia wanted her to cancel the procession, but John knew she couldn't. Some of the cardinals were pushing back at her. She didn't think they suspected the truth of who she was, but they were waiting for an excuse to knock her down. They did not like the changes she was discussing. She did not want to give them any chance to accuse her of avoiding her duties. Besides, starting tomorrow she would have all the rest she needed.

So she'd carefully dressed in her processional robes, long and white with silver and blue embroidery lining them. Her tall papal hat she secured last, before she stepped outside, allowing Ignatius to help her onto her horse.

They wound their way through the streets from St. Peter's to the Lateran Palace. It was expected that her comings and goings were an event in Rome, even her daily commute from the church to her residence. But as horrible as she felt, she viewed this as one of her most important duties. So much of what she did was behind walls, doors, and gates. She was supposed to be the steward of the people, which meant she needed to be out amongst the people. She had seen the change come over someone when she caught their eye and gave them a nod. For people struggling to survive from day to day, the least she could do was sit straight in her saddle and give them that small glimpse of hope.

Twelve cardinals followed, but Lucia was directly behind her, walking. Her head bowed, she gave the appearance of being a submissive servant, ready for the orders of the Pope. But John could feel her gaze through her lashes. Ignatius had taken her arguments that she was fine at face value. But Lucia, she knew better. She knew John better than anyone. She was not fooled.

Ahead, Ignatius turned down the Via Sacra, the Sacred Road. It was the most direct route from St. Peter's to the Pope's residence.

John gripped the reins as pain sharper than any before rippled through her. Wetness slid between her legs. Blood began to stain her cassock. The sweat that had broken out on her forehead as she'd taken her mount now dripped down the side of her face. She bit her lip trying to contain her scream. Unconsciously, she yanked on her reins, pulling the horse to a stop as a second pain followed the previous one almost immediately. A gasp of pain burst from her lips.

Lucia gripped her leg. "Your Holiness?"

"I—" Pain stole her voice as her vision dimmed. She felt herself falling from her perch.

Lucia propped her up, keeping her from falling. "Ignatius!"

Ignatius grabbed her from Lucia before she could hit the ground. "Your Holiness!"

She gripped his tunic. "The baby," she whispered before she screamed. She could feel the child crowning. *No, no. This cannot be happening.*

Ignatius clutched her close. "We need to get her—"

"There is no time." Lucia pushed aside John's long robes, crouching in front of her. "I need your knife."

More pain lanced through John, so strong she did not care about anything happening around her. All she wanted was for the pain to stop. She pushed with everything she was worth, Ignatius holding her tightly to keep her from collapsing.

"What is wrong? What is going on?" the cardinals called behind her.

John could not answer them as pain gripped her again. She pushed. Blessedly, the pain disappeared, the pressure as well.

She sagged against Ignatius in relief.

Then the baby cried out.

Everyone in the alley went still before the mutters began, disbelief followed by anger. Fear cut through the relief brought on from the absence of pain as she read the violence and betrayal in the rising voices.

John's gaze flew to the bundle in Lucia's arms as she stood.

"A girl," Lucia said quietly.

"Get her away. They will kill her." John gripped Ignatius's arms, nodding at Lucia, who held their child. "You must them get them both away."

"Blasphemer!" came the yell from the crowd before the first rock flew.

Ignatius stared down at her, his loyalty torn. "But they will kill you."

John knew he was right, but that changed nothing. Her fate was sealed. But her daughter's, her friend's, her love's, they could all be spared.

"Leave me. I am the one they want. Save her. Save our daughter. Lucia knows what to do."

They had made a plan, one John had never thought they would have to initiate. She had delivered too early. But God did indeed work in mysterious ways. If this was His plan, then she would gladly trade her life so that her daughter could live.

Lucia cried out as a rock hit her. John pushed at Ignatius. "Go, go! Before it's too late!"

Ignatius tightened his embrace before gently releasing John to the ground. He pulled his sword with one hand, pulling on Lucia with the other. He stormed through the crowd, knocking people back.

John watched, not even having a chance to say goodbye to any of them. But it was better that way. No words would ever be enough. A rock slammed into her shoulder, another her chest. She blinked in pain. The crowd surged toward her. Cardinal Segnillio threw a rock, catching her under the eye. The rest of the cardinals joined in, their faces masks of hate. More rocks flew, so many that she could not tell who threw them or from what direction. They seemed to come from everywhere at once. Pain lanced through John, followed by a blessed numbness. Hands reached her, tearing at her garments. And then feet stomped on her, replacing the rocks.

She looked up into the eyes of a man, his eyes wild, spittle flying from his mouth as he yelled vulgarity after vulgarity.

I forgive you, she thought just as he raised his foot and stomped on her head. Then she thought of nothing at all.

～

VINCENTO CORDALIO, Bishop of Padua, raced through the streets, his heart pounding, his tunic covered in blood.

The blood of the Pope. That treacherous slut.

He shoved through the door of the Lateran Palace, pushing the door closed behind him.

"Wait, wait. Let me in." Cardinal Segnillio pushed in behind him.

Together they shoved the door closed, pulling a long piece of wood across it to secure it. Both men leaned heavily against the door, their breathing ragged. Vincento raised a shaky hand and wiped the sweat from his face. "How is this possible? She was a woman?"

"She is the Devil come to destroy the Church. We did God's work today."

Vincento looked down at the blood staining his tunic. "How did we not know?"

But he knew the answer. Bathing did not happen often, so there'd be little opportunity for someone to uncover the ruse. With clothes hiding shapes, it was possible. But how had she been able to complete her studies? She was a *woman*.

Segnillio pushed off from the door, crushing his cap in his hands. "We can never let this be found out. She must be stricken from our books. We barely survived the Great Schism. This coming so close on its heels; the Eastern churches will use it to pull more of our members."

Vincento nodded. Segnillio was right. The Great Schism of 1054 had separated the Church, removing all the Eastern Orthodox churches from the Roman Catholic Church. It had halved the Church's power. Already weakened, it would not be able to easily swallow a hit of this magnitude.

"She will be stricken, but more must be done. We must protect the Church at all costs. It is too fragile."

"How?"

Vincento paced, his heart still beating fast, but his mind moving faster. "A small group, dedicated, with ranks of spies and warriors under their control. We will identify threats and stop them before they can cause harm."

Segnillio nodded his head slowly. "Yes, but it must remain secret. The members cannot know. Most of the priests, and even the Vatican hierarchy, must not know. It will be our sacred duty to ensure this"—he sneered—"and any other situations never occur again."

Vincento extended his hand. "In God's name."

Segnillio laid his hand on top of it. "In God's name."

CHAPTER 1

ROME, ITALY

PRESENT DAY

Torches flickered in the dark caverns underneath the Vatican, causing shadows to dance along the earthen floor and the dark spaces. Over four million tourists visited the Vatican each year, but none were able to access these areas of the necropolis underneath its hallowed halls. That access was restricted to only a few who had proven their loyalty and dedication over the years.

Cardinal John Moretti walked along the ancient dirt paths, breathing in the stillness. Normally, walking down here brought him peace, being this close to Simon Peter made him feel connected to God and the Church in a way nothing else did. The Vatican had been built on the site of St. Peter's grave, although construction had not begun until the fourth century A.D. Most of the original structure had been destroyed or replaced over time, but the catacombs and trails underneath the Vatican remained untouched, at least the parts hidden from public view.

But today, he found no solace. Today, he could not get the images beamed around the world from D.C. out of his mind. The powers of Elisabeta Roccorio and Delaney McPhearson were truly terrifying. The world had breathed a sigh of relief when Roccorio had been killed. It was better for the world that she was gone.

But Delaney McPhearson still lived. The funnel of lightning and wind she displayed while keeping the agents of the U.S. government at bay were only a taste of the power she would no doubt yield at some point in the future. The world saw her as a savior of humanity, but Moretti saw her for what she truly was: the downfall of humanity, the antichrist. In the prophecies of the antichrist, it was always the same: The antichrist would be embraced as a savior, and they themselves might think of themselves as a savior before their true nature revealed itself and the world trembled at their feet.

But I will not let that happen. I will stand between McPhearson and the damage she would do.

It was his sacred duty. When he had joined the Church, he had joined a brotherhood within it, sworn to protect the Church and the papacy from all harm. Scattered throughout the world, their members had protected the Church from scandal, from danger, and sometimes from enemies within, all in the name of God. And tonight, they would allow a new member into their inner council.

John made his way slowly up the hill, bowing his head at the grave of St. Peter. Peter was a man who had taken on the mantle of building Jesus's following, paying the ultimate price for that devotion. He had spread Jesus's word to the world. None of this would have been possible without him.

But all of that was now being put at risk.

"Cardinal Moretti." A tall man with dark hair and a heavy Spanish accent stepped out of the shadows.

John inclined his head. "Cardinal Francisco."

Both men turned as three other cardinals joined them: Cardinal Antonio Ribraldi, Cardinal Luke Park, and Cardinal Paul Tegano. All the men were in their sixties, except for Tegano, who had just passed the seventy mark last week. A sixth member was decades younger than his brothers. Father Sebastian Gante was thirty-six. He was young, but he had proven his loyalty to the cause over and over again.

And the cause was no less than the protection of the papacy, and by extension, the very world. The Brotherhood rarely met. They did not like to draw attention to themselves. But the events in D.C. had forced their hand, requiring them to determine a new course of action.

John's gaze swept across each of the men. "We must decide tonight what to do about the recent events."

"What is the Pope's view?" Tegano asked.

John paused. "He has been aware of the Fallen's existence since he was made Pope, of course."

It was the Brotherhood's job to inform the Pope after his inauguration of all the hidden components of the Church that he may need to be aware of. Each Pope, going back centuries, had been aware that there were certain individuals in this world who were blessed or cursed, depending on the Pope's perspective, with extra abilities. But never before had a Pope had to publicly acknowledge their existence.

"But he is not convinced that all individuals with abilities are destined to be evil. He believes they, too, have a chance at redemption."

Ribraldi gave an inelegant snort, his large stomach joggling with the effort. "Redemption. They are Satan's soldiers. There is no saving them."

"Agreed," Moretti said. "But that is not what I have brought you here to discuss. We need to determine what is to be done about the ring bearer."

Silence descended across the space before Tegano spoke. "It is not the actual ring of Solomon she wears, is it?"

"From our reports, it does indeed seem to be."

"What does the Tome say?" Ribraldi asked.

"It's been slow reading. We only remembered we had it when Roccorio made her first announcement."

Moretti had been annoyed at how off guard they had been caught when the Fallen were so publicly revealed. They had, of course, known of the Fallen's existence for hundreds of years, but the Fallen had always stayed hidden. Roccorio's announcement had gone against a millennium of intel on the Fallen's activities.

But that announcement had forced them to reevaluate the Fallen. They had been a quiet nuisance. But now the world knew who they were. And the whole world was changed by that knowledge.

Moretti did not like being caught off guard, especially since they had the Tome of the Great Mother in their possession. It was perhaps the greatest repository of information on the Fallen in the world, in perhaps the history of the world. But it had simply sat on a shelf until recent events had forced them to pull it from the shelf and see what knowledge it could offer.

"I have scholars reviewing it. Preliminary analysis indicates the ring bearer has been called in times past to combat a rising threat from the Fallen."

Ribraldi scoffed. "But she's a woman. Surely she would not be God's chosen one."

"I agree. It seems unlikely." Moretti paused. "There is one other issue that harkens toward a critical point for the Church." He nodded at Father Gante, who produced his phone with a picture from the failed coronation already on the screen. A man was pictured there, his arms wrapped around the ring bearer as she bled.

"Who is this?"

"That is the question. We know he goes by the name Drake. He was a Las Vegas entertainer."

Tegano frowned. "Why does he matter?"

John nodded at Gante, who swiped to another picture. "He was also Sir Reginaldo Lopez from the sixteenth century. Even a duke from England in the fourteenth century." The picture shifted again.

Park's eyes went wide. "He has reincarnated?"

"No. We believe he has lived throughout these times."

"So who *is* he?" Ribraldi demanded.

Gante held up his phone with a picture of a statue from Castel Sant'Angelo. Each of the cardinals gasped. "It cannot be."

"Are you sure?" Ribraldi asked.

John shook his head. "No. I am not sure. But we have to prepare if he is God's soldier. We need information."

"What do you suggest?"

"Gante will gather the information for us. He will be the Vatican's representative and interview Patrick Delaney and Delaney McPhearson. He will get close to them and get us the information we need."

"But if this man is who you suspect, is it possible that Delaney McPhearson, rather than being God's chosen, is the Devil's?"

John nodded, his voice grave. "If Drake is God's soldier, then Delaney McPhearson may very well be the antichrist, and we *need* to protect the Church."

"Do we agree?"

All the men nodded back at him.

John extended his hand. "In God's name."

Each man placed their hand forward. "In God's name," they said in unison, their words echoing across the ancient necropolis.

CHAPTER 2

CHICAGO, ILLINOIS

THREE MONTHS LATER

The van tore around the corner. Two wheels lifted up in the air as the remaining two squealed in protest. Delaney McPhearson's teeth rattled as the wheels touched back down, but she didn't yell at Jake Rogan, who was behind the wheel. She saved her ire for the officer on the other side of her earpiece.

"What the hell were you thinking, breaching without waiting for us?"

"We have been trained to—"

"Shit!" Jake swerved as gunfire sprayed across the windshield. The glass was bulletproof, but a dozen indentations showed exactly how much damage the barrage could have done.

Jake yanked the wheel to the left. They bounced over the curb as they barreled into a parking lot hidden from the warehouse and storefronts down the street.

"How many hostages?" Laney demanded, cutting the officer off.

"We're not sure. We think it might be—"

"Fourteen," Jen Witt said, cutting off the sergeant.

"Where are you?" Laney asked.

"On the roof. They've got fourteen hostages, eight of them kids, and I've counted twelve bad guys, all heavily armed. There may be more, though, because the skylight I'm looking through has no view of the offices in the back."

"Got it. Sergeant, where are your men?"

"On the southern end of the street you just came down. Now look, we have the situation—"

Laney cut off his channel. She did not need to hear his opinion right now. She needed to try to figure out a way to make any of this work, and a guy who jumped the gun while knowing help was on the way was not going to be much help with that.

Just this morning, the higher-ups in Chicago had contacted the SIA about one of the gangs outside of Chicago now being led by a Fallen named Dirk Magnet. Laney wasn't sure what the man's parents were thinking of, naming him that. There were no good career options predicted with that name.

Dirk was running guns and terrorizing the neighborhood, demanding protection money. No one had said a word until a twelve-year-old had ended up in the hospital, shot in a war between the new gang and the one that had once controlled these streets.

Sadly, this was not a new story. Ever since the botched coronation, some Fallen had taken the loss of their leader as a signal that they could do whatever they wanted. Apparently, for them, that did not include being a productive, law-abiding citizen. The SIA had been run ragged the last few months, going from one incident to the next.

Laney, Jake, and Jen were supposed to analyze the situation and figure out the best way to neutralize Dirk. They had just touched down in Illinois twenty minutes ago. They'd been on route to police headquarters when they'd gotten word that some hothead sergeant had decided he didn't need to wait for the SIA. They'd moved in ten minutes ago, and all hell had broken loose. As soon as the gang members caught sight of the cops, they opened fire. Two officers had their necks broken by the gang leader before a lucky shot had slowed him down. Now the gang was holed up in a warehouse with hostages they had grabbed from the surrounding buildings. It was not looking good.

She switched the officer's channel back on. "Sergeant, have your people set up a perimeter and keep up surveillance. Let us know if anyone tries to leave the warehouse."

"Fine." Laney could hear the man gritting his teeth over the line. "Do *you* have a plan for infiltrating?"

"I'll get back to you shortly with that." She disconnected the call, then turned to Jake while touching the mic at her throat to include Jen in the conversation. "So the police department that created this FUBAR situation would now like to know what we are going to do to fix it."

Jen snorted. "Figures."

"Any ideas?" Laney asked.

"Develop time travel, go back in time fifteen minutes, and tell the cops to freaking wait?" Jen grumbled.

Laney smiled. "Great idea. But any ideas that do not involve the plot from a dozen or so sci-fi movies?"

Jake shrugged. "We could do the usual."

Laney blew out a breath as she opened the car door. "Great. Winging it again."

CHAPTER 3

Laney rolled her neck, trying to work out some of the stiffness there. They'd rushed here from Arkansas, where they'd been training a special law enforcement unit to deal with Fallen situations. Before that, she'd spoken to a teen group aimed at runaways. She'd been moving pretty much ever since everything that happened in D.C. There'd been interview requests, which she'd turned down, and hearings on the Hill, which she couldn't turn down. Plus, she'd been working with local, state, federal, and foreign governments along with the SIA to address the growing Fallen issue, which meant right now she was tired and cranky.

Jake stood next to Laney as she peered around the corner of the building at the end of the alley to check out the warehouse. She leaned back. "I saw four gunmen. Two outside. Two inside."

Jake pulled the slide back on his Beretta. "Okay. Let's try to take these guys into custody with as little property damage possible."

Laney snorted. "Yeah, I'd hate to make the accountants unhappy." That was another new addition to their lives: paperwork.

The warehouse in question was in fact owned by the city and

slated for destruction, but the new guidelines that the government had put in place for SIA agents required that any property that was damaged needed to be documented. They would have to write up every broken window, dinged doorway, and scratched paint job. So each time a bullet or body dented a piece of property, they needed to account for it in a report. Honestly, the amount of paperwork that now came with her job of *saving lives* was almost enough to make her turn to the dark side.

Almost.

"So what's the plan?" Jake asked.

Laney peered around the building. "Jen, can you get into the warehouse?"

Jen's voice was dry. "I'm going to ignore the insult in that question and chalk it up to a lack of sleep."

Laney smiled. "Okay. You are responsible for getting the hostages out when the gunmen become distracted. Jake, you cover her."

"What's the distraction?" Jake asked.

Laney sighed. "I thought I'd go talk to them."

Jake raised his eyebrows. "Seriously?"

Jen was less polite. "That sucks."

Laney sighed. "I know. But it's all I've got right now."

CHAPTER 4

Laney put her hands up and stepped around the corner of the building. She hated this part. She now had the abilities of the Fallen: the speed, strength, and healing, along with her abilities to control the weather and communicate with animals. Her ability to order the Fallen, however, was no longer in her bag of tricks.

She was pretty sure she was immortal, though. The Omni combined with her blood should have done the trick. But being the only way to test that was to have someone give her a mortal wound, she had yet to determine if that was true. Of course, there had been some very helpful Fallen who, over the last few months, had made attempts to get her an answer to that question.

So as she walked down the street, her hands up, her eyes scanning the warehouse in front of her, she knew there was a chance she could die. She just had to hope she was a little better than Dirk. She smiled at the gunmen, who looked at each other and then back at her.

"No guns. I just want to talk," Laney called out, continuing to move toward them.

One of the men squinted, making Laney think he needed

glasses, which was good. Hopefully he would not recognize her until she got closer.

"Jen?" she whispered into her mic.

"In place."

"Shit! That's Delaney McPhearson!" The other guy apparently didn't need glasses and opened fire.

"Go!" Laney yelled. She blurred forward, leaping on the dumpster near the door to avoid getting shot. She jumped down on one of the gunmen, slamming him across the space and into the other one. They crashed into the wall. Jake sprinted up behind her. Laney didn't wait for him, knowing he'd make sure the two guards were out. Glass shattered as gunfire rained into the street.

The door was covered, so Laney went through the window, ignoring little cuts that the shards of glass left in her skin. In a glance, she took in the warehouse. New electronics still in their boxes were stacked through the space on pallets by the loading dock along the back. Empty boxes were also scattered throughout the space, along with a forklift and another dozen empty pallets. Long windows lined the walls and staircases leading up to her right and left. A catwalk was strung across the third story, and people were being ushered across it toward the roof.

Skylights dominated the ceiling. One crashed in as Jen burst through, landing on the catwalk with the grace of a ballerina. She sprinted across the space as Laney turned for the two gunmen who'd been positioned at the door and other window.

Laney tackled the gunman near her as he turned, her shoulder crashing into his hip as she yanked his ankles back. He fell hard, his head hitting the ground with a noticeable *thunk*. Laney stomped on his chest as his partner turned. She shot out with a side kick, catching him mid-chest before slamming a round kick into his knee. He screamed, dropping his gun and reaching for his obliterated knee. Laney kicked the gun away.

Screams sounded from up the stairs, followed by gunfire. The gunfire cut off, but the cries remained.

"We've got a problem, Laney!" Jen yelled through her earpiece.

"On my way." Laney sprinted for the stairs. Four gunmen were on the second level, heading down. Laney went through them like they were bowling pins. Each man plunged over the side to the floor of the warehouse below.

She felt the tingle of the Fallen as she reached the third level and ducked as one leaped from the shadows, swinging a large machete at her head. Laney jumped back, landing on the catwalk as he retreated back a few steps.

He was not what Laney had been expecting. He had short blond hair artfully held in place with product. His blue eyes sat in an almost orange face that Laney was pretty sure was regularly tanned at a tanning salon. He wore a pink polo shirt with chino shorts. She glanced at his feet before looking back at him.

"Loafers? You're supposed to be a big badass gang leader, and you're wearing loafers without socks? Have some self-respect, man."

"The clothes make the man," he growled, jumping toward her.

Laney tried not to groan at the cheesiness. To be honest, the aging frat boy in front of her just ticked her off. He swung widely with the machete, letting her know he had no skills. He was relying purely on brute strength.

She shook her head. Like a lot of Fallen, he figured because he was stronger than humans, he didn't need anything other than that strength. Stupid, stupid boy.

A scream sounded outside.

"Laney!" Jen yelled.

"Okay, enough." Laney stepped forward as the machete swung past her. He shifted, but Laney redirected the knife to his knee with the back swing. He screamed as she sliced across his knee. She slid the knife past before burying it in the back of his thigh. He screamed again, tears streaming down his cheeks. She reached over and snapped his neck.

Jake was already rounding the stairs, pulling out the syringe case. "I got it. Go!"

Laney burst through the door to the roof. Jen stood on one end of the roof, her legs bent, muscles straining as she held on to the fire escape that had been wrenched away from the building. Another group of five people huddled near her. Three men were holding on to the railing with Jen, trying to keep it from plunging to the ground.

Screams sounded from the fire escape. Laney sprinted for the edge of the building, but she couldn't see the fire escape from this angle.

A catwalk connected the two buildings. She leaped on it, and it groaned under her weight, but she moved to the middle anyway, where she could see the group of people clinging to the fire escape that swung in the air. There were eight people hanging on to it. Four of them were just kids.

Calling on the wind, she steadied the fire escape. With a groan, the metal Jen held snapped.

"No!"

The fire escape jolted, but Laney slammed wind into each person, keeping them on it and the escape pinned to the side of the building.

"I've got them!" Laney yelled. "Start pulling—"

A second groan of metal rang out before the catwalk shuddered. Laney plunged toward the ground, along with all eight people from the fire escape.

CHAPTER 5

The ground was coming up fast. Laney lashed out with the wind, cushioning the group. They were spread out, but she managed to get them all and stop their descent. At the last second, she managed to get a little wind underneath her, slowing her, but she still slammed down harder than she liked. Dust and concrete flew in the air.

The air emptied from her lungs. Pain lanced through her back and skull. Her control wavered, but she reinforced the wind, managing to get the people to the ground, touching them down lightly. She blinked her eyes, trying to focus, but everything was blurry, disjointed.

Definitely have a skull fracture.

"The rest are coming down with me," Jen said through her earpiece.

"Great," Laney mumbled, not moving from her spot as the police hurried over to the group, who sat stunned, staring up at the top of the building.

A black helicopter hovered to the right of her vision. She turned her head, pain lancing through it.

Yup, definitely a skull fracture. The chopper hovered for only a few more seconds before it flew off.

Jake hustled over, sweat on his brow, his eyes large as he knelt next to her. "Lanes, you okay?"

Laney grunted, not even trying to move. She'd heal. But it didn't stop the pain from each of the injuries. Right now everything hurt so bad she wanted to bite her tongue off. She held up a finger to get Jake to wait just a second. She closed her eyes, breathing shallowly as the pain began to lessen.

After a minute, she opened her eyes. "Yeah, I'm okay."

Jen materialized next to her, nodding toward what remained of the fire escape. "Think we have to report that?"

"Oh, crap. Yes, and the catwalk." She pictured the paperwork that would be required and contemplated flinging herself off the building again. It would be less painful.

Jake helped pull Laney up, nodding to where the chopper had been. "Our friend was back."

Jen stared up at the sky. "Yeah. Saw them earlier. We still can't get an answer on who they are?"

Laney shook her head and rolled her neck, most of the pain just a dull ache now. "Nope. Apparently Stanton thinks that is not need to know." Sourness filled her at the thought of the government representative.

Jake grinned at Jen. "Speaking of which, I believe it is Laney's turn to brief him."

Laney groaned. "No, I'm sure I did it last time."

"Nope, that was me," Jake said.

"And for some reason, he's requested I don't do any of the debriefs," Jen said.

Laney laughed. "Yeah, well, when you terrify the government official to the point that they pee their pants, they tend not to want you to speak with them. Maybe I should try that . . ."

"Laney," Jake warned.

"I know, I know." Laney sighed. She would love more than

anything to avoid these stupid debriefings, but she also knew they were all on a bit of a short leash with the government. "Fine. I'll speak with Buttface."

Jen snorted. "Maybe don't call him that to his face."

"I make no promises."

CHAPTER 6

WASHINGTON, D.C.

Senator Bart Shremp's black Escalade hurtled down the 295, heading for a quick meeting before a fundraising cocktail party. His appointment to head the Committee on Enhanced Individuals (CEI) had raised his profile in Washington, which of course made him the man people wanted to meet and fund. His schedule since the appointment had been jam-packed.

Everything was falling into place. In the next presidential election, he'd planned on dipping his toe in, make sure people knew who he was, but then he would seriously run in the election after that. He'd always planned on running for president two election cycles from now, but with his new position, if he played his cards right with this whole enhanced individuals thing, he could run seriously in *this* election cycle. People might just be calling him Mr. President a mere three years from now.

And I have the Fallen to thank for that.

The public was terrified of them. Shremp was too, but unlike the general public, he had around-the-clock protection. The frequency of Fallen incidents had dramatically increased in the last three months, and Shremp had made sure he fanned those flames of panic. People were less concerned with civil liberties and due process when they felt they were in danger, which had made it easier to get his legislation passed recently. Besides, scared people were looking for someone to step in and assure them that they would protect them from the big bad. Shremp planned on being that person and riding that all the way to the Oval Office.

He looked at his aide Adam, who sat next to him, working quietly on his tablet. "What are the polls saying?"

Adam Hinkel had joined Shremp's office two years ago as a young, eager intern. Shremp had seen the hunger in the kid's eyes to help his country and had managed to parlay that into a highly competent, if young, chief of staff.

Adam swiped to another screen, his eyes scanning the report as he spoke. "Most people believe that the Fallen do present a risk to our nation's safety. But those numbers are falling."

"Falling? Why?" he asked, even though he knew.

"The pollsters are attributing it to two factors. First, Delaney McPhearson and the SIA's highly publicized efforts to curtail any Fallen incidents."

Shremp grunted. That woman and her exploits had chased him off the front page on more than one occasion. Perhaps most gallingly, though, was she didn't even seem to want the attention. She never did interviews. But her silence only seemed to make the public more intrigued by her. He couldn't count the number of debates he'd overheard both onscreen and off as to whether she was a savior or a villain.

"And the second?" he asked.

Adam handed him the tablet. "The Chandler Group's public relations campaign."

Shremp glared at the image frozen there. Molly McAdams, the smiling face of the Chandler Group's PR campaign to humanize the Fallen. He had to admit they had chosen well. She was young, fresh-faced, and not even slightly threatening. She was the personification of young and innocent.

He flipped through to the next picture. Molly was smiling, her eyes closed as a giant leopard leaned in to her, his eyes closed as well. The cat's name was Zane. He was also part of the Chandler public relations campaign. Once people had learned of the genetically modified cats, panic had ensued.

But Chandler had been prepared. He'd had the photos of Zane released almost immediately, along with the backstory of how Molly and Zane had aided people on the Day of Reckoning, the name given to the day when Samyaza had set off a bomb in the western part of the United States and ordered her Fallen to rampage through the streets all over the globe. And now it was well known that Molly and Zane were the best of friends. The two of them even did public appearances together.

Shremp growled. The two of them had blunted all the impact of the fear the news of the genetically altered leopard had been developed to create. He'd spent hours crafting the release to make sure people were terrified

"That young girl, Molly McAdams, has been a real hit with people," said Adam. "She's got a sweet girl-next-door quality to her. There's been testimonial after testimonial about how she helped save people on the Day of Reckoning. The media started highlighting more stories about the Fallen helping people, which has affected public sentiment."

Shremp was barely able to keep himself from throwing the tablet back at Adam. "What about *our* campaign?"

"We have exposés about the increase in Fallen incidents across the globe. And a few stories about the rash of vandalism out—"

"Vandalism? Vandalism? These monsters are destroying lives, and we're focusing on *vandalism?*" Shremp stewed. *God, I'm surrounded by incompetents.* "They have a poster girl for the good the Fallen can do. You need to find me a poster boy for the bad.

What about that incident in Chicago? Didn't one of them take over a town or something?"

Adam's fingers moved quickly over his tablet. "Not a town, but he did control a few square blocks. And the neighborhood was terrified of him."

"What about murders? Did he kill anyone?"

"He's suspected in a dozen murders, as well as extortion."

"Good, good. That will play well. He took some hostages, right?"

"Yes. Two dozen."

"Even better. Let's make sure the media focuses on him, and find me some others we can focus on."

Adam nodded, his hands flying. His head snapped up. "You know Delaney McPhearson is the one responsible for stopping him, right?"

Shremp frowned. Ugh. He'd forgotten about her role in his apprehension. God, he really hated that woman. So damn arrogant and dismissive. She'd waltzed into her first joint chiefs meeting like she owned the place. Then she'd simply dismissed the authority of all of those in the room as if she was ordained by God.

He paused, an idea forming. *Ordained by God...*

"I need you to compile a list of mass murderers, serial killers, or any other kind of massively damaging individual that believed they were doing the work of God."

Adam frowned. "Okay. What's the angle?"

"I'm not entirely sure yet. But Delaney McPhearson is portraying herself as God's soldier. Maybe we should remind people of the damage done by others who claimed the same."

Adam stared at him for a long moment. "I'm not sure that's accurate. She's not really portraying herself as anything. She doesn't do any interviews at all."

Shremp narrowed his eyes. "Then her people are portraying her as God's soldier. She's no doubt orchestrating things behind the scenes while publicly looking as if she wants nothing to do with publicity."

"Maybe." Adam drew out the word.

"Is there a problem here, Adam? You know Delaney McPhearson is a danger to our society, don't you?"

Adam licked his lips, glancing out the window for a second before turning back to Shremp. "But she . . . she saved us. All of us. The entire world. She nearly *died* saving us."

"Did she really? Or was that all just a nice little public relations coup? Making it look like she was truly suffering? Besides, that was three months ago. The question you should be asking, the question *everyone* should be asking, is what danger does she pose to us *now*."

Adam still didn't move, his hands unnaturally still above his tablet.

"Are we going to have a problem with this? Because I assure you, I can find someone who—"

"No, no. I've got it. I'll—I'll get you the information."

"Good." Shremp sat back with a smile, picturing himself walking down the steps of the U.S. Capitol to be inaugurated as president. It was so real he could practically taste it. And all he had to do was make sure everyone knew how dangerous the Fallen were to society and place himself in position as the man with answers.

And he knew exactly how he was going to do that.

CHAPTER 7

BALTIMORE, MARYLAND

Stanton Calloway clicked his pen shut. "Well, that seems to cover the situation. Next time, you need to try to capture the subject with less property damage. You are not given carte blanche to do whatever you want. You are a representative of the government, Ms. McPhearson."

"*Dr.* McPhearson, Stan."

He glared. She smiled in response, knowing he hated the shortened version of his name. But being she had refrained from Buttface, she thought she deserved to get slightly under his skin.

Stanton loaded his legal pad and pen into his briefcase. The lights of the conference room bounced off his shining bald dome, rimmed in black hair. He was only thirty-two, but his hair was already half gone. His unusually large forehead made his small eyes look even smaller. His tiny mouth was pursed as he snapped his briefcase shut. And Laney couldn't help but agree with Jake— he really did look like an alien. Maybe they should cut him just a little to see what color his blood was.

Stanton glared at her. "The government is watching your actions closely."

"Yes, I've noticed." Ever since the coronation, the government had taken an active interest in Laney's activities. While they were allegedly now all on the same side, Laney certainly did not feel that way. All members of the SIA had to detail every incident in excruciating detail, to the point that people had been suspended for failing to detail minor issues. Jake had been suspended once because he'd failed to mention that during a car chase they'd had to drive along a sidewalk for about twenty feet.

It was ridiculous.

"Speaking of close government relations, who's in the black helicopter?"

"I'm sure I don't know what you mean."

Laney studied him. She believed him. As pompous and condescending as the man was, he was, in actuality, just an errand boy. He probably didn't have clearance to know. *Just like me.*

"Good day, Ms. McPhearson." Stanton strode for the door.

Laney stuck her tongue out at his back.

"Well, that is very mature," Drake drawled as he stepped into the room.

"God, I hate that guy."

"Can't say I blame you. He looks like a hot dog with eyes."

Laney smirked. "I was thinking of a younger version of Mr. Burns from the Simpsons."

"Never seen it."

"What? How is that possible?"

Drake shrugged. "Not much of a TV watcher."

"You know, the next time we have some downtime, we are totally doing a veg out on the couch and have a TV marathon."

"The next time we have time? So I'll pencil us in for thirty-seven years from Tuesday?"

Laney dropped her forehead to the conference table, her hands over her head. "Yeah, that sounds about right."

Honestly, she could not remember the last time she had relaxed a little. She always seemed to be running from one situation to the next. Drake was doing the same, although not officially. While many people contacted the SIA when there was a Fallen situation, some contacted the Chandler Group directly, not wanting to involve the government. Drake looked into those cases, since he also was not a big fan of the government. He'd been doing a lot of good, but it meant they were often heading off in opposite directions.

"Want to get some lunch?"

Laney didn't take her head from the table. "Not really."

Drake laughed as he pulled her back and slid into the seat next to her. "No moping. What's going on?"

She sighed. "I don't know. Today it's just all getting to me."

"What's all?"

She threw her arms wide. "All of it! I mean, Jen, Jake, and I just caught a Fallen who'd been running a gang outside of Chicago that was terrorizing a neighborhood. I'm not expecting a ticker tape parade, but I don't think it would be out of line to not be treated like public enemy number one. I mean, I did save the world from Samyaza. I think I've earned a little trust."

Drake shook his head.

"What?"

"Yes, you saved the world. But what you earned from the governments of the world is fear. You showed them how you are more powerful than any of them. Right now, they are scared of what might happen if you decide to turn that power against them and try to run things."

"I wouldn't do that. I have zero interest in running anything. In fact, a life with very few responsibilities sounds fabulous."

Drake watched her for a long moment. "You are an unusual creature. You have all this power, yet no ambition to use it for your own gain. That is not something politicians will ever be able to understand. Their whole existence revolves around attaining more power."

Laney shuddered. "Good thing they're not the ring bearer."

"Yes, it is. Any word from inside the government? About what they're planning?"

Laney shook her head. "Matt's been shut out. So has Nancy, or at least that's what she says."

"You don't believe her?"

Laney shrugged with a smile. "She *is* a politician."

He returned the smile with an incline of his head. "That she is."

Drake's words rolled through Laney's head. While on paper it looked as if Laney and the government were working together, she knew they were keeping her at arm's length. It definitely wasn't a partnership. More like they were hunting with a dog they didn't entirely trust and therefore kept a gun on. But what if it was more than that?

"You really think they're plotting against us?" she asked.

Drake nodded. "Us and you specifically. I've been around a long time. And one thing I know for certain is that people in charge want to attain power. And if they can't attain it, they want to destroy it."

CHAPTER 8

LANGLEY, VIRGINIA

The halls of the CIA headquarters were bustling as David Okafur headed for his new office. Suited men and women hurried past him with coffee, folders, and briefcases. A few gave him nods, although he didn't know them, and they didn't know him. But in an office setting, that's what you did. Nodded at people you didn't know to show that you belonged, even if you were not entirely sure if they did. The CIA was no different.

He turned down a hall, walking past row after row of desks. A single desk sat outside a single door at the back of the room. Chang Kim looked up from behind the desk as David approached. "The video feeds are on your account."

"Thank you."

"And Director Heller asked to see you in an hour."

"All right. Can you grab me a coffee?"

Chang nudged his chin toward the door. "Already on your desk."

David nodded his thanks as Chang buzzed him into his office. Chang was not some simple assistant. He and David had worked together for fifteen years now. Chang was a whiz at computers, paperwork, and organization. But he could also hit a target at 1500 yards, disable multiple opponents, and slip in and out of secured locations without raising any alarms. David knew that in the not-too-distant future he'd have to get Chang out of the office. He, like David, got a little stir crazy being around suits for too long. Three months was definitely hitting that limit.

There was a small issue in El Salvador he could send Chang on. A quick in and out. He could do it over the weekend. Planning to send him the details after he met with Heller this afternoon, he settled behind his desk to write up his report.

Twenty minutes later, he pushed back from the desk, satisfied he'd detailed everything accurately. This was the seventeenth incident Delaney McPhearson had been involved in that he had documented. It was the twelfth he'd been in the chopper for. Chang had installed a tracker on the SIA computers so that they were notified of any impending raids. After the first five, David had insisted on being on site to watch the other ones. Even with the chopper recordings of the incidents, it was difficult to believe what was occurring. David had wanted to see it with his own eyes.

Even then, it had been shocking. The Fallen moved so fast. He could barely discern their movements. Even with all his skills, he knew he would be no match for them.

And then there was Delaney McPhearson. Her abilities, all those of the Fallen with the added ability of being able to control the weather, she was more terrifying than all of them. When he began this mission, he knew exactly how dangerous that much concentrated power would be in one person's hands. Those first few incidents had done nothing to lessen that concern.

But then there had been incidents like today. Instead of protecting herself, she had protected a group of strangers, lowering them safely to the ground while she plunged to the concrete. He knew she would recover from the fall, but she would also feel every broken bone, every bruised surface. Yet she chose the pain in order to protect a family she did not know. He was beginning to think that perhaps whoever had given her those abilities knew exactly whom they were choosing when they did so.

And *that* might be more terrifying than even her abilities. David had lost the ability to see the goodness in most people he came in contact with. On behalf of the U.S. government, he had killed drug lords, politicians, just generally bad people for the better part of two decades. Without fail, everyone they aimed him at had done something so deplorable that he viewed their removal from the gene pool as a true public service.

But Delaney McPhearson did not belong in that category. So he wasn't entirely sure he agreed with the government aiming him in her direction, even if right now it was only for simple reconnaissance.

Chang's voice over the intercom broke into his thoughts. "The director is moving up the meeting. He expects you in fifteen."

"Tell him I'll be there."

"Sure thing."

David scanned the report again. Satisfied, he sent a copy to Heller while sending another copy to his encrypted off-site storage site. He pushed back from his desk. He trusted Heller, for the most part. But if anyone tried to burn him if and when news of this surveillance got out, he planned on taking everyone down along with him.

CHAPTER 9

BALTIMORE, MARYLAND

The Chandler Estate was incredible. That was the thought that kept running through Mary Jane McAdams's mind as they wound down the driveway toward Sharecroppers Lane. Jake had driven them past the main house first. Mary Jane couldn't help but think of pictures of Monticello when she saw the large imposing building. Jake explained that both wings of the large building had been damaged in the attacks, but Henry had quickly had them reconstructed, wanting to get life back to normal as quickly as he could for everyone on the estate.

Now Jake had turned onto Sharecroppers Lane. The street was adorable with stone-covered cottages lining it, each with a small wooden porch and overflowing window boxes. A few had fences —short stone ones or picket fences. She sighed, a smile on her face.

Mary Jane's oldest son, Joe, popped up from between the seats. "What's a sharecropper?"

"A farmer who rents land and pays through part of their crop."

"Oh."

Joe sat back, and Mary Jane glanced into the back. All four of her kids were looking in awe out the windows.

She was struck by how alike they looked with their red hair and blue eyes. She smiled. They all looked like slightly different versions of one another. Joe was sixteen and had really started to put on muscle in the last year, making him look more man than boy. Shaun was starting to fill out too, but he still had that wide-eyed-boy look.

Her youngest was two-year-old Susie, whose red hair was in pigtails that had started to come undone on the flight down. But seeing as how she'd been asleep when they landed, Mary Jane hadn't wanted to wake her by fixing them. Molly looked like what Mary Jane assumed Susie would look like in another ten years with her thin frame and bright blue eyes, her curly red hair also contained by two long braids. Mary Jane always thought of *Anne of Green Gables* when Molly wore her hair like that. But Molly, for all her youth and innocence, had grown up a lot in the last year.

"This is you guys." Jake pulled to the side of the street in front of a cottage with a light rock facade, black shutters, a white covered porch, and a short rock wall with a wooden gate. Colorful petunias in purples, pinks, and white flowed over the window boxes, cascading down the side of the building.

Jake looked over at her with a smile. "Like it?"

"It's magical."

"Awesome." Shaun flung open the door and jumped out. Joe was right behind him.

Molly climbed over the back seat. "I've got Susie."

"Thanks, honey." Mary Jane rolled down the window. "Boys! Get back here and get the bags!"

"Mom," Joe grumbled while Shaun stared up at the sky as if to ask why his life was so difficult.

Mary Jane tried not to get annoyed at them. Or at least more annoyed. "Yeah, yeah, I'm horrible. Go get your stuff."

The boys grumbled, pushing each other as they made their

way to the back of the SUV. Mary Jane caught Molly's grin in the rearview mirror and returned the smile. "Remind me again why I had your brothers and didn't just skip ahead to you two?"

Molly pulled Susie into her arms as the back door opened. "Because you had to perfect the recipe. They were the trial kids."

"Heard that." Joe grabbed a bag.

"You were supposed to." Molly climbed out of the car.

Mary Jane looked at Jake. "Still think us moving to the estate is a good idea?"

He leaned toward her. "Absolutely."

Mary Jane leaned in toward Jake for the kiss, a tingle running through her as his lips touched hers. Jake was . . . unexpected. When Billy had died, Mary Jane had never given another thought to romance, not for her. Billy was her husband. When he died, she became his widow. As far as she had been concerned, that was the end of her romantic story.

But Jake, with his strength, his heart, how could she not fall for him? And the fact that he not only put up with her kids but actually seemed to really like them? That was just the icing on the cake.

"Oh, get a room," Shaun said from the back of the car.

Heat flooded Mary Jane's cheeks as she broke away from Jake. "Shaun!" But Shaun just grinned as he closed the tailgate.

"I'll go show them inside." Jake stepped out of the car and grabbed one of the bags from Joe before heading into the house.

The boys followed him in, but Molly stood looking around, holding Susie, a smile on her face. That smile was worth everything to Mary Jane after these last few months. Mary Jane stopped next to her. "What do you think?"

"It's beautiful."

Mary Jane put an arm around her waist. "Yes, it is."

Molly's head whipped down the street. Mary Jane tensed knowing Molly sensed something, but then she grinned. A large yellow-and-black Javan leopard sprinted down the street. Mary Jane stumbled back, but Molly stepped forward. "Zane!"

Zane screeched to a halt before he ran Molly and Susie over. Then he gently lifted himself onto two paws, placing his front paws on Molly's shoulders and licking her face. With another gentle lick to the top of Susie's head, he dropped back down to the ground, leaning against Molly.

Heart pounding, Mary Jane reached over and took Susie. Molly immediately dropped, throwing her arms around Zane. "I missed you."

Zane buried his head in Molly's chest.

Mary Jane watched on in awe. Jake had brought Zane with him when he'd come to Boston on the Day of Reckoning. Zane and Molly had gone together throughout the neighborhood for days, helping people out. They'd established a strong bond as a result.

Molly stood up with a giant smile. "Is it okay if Zane and I go check out the house?"

"Uh, sure."

Molly started for the house, then turned back, kissing Mary Jane's cheek. "Thanks, Mom."

Mary Jane watched the two of them head through the gate as Jake held it open for them. He moved to Mary Jane's side. "I see Zane found you."

Mary Jane just nodded, absentmindedly rubbing Susie's back, watching the doorway where Molly and Zane had disappeared.

"You sure you're up for this?"

She gave a nervous laugh. "Hey, I've been saying for years what our house was missing was a giant genetically enhanced leopard."

Henry had agreed to let Zane stay with the McAdamses for a trial run. Zane and Molly were already part of a public relations campaign the Chandler Group had come up with to help people accept the existence of Fallen. And Zane had been out to Boston a bunch of times. But now it was official: He would be the newest member of the McAdams family.

"Mary Jane?"

She looked up into Jake's eyes before spying Molly through the windows, smiling from ear to ear. That was a sight more rare these days than a genetically enhanced leopard. Ever since people learned what Molly could do, she had lost a lot of friends. School became really tough. Kids had started bullying her, both in person and online. And the people that wanted to spend time with her wanted to because of what she could do, not because of who she really was. It was tough. She had started to retreat into herself, spending less and less time with her friends. Even soccer had become impossible with the media always there. Normal life had become a thing of the past.

But Zane, he just loved Molly with no ulterior motives. As a mom, she knew she would do whatever it took to keep her kids safe and happy. Apparently, in today's world that included allowing a giant leopard to live in their house and moving hundreds of miles from the home they'd always known.

When Jake had learned how bad things were getting for Molly, he had suggested they move to the estate. At first Mary Jane had said no. But when she'd found Molly crying while sleeping three nights in a row, it had been the last straw. She needed to find a way to bring her daughter some peace. So she'd packed up all their belongings and headed south. It might be temporary until things calmed down, or it might be forever. But right now her family needed the calm, the normalcy that the estate could hopefully offer.

So they had pulled up stakes for the foreseeable future. It was definitely going to be an adjustment.

"This is good. Good for Molly, good for Zane. Good for the world. They need to see that the Fallen are just normal people. And who looks sweeter than my little girl?"

Susie reached out her arms. "Jake!"

Jake took her, holding her with one arm while pulling Mary Jane close with the other. "It'll be all right."

Mary Jane breathed deep. "I hope so."

CHAPTER 10

LANGLEY, VIRGINIA

Bruce Heller, deputy director of the CIA, was on the phone when David arrived. He waved David in and gestured to the coffee machine in the corner. Popping a pod into the Keurig, David brewed himself a cup. By the time his coffee was ready, Bruce was off the phone. He indicated a chair in front of his desk. "Didn't get a chance to read the report. Take a seat. I'll read it quickly."

David settled into a chair with a nod. "Take your time."

Bruce only smiled in response, his gaze already shifting to his computer screen. David knew the reason behind the smile. Bruce could read faster than anyone David had ever met. Most people who criticized speed-reading argued that people retained very little of the information, being that they scanned more than read. But as far as David could tell, Bruce retained everything.

Bruce let few people know about that ability. He liked to watch other people when they thought he was busy absorbing information in a report. But with little more than a glance, Bruce could digest and retain the information in front of him. Just another spook trick he still had tucked up his sleeve.

David had only taken his second sip when Bruce spoke. "Impressive. They work well as a team."

"That they do. They also have a law enforcement approach with the protection of bystanders being the priority."

"And Jake Rogan?"

"Surprisingly useful." When David had begun these reviews, he'd been sure that Laney would carry all the weight, delegating only when necessary. But that wasn't how it worked. Everyone played their part, even the non-enhanced individuals.

"Seems to be quite a few effective non-enhanced individuals in the SIA. The reports on that Mustafa Massari and Jordan Witt demonstrate equal effectiveness." Bruce's watch beeped. He looked down with a frown. "The reason we moved the meeting up is we have a guest coming to join us."

David grunted. "Fabulous."

A knock sounded at Bruce's door. Buttoning his suit jacket, David stood as Senator Bart Shremp, chairman of the Senate Foreign Relations Committee and newly appointed chair of the CEI, strode in.

"Good, good. You're both here." Shremp slipped his coat off his shoulders, extending it toward David.

David looked at it with distaste. "*What* exactly do you expect me to do with that?"

Shremp's face reddened.

"Sandra," Bruce called. His assistant hurried in and took the senator's jacket. "Can I get you some coffee, Senator?"

"Yes, black, four sugars."

They all waited as the coffee brewed. Sandra placed it on the desk in front of the senator. "Is there anything else?"

"That will be all. Thank you, Sandra," Bruce said.

With a nod at Bruce and a small smile for David, Sandra exited the office. Shremp watched her retreat, his eyes focused on her long legs. "Nice view you have here, Bruce."

Bruce waited until Shremp met his gaze. "Sandra is a master of espionage who spent a decade in the field. She has more commendations by the bureau than almost anyone I know. She could kill you before you even realized she was in the room. I suggest you treat her with more respect."

Shremp grunted. "Don't get all huffy. Just making an observation."

"An unnecessary one," Bruce said. "Now, you called this meeting, what can we do for you?"

Shremp crossed his arms over his chest. "I'd like an update on your progress regarding the Omni."

The Omni—the substance that Elisabeta Roccorio had mentioned in her recording for the governments of the world. The one that would give an ordinary human the power of the Fallen. The President had made it clear that it was the most important piece of intel she was looking for. She had multiple labs analyzing Fallen blood to no avail. Other countries across the globe were doing the same. At first David had expected them to be able to figure it out. But now he wondered if they ever would. They seemed no closer than when they started. And he knew for a fact they had recruited the top minds in the scientific communities to work on it. Well, all the top minds not employed by the Chandler Group.

Delaney McPhearson had refused to provide a blood sample, had refused to acknowledge even knowing about the Omni, never mind offering up where to find it. But the world had seen her shot, and then shot again by her own people. She claimed she had healed on her own, that the bullets were merely normal bullets. But she had kept the Secret Service agents at bay while she destroyed something on the western front of the U.S. Capitol. She refused to say what exactly it was.

At first David thought she was trying to keep the formula for herself, to keep the power for herself. But the more he watched her, the more he was coming to accept the realization that if she had the information, she was keeping it to herself because she did not trust the government with that knowledge. As he looked at the slovenly U.S. senator sitting across from him, he couldn't exactly blame her.

"Have you made any inroads in determining what labs or personnel she used to create the Omni?" Shremp asked.

Bruce didn't look at David as he responded. "No, we have not, although we are continuing to investigate."

That was a bald-faced lie. They had narrowed it down to two individuals. Delaney McPhearson would not trust the information to just anyone, and certainly not to some large lab. No, it would have to be someone in her inner circle. The two most likely candidates were Danny Wartowski and Dr. Dominic Radcliffe. Wartowski had the intelligence, that was certain, but he tended to stay on the more technological side of things. David's money was on Radcliffe. He was a hermit who lived in a bomb shelter on the Chandler property. But he had a slew of degrees ranging from nuclear biology to chemical engineering. He was also, according to reports, considered family by Delaney. She would trust him.

Shremp turned to David. "What about you? Do you have any ideas who she would have create the Omni for her?"

David shook his head. "Not a one."

CHAPTER 11

ROME, ITALY

John walked down the long hall to the Pope's private residence. He had traveled these hallways many times, but he had no illusions that one day he himself would be Pope. He was committed to the Church, but his past indiscretions made him completely unworthy of the highest role within it. Instead, he'd dedicated himself to protecting it from all threats. And sometimes that meant keeping what he knew from the Pontiff himself.

He knocked on the door.

"Come in," came the muffled reply. John opened the door. Pope Innocent XV turned from the window, watering can in hand, a smile on his face. "John. It's good to see you."

John inclined his head. "And you as well, Your Holiness."

Innocent chuckled. "I told you there is no need for formality when we are alone. We have been friends too long to be formal now."

"Yes, Your Holiness."

Innocent shook his head, placing the watering can on the floor near the window. "What am I to do with you?"

"I have a report on—"

Innocent put up his hand. "That can wait. Now, come sit. Tell me how *you* are doing. And then you can tell me how the Church is doing."

And in John's mind, this was what made Innocent a great Pope. He was honestly and genuinely interested in the people, all the people. Regardless of their creed, ethnicity, even regardless of their intentions toward him. John took a seat at the small dining table and spoke with Innocent about the events of the week, leaving out anything having to do with the Brotherhood. It was established to protect the papacy, and that meant keeping the papacy unaware of its existence, even as it ensured his existence.

As John and Innocent chatted, John felt the lightness he always felt when he was near His Holiness. Each time, that feeling confirmed the rightness of his calling. Protecting the Church, protecting this man, was the most important role of his life. Because the Pope represented the power of good. And John would make sure he was able to fulfill his mission.

Innocent wiped at the sides of his mouth, pushing his plate with the crumbs of his pastry forward. "Now, on to business. I have decided that I will send you to the United States to speak with the President."

Surprise flickered through John along with anticipation. He had been planning on asking the Pope to allow him to go. Yet again, this just proved that He was supporting his plans. "I would be happy to."

Innocent glanced out the window, his voice soft. "The world is much changed in this last year. The existence of the Fallen has changed us all, in ways I'm not sure we even yet realize."

John knew he was right. Although, unlike the rest of the world, he had known of their existence earlier. But they were not what truly concerned him, especially now that Elisabeta had been taken care of. No, his concern was Delaney McPhearson. Elisabeta had been gathering Fallen to her to unleash across the world. But so too had Delaney McPhearson. And her troops had not been scattered. If the reports were true, they were growing in number. And she was being looked upon as a savior.

A false one, he thought, gripping his china cup.

"John? What's wrong?" Innocent frowned at him.

John wiped his face of emotion, shaking his head. "Just thinking of the damage Elisabeta could have caused had she not been stopped."

"Yes. We are lucky Delaney McPhearson exists."

"Hm." John took a sip of tea. Innocent did not believe Delaney McPhearson was the antichrist. But then, of course, he saw the good in all. His faith in humanity was his greatest gift to the world, and in John's personal opinion, his greatest weakness.

"If you could also try to persuade Patrick Delaney to give an accounting, that would be of great aid. I would like to hear what he thinks of all of this, being he has been closer to it than any of us."

"You could just order him to return."

Innocent nodded. "I could. But I believe Father Patrick is on a path ordained by a power greater than I. He has faced many trials, and I fear will continue to. But he is where he should be. But should he feel ready to speak, I would be very happy to listen."

John tried not to be annoyed. Innocent could order Patrick to return, demand answers. He had that power, yet he wielded his power rarely. John tamped down his feelings of annoyance. The Pope was not a man who coveted power or tried to sway people to his side. But sometimes John worried his unfailing belief in free will would lead to his downfall.

And John could never allow that to happen. Patrick Delaney needed to answer some questions. It was disrespectful to the whole Church that he had not done so already.

"Now, the President will ask about our view on the Fallen."

"Has that changed?"

"Not publicly. The cardinals believe we need to take our time and not rush to judgment in the open. We believe they are genetically gifted individuals."

"And privately?"

"We are a religion based upon the belief that the son of God walked among us and showed us the way to move forward. Why would angels not still walk among us, especially those banished from Heaven? I believe the Fallen are how they say they are, fallen angels, and that like all people, they can choose to do good or to not."

"And Delaney McPhearson?"

Innocent smiled slowly. "She is more difficult to identify, isn't she? But I have been reading more in the archives, the early writings of the Church. And I believe we have done a disservice to women. I believe that Jesus wanted Mary to be the future of the Church along with Simon Peter. He believed in the equality of women. So why not send us a female savior this time?"

"Savior? You don't mean she is the child of God?"

"A child, not *the* child. But I do believe she is a force of good. And we should support her."

John was aghast. What Innocent was saying went against thousands of years of Church teachings. The last Pope who had proffered such views had died a short time later.

Innocent smiled wider. "I see I have shocked you."

"I am just concerned. I am not sure the Church is ready to hear such things."

Innocent shrugged. "Perhaps, but that does not mean they do not need to be said."

"Please do not say anything until I have had time to determine any security issues that such a statement would bring about."

"I have no intention of saying anything until after my trip at the earliest." Innocent stood.

John sighed with relief. Innocent was leaving for a two-week trip through Asia tomorrow morning. "Good. That is good."

Innocent clapped him on the shoulder. "Do not worry so, John. It is God's work we do."

John stood, bowing his head. "Yes, Your Holiness. It is."

CHAPTER 12

BALTIMORE, MARYLAND

It had been a week since the Chicago incident. Laney had done a handful of trainings and had helped out one police department with a Fallen incident, but she'd slept every night in her own bed. It had been a long time since she'd done that for a full week.

This morning, the estate was quiet as Laney made her way down the path from the main house to Sharecroppers Lane. After Samyaza's botched coronation, the place had been crawling with agents from almost every agency with initials. The last of them had finally taken their leave about six weeks ago, and life had started to slowly go back to normal. Well, at least what passed for normal around here.

The McAdamses being here helped. Even though they'd only been there for a week, they were now a fixed part of the Chandler family. They added a new energy that was great to be around. And Jake seemed so much more relaxed with Mary Jane close to him. The boys fit in well, and Molly, well, she'd really bloomed. Laney prayed that this place offered Molly a soothing balm to the chaos of the past few months.

Henry had started to take contracts again, after he and Jen had taken a small trip away. They were both better, but the loss of Jen's pregnancy still weighed on both of them. Laney would catch Jen staring off into space at random times, and then she'd try to pretend everything was fine. She'd thrown herself into her SIA work. Sadly, there'd been more than enough to keep her busy.

Naively, Laney had thought that when Samyaza died, the Fallen would largely crawl back into the shadows. But they'd done almost the opposite. Reports of Fallen incidents had exploded across the globe. Thefts, assaults, murder—they all seemed to have slipped their leashes. But most incidents were in the grand scheme of things, relatively minor. The problem was that now those incidents required more investigation. Fallen would rob a bank in one state or even a country, then slip across the border and disappear before anyone was the wiser. They'd had to hire more agents and more analysts to pore over video feeds and try to get descriptions. It was time-consuming and frustrating. Laney had removed the largest threat. But in so doing, she had unleashed a slew of smaller threats. It was like a giant game of whack-a-mole. You slammed one down and three more popped up.

Laney blew out a breath, running a hand through her hair. *Ugh.* Tension crawled over her skin. She felt responsible for it all, even though taking down Samyaza had been necessary. The world would be in a much worse situation if she hadn't. But damn it, it would be nice if a girl could catch a break every now and then.

Drake had been called off on another incident. It was only in upstate New York. It was supposed to be small, so it shouldn't take too long. Laney had offered to go along, but Drake had insisted she needed some time off. She had halfheartedly argued with him, but in her heart she knew he was right. She needed a little downtime.

Spying her uncle's cottage, she rubbed her hands over her face as if she could wipe away all traces of her tension and worries. She didn't like adding any more to his burden. The new addition to the cottage came into view as she approached: a wheelchair ramp at the back of the house along with a widened automatic door.

Despite their hopes, her uncle's injury was not temporary. Henry had flown in every single expert he could find. But after examining her uncle and his records, they all came to the same conclusion: There was nothing that could be done to return the function to his legs.

Laney had told herself she was prepared for that. But she hadn't been. It had been a blow. Her uncle had always been this wall of strength, and to see him brought low, it was hard. She knew he was keeping his own fears and concerns from her. He still thought of her as the child and him the adult, at least when it came to his own emotions.

But according to Cain, Patrick had had some dark moments. Cain had been there for him during those times. Laney said yet another thank-you that the immortal had come into their lives. He had become the friend that she had not realized her uncle needed. He had been by his side for the last few months, always ready to do whatever was needed. Who knew the world's first murderer would end up being an incredibly dedicated friend?

Laney pushed through the back gate of the stone fence that surrounded the cottage. The windows were open. The opening refrain from *Mickey Mouse Clubhouse* wafted out to greet her. She smiled, picturing Nyssa sitting curled up on the floor with her milk, bopping along. She loved that show.

Nyssa was the reincarnation of Victoria, Laney and Henry's mother. It had taken a little time for both of them to adapt to the fact that their mother was a two-year-old who could barely talk. It still took her aback.

The back door opened. A tall black leopard slunk gracefully through the door. The fluidity in Cleo's movements always amazed Laney. She moved without effort but was full of grace and regality.

Cleo stopped in front of Laney, who reached down and ran a hand through her fur. "How's everybody doing, girl?"

An image of Patrick sipping tea in the kitchen while Cain read the newspaper wafted through her mind, followed by an image of Nyssa leaning against Tiger while watching her show. Laney smiled. Tiger was another addition to her unusual family. Once Tiger had met Nyssa, he had refused to leave her side. And Nyssa did not want to go anywhere without her four-legged friend.

And with all the craziness in their lives, no one even batted an eye at the idea. Everybody just shifted a little to the side to make room for another giant cat in their lives.

Run?

Laney shook her head. "Not yet. I want to check on everyone."

Later.

"Yes."

An image of Calloway flitted through her brain. He had been the reason she'd been up at the main house. He'd wanted to discuss a draft of new regulations for the SIA. They were horrible. It had not been a pleasant meeting.

"Yeah, I saw him."

Bite him?

Laney laughed. "No."

Should have. Cleo brushed past her, slinking out the gate.

Laney smiled. *You are not wrong.* She walked up the ramp and let herself in the back door. Patrick looked up from his crossword, his reading glasses perched on the end of his nose.

Laney forced a smile onto her face. He had aged in the last few months. His shoulders were a little more hunched. There was more gray at his temples and throughout his red hair. His face was also thinner. He looked fragile. And that terrified her.

But his blue eyes still twinkled when he smiled. "Ah, there she is. How'd the meeting with old Sourface go?"

"Buttface, Uncle Patrick. The nickname is Buttface." She leaned down and kissed his forehead.

He shuddered. "That's a horrible nickname. I prefer mine. Anyway, how'd it go?"

Cain offered a cheek. Laney gave him a kiss as well before heading to the counter to pour herself some tea in the cup waiting for her. "Oh, the usual: Couldn't you have used less violence? Was it necessary to destroy the skylights by jumping through? Couldn't you have opened them and slipped in? Wasn't there a quieter way you could have disarmed the two dozen armed gang members and their Fallen leader?"

Cain arched an eyebrow. "I take it he did not use those exact words?"

Laney shrugged. "I'm paraphrasing. I feel like they're trying to build a Capone case against us. They can't get us for the crimes they think we've committed, so they're trying to find a financial angle to take us down." She grabbed a snickerdoodle before taking a seat. "I swear, they're going to charge me for every single cost related to any of these incidents."

Cain cracked his newspaper as he refolded it. "Good thing I have billions hidden all over the world."

Laney's mug stopped halfway to her mouth. "Billions?"

Cain's black eyes focused on her. "Immortal, remember? Got pretty good at reading the markets."

Laney caught her uncle's gaze with a smile. He shook his head. "I remember wearing shoes with holes in them for a full year because we couldn't afford new ones," said Patrick. "I hated when it rained." He shuddered.

Cain snorted. "I remember when we did not have houses, just caves we lived in. They were always damp."

Laney rolled her eyes. "Yes, you have both struggled mightily. This new generation has no idea how good they have it."

Cain didn't take his eyes from his newspaper. "Good of you to notice."

Patrick nodded his agreement, making Laney smile as she took a bite of her treat. "Could I get the entertainment section?"

Cain rummaged through the paper, pulling out the section. "You're sure you don't want the news section?"

"Am I in it?"

"Well, yes."

"Then no. I'll stick with the comics."

~

IT HAD BEEN AN ENJOYABLE MORNING. Laney sat with her uncle and Cain reading the paper, then she'd taken Nyssa for a walk along with Cleo and Tiger. They'd run into Mark Fricano and Dylan Jenkins, two of Jake's former Navy SEAL buddies who were part of the Chandler Group security team, who played peek-a-boo with Nyssa amongst the trees. Then Nyssa had gone down for a nap and Laney had curled up with her.

When she'd awoken, Cleo was sprawled out next to her, all her paws up in the air. Tiger was lying across the bottom of the bed. Nyssa was curled in tight next to her.

Laney ran a hand through Nyssa's soft curly red hair. She was a beautiful little girl who always seemed to be looking for an opportunity to laugh. Even without knowing she was the oldest soul in the world, she was truly an amazing little girl.

Cleo rolled to her side, lifting her head up. *Visitor.* Tiger lifted his head from the end of the bed as well.

Laney nodded, sliding off the bed without disturbing Nyssa, who rolled onto her stomach, her arms thrown wide. *Stay with her.*

Tiger and Cleo nodded back at her.

The house was quiet as she closed the bedroom door behind her. Cain and Patrick had gotten into the habit of taking a morning nap as well. Laney hurried down the stairs, getting no sense of the visitor on the other side of the front door, which meant they were neither Fallen nor Nephilim. Being they had been let into the estate, she knew they were no threat. In addition to checking people at the main gates, Henry had installed additional guards at the end of Sharecroppers Lane to check IDs, even when on the estate.

She ran across the foyer to fling open the door before whoever was coming up the steps could knock or ring the bell and wake everyone up.

A man of average height with dark hair and eyes started as he placed a foot on the porch. "Laney. Good morning."

Laney put a finger to her lips, closing the door behind her.

"Ah, nap time?" The man stepped fully onto the porch, his jacket falling open to reveal his black clothes and the white collar of a Roman Catholic priest.

She nodded as she directed them to the porch chairs. "Yes. How are you, Bas?"

Bas was Father Sebastian Gante, formerly residing in Rome, Italy. He had arrived in the States two days after the Washington D.C. incident to get her uncle's statement for the Church. And he had not left.

Bas took a seat with a sigh. "Father Invencio is being, shall we say, difficult this morning."

Father Invencio had been put in charge of the Church's newest task force charged with investigating the veracity of the fallen angel claims. With all the press Samyaza had received, the Church had received demands from its members to know if Elisabeta Roccorio had indeed been Samyaza, if the Fallen were truly fallen angels, and to know what exactly Laney's role was in the whole debacle. Unable to avoid the very public nature of the issue, they had created the task force and dispatched Bas to speak with Patrick.

No one had trusted him when he first arrived. No one even wanted to speak with him. But Laney was definitely warming up to the young priest. He seemed no less happy with the Church's hierarchy than her uncle was these days.

"What's Invencio's issue now?"

"He does not think my last report was detailed enough. He wants more pictures next time."

"Are they springing for a camera for you?"

"Apparently one should be arriving in the morning." Bas's smile faded. "Laney, I know you are going through a great deal, but I do need to interview you. It is always your right to say no, of course, but the Church is growing restless, and I fear they may send someone else if you do not speak to me."

Laney studied the priest. He was in his midthirties and had been born and raised in Italy. He'd joined the Church when he was twenty and had worked almost exclusively in Rome since that time. He was an insider. Yet for some reason, she trusted him.

But trusting him was not the same as being willing to reveal all her secrets. "I still don't understand how the Church can claim to know nothing of my role in history. They must have known about the ring bearers."

"I don't see how they could not have known either. It does not make sense. But that is their official statement." There was no guile in the priest's face or voice. He seemed as perplexed by their apparent denial of knowledge as she was.

"You see why I would have difficulty sharing information when I feel they are not being truthful?"

"I do. I have spoken with them, but Father Invencio is adamant that they know nothing about a ring bearer."

Silence fell between them while Laney wrestled with the correct course of action. She had no interest in making her uncle's life harder than it already was, and she knew how much pressure the Church was putting on him to provide answers. They even wanted him to come to Rome to give an accounting. She just had a feeling that revealing all she could do and what she knew was not the right move.

Bas reached out and patted her hand. "It does not have to be today. I know you have had a long week already."

She narrowed her eyes. "How do you know that?"

"The news. Your exploits in Chicago have been covered on all the major channels."

Laney groaned. "Oh, crap."

Bas laughed, a deep rumble. "It was good. They said you were like a superhero, or maybe a saint."

"Ugh. I wish they'd stop talking about me altogether."

"I do not think that it's going to happen." Bas stood up. "How about if I make lunch for everyone? A good meal makes everything better."

Laney stood up as well, her stomach grumbling in anticipation. Bas was a great cook. She had been lucky enough to partake in more than a few of his meals since he'd arrived. "I think that sounds like a great plan."

"Will you help me?"

"I'd be delighted."

CHAPTER 13

Aromas from the kitchen drifted down the hallway as Patrick pushed open his bedroom door. Oregano and basil with a little hint of Parmesan, which could only mean one thing—Bas was here. He'd been suspicious of the young priest when he'd arrived from Rome. The Church hadn't been overly sympathetic to Patrick's trials as of late, at least when it came to information. They were demanding an accounting. He'd spoken to them by phone and had answered most of Bas's questions. But there were certain things that he would not tell them.

Such as how Elisabeta had become immortal and then mortal again. The world did not need that knowledge floating around.

He banged the side of the wheelchair into the door frame, having misjudged the distance. He'd yanked his fingers back in time, just managing to avoid crushing them between his chair and the door frame.

They had converted the dining room into a bedroom with an attached bathroom, all designed to accommodate his wheelchair. Henry had it ready to go for him as soon as the doctor okayed him to go home. At first he'd resented the chair, and he still had dark moments, but it seemed selfish when Kati, Maddox, Zach, and thousands of others had lost their lives. Still, for an active man, it was a struggle to accept.

Conversation from the kitchen drifted down the hall along with the scents. He smiled hearing Laney's voice. She sounded good, relaxed. She'd taken on so much lately that these little moments of normalcy warmed his heart.

Nyssa appeared in the hallway, a giant smile on her face. She hurried toward him, Tiger slinking along behind her. She threw herself on his legs with a squeal of joy. He rested his hand on her red curls. "Hello, little love. Did you have a nice nap?"

She looked up at him, her arms still wrapped around his legs, nodding. Tiger nudged Patrick's other hand. Patrick rubbed his head. "Hello, Tiger. Good to see you too."

Tiger's head snapped up, and he stared at the door. Patrick looked over in time to see the mail fall through the slot in the door. With a happy squeal, Nyssa ran over, gathering it in her arms. A few pieces fell. Tiger picked them up in his mouth. Patrick had seen a show about training rescue dogs to be service dogs and wondered for a moment if he could get one of the cats to be his service animal. It could come in useful.

"May I see those?" Patrick asked.

Nyssa shook her head, holding them tighter to her chest and taking a step back.

She loved mail. He wasn't sure why, but she loved playing with each envelope or flyer that slipped through the slot. The batch in her hands right now looked like it was mostly junk.

"All right. Why don't you go show Cain what you found?"

She smiled and ran down the hall. Tiger dropped his three pieces in Patrick's lap before trotting after her. Patrick wheeled behind them with only a quick glance at the mail in his lap. The letter on top was from a hearing aid company. He rolled his eyes. He'd received more and more medical device advertisements since he'd been shot than he'd received in his whole life. Whoever manufactured the wheelchair must have sent out the announcement that he was now looking for every medical invention ever created.

As he rolled into the kitchen, Laney looked up from the island. "Hey. Lunch will be ready in five."

"Smells great. Good afternoon, Bas."

Bas nodded at him, plaid oven mitts on his hands. "Good afternoon, Patrick. You look well."

"And you lie poorly. But it's still nice to see you."

He rolled over to the desk in the corner of the kitchen and picked up the three pieces of mail Nyssa had allowed him, tossing the advertisement on the desk. He'd shred it later or give it to Nyssa. A second advertisement asking if he was happy with his electric company was next. It joined the first. He sighed, thinking of the amount of trash the postal service delivered. No wonder the landfills were filling up at alarming rates.

The third envelope gave him pause. It was from the Executive Office of Immigration Review. Patrick frowned. He had a green card, as he was still a British citizen. He'd thought about getting his American citizenship years ago, but he'd never quite gotten around to it. He'd never seen the need.

He paused. He'd sent in his ten-year renewal form months ago, but now that he thought about it, he realized he'd never received anything back. With everything going on, it had simply slipped his mind.

But now that glaring omission of a response was like a neon sign in his mind. Since the coronation, there'd been a crackdown on immigrants in the United Sates. They'd been deporting more and more. People without criminal records who had lived here for decades had been forced to leave their families and their lives behind.

It's nothing. I'm sure it's nothing, he tried to tell himself. But there was a noticeable tremor in his hands as he slid the envelope open. He pulled open the single sheet of paper. The seal of the

United States government was at the top, a form letter beneath it. He read slowly, his mouth falling open.

Laney walked over wiping her hands on a towel. "Uncle? Are you all right?"

He stared up at her, his mind blank for a moment.

"Patrick?" Bas stood behind Laney, concern etched on his face.

He swallowed. "I think . . . I think I'm being deported."

CHAPTER 14

ALEXANDRIA, VIRGINIA

The coffee eased down David's throat as he scanned the headlines on his tablet. More Fallen incidents had been reported. There was a growing call for information and a quieter call for them to be rounded up. David stared into the small backyard of his townhome. He'd seen these times before—not in the United States but in Iran, in El Salvador, in Russia. None of them ended well for those caught in the crosshairs. And as much as he would like to think his fellow Americans would be more magnanimous in their views, he also knew that paranoia was contagious. In this world of instant messaging, it seemed the loudest voice, not the most accurate voice, was given the most credence.

His partner of eight years, Rahim Nabavi, placed a kiss on his forehead, laying a hand on his shoulder. "What has you looking so gloomy this morning?"

David squeezed his hand before Rahim took the seat across from him. "Nothing, just the news."

Rahim was a lawyer with the Immigration Fund. He spent his days trying to help people who came from horrific situations to make a better life in the United States, much like Rahim had done. He wrangled red tape to get people coming from war zones, crime zones, and all-around horrible places housing, jobs, and legal standing. He was, in David's opinion, one of the best and most moral people he had ever met. The irony of the extreme differences in their professional lives was not lost on him.

Rahim frowned, the skin between his dark brows wrinkling. "They're increasing the calls for something to be done about the Fallen?"

"Yes." David paused. "What do you think of it?"

Rahim looked across the table, his face tensing for a moment before he shrugged. But David saw the movement and wished he could take his question back. He knew what Rahim would think. "I'm sorry. I shouldn't have—"

Rahim's hand shot out, taking David's hand. "No, no. What happened to me was horrible. But it is not my horror alone. Hate and ignorance is not relegated to only my former government."

David knew that was true, but he hated when he brought up Rahim's past, even unintentionally. Rahim was from Iran, a country that still executed people for being gay. Rahim had been David's informant for a few missions. Over time, they had fallen in love. But David had never seen himself as someone who had a normal family life. Besides, he and Rahim lived worlds apart.

But then Rahim had been picked up by the Iranian police for protesting the execution of one of his friends, and it was his turn to stand on the execution block. By the time David reached him, Rahim had been beaten so severely David could only recognize him by the scar on his leg from a childhood accident. He had smuggled Rahim out of the country and used his pull to get him asylum. Rahim had become an American citizen six years later. Now he tried to help others going through nightmares similar to his own. He was doing extremely well, but every once in a while the nightmares reminded him of his life before and haunted him for days. So David did everything in his power to keep their home life peaceful. But sometimes real life had to intrude.

Rahim stirred his coffee. "I see the signs here: the intolerance, the fear. None of it is good."

"But unlike your situation, these people, these Fallen, have the power to inflict real damage."

"Or commit great acts of good. There are good people. There are bad people. No one should be judged based on one aspect of who they are. It tells you nothing of their heart."

"No, it doesn't." David studied his partner, seeing the dark circles under his eyes. "You know, I think I have a quiet day. Perhaps I'll work from home, then we can go out to lunch."

Rahim smiled. "I'd love that. I'll call the office and tell them I'm working from home as well."

The doorbell rang. The smile slipped from Rahim's face. "I think that means your day is going to get a little more busy."

"Perhaps not. It could just be the paper boy," David said as he stood.

"Ha ha. We don't get the paper delivered."

"Well, maybe he's looking to change that. You eat. I'll see who it is." David walked to the counter and pulled out the drawer on the end. He pretended not to see Rahim tense just as Rahim pretended not to see David pull out the Walther PPK before heading to the front door.

David stopped halfway down the hall at the monitor that displayed the front stoop. There was a single man David did not recognize standing there behind the bulletproof door. He was tall, and he wore a suit and a dark raincoat. David punched the intercom. "Can I help you?"

The man leaned toward the speaker. "Mr. Okafur, I am Secret Service Agent Sheffield. I have been sent to retrieve you for a Tango meeting."

David flipped open his phone, pulling up the morning's security screen. "Authorization?"

The agent rattled off a series of ten numbers and letters. They matched.

"All right. Give me five minutes."

He snapped off the intercom and turned to find Rahim standing in the doorway of the kitchen. "I guess our lunch is off."

David walked over to him. "Not necessarily. I'll see what I can do. If not, maybe we could do dinner."

Rahim kissed him softly. "Be careful."

"Always."

Rahim turned back for the kitchen. David watched him for a moment. Rahim added a softness to David's life that he had never realized he had been missing. He was immensely grateful for that. He turned and hustled up the stairs, his mind already shifting gears. A Tango meeting. Apparently the President wanted to chat.

CHAPTER 15

BALTIMORE, MARYLAND

"This has to be a mistake." Laney gently took the letter from her uncle's hands. He didn't try to stop her. His face had taken on a pallor she didn't like. She quickly scanned the document. "It says you failed to renew your green card."

"No, no. I sent in the paperwork. I did it from the cabin in Pennsylvania."

"How did you mail it?"

"Certified mail. We were in the middle of nowhere. I wanted to make sure it got there. I received a receipt telling me it had been received. They got the paperwork."

"I'll call Henry. I'm sure it's just a clerical error."

Bas nodded. "Laney's right. Let's not worry until we have to. And the lunch is ready. Let's eat. I'm sure by the time we're done, this will all be sorted out."

Patrick nodded. "I'm sure you're right."

"I'll call Henry right now. Do you still have a record of the mail receipt?"

"Yes."

"Send it to me. I'll get it to Henry. Let's not worry until we have to."

"All right." Patrick pulled over the laptop and began to input his password. Laney turned for the back door, wanting to make the call in private. But as she did, she caught the tightening of Bas's jaw. He looked bothered. She shook her head. Of course he was bothered. Anyone could see her uncle didn't need this stress right now.

∽

LANEY HAD CALLED HENRY. He promised to have his people look into it immediately. She didn't feel comforted, but she'd straightened her shoulders and plastered a smile on her face. She opened the door as Bas was pulling the lasagna from the oven, placing it on the island next to the garlic knots and salad. "That smells delicious."

And it was. Whoever taught Bas to cook had her heartfelt appreciation. They only spoke about the letter for a moment when Cain, with his dark glasses on, entered the kitchen with Nyssa. But then they kept the conversation light. Bas told them stories about his first days at the Vatican, which had them all laughing, even Cain.

Bas turned to him as he wiped his mouth, pushing his plate away. "Have you been to Rome?"

Cain nodded. "Many times. It's changed a great deal over the years."

"How so?"

There was a small pause. Bas did not know who Cain truly was. Every once in a while, keeping it that way seemed fraught with difficulty. Bas thought Cain's name was a shortened version of McCain, his last name. It was not a brilliant cover. But they had been scrambling when Bas had shown up and Nyssa had called Cain by name. Bas thought Cain was an expert on ancient languages, which technically was true.

Cain took a sip of water, looking not even slightly nervous. "Much more traffic, more tourists."

Bas nodded. "Yes, when I was a child, you could walk the streets much easier."

"Hmm, these rolls are delicious. Where did you learn to cook?" Laney asked.

"The cook at my school, Sylvia. She was a wonder in the kitchen. I would pester her until she'd let me help out."

Laney frowned. "Were you at a boarding school?"

Bas didn't meet her eyes. "Of a sort."

Laney's phone rang before she could follow up. Like Cain, Bas seemed selective in the information he shared. His childhood tended to be completely off limits.

"It's Henry." She snatched the phone from the table and quickly turned it on. "Hey, Henry."

Henry didn't bother with pleasantries. "I had Brett speak with the immigration office." Brett was Brett Hanover, the head of Henry's legal department.

"Hold on, Henry. I'm putting you on speakerphone." She pressed the speak button. "Okay, go." She placed the phone closer to Patrick.

Henry's voice rang out through the kitchen. "The office is saying they never received his paperwork."

Laney leaned forward. "But he has a receipt saying they did."

"Brett pressed that point. After some back and forth, they've agreed that Patrick will not be deported, but he has to renew his green card again, this time in person."

Laney met her uncle's gaze and smiled. Okay. It would be an inconvenience but still doable.

"That's great. Thank you, Henry," Patrick said.

"Well, don't thank me yet. Since the coronation, the government has really been cracking down on foreigners in the country. They've initiated a new requirement for green card renewals."

"What is it?" Laney asked.

"The person must return to their country of origin to renew their green card."

Laney's mouth fell open. "That's insane. Why on earth would they do that?"

"I'm not sure. But it means Patrick needs to go overseas to renew his card."

Laney studied her uncle. He was so fragile right now. An overseas trip was a huge burden. "There must be some exceptions."

"I'm afraid not. The deadline is one week from now. I'm going to make arrangements. Let me know when you want to leave and who's going."

Laney nodded. "Thanks, Henry." She snapped off the phone.

Patrick met her eyes, but there was no joy in his voice. "I guess we're heading back home."

"I guess we are."

Her gaze slipped to Cain and the concern behind his glasses. "This is ridiculous. Patrick's still healing. He's in no shape to take a transatlantic flight."

"I'll be fine." Patrick pushed back from the table. "I just need a minute." He rolled himself to the back door and let himself into the backyard.

No one spoke as he headed outside.

Cain leaned toward her. "I don't like this, Laney. With all that you've done, there should be a way to get his paperwork through. He's been here for nearly fifty years."

Laney watched the empty door and couldn't help but notice the slight shake in Bas's hand as he picked up Patrick's plate and headed to the sink. "I know. Something smells off. I just don't know what it is."

CHAPTER 16

WASHINGTON, D.C.

The tunnel was quiet except for the sound of footsteps. Secret Service Agent Sheffield led the way. His tall companion, who'd held open the door to the dark black Yukon and who had not been identified, now walked behind David—not a situation David was comfortable with.

David was aware of every move, breath, and footfall of the agent. He'd already identified his tics. He favored his left leg. His eyes would immediately shift to any movement in his peripheral vision. He kept opening and closing his right fist, suggesting an injury. All were factors that David could and would use to his advantage if necessary.

Not that he expected any problems. He'd walked this very same tunnel at least six other times to meet with the President. They always met at the same location. David wasn't surprised by the choice of location. The President had been holding more and more high-level meetings in the tunnels. The scuttlebutt was that it was due to the President's own fears that had driven her underground, but David knew it was due to the concerns of the

Secret Service. A Fallen had gotten way too close to the President on the Day of Reckoning, and they were well aware of how lucky she had been to escape injury. Not everyone on her detail had been.

He was currently walking in the tunnel that linked the White House to the Vice President's courtyard. He supposed he should be flattered—very few even knew these tunnels existed, never mind got to walk them. But he did not like being summoned like a houseboy.

Ahead, the door to the conference room stood flanked by four Secret Service agents. An additional six were no doubt stationed along the tunnel the President had taken in. He'd passed two more at the entrance he had used.

Sheffield nodded at the agent by the door. "Open it up."

The agent unlocked the bulletproof door, stepping back to allow David to enter.

David stepped through, scanning the room for any threats. Two agents stood on the other side of the door. Two on the opposite side of the room. The President stood with her aide at the conference table. All par for the course. But there was one extra attendee at today's meeting: a man in a long black cassock, a red sash around his waist, a red cap on his head, and a long rosary around his neck.

David had been waiting for the Roman Catholic Church to become involved. Although he had to admit, he was surprised that the President would include them in one of these briefings. He strode over to the table. "Madame President."

The President shook his hand. "Mr. Okafur, I'd like to introduce you to Cardinal John Moretti."

David shook the cardinal's hand. "The third highest ranked Vatican official."

The President's eyebrows lifted. "You know your Church hierarchy?"

David shrugged. "I am a man of hidden depths."

"So it would seem." The President gestured for the men to take a seat as she did the same.

David nodded to the President's aide, Alicia Lopez. "Alicia."

"Mr. Okafur."

Alicia was always in attendance at these meetings to take copious notes, for the President's eyes only. She was also trained at Langley, a fact the President was aware of and perhaps counting on should David get out of hand. David had even taught her hand-to-hand at the academy when he'd been grounded due to his face becoming a little too well known in certain parts of the world.

The President clasped her hands in front of her. "Now, tell me your impressions of the latest Fallen incident."

David quickly ran down the incident outside Chicago, keeping to the facts.

When he was done, the President frowned. "Delaney McPhearson fell three stories? Why didn't she use her abilities?"

"She was using them to keep a family from falling to their death. She had to choose, herself or them. She chose them."

The cardinal waved away his words with a scoff. "But she will heal. They will not."

"Yes, but she will feel the pain of the fall. Nothing in her abilities or any of the Fallen's prevents them from feeling pain. With a fall like that, she will have broken ribs, her back, a skull fracture is possible. It would have been extremely painful."

The cardinal studied David. "You sound like you admire her."

"I am merely making sure you have a complete picture of McPhearson's abilities and those of the Fallen. Assuming they do not feel pain is a mistake. They do feel it. They just heal from it quicker than normal humans."

"Thank you, David. Now, tell me what you have learned about Father Patrick Delaney," the President said.

This time David *was* surprised by the request, although he was careful to keep any of the surprise from showing on his face.

"Patrick Delaney is a Roman Catholic priest, age fifty-eight. He has been stationed in the United States for most of his career, although his work has taken him—"

The cardinal cut in. "Yes, yes. But what is his relationship like with Delaney McPhearson?"

David paused for only a second. "As you know, he has raised her since the age of eight, an unusual arrangement for a priest. They are extremely close. More father/daughter than uncle/niece. Through these last few years, when her abilities came into being, he has been a constant source of strength and support for her."

"So they are connected, emotionally bonded?" the cardinal asked.

"Very."

The cardinal leaned in. "I have heard that she is close to many people."

David frowned. Where was the cardinal going with this line? "That is true. She has a wide circle of people she cares deeply for."

"Would you say she cares for her uncle more?"

David frowned. "I doubt she would characterize it that way, but that is probably accurate."

The cardinal and President exchanged a look. David was barely able to contain his frown. Why the focus on the uncle? He was sidelined from most activities due to his injury. "You are aware that Father Patrick sustained an irreversible spinal injury and is confined to a wheelchair?"

"Yes. It is a shame," the President said.

David almost believed her . . . almost. He decided to switch gears. "If I may ask a question."

The President nodded.

"What is the Church's view of the fallen angel problem? And of the existence of a ring bearer?"

A sneer flitted across the cardinal's face before he covered it. But David saw it and knew it said more than his words. "The Church is not publicly commenting on either of those issues."

"Cardinal, David is in charge of the investigation into the ring bearer. The Church's view may hold some bearing into his work. David will not be revealing any information discussed here." The President speared David with a look, and he nodded in response.

The cardinal pursed his lips, studying David. Finally, he crossed his arms over his chest. "We view the Fallen problem as a genetic anomaly. The individuals with these abilities are not the reincarnation of fallen angels. The people cried to God for help, and he answered them, banishing the fallen angels to a pit in the desert."

"What of the argument that they were only banished there for seventy generations or until the world was destroyed? And that when those seventy generations passed and the world was not destroyed, they were released?"

The cardinal's eyes narrowed. "Those teachings are not recognized by the Church."

"And the ring bearer?"

The cardinal tried to keep the derision from his voice, but in David's opinion, failed. "The ring bearer, as she calls herself, is not an agent of God. God would not bestow such powers within one individual."

"And if He did, it would certainly not be a female," David said. The role of women in the Church had not been determined by Jesus but by his followers after his death. And Simon Peter's animosity toward Mary Magdalene was well documented long before Jesus's death, never mind after it. It was clear Simon Peter could not understand why Jesus put such faith in her. Although the Catholic Church argued for a less prominent role for women, other historical documents suggested that Mary Magdalene was a disciple, if not *the* disciple. And that she and Peter had very different views on how the followers of Jesus should move forward after Jesus's death.

The cardinal glared at David. "Women are an important part of the Church, but they are not the equal of men. There is a reason Jesus's apostles were only men. There is a reason he chose Simon Peter to lead his flock after his death. If the ring bearer were ordained by God, he would be a male. Women are too delicate for the position."

David snorted. "Delaney McPhearson does not strike me as particularly delicate. And I believe other religious leaders do support her as being ordained by God."

"That may be, but we are God's chosen representatives here on Earth."

"Oh, are you?"

"Yes, we are."

"I'm sure the Jews would be surprised to hear that, as would the Muslims."

"They are also children of the book. But the Holy Catholic Church is God's authority on Earth. The Pope is infallible. His words are God's words."

"I see," David said. "So the view of the Church is that both groups are genetic anomalies."

"We do not see them as separate. Delaney McPhearson is a genetic anomaly, just as the Fallen are." The cardinal cupped his hands together in front of him. "God has asked us to be humble. To be thankful. These Fallen are aberrations, not created in God's image."

"If they are not created in God's image, then whose image were they created in?"

The cardinal smiled. "Not God's."

"And what about their nature?" the President asked. "Are they good or evil?"

"As I said, they are *not* created in God's image."

David's eyebrows rose. *Well, that's damning.*

The President nodded at the cardinal. "Thank you for your input, Cardinal Moretti."

The cardinal stood. "Thank you, Madame President. I look forward to our cooperative efforts in the days to come."

The President nodded. The cardinal left the room. Cooperative efforts? The U.S. government was working with the Roman Catholic Church? That seemed problematic. Apparently the separation of church and state didn't extend to cover incidents involving the Fallen or McPhearson.

David studied the President as she silently watched the door close behind the cardinal. "Is there anything else, Madame President?"

"Yes." She turned her gaze from the door. "You have no doubt heard of the unrest in the populace that has arisen due to the existence of the Fallen."

"Of course. I was under the impression the unrest was only due to small pockets of individuals. That the larger population, while wary, is more open to the Fallen."

"The resistance to the Fallen is small, perhaps, but vocal. You have been studying this problem for the last few months. What is your view on the Fallen issue? Are they a danger to the public?"

All the incidents of the Fallen flew through his mind, but the last image was not one of the Fallen. It was of Rahim. The Iranian government had listed him as a danger to society's moral fabric, which was why he had been slated to die. What a loss to the world if they had been allowed to carry that decision through.

Still, David chose his words carefully. "Some of them are extremely dangerous, such as this individual in Chicago, Dirk Magnet. If Delaney McPhearson and her agents had not taken him down, he would have done a great deal of damage. But Delaney McPhearson has Fallen and Nephilim on her team. There are no doubt countless others in the shadows just living quiet lives. I think much like the unrest, the loud ones are the ones we are focused on. But I think like all people, there are good ones and bad ones."

"But you do think they are dangerous?"

David had a feeling the President did not want a balanced

opinion in the dangers of the Fallen. She wanted justification for whatever she already had in mind. "Some of them are, yes."

"Thank you, David. That will be all."

David stood. "Madame President." As he turned for the door, he couldn't help but wonder what the President had planned. One of the Secret Service agents opened the door. Sheffield and the tall agent were waiting for him.

David began to follow Sheffield back down the hall when he heard footsteps heading toward the room from a different hallway. He slipped his hand into his pocket, pulling open the stiches inside. He pushed his house keys through the newly created hole. "Oh no."

He scrambled to the ground to get them, quickly pulling his lace on his left shoe loose. Grabbing his keys, he continued kneeling as he began to slowly tie his shoe. "Give me one second."

From the other passageway, three men emerged turning onto David's hallway as David finished and stood. "My apologies, gentlemen. Shall we?"

Sheffield and his silent partner said nothing, just headed back down the hall for the exit.

David also said no more as he followed them back to the Yukon. But his mind was swimming, picturing the man being escorted to the conference room. Why was the President meeting with the U.S. Attorney General right after meeting with David? As he climbed into the back seat, he had a sinking feeling he knew.

And Rahim was not going to be happy.

CHAPTER 17

Cardinal John Moretti walked down the long hall, escorted by the Secret Service agent. The meeting had gone better than planned. The agent opened the door leading to the exit outside the White House gates.

"Cardinal, if you'll follow me."

"Actually, I think I would like to take a walk. My car will meet me."

The Secret Service Agent looked around. "I'm not sure that is safe."

A dark black Cadillac pulled up to the curb. A tall man in priestly black stepped out, nodding to the cardinal and the agent.

"Ah, here is my security now. Thank you for all your help, Agent." John smiled but made sure the agent knew he was not requesting being able to walk but informing the agent of his plans.

The agent stiffened before nodding his head. "I hope you enjoy the rest of your trip."

"Thank you." John started down the street as Father Pedro joined him. Pedro walked next to him but said nothing as he continually scanned the street. John pulled out his phone and dialed.

Cardinal Francisco answered. "Si?"

John smiled. "It went well, better than expected. The President has agreed to help make her uncle available to us."

"But how does that get us her?"

"She will not let him go alone. If she accompanies him, we will have our shot."

"Excellent. I have to admit, I did not think this idea of yours would work. In the past, the Americans have been very protective of their citizens."

"But that was before Delaney McPhearson demonstrated she could be more powerful than the President if she chose to be. Now the President is trying to crowd Delaney McPhearson off her stage. Being we are offering such an opportunity, she jumped at it."

"Well done, Cardinal. The Brotherhood will be pleased. You bring honor to our ranks."

"As always, we do this not for glory but to protect the papacy. Nothing is more important to me."

"And me either. I will be home tomorrow morning. We will need to discuss next steps."

"I have already begun the preparations. Come by my villa. We will eat and plan."

"I look forward to it."

John disconnected the call. He stopped turning. He could just make out the dome of the U.S. Capitol Building. All the power the Americans had, and it paled in comparison to the power Delaney McPhearson could unleash with her followers. The President didn't truly see the danger. She looked at McPhearson as a political issue. But John knew she was so much more than that. She was the greatest threat mankind had seen, perhaps ever. She was not just a threat to lives but to people's very souls.

But there was one within the U.S. government who did see Delaney McPherson for the threat she was. He might be coming at the issue from a different angle, but their goals were the same: to neutralize Delaney McPhearson.

Moretti had spent years collecting favors and information all over the world, including in D.C. Now was a perfect time to put those contacts into play. He pulled out his phone and dialed.

A young professional voice answered. "Senator Shremp's office."

CHAPTER 18

BALTIMORE, MARYLAND

"Are you sure you don't mind? I don't want to impose." Cain stood in the living room of the McAdamses' new home, looking around, unsure.

Mary Jane squeezed his arm. "Nonsense. The girls are having a great time. I'll give them some lunch, put them down for a nap. Go take some time."

Cain looked over to where the girls were playing on the floor, Tiger dozing near them. It was hard to tell Nyssa and Susie apart in a glance. Both had light, curly red hair, bright blue eyes, and a skin tone that promised that a lifetime of sunscreen would be required. They were also the same height. They could be mistaken for twins. And they acted like they belonged together. When Cain had brought Nyssa over that first day, the two girls had taken one look at one another and hit it off. They had been inseparable ever since.

Mary Jane herself had hit it off with Nyssa's guardian, Cain. She'd been a bit taken aback by his name at first. I mean, who would name their child Cain? But the man himself was lovely.

Considerate, attentive to Nyssa's every need, and he knew so much about history! She and Cain had spent hours talking the first day they had met.

But she recognized the need for him to go spend some time away from Nyssa. Laney had taken Patrick to meet with the Chandler lawyers about his green card, so Cain was on his own. She stepped in front of Cain. "You are a wonderful father. But all parents need to take a little time for themselves. So go, run a few errands, have a coffee solo. Just take a little time. Nyssa will be here waiting for you when you get back."

"Are you sure?"

"I'm sure."

"Maybe just an hour," Cain said, looking at Nyssa. At least, Mary Jane thought he was looking at Nyssa. It was hard to tell with those dark glasses of his. He never took them off, even indoors.

"Go. Enjoy yourself."

He leaned down and kissed Mary Jane's cheek. "Jake is lucky to have you."

Mary Jane smiled. "You are too sweet."

"All right. I'll be back in a little while. If there are any problems—"

Mary Jane escorted him to the front door. "I have your cell phone number and will call. Now shoo."

"All right." He paused, standing in the doorway before he slipped out the door.

Mary Jane shook her head as she turned back to the living room. Cain really needed to make some time for himself.

A chuckle snapped her head up. She narrowed her eyes at Jake, who stood leaning against the doorway of the kitchen. "And what are you laughing at?"

"Cain. I'm not sure he's ever been handled like that before."

"What? He's got a lot on his plate. Taking care of Nyssa and helping Patrick adjust. Now with Laney and Patrick busy, it's the perfect time for him to take a little break."

Jake shook his head, walking toward her. "Only you would see that. The rest of us see him as invulnerable."

"He's only human. And we all need a little help."

"I suppose we do."

The back door swung open. Cleo strolled in, kicking the door shut behind her. She nodded at Jake and Mary Jane before strolling into the living room. After a quick lick of each of the girls, she curled up next to Tiger and closed her eyes.

Mary Jane puffed out an incredulous laugh. "I know these leopards are smart, but every time Cleo opens that door and then shuts it behind her, I am amazed. I can't even get the boys to reliably do that."

"Speaking of your boys, they called while you were trying to get Cain out of the house. They wanted to know if it was okay if they ate lunch down at Dom's. Something about a *Minecraft* marathon."

The back door flew open. Mary Jane's hand flew to her throat as Molly zipped in. Theresa, a Fallen the same age as Molly with blonde hair and big blue eyes, appeared right behind her.

"Hi, Mom."

"Hi, Mrs. McAdams."

Trying to talk around her heart, which had leaped into her throat at their appearance, she glanced back at the door they had left open. "Hi, girls. What are you up to?"

"Jen and Noriko are going to get burgers in town," Molly said.

"They wanted to know if we could join them," Theresa said.

Molly clasped her hands in front of her. "Please?"

"Please?" Theresa echoed.

Mary Jane tried not to smile. While she was happy the boys had hit it off with Lou, Rolly, Danny, and Dom, she was over the moon that Molly had hit it off so well with Theresa. These last few days had been the first ones where Molly actually looked relaxed since the Day of Reckoning. Theresa had spent the night every night since they'd arrived, and the two could be heard giggling away in Molly's room. The sound lightened the weight on Mary Jane's shoulders immensely.

"Yes, yes. Just bring me back a burger and shake."

"Me too," Jake said.

"Okay." Molly sprinted over, kissing Mary Jane's cheek. "Love you, Mom!"

"Love you too. Have fun." The two girls grinned at her before sprinting back out the open door. This time, they remembered to close it.

"What's that smile for?" Jake asked.

Mary Jane wrapped her arms around Jake's waist. "I think things may finally be turning a corner for Molly."

"I'm glad."

She leaned her head on Jake's chest. "Me too."

CHAPTER 19

The traffic was surprisingly light as Jen made her way toward downtown Baltimore. "Have you ever been to the inner harbor?" Noriko, who sat in the passenger seat, asked Molly.

"No. This is my first time in Baltimore."

"There's a really great aquarium and a really cool scavenger hunt you can do. Maybe we can take your whole family there tomorrow."

Molly smiled. "That would be great. Thanks."

Jen returned the smile in the rearview mirror. She really liked Molly. She was quiet, sweet, even bordering on shy. But on the day of the attacks, she had gone out there to help as many people as she could. That was the reason that she and Henry had asked her to be the face of the new public relations campaign. She was a great choice. Straight-A student, wholesome look. They couldn't have chosen better if they'd gone to a casting agent.

Sadly, they were going to need that kind of good press. Jen did not like the hot topics on the talk shows or the views being spouted by the talking heads on the twenty-four-hour news networks. Protests had sprung up in some major cities, but they hadn't made it to Baltimore yet. And so far, the ones in other cities had been pretty small. But Jen had a feeling that would change soon enough.

Jen slowed at a red light, and Theresa gasped in the back seat.

"What is it?" Noriko asked.

Theresa just pointed out the window. Jen followed her finger to the graffiti on the side of the building. It said "Death to the Aberrations."

The Aberrations—the title bestowed upon those with abilities by the pundits trying to drum up outrage.

The light turned green. Jen hit the gas. "It's just a bunch of idiots. It doesn't mean anything."

But the mood in the car had shifted from happy to wary. Molly and Theresa scanned the street as if looking for a threat. Even Noriko was tense in the passenger seat. With relief, Jen saw the Burger Joint parking lot coming up quickly. Pulling into the lot, she put the car in park. She turned to look at the two frightened girls in the back seat.

"You are not aberrations. You are strong young women. And one day you will be a force of good of this world. Okay?"

They nodded back at her.

"Okay. Now let's go get some milkshakes." Jen stepped out of the car as a beat-up Nissan Sentra drove slowly by on the road. The occupants all stared at Jen and the girls as they got out of the car.

A chill crawled over Jen, but she got no sign that they were anything but human, and therefore not a threat. She forced a smile to her face. "Let's eat."

⁓

THE BURGER JOINT was filling up as Jen pushed the door open as they came back out into the parking lot an hour later. The lunch had started off a little tense, but as time wore on and the carbs were consumed, everyone's mood improved. Molly laughed as she scooted out behind Noriko. "There is no way Zane did that."

"I'm telling you," Noriko said. "He took one of the guards' shoes and hid it in the top of the oak tree. None of us know how he managed it, but I swear he did it."

"You sure you still want him to come live with you?" Theresa asked.

"Absolutely. Besides, if he hides anyone's shoes, it'll be the boys'. I'm totally okay with that."

Everyone laughed, and Jen was still smiling as she started across the parking lot. But then she went still as she caught sight of her car. "Freaks" was spray painted across the passenger side. "Die" was sprawled across the front.

"Oh my God." Noriko's mouth dropped open next to her.

Molly stumbled forward, looking unnaturally pale. "Who would—"

Jen's head snapped up, her vision narrowing as someone disappeared around the side of a building. She took off like a shot. Three men, all in their early twenties, sprinted down the street. Jen ran past them, materializing right in front of them. The guy in front screeched to a halt, lurching back and nearly losing his balance.

"And where are you running to?" Jen asked.

"None of your business." One of the ones behind the dark-haired man stepped out, a can of spray paint falling from his pocket.

"Really?"

The third one grabbed his friend and turned to go, but Theresa and Molly blurred into the space just behind them.

The men stumbled. "Freaks," one muttered, spitting at Molly's feet.

A police siren rang out before a patrol car slid into the curb. Two officers stepped out of the car. An older officer with gray at his temples stepped forward, his partner, a younger female, stayed by the car. "What's going on here?"

Jen didn't take her gaze off the men. "Officer, these men here just vandalized my car with spray paint."

The officer studied Jen. "I know you, don't I?"

"Agent Jennifer Witt, with the SIA."

"You're one of them Fallen," the officer said.

Jen didn't like his tone. "I'm a federal agent, and these men need to be placed under arrest."

The officer crossed his arms over his chest. "Did you see them spray paint your car?"

Jen gritted her teeth. "No."

"Then it seems to be your word against theirs."

"You are conveniently forgetting the spray paint can right there and the marks all over their hands."

The officer shook his head with a shrug. "Still not enough to make an arrest."

Jen flicked a gaze at him, noticing the stance and derision barely hidden behind the scowl on his face. "Let me get this straight, you are refusing to place these men under arrest?"

"You got that right."

Jen looked at the man's badge. "All right, Officer Benson. I'm sure my boss will have a lovely little chat with your boss about this."

The female officer stepped up, handcuffs in her hands. "You want me to secure them while you call for transport?"

Benson turned to his partner. "What the hell do you think you're doing?"

"My job," the officer answered. "What do you think *you're* doing?"

He narrowed his eyes. "You don't want to do this, Stein."

"No, sir, I think *you* don't want to do this. My job is to enforce the law. That's what I'm going to do." Stein nodded to the men. "Up against the wall."

The smirks dropped from the men's faces. They looked to Benson, who scowled in response.

Stein stepped forward. "I *said*, up against the wall."

The men faced the wall. Stein snapped cuffs on the first man before pulling two zip ties to make cuffs for the other two. Secured, she ordered them to sit.

While Stein was securing the men, Jen called the SIA, who contacted the Baltimore PD to send an additional squad car over.

Benson stormed back to his cruiser.

Jen stepped next to Stein. "You going to get in trouble for this?"

Stein shrugged. "Maybe. But I signed up to enforce the law, not look the other way because of someone's prejudice."

"Well, thank you."

"You're part of the Chandler Group, aren't you?"

Jen nodded.

"You know Delaney McPhearson?"

Jen smiled. "I do."

"Then tell her to not listen to the garbage a lot of people are spouting on the TV. They're just trying to get ratings. You guys have a lot of people pulling for you."

"Thanks, Officer Stein."

"Thank you, Agent Witt."

CHAPTER 20

The next morning, breakfast had just finished when Henry knocked at the back door of Patrick's cottage.

"Come in!" Laney called as she started to gather up the dishes.

Henry stepped in, smiling at the sight of Laney by the sink. "She stops villains at night and does dishes in the morning."

"Ha ha."

Henry kissed her cheek, then snagged a Danish from the plate on the counter next to Laney. He leaned against the counter, his feet crossed at his ankles. "Where is everybody?"

"Cain, Patrick, and Tiger took Nyssa for a walk. Drake is grabbing a shower."

"He's not helping with the dishes?"

"He *made* the breakfast, so I volunteered to do the cleanup." Laney placed the last of the dishes in the dish rack and wiped her hands on a towel. "So are you just swinging by to chat or is something up?"

"I heard back from Brett this morning."

Laney tensed. They'd been playing back and forth with the governments for the last few days, trying to figure out where exactly they were supposed to renew Patrick's green card. One day it was Scotland, then it was London. Then they weren't sure. If Laney didn't know any better, she'd swear they were stalling. "And?"

Henry let out a breath. "The final word came down this morning."

"The final final? Or the final until an hour from now?"

"No, they've assured Brett this is it."

"Okay, so where are we heading? Scotland or England?"

"Neither. They're saying because Patrick works for the Church, he needs to renew his visa at the Vatican."

Laney's jaw dropped. "What?"

"I know. It makes no sense. But their argument is that being the Vatican is in fact its own country, they should be the one to issue the visa."

The Vatican was the world's smallest country at only two square miles. Officially, it had only 600 citizens, although millions visited it annually. It also had its own television and radio stations, post office, banking and postal system, and newspaper. It even had its own police and security force.

While Laney knew all of that, it didn't change one basic fact. "But he's not a citizen of the Vatican. He's a citizen of Great Britain."

"I know, but apparently a new executive order was put into effect yesterday. Fallen or their family members who work in the United States must receive approval through their country of origin and the country that is employing them."

"That seems oddly specific," Laney said dryly.

"Yeah. If I were the paranoid type, I'd say this is an obvious ploy to get Patrick to Rome." Henry paused. "What do you want to do?"

"I *want* to tell them all where they can stick their new rules."

Henry smiled. "Okay. So what are you *actually* going to do?"

Laney sighed. She really did not like any of this. She also didn't like the mood of the country right now. She could feel the tide shifting against the Fallen. Somebody, she didn't know who, had started pushing anti-Fallen stories on the news and had started a virulent anti-Fallen social media campaign. And she was worried that the incident with Jen, Noriko, and the girls the other day was only the tip of the iceberg. "I really don't want to be out of the country right now. With everything that's happening, I feel like I need to be here."

"I can go for you."

Laney looked at her brother, an overwhelming sense of gratitude welling up inside her at the fact that she had found him. "Thank you. But I owe my uncle. He's been there for me my whole life. I have to go."

"I understand. I'll have a jet ready to go tomorrow morning. Hopefully you'll only be on the ground in Rome for a few hours."

Laney nodded but didn't say anything because she had a feeling a storm was about to break. And she just couldn't tell where she should be to help hold it back.

CHAPTER 21

ROME, ITALY

The hallway was lined in priceless paintings. John's steps echoed off marble tile that dated back to the sixteenth century. A fresco lined the ceiling, painstakingly uncovered thirty years ago when John had bought them home prior to becoming a priest. While John had divested most of his trappings of wealth, his home was the one thing he had never been able to let go. It had once belonged to a Doge who had spared no expense in its creation and decoration. John in turn had spared no expense in bringing it back to that original glory.

It was good to be home. He hurried down the hall to his office. His assistant stood up from behind his desk as John entered. Father Nikhil Longsly had been assigned to him by the Church. He was not part of the Brotherhood, although he did at times unwittingly do their bidding.

John strode across the room. "Well?"

"Father Patrick was informed that he needed to renew his passport here in Vatican City."

John smiled. "Excellent."

"Forgive me, Your Eminence, but I do not understand why he is coming here. As a British citizen and a U.S. green card holder, shouldn't he resolve this issue in one of those countries?"

"The Fallen have changed many things, my son. Including bureaucracy."

Nikhil frowned, his eyes still showing his confusion. "Uh, yes, Your Eminence."

"Now, how about some lunch? I find myself famished."

"Of course. I will see if the cook has prepared anything." Nikhil headed for the door.

John accompanied him to the door. "Be sure to make a plate for yourself." He clapped Nikhil on the shoulder as he stepped past John, then closed the door. He walked over to his desk, flipping through the papers Nikhil had been working on. Nothing of importance. He picked up the phone. Father Ezekiel answered on the first ring. "Yes?"

"Ezekiel."

"Father Moretti, it is a great honor." He dropped his voice. "All the preparations have been made."

"Excellent. Where will it take place?"

"The Castel Sant'Angelo. It seemed a fitting location, given the mission."

"Yes, indeed." Castel Sant'Angelo, where those who dared to go against the Church were tried and dealt their punishment.

"My only concern is that the steps we have taken are not enough. The ring bearer—"

"—is a woman. Do not make her out to be more than she is. Yes, she has abilities, but our brothers are well matched for her."

"And what of—"

John cut him off quickly. "Yes, he is another issue. He must not be harmed in any way."

"I'm not sure I can guarantee that. What if he fights us?"

"Do not fight back. Do not let him leave with the ring bearer, but no harm is to come to God's soldier."

"Yes, yes, sir." Ezekiel paused. "It is a great honor, sir, to be entrusted with this mission. To be alive at this time, to be part of God's plan, it is very fulfilling."

"Yes." John nodded his head. "I could not agree more."

John and Ezekiel spoke for a few more minutes, finalizing plans before John hung up. He sat back in his chair and pulled out his phone. He pulled up the picture from the coronation. Delaney McPhearson lying on the dais, soaked in blood, cradled in the arms of the man the world knew as Drake, Las Vegas entertainer. He zoomed in on the man's face, the agony splashed across it.

He cares for her. That could be a problem. But he shook his head, clearing the thought. *No. Once he learns who he is, once he remembers who he is, any feelings he has will be subsumed under his duty.*

Yes, soon God's soldier would be their best weapon in the fight against Delaney McPhearson.

CHAPTER 22

BALTIMORE, MARYLAND

A Dornier 328 jet raced down the runway and burst into the sky. Laney watched it with awe. She understood the mechanics of aviation, but that moment of takeoff always filled her with dread, hope, and a sense of magic. Hopefully they'd be flying back at this time tomorrow.

"Still watching the planes, I see." Patrick came to stop next to her at the airport terminal's window.

"I still can't believe they can get up into the air."

Patrick smiled. "I remember being with you and your mom at JFK, waiting for your dad to arrive home from a business trip. Your face was glued to the glass watching the airport personnel scurry around the tarmac. You even got into a little dance off with one of the guys loading suitcases onto a cart below."

"I did?"

Patrick's smile grew brighter. "It is one of the best memories I have from your childhood. It never fails to make me smile. You were wearing this bright green shirt with a unicorn on it and a pink tulle skirt. You were four."

Laney smiled, not because she remembered the moment but because Patrick obviously relished the moment. An image of her adopted mother flitted through her mind. With all the talk about Victoria in recent years, she supposed people thought of her as her true mother. But Fiona Delaney had loved and raised Laney until she and Laney's adopted father were taken from her when Laney was eight. She was the first person Laney thought of when she thought of her mother.

Patrick's little stories about their time together brought her both a sense of connection and loss. How different would her life have been if her parents had never died? If Patrick hadn't been the one who raised her for the majority of her childhood? If her parents had been alive when she realized she was the ring bearer? Would it have made it easier or would it have been harder? She turned back to the window. She didn't often go off into the world of "what if," but sometimes she had to wonder how different her life could have been.

Drake strode in through the terminal entrance. He smiled, heading to Laney and Patrick. "Good news—no bombs on board. The captain checks out, and all the radar systems are working."

Laney wanted to roll her eyes at his overprotectiveness, but she was glad for it. She might survive another missile attack on a plane, but her uncle certainly wouldn't.

"Radar systems?" Patrick asked.

"It's nothing. Just after that little incident with Samyaza, Henry made sure that there were missile defense systems added to the private planes we use," Laney said.

"'Little incident'?" Patrick asked. "You mean when she blew your plane out of the sky?"

Drake placed his hands on the back of Patrick's wheelchair. "That's the one! Now how about I escort you to the plane while Laney deals with an uninvited guest."

Laney frowned. "Uninvited guest? Who?"

Drake tilted his head back toward the terminal's entrance as the doors slid open. Stanton Calloway stepped through, looking around the terminal for a moment before making a beeline for Laney, Patrick, and Drake.

Laney groaned. "Oh, come on."

"Well, I think that's our cue," Patrick said. "Onward, Drake."

"Thanks, thanks a lot," Laney grouched as Drake pushed Patrick quickly toward the exit leading to the runway.

Laney turned to watch them through the glass as they made their way to the Chandler jet.

In the reflection of the glass, she saw Stanton stop behind her. "Ms. McPhearson."

Laney gritted her teeth, not turning around. "Doctor."

"The government has given you permission to leave the country."

This time Laney did roll her eyes before turning around. "I know, Stanton. That's why I'm here."

"Yes, well. They wanted me to remind you that when you leave the United States, you are also leaving the protections of the United States behind. You will be expected to comport yourself within the legal restraints of the country you are visiting."

"Yes, I am well aware."

"Also, you will have no legal authority. The government has suspended your SIA credentials while you are out of the country."

"What? Why?"

A smug smile crossed his face. "If they wanted you to know, they would have told you."

Laney smiled back just as smugly. "So they didn't tell you either, huh?"

Stanton's tiny mouth shrunk even more as he pinched his lips. "You are expected to be a representative of the United States and acquiesce to any informational requests that might be made of you by the Vatican committee on the Fallen."

Laney snorted. "No."

Stanton glared. "The United States government has assured the Vatican you would cooperate."

"Well, you really should have checked with me before you did that."

"A representative will meet you. You are expected to answer—"

Laney held up a hand. "Let me stop you right there. I will answer questions when and if I choose to. Not when the United States government orders me to do so."

Stanton narrowed his eyes. "You are making a mistake."

A flippant retort was on the edge of her tongue, but she bit it back as she studied Stanton. There was more confidence in his tone today. A little extra something in his eyes. She stepped forward. "What do you know?"

Stanton took a step back. "More than you. You should do what the government says. You are after all, still a citizen. Unlike your uncle." With that, he turned and headed for the exit.

Laney watched him go, a feeling of dread welling up in her stomach. That was a threat. The government had just delivered her a threat. But what the heck was it about? Answering the questions of the Vatican? Why would they care if she did that, especially being she hadn't even answered *their* questions.

What am I missing?

A blur blew through the doors. Drake stood in front of her. "All aboard who's going aboard."

She kept her gaze on the door Stanton had exited through before turning to Drake. "Right. Let's go."

"Hey." He grabbed a hold of her shoulders and tipped her chin up. "What's going on? Did Stanton upset you?"

"No, not him." She shook her head. "He warned me to not break any laws while out of the country, told me my SIA badge would be of no use."

Drake shrugged. "So?"

"I don't know. There was something about his tone. I feel like I'm missing something."

"Is there anything you can do about it right now? Do you want to stay? I could accompany—"

"No, no. Uncle Patrick is the priority right now. We'll go. Get his green card taken care of and be right back."

Drake kissed the back of her hand. "I love how completely naive you are about the efficiency of government bureaucracies."

She slipped her arm through his. "Come on, my notoriety must be good for at least getting through a little red tape."

"You're right. Twenty-four hours, probably less."

She nodded as the doors slid open and they stepped outside. A cool wind blew back on them, making her shiver. She tried not to take it as an omen.

Twenty-four hours.

CHAPTER 23

Mary Jane stood over the crib. The girls had gone down for a nap, their hands clasped together in the crib. Tiger, Cleo, and Zane had swung by just before naptime. Now they were sprawled out on the floor of the girls' room. The group of them napping together at either her or Cain's house had become the new normal.

She backed silently out of the room. Her boys were down at Dom's. Jen and Noriko had picked the girls up a few hours ago to take them back downtown. Jen wanted to cover the bad memories with good ones. And it seemed to have worked. Molly had called an hour ago, and she'd seemed really happy. Mary Jane hoped she'd pushed the ugliness from her brain. But Mary Jane had spent a few sleepless nights because of it. She headed down the stairs, hearing Jake on the phone.

"It's okay. Do what you need to do. Everything's quiet here." He paused. "Okay, will do. Try to enjoy yourself." He disconnected the call.

"Laney?" Mary Jane asked.

"Yeah. Apparently the Vatican, who has been desperate to

speak with them for the last few months, has yet to meet with them."

"Why not?"

Jake shrugged. "They don't have a clear answer on that. But it has at least given them a chance to play tourist."

Mary Jane smiled and then tried to cover a yawn.

Jake laughed, taking her hand and leading her to the couch. "Come on, Sleepy. Close your eyes for a little bit."

Mary Jane curled up on the couch with Jake. Jake rubbed her arms. "I could get used to this."

"Me too."

Jake's phone beeped. Mary Jane's sounded from the kitchen at almost the same time. Jake grabbed his from the coffee table. "It's a news alert. The President is making a statement . . . about the Fallen."

Heart beginning to pound, Mary Jane grabbed the remote and turned the TV on, quickly switching to a twenty-four-hour news channel. Jerome Fontane was sitting at the news desk, his face serious.

"We will shortly go live to the White House, where President Rigley is preparing to deliver a statement on the enhanced individuals that the world learned about on the Day of Reckoning. Protests against the enhanced individuals have cropped across the world as people worry about the power imbalance between these much stronger humans.

"Pressure has been mounting on the President and other world governments to develop a policy regarding the Fallen. Reports from around the world suggest that most governments are keeping track of the Fallen within their borders. There has also been a marked spike in violence both committed by enhanced individuals and against them."

Jake laced his fingers through Mary Jane's. She held on tight. Cleo slunk into the room, sitting on the ground on Mary Jane's other side. Mary Jane rested her other shaking hand on Cleo's back. Mary Jane had been telling herself everything would be fine. That Molly would be fine. But in the back of her mind, she'd known this moment was coming.

Jerome paused. "I am receiving word that the President is about to issue her statement. We go live now to the White House press room."

The screen image shifted to the familiar White House press room with its white walls and blue carpet. The podium at the front of the room was empty, but then there was a rustle of energy. President Rigley appeared from the doorway to the left of the screen before taking her position behind the podium.

The reporters leapt to their feet. But President Rigley just raised her hand, and they quieted down. She nodded.

"Good afternoon. The Day of Reckoning was a watershed moment in world history. The existence of a group of humans with the supernatural abilities of strength, speed, and healing became known to violent effect. On that day, Elisabeta Roccorio, in her attempt to take over all world governments, killed one million Americans. Such a crime cannot go unanswered, even though the catalyst for those actions died."

"At Laney's hands. I see she didn't mention that," Jake growled.

"But Elisabeta did not work alone. She would not have been able to commit her acts of atrocity without the aid of other Fallen." The President took a deep breath.

Mary Jane did as well. Jake squeezed her hand, but she barely registered it, the sense of impending doom overriding everything but the President's voice. Mary Jane felt like she was on the edge of a cliff, knowing the words the President next uttered would shift her world forever.

"Beginning immediately, all Fallen within the boundaries of the United States government are required to register at the newly appointed Agency of Enhanced Individuals. Individuals with enhanced abilities who fail to register within three days will be arrested."

"Under what charge?" a reporter yelled out.

The President paused. Mary Jane thought she was going to ignore the question, but she didn't. "In my office, I just signed Executive Order 2157, the Protection of Humanity Act. It declares that any individual with enhanced abilities who fails to register will be considered an enemy of the state. I fully expect the Congress to take the order and legislate it into law. But as time is of the essence, I have used the executive order privilege to begin the process of protecting American citizens."

Mary Jane gripped Jake's hand tighter, disbelief running through her. *But Molly's an American citizen. Who will protect her?*

CHAPTER 24

After dropping that bomb of an announcement, the President stepped aside and let the press secretary answer the flurry of questions from the press corps. Mary Jane sat there feeling numb. Jake wrapped a blanket around her shoulders when she started to shake.

All Mary Jane could picture were other points in history when governments required people to register. In the United States, it was Japanese citizens during World War II, but not German citizens. And of course, in Germany it was the Jews. Both of those situations resulted in camps. In the United States camps, American citizens had lost all of their property and watched their families be treated like second-class citizens in their own country.

In Germany, millions had lost their lives. She gripped the blanket around her, picturing the mounds of eyeglasses left behind at the concentration camps, the piles of suitcases, and the bodies that were left out because there was simply no space to hide them.

"The girls are up," Jake said softly. "I'll put a show on for them upstairs, okay?"

Mary Jane nodded numbly. Cleo placed her head in Mary

Jane's lap as Jake stepped out of the room. Mary Jane looked into the large cat's eyes, tears pricking at her own eyes. "How am I going to keep her safe, Cleo? What am I going to do?"

The front door flew open. "Mom?"

Wiping her eyes, Mary Jane leapt to her feet, hurrying into the hall.

Molly's hair was wild, her eyes bright with unshed tears. "The President—she—Mom—"

Mary Jane just opened her arms. Molly nearly bowled her over as she ran into them. "I will not *let* anyone hurt you."

Molly shook her head. "But, Mom—"

Mary Jane placed her hands on her daughter's cheeks and lifted her face so she could see her eyes. "You listen to me, Molly Jane McAdams—*no one* is going to hurt you. Do you hear me? No one."

Molly nodded, tears sliding down her cheeks. Mary Jane crushed her back to her chest, just noticing Theresa standing in the doorway, looking uncertain, biting her lips to keep her own tears back. Mary Jane held out an arm to her. Theresa flew down the hall, her shoulders shaking.

Mary Jane held the two sobbing girls, the girls the United States government was so worried about, and anger burned through her. How dare they terrify these girls this way. This country had been built on independence. It was also supposed to run on justice. There was nothing just in this government order.

Jake walked down the stairs, placing his phone in his back pocket. He glanced at the two girls, his gaze worried before he looked at Mary Jane. "That was Henry. He wants me at the main house to talk about the executive order. He managed to get a copy of it."

And it's not good. Mary Jane heard the words as easily as if Jake had said them. Mary Jane squeezed the girls' shoulders. "Okay, you two. Let's dry those eyes. Go to the kitchen and get yourself something to drink. I'll be right there."

Molly stepped back, wiping her eyes. Mary Jane wiped a tear she missed. "It will be okay." She leaned forward and kissed her forehead, then did the same for Theresa. "Go on."

The girls walked side by side, both looking fragile despite the strength that coursed through them.

Cain stepped into the open doorway. "Mary Jane, I just heard. What do you need?"

"Can you watch Susie for me? And Molly and Theresa are in the kitchen. They're terrified. I'm going with Jake to get more details."

Jake shook his head. "Mary Jane—"

"I'm *going*." She flicked a gaze to the kitchen.

Cain walked to Mary Jane until he was only a foot away. "I'll look after them as well. I'll take everyone down to Dom's. His place has a way of making people feel safe. I'm guessing it's the multiple blast doors."

Mary Jane gave him a watery smile. "Thank you." She reached up and kissed his cheek. "You're a good man."

Cain's mouth popped open, and he swallowed. "I should go check on the girls." He headed up the stairs.

"They're in the master bedroom," Jake said as he passed.

Cain nodded his acknowledgment.

Jake made his way down to Mary Jane as she took some deep breaths to try and calm the emotions running through her. "You all right?"

"No. You know what? Let me talk to the girls some more, then we'll go talk to Henry." She turned to the kitchen before she paused, looking back at Jake. "What about Laney? Do you think she knows?"

Jake pulled out his phone. "I'll make sure she does."

CHAPTER 25

Jen stepped out of the car down the street from Mary Jane's house on Sharecroppers Lane. The girls had bolted from the car as soon as they arrived.

Noriko exited from the passenger side as Jen's phone beeped. It was a text from Henry.

"What is it?" Noriko asked.

"Henry wants me up at the main house immediately."

A slight disturbance in the air had Jen whirling. As a Nephilim she couldn't sense Fallen, but she was beginning to recognize the signs. Gerard materialized next to Noriko.

Noriko stumbled back. "Gerard?"

He reached out, steadying her, his blue eyes raking her in and apologizing all at once. "Sorry. I need to get you to the cats. Henry's orders."

Noriko looked over at Jen, conveying her concern.

Jen waved her away, her heart beginning to pound. "Go, go."

Gerard picked her up, and they were gone.

Jen's stomach dropped. While all of them could cover distances quickly, they tended not to take passengers unless it was an emergency.

Oh no.

She looked back at Mary Jane's porch as Cain hustled up the steps. The girls were in good hands. Besides, information was what everybody needed right now, not empty platitudes. And Henry was the one most likely to have those.

Leaving the car, she bolted for the main house, her thoughts moving almost as quickly as her feet. When she'd been driving home, she'd been happy at the idea of bringing the girls a little happiness after the last trip downtown. But the President's order had ripped that away from all of them. Jen knew the executive order was much more than a political calculation or even an effort to protect the public. It was the opening salvo in a war against the Fallen—*all* of the Fallen.

For a moment, she wondered how she would have responded had she still been pregnant. She would have been about six months along right now. The grief hit. She stumbled, slowing to a walk. She took a breath, bending at the waist as her heart pounded. She hadn't been planning on a child, but she had wanted that child more than anything. Losing her was like someone had ripped out a piece of her heart. A piece she would never get back again.

Lock it down, she warned herself. *You have other people to worry about right now.*

She took some breaths, her breathing returning to normal in only a few seconds. She had gotten good at this. Shoving down her grief, focusing on something else so it didn't overwhelm her. But she knew that one day she wouldn't be able to shove it away anymore.

She jogged at a normal pace around the side of the main house and entered through the front foyer. She took the stairs two at a time. In only a few seconds, she was walking through the doors to Henry's office, her focus back on the current crisis but with a small twinge of grief lurking in the back of her mind like it had for the last three months.

Henry looked up from his desk, his cell phone to his ear. "Yes. Have them all moved immediately. No, you won't have to get them in the truck. Noriko should be arriving any minute to organize them. I've sent a security team to escort you. Call me if you have any issues." He disconnected the call.

Jen moved over to the desk. "You're moving the cats?"

"And the kids from the school. The cats are going to the fallback location we set up after the fire at the preserve."

"Do you think this is necessary?"

Henry's cell rang as he handed her a single sheet of paper. "This is the executive order. Read it."

Jen took the paper as Henry answered his phone. "Brett, thank goodness. Have you read the order?"

Jen ignored him as she made her way to the couch, already reading. With each sentence she read, her horror grew. She read the entire document three times before Henry joined her on the couch. She looked up at him in disbelief. "This can't be legal."

"Brett is already drafting an injunction to stop it. But being it's Friday, he won't be able to submit it to the court until Monday."

"And until then?"

"Until then, this is the law of the land."

Jake appeared in the doorway, Mary Jane next to him. Jake looked between Henry and Jen. Jen tried to wipe the shock from her face, but she was pretty sure she failed miserably at it when Mary Jane's terrified gaze met hers.

"How bad?" Jake asked as he walked over, Mary Jane's hand clasped in his.

"You should sit," Henry said quietly, his gaze on Mary Jane. She all but collapsed in the club chair across from Jen.

Jake pulled the other club chair over next to her, taking her hand again. "Cain is taking the kids down to Dom's. I got through to Laney. I had to talk her out of coming home. She really doesn't like that the President issued this while she's in Italy."

"I don't either," Henry said. "The timing is a little too coincidental."

"Are they even going to let her back *in* the country?" Jen asked.

Henry did a double take at her, his eyes growing wide. "I don't know the answer to that."

"Have you—" Mary Jane swallowed. "Have you read the full executive order? I tried to find a copy online, but it wasn't available yet."

"I managed to get a copy." He took a breath. "You need to prepare yourself but also know we are going to do everything in our power to fight this."

Jake pulled Mary Jane's hand closer to him. "Tell us."

Henry's voice was calm, without emotion, but it didn't help make the news any less stark. "As the President explained, all people with enhanced abilities will have to register with the government. What she didn't mention was that the government has reserved the right to hold anyone with enhanced abilities without probable cause for an indefinite amount of time for any reason."

"That's insane," Jake said.

"That's the *PATRIOT Act*," Jen said. "Only this time it's going to be aimed at American citizens. And that's not the worst part." Jen looked at Mary Jane and just couldn't get the words out.

Henry carried the story for her. "They also reserve the right to take any enhanced individual in for what they are calling a physical exam."

Mary Jane's mouth fell open. "They—they want to experiment on them?"

Henry shook his head. "It could just be checking reflexes or blood or—"

"But without their consent. They are saying that they have complete control over the bodies of these Fallen. Of my daughter."

Henry nodded. "That's our interpretation as well."

The door to the office creaked as Cleo walked in. Jen tensed. "What are we going to do about the cats?"

"Hide them. There is no other choice," Henry said.

Cleo sat down, staring at Henry. Her demand for information was as clear as if she had spoken.

"The government has declared that any genetically enhanced animals are to be immediately placed in U.S. custody. Any animals outside of U.S. custody are to be shot on sight."

Mary Jane gasped. "No."

Cleo leaned over and licked her hand. Jen nearly lost it right there.

Henry looked at Cleo. "You need to get Zane and Tiger. You need to go into hiding until we can figure this out. We're going to fly you guys to meet the rest of the cats."

Cleo met his gaze and then walked out of the room.

"Do you think she understood all of that?" Mary Jane asked.

Jen watched her go. "Oh, she understood. The question is whether or not she agreed with it."

CHAPTER 26

Twenty-four hours later, Mary Jane sat in the living room of the cottage on Sharecroppers Lane. The boys were in the kitchen with Lou, Rolly, and Danny. Theresa and Molly were upstairs with Nyssa and Susie.

Cain walked in from the kitchen, a tray in his hands. He placed it on the coffee table and then placed a cup of tea on the coaster next to Mary Jane. "Here. Patrick always says a good cup of tea can help any situation."

Mary Jane smiled, even though it was the last thing she felt like doing. "Have you heard from him?"

A tremble ran through Cain's hands as he poured himself a cup of tea, but his voice didn't waver. "Yes. He wants to return, but without the situation with his green card being resolved . . ." He shrugged.

"How's Laney?"

"Anxious about all of us. But the Vatican is supposed to see them this morning. They should be on their way back within the next day. And hopefully, all we'll have to report is how worried we all are."

Mary Jane didn't know Laney well. She and Jen had come by

to help train Molly a few weekends, but since she'd moved her family here, she'd gotten to know her a little better. She was a confident woman but also friendly and warm. It was hard to reconcile that with the all-powerful woman she had seen in D.C. just three months ago.

But it was that image, the woman who had risked everything to defeat Elisabeta, that Mary Jane held on to. Because Mary Jane knew that she would do the same to protect those she cared about. And she prayed for everything she was worth that Molly now fell under that umbrella.

But even with all of Laney's abilities and Henry's connections, the forces arraying against those with abilities seemed insurmountable. Since the President's executive order had been broadcast, the floodgates on news about the Fallen had burst wide open. Stories of incredible good and incredible evil jockeyed for top positions on social media. There were reports of people being detained in foreign countries, being whisked away in the middle of the night. And it wasn't just people with enhanced abilities that were being rounded up. Whole families were being grabbed.

Mary Jane took a shaky drink. *It will be all right. This is the United States of America. That won't happen here.*

Shaun and Joe appeared in the doorway. Mary Jane forced another smile to her face. "Hey. Are you heading over to the bomb shelter?"

Shaun shook his head as he took a seat next to her. "No. Danny, Lou, and Rolly just left. We thought we'd watch it with you."

She gripped his hand, squeezing her thanks. She hadn't asked them to stay. She liked how well Joe and Shaun got along with the other teenagers, but she did want them here. All day, advertisements for tonight's showing of *DC Tonight* had been broadcast across social media. The producers claimed they had explosive information about the government's role in understanding the Fallen. But no leaks had come out to indicate what they were going to reveal. Mary Jane was hoping for the best but trying to prepare herself for the worst.

The front door opened, and she heard Jake's familiar footsteps. She let out a breath, feeling some of the tension leave her chest. Nothing had changed ostensibly, but having Jake there eased some of her fear. He helped share the burden of her worry.

His eyes focused on Mary Jane as he walked into the room, a small smile crossing his face. "Hey."

"Hey," she said.

Shaun started to rise, but Jake waved him back down, taking a seat in one of the club chairs. "You're good where you are."

"Where are Henry and Jen?" Mary Jane asked.

"Down at Dom's. They wanted to be there for the kids in case this broadcast is difficult."

Molly and Theresa walked in, carrying Nyssa and Susie.

"Hello, my little ones." Cain walked over to them, holding out his arms. Both toddlers reached for him, and the girls transferred them to his arms. Cain looked over his shoulder. "I'll take the girls to the kitchen and get them something to eat. I'll keep them busy during the broadcast."

"Thank you," Mary Jane said.

He nodded before heading down the hall. Tiger followed Cain, but Cleo and Zane lay across the doorway, as if they wanted to keep a view of both rooms.

Molly curled up on the floor, leaning on Mary Jane's legs. Theresa sat next to her, her arms wrapped around her knees.

Jake grabbed the remote, nodding at the muted set. "It's starting."

The last refrain of a chain restaurant jingle drifted through the room. Tension filled the silence as the opening of *DC Tonight* began to play. Once again, Jerome Fontane looked out into the audience.

"Good evening, and welcome to *DC Tonight*. Twenty-four hours ago, President Margaret Rigley authorized an executive order that requires all enhanced individuals to register with the Agency of Enhanced Individuals within a week.

"*DC Tonight* learned of the new agency about seven days ago and has been investigating it ever since. The agency falls under Homeland Security, but more specifically, it falls under the External Threats Task Force."

Jake sucked in a breath, his jaw tight. But Mary Jane didn't ask what was wrong because she had the feeling Jerome was about to explain it all to her in excruciating detail.

"The External Threats Task Force works under the auspices of Homeland Security and is an extremely controversial group. They act with very little oversight within a terrorism framework that is already criticized for being too harsh and failing to provide basic constitutional protections. Placing the agency under the auspices of this group is a bad omen for the treatment that enhanced individuals in the United States can expect."

Jerome took a deep breath. "And that brings me to the agency known as the Special Investigative Agency or the SIA. For years, the SIA has worked quietly behind the scenes, apprehending enhanced individuals who have broken the law. The normal criminal justice system—and more importantly, the correctional system—are not set up to handle an enhanced population. Which is where the SIA stepped in.

"When we first learned of the SIA, we were concerned about their methods. Enhanced individuals did not receive a trial. They did not receive any sort of legal representation. They were simply ruled guilty by the SIA and put on ice.

"But at the time, in their attempts to keep the existence of the enhanced a secret, it was the best option. And in our review, the individuals targeted by the SIA, if brought to trial, would have almost undoubtedly been found guilty.

"The enhanced were then kept in a drug-induced coma, unable to access their abilities while the SIA looked for alternative methods to hold them. There weren't many options. No facility was strong enough to contain them. And while they were held there, they were just that—held there. They were not otherwise mistreated.

"But then the External Task Force took over under the stewardship of Moses Stewart." An image of a man in his forties, glaring at the photographer, appeared on the screen.

"Moses Stewart had a different idea of how the enhanced individuals in his charge should be treated. We managed to obtain a recording of the SIA's treatment of the enhanced under Moses Stewart's leadership. I warn you, the video you are about to see is graphic, and parents are strongly encouraged to remove their children from the room."

A graphic content warning sign appeared on the screen for five seconds before the recording began. It was a security tape of what looked at first like a hospital room. There was a man lying on a bed. Mary Jane leaned forward with a squint and noted the restraints keeping the man there and some sort of IV. Two men dressed all in black with an insignia on their long sleeves stepped in. There was no sound, which made it all the more eerie as they moved toward the bound figure.

On the floor, both Theresa and Molly inched closer to Mary Jane. She stroked Molly's hair as Shaun squeezed her hand. Both of the men in black pulled batons from their belts.

"Oh God." Molly hid her face in her hands. The men struck the man in the bed repeatedly, over and over again. The prone man offered no resistance. It went on for two minutes without pause as they struck at him. Blood began to drip from the bed to the floor. By the time they were done, it had shifted from an occasional drip to a steady stream. The men stepped back, and one of them spit on their victim before leaving the room.

Mary Jane's hand flew to her mouth. She worried for a moment she was going to be sick.

The image began to fast-forward as Jerome began to speak

again. "The man was left there, bleeding, injured and without aid for a full day."

"Mom," Molly said, her voice shaking. Mary Jane wrapped her arms around her.

Jerome reappeared on the screen. "Those men were agents employed by the United States government. And that scene was replayed in every cell of the SIA's secret facility in Lowell, Ohio. We reviewed each of those recordings. Each inmate was beaten and left without medical care. None of the individuals were in any state to fight back or defend themselves. They were completely defenseless."

Jerome took a deep breath. "Some may say these individuals got what they deserved. Each of them was indeed locked up for a violent offense. But they posed no threat at the time they were beaten. Physical punishment is *not* part of the United States system of justice. It was Dostoevsky who said that 'the degree of civilization in a society can be judged by entering its prisons.' These individuals were in our prisons, and this is how we treated them. What does that say about us as a society?

"Now our government is saying we should trust them with the names of the enhanced individuals within our country. Individuals who have broken no laws. Many of whom protected people on the Day of Reckoning. Yet the United States government has suspended their constitutional protections and said they could be subject to incarceration and submitted to experimentation at the hands of the same government that allowed this to happen.

"Is this what our government has become? Is this who we have become? Have we let fear push us to a point where we lock up innocent victims? When Josef Mengele conducted his experiments, he was reported to switch between affection for his charges and a callous disregard for their suffering. Are we going to use the same argument? History did not judge Nazis kindly. If the United States continues on this path, I do not think we will be judged any less harshly. We'll be back after this commercial break."

Jake muted the set. No one spoke. Mary Jane couldn't think of a single thing to say.

Theresa finally broke the silence. Her voice shook. Tears had traced their way down her cheeks. "Can they really do that to us?"

Mary Jane just shook her head.

Joe sprang to his feet. "We can't let this happen. It isn't right."

"But what can we do?" Shaun asked, his chin trembling as he looked at his little sister.

"We fight," Jake said quietly. "We fight them every step of the way."

CHAPTER 27

ROME, ITALY

Laney was fit to be tied. They'd been in Rome for three days without getting anything but the runaround from the Vatican. She had the distinct impression they were stalling. No bureaucracy could be this incompetent.

Then she'd seen the news report this morning on *DC Tonight*. Already there were protests, people taking sides.

Yes, they deserved that treatment.

No, they didn't. It isn't what America is.

And here she was, twiddling her thumbs. She'd called Henry first thing this morning after she'd seen the broadcast. Henry assured her that everything was fine, but she could hear the tension in his voice. But she couldn't press him for more information. It was a safe bet that their conversation was being recorded. She knew him, though. She knew he was making plans. No doubt he had arranged to whisk the kids away at the first sign of trouble. The *DC Tonight* revelation on top of the executive order—they were storm clouds along the horizon. Trouble was coming.

"It's okay if you want to go home. I can handle this on my own," Patrick said.

Laney shoved her feelings aside and shook her head as Drake brought Patrick's wheelchair to a stop at the entrance to St. Peter's Square. "Of course not. Henry has everything under control. And when else will I get a chance to see behind the scenes at the Vatican?"

"I'm not sure you'll be able to see much more than long hallways," Patrick said.

"That's all right. I'll enjoy the peace."

"And I'll be there if it gets too boring," Drake said.

Patrick winced. "Well, that's . . . something."

Drake leaned down. "I'll be on my best behavior." He nodded toward the giant Egyptian obelisk in the center of the square. "I helped deliver that. It originated in Heliopolis. Caligula originally brought it to Rome, where it was positioned in a place of honor to oversee the Circus of Nero." Drake frowned. "It always seemed an odd thing for the Church to want, given those two associations with it."

Patrick gaped up at him. "I actually didn't know that."

"When the obelisk was placed here, that was all that was here. The rest wasn't built until a hundred years later," Drake said.

Laney had to admit it was quite a sight. She had been to St. Peter's Square twice before, both with her uncle. Her reaction to it was no different than the two times before—it took her breath away. St. Peter's Basilica was straight ahead, built to mark the spot where St. Peter had been crucified. In front of it was St. Peter's Square. It was a massive space, with an almost semicircle of four deep colonnades on the perimeter. Sitting atop the colonnades, looking into the square, were statues of one hundred and forty saints.

Drake pushed on Patrick's handlebars, and they began to make their way through the square in the early morning light. Laney couldn't help but think of all the people and power that this place had represented over time. For the most part, she liked the current Pope. He seemed like a good man, a very good man. She just hoped those who served the world under him were just as good.

Patrick put up a hand, stopping Drake from pushing him farther. "I think I'd like to wheel myself around for a bit. We have a little time."

"Of course. We'll meet you at the entrance when you are ready," Laney said.

Patrick smiled and started to wheel away.

Laney watched him go. He was putting on a brave face, but she knew the executive order and the broadcast from the President had shaken him as well.

Drake took her hand. "We can go home."

Laney shook her head. "No. We can't. Not until my uncle finishes his business here. Until he gets this sorted out, he can't come back with us, and I won't leave him here alone."

"He looks tired."

Laney nodded, a smile creeping across her face. "I think your tour yesterday took a lot out of him."

Drake grinned. "I just wanted to make sure he saw the Rome I know."

Laney smiled back at him. The Vatican had kept pushing her uncle off each time he inquired when he was going to get to speak with someone regarding his status. So Drake had done his best to distract Laney and Patrick. For the last three days, they'd been touring the city and surrounding areas with Drake taking it upon himself to show them around. He had been the world's most enthusiastic tour guide. He'd gotten them behind the ropes at every single tourist spot they had gone to and even at a few spots that did not have any official tour. Her uncle, while tense when they had arrived, had slowly relaxed, soaking in the history. His eyes had sparkled in a way Laney hadn't seen since before he'd been shot.

"Thank you for all you've done." Laney leaned toward him, but her phone beeped, halting her forward momentum.

Drake sighed dramatically. "Foiled again."

Laney gave him a distracted smile as she read the text. "It's from my uncle. The Vatican is ready for us."

"And yet you don't look happy."

She forced a smile to her face. "No, no. This is good. Hopefully we can wrap all this up today and be on our way home tonight."

Drake squeezed her cheek. "Aw, look who's still overly optimistic about large bureaucracies."

She swatted his hand away. "Fine, tomorrow at the latest. But it does mean this is finally coming to an end."

This time it was Drake whose smile faltered for a moment. But Laney pretended not to see it. She wanted to believe that Drake thought that everything would be fine.

After all, at least one of them should believe it.

~

PATRICK WAS WAITING for them near the basilica's entrance. He had more color in his cheeks, but he still looked a little tired.

Laney frowned. *Maybe this was too much for him. I should—*

"Father Patrick!"

A small, thin priest hurried over from the entrance. He had curly dark hair and an unfortunately hooked nose. He was accompanied by two younger priests. If not for their clerical collars, their build would suggest they were security.

The priest stopped in front of them and gave them a big smile. "Welcome to the Vatican! We are so excited you could join us today. I am Father Ezekiel."

Laney looked at Drake, who was staring at the man like he was some form of unappealing luncheon meat.

"Thank you, Father Ezekiel," Patrick said.

"We have a full day scheduled, including a tour. I thought we could start with—"

Before Laney could interrupt, her uncle did. "I'm afraid we are in a bit of a time crunch. We have been in Rome for three days, and as I'm sure you have seen the news from the States, you can understand our need to get back as quickly as possible."

"Yes, yes, of course. The tour can wait for another time. This is Father Michele and Father Angelo. They will escort you to your first meeting."

Both priests nodded. Father Angelo moved behind Patrick's wheelchair.

Laney blocked the priest's way. "That's not necessary. I have it."

Ezekiel's face fell. "Oh, I'm so sorry. There are no outsiders permitted in the parts of the Vatican we will be in." His smiled returned. "But Dr. McPhearson, Mr. Drake, I would be honored to give you a tour of the Castel Sant'Angelo while your uncle conducts his business. It will only take an hour or two, and your uncle should be done by the time we return. I assure you, this is a tour that no other tourist gets."

Laney paused, studying the man. He smiled, but it didn't seem to reach his eyes. She turned to her uncle.

He patted her hand. "It's all right. Let's just get this over with."

"If you need me, you call. Drake and I will be right there."

"I know. Now go, see the castle, then tell me all about it on the trip home."

Home. Just the word sounded wonderful. "All right." She leaned forward and kissed his cheek. He gave her a little wave as Father Angelo wheeled him away.

Ezekiel gestured to a side entrance. "If you'll follow me. I have a car waiting for us."

Laney inclined her head. He hurried toward the entrance. Laney began to follow, Drake falling in step next to her. He leaned down, his lips brushing her ear. "Watch your step, ring bearer. This place has changed much over the years, but one thing remains the same: There are wolves within these walls."

CHAPTER 28

David strode through the airport in Rome, skirting around a family whose two young children were crying in earnest. He stepped out into the bright sunshine, enjoying the feel of the sun on his skin after the long flight. Within an hour, he had stopped at his apartment, gotten changed, and was back out on the street, slipping into the tourist pedestrian traffic.

He buttoned his suit jacket as he stepped to the curb and raised his hand to hail a cab. He had let Bruce know he was heading to Rome. Laney accompanying her uncle was not out of character for her. But after the executive order, he was surprised she was still here. Of course, his sources told him the Vatican, which had been desperate to speak with her uncle for the last few months, had not met with them yet. *That* was surprising.

David was not a fan of unpredictability. He studied his marks inside and out. He could always predict what they were going to do. It was what made him so good at his job. He had an inkling of what the Vatican's angle was, and if he was right, it would not be good for Delaney. David wasn't sure it would be so good for the United States either, even though he was pretty sure they were in cahoots with at least some individuals at the Vatican.

Perhaps she's just good. Rahim's words slipped into his mind. The more reports he read on her, the more he thought his partner might be right. And that could explain why he was having such a difficult time with this particular mission. His targets almost always had selfish motivations: money and power being the top two. Altruism? Family? Those had never made the cut in any of his cases. He had one overlord who'd killed his entire family because he thought his wife was cheating on him. She wasn't. Family ties? Those rarely offered any protection.

Shremp wanted something that he could use to take Delaney down. *His* motivation was clear: power. Shremp believed if he could take Delaney down, it would cause his own political star to rise. He didn't care if the story he crafted was true or not. He just wanted it to look damaging enough to thrust him into the spotlight as the hero.

He grunted. Shremp wanted everyone to view him as a hero, and Delaney McPhearson, who had saved thousands if not millions of people, was uncomfortable with the title. But that's how it always seemed to be. Those with the right to the honor felt unworthy of it, and those without the right felt entitled to it.

David lowered his arm as a taxi approached. The driver eyed his outfit and spoke in English. "Where to?"

David slid into the back seat. "The Vatican."

CHAPTER 29

Father Ezekiel led Laney and Drake to a sleek black Mercedes. Two Swiss Guards on motorcycles were in front of the sedan and another two behind. The motorcycle security escorted them through the streets.

Laney tried to focus on the scenes flashing by her window, but all she could see were the scenes from the broadcast last night.

Drake took her hand. "None of that."

"What?"

"There is nothing you can do back home. Until the government does something, we have to wait. We might as well wait while touring an ancient castle." He leaned over and nuzzled her neck. "Of course, I can think of more pleasurable ways to pass a few hours."

Laney blushed, dropping her voice. "There are two priests in front of us."

Drake shrugged. "Archangel. I outrank them."

"Ah, here we are!" Ezekiel proclaimed as they crossed over the Ponte Sant'Angelo, the bridge that connected the mausoleum to the city. Laney stared at the array of winged angels that had been erected along the bridge during the baroque period, watching their passage. They were beautiful.

The driver pulled to a stop in front of the main entrance. The drive in front was empty, as the site didn't open to the public for another two hours.

Laney and Drake exited the car from opposite sides. The Castel Sant'Angelo loomed above them. When it had first been constructed, the castle had been the tallest building in Rome. But in the modern day it was dwarfed by a multitude of other structures.

Laney slipped around the car to stand next to Drake. He stood still, staring up. Shielding her eyes, Laney followed his gaze to the tallest point of the Castle. "What is that?"

Drake said nothing, his gazed fixed on the top of the fortress.

Father Ezekiel followed his gaze nodding. "Ah, yes, you see the avenging angel that guards the castle. It's quite a sight. Now, if you'll follow me."

Ezekiel hurried on, not waiting for a reply.

Drake extended his arm to Laney. "We better hurry up before the good father leaves us behind."

"I think I'd be okay with that."

"I'm willing to ditch him if you are."

Laney was tempted, really tempted. But she didn't want her and Drake's behavior to reflect badly on her uncle. She sighed. "No. We should stick with him."

"Fine. But I have a felling this will be the most boring tour in the castle's long history."

Drake was not wrong. The good father led them through room after room, reciting endless facts about the castle. Laney made noncommittal noises every now and then, tuning him out as she let her own imagination run as she looked at the incredible space.

The castle had originally been built as a mausoleum for Roman Emperor Hadrian and his family in 134 A.D. Other emperors were also entombed there, their ashes kept on the treasure room of the mausoleum until 217. In 401, the site was turned into a military fortress. In the fourteenth century, the papacy took over the site and turned it into a castle. Pope Nicholas III even had a tunnel created that led from St. Peter's Basilica to the castle.

While the castle currently showed off priceless works of art and gorgeous marble floors, it also had a darker history. Prison cells had been added under the reign of Pope Alexander IV Borgia. It had been used as a prison and a site of executions, which Father Ezekiel pointed out as they stepped into the courtyard.

"Executions were held here," said Father Ezekiel, "when an individual was found guilty of blasphemy."

Laney nodded, picturing the horrible scene. "Giordano Bruno was held here, isn't he?"

Ezekiel nodded. "It was a difficult time in the Church's history. They could not adapt well to the changes of the day."

Bruno had had the audacity to suggest that the stars seen in the night sky were actually suns in their own right. And that exoplanets surrounded each sun. He therefore concluded that some of these planets may foster life. He even went as far as to suggest that the universe was infinite and that the Earth was not its center. In fact, he argued there was no center. While he was charged for his pantheistic views, he was also tried for denying multiple Catholic doctrines such as eternal damnation, the Trinity, and the divinity of Christ. In addition, he was well known for supporting the notion of reincarnation. That last one made her pause. The Church did not recognize reincarnation. According to the Church, you died once and were judged for your actions on Earth.

But Laney now knew that wasn't true. She had been born time and time again, as had almost everyone she knew in her current life. Did the Church still have such a strong stance against reincarnation? Could they, in light of recent events and the outing of the Fallen?

Laney realized they probably still did. If recent statements were an indication, the Church still had difficulty in adapting. The Church had declared Elisabeta was not the true Samyaza and that the Fallen were no more than genetically enhanced individuals. Obviously they were not as accepting of information that was clear to everyone else.

She turned to speak to Drake and realized he was no longer at her side. He had walked across the courtyard and now stood staring at a statue of a winged angel. It was the same one they had seen from the ground.

Ezekiel fell in step with her as she crossed the courtyard to join Drake. "Who is that?" Laney asked, nodding toward the bronze statue of the angel on high, seen pulling his sword from his sheath, his wings spread.

"That is the Archangel Michael, preparing for battle. The statue was created by a Flemish sculptor named Peter von Verschaffelt in 1798. That is the sixth version of the statue."

"The sixth?" Laney asked.

Ezekiel nodded. "Yes. The first was wood and did not survive the elements. The second was marble but was destroyed by angry Roman citizens in 1379. The third was also marble, but the wings were bronze and were destroyed by a lightning strike."

"A lightning strike?" Laney pictured what that must have looked like. It would have seemed as if the hand of God had come down.

"The fourth was also bronze, but then it was destroyed to create cannonballs in the early sixteenth century. The fifth, which can be seen in the courtyard, was damaged by weather. And finally, the sixth is what you see now."

Laney stared up at the statue. "Poor Michael. This world doesn't seem to have been kind to him."

"No, it hasn't," Drake said quietly.

Laney frowned. Drake was awfully serious. He had been more so ever since they arrived at the castle.

Ezekiel clasped his hands. "Well, let us check out where they once held the prisoners, shall we?"

Drake's shoulders shifted as if he was shaking off whatever had come over him. He raised an eyebrow at Laney as Ezekiel took off once again, not waiting for them. "He's awfully excitable, isn't he?"

Laney was heartened to see her Drake return. "Yes, he is. Apparently the cells are not to be missed."

The section of the castle Ezekiel led them to was obviously not on the official tour. It was colder. The walls were crumbling. Ezekiel stood at the end of the hall, outlined in a doorway. "This way. This way." He disappeared from view, but Laney could hear his footsteps clearly.

"I guess we're heading down."

The doorway led to a stairwell that Laney was surprised to see had electric lighting. It looked so ancient she wouldn't have been surprised to see torches. Drake grabbed Laney's arm as she was about to step.

"What?" she asked as he cast his gaze around.

He shook his head, releasing her hand. "Nothing. I just seem to be spooked."

She leaned forward with a smile, keeping her voice low. "Spooked? Archangels can get spooked?"

He returned the grin. "Apparently today they can. Now hurry up before Ezekiel gives us detention."

Laney chuckled as she headed down the stone steps. Ezekiel did remind her of some of the priests she'd had in high school. The stairs ended one level down. Ezekiel once again was about thirty feet away, waving them on. He disappeared in a doorway.

As soon as they appeared in the doorway, Ezekiel waved from another doorway, disappearing inside. Three more doorways and it was the same process: Ezekiel a good distance ahead, disappearing and expecting them to follow.

"I'm feel like we're playing a game of cat and mouse," Drake murmured.

"Yeah," Laney said, beginning to feel a little spooked herself as she made her way down yet another set of stone stairs.

Stepping onto the floor, Ezekiel, grinned, waving toward the wide hall behind him. "We have arrived."

Laney stepped past him. Cells had been carved out of the rock in the ground. Metal bars had been placed from floor to ceiling with a single door. It was cold and damp. Not liking it, Laney shivered, feeling a great deal of sympathy toward anyone who had to spend any amount of time in here.

Ezekiel waved them toward the third cell. "This is the cell that Bruno himself stayed in. In the back corner, he even carved an inscription. Go see."

"I'm good here," Drake said.

Ezekiel's face fell. "But it's the best part."

Laney sighed. "Okay. Where is it?"

"Right along the back wall down at the bottom right. Go ahead, Mr. Drake."

Laney tugged on Drake's sleeve. "Come on, Mr. Drake. Let's go see."

Laney stepped into the cell, Drake right behind her. She walked to the back wall and crouched down, but she couldn't make out anything scraped into the wall.

"Drake, do you see any—"

The metal door to the cell slammed shut. Laney jumped to her feet and whirled around. "Ezekiel?"

But the only response was the sound of hurried footsteps as Ezekiel fled up the stairs.

CHAPTER 30

Laney stared at the locked cell door in disbelief. She turned to Drake. "Did he just lock us in an ancient jail cell?"

Drake's voice was dry. "So it would seem."

Laney laughed. "Wow. He really has no idea who we are, does he?" She focused for only a moment before a wind ripped the door off, slamming it into the wall across from them.

Drake offered her his hand. "Shall we, my dear?"

Laney placed her hand in his. "Let's."

They stepped out of the cell as tingles ran over Laney's skin. She pulled her hand from Drake's, turning to the stairs. "You feel that?"

"Yup."

Laney thought about sprinting up the stairs but immediately discarded the idea. The stairwell was narrow, and whoever was coming for them would have the higher ground. The hallway between cells, while not ideal, was a better location to face off with whomever Ezekiel was sending.

Next to her, Drake bent his back leg, hands coming up, getting into a fighting stance. "Looks like the good Father Ezekiel is not quite so good."

Laney didn't have time to respond as two figures blurred into the room. They stopped at the bottom of the stairs. Both wore long brown monk cloaks. More footsteps pounded down the stairs behind them.

Laney eyed the two silent monks. "Just who are you supposed to be?"

Their only response was to draw two long wicked knives from the sleeves of their robes.

"They, Laney, are the bad guys," Drake said.

She sighed. "Why are we always running into bad guys?"

Three more men, also in brown robes, burst out of the stairwell, guns in hand. Laney's gaze flicked toward them, which was all the distraction the men at the bottom of the stairs needed. One leaped toward Laney, swiping at her with the knife. She dodged back for the first strike before zipping forward, arresting the man's backstroke. She redirected his movement to his own thigh, slicing high and then whipping the knife back to slice the back of his knee. The same move she'd used on Dirk Magnet not that long ago. If a human, he'd be unable to walk, the tendon at the back of his knee severed. But Laney knew that this man's wounds would knit closed soon enough.

She stripped the knife from his hand, plunging it into the back of his thigh. Then she slipped one hand at the back of his head, the other toward the top, and wrenched it to the side with a quick snap.

The snap was not loud enough to drown out the slide of the weapon of one of the men on the stairs. She grabbed the Fallen before he could drop and used him as a shield as the men opened fire. Ducking down, she pushed the man toward the men on the stairs as bullets slammed into him.

Ezekiel's head popped out of the doorway. "Do not kill God's soldier!" he shrieked.

Laney grunted. If they weren't trying to kill her, they probably shouldn't be shooting at her. Bullets slammed into the monk she was using as a shield, but she kept moving forward.

Drake took a different approach and just flung his guy at them. He knocked two over like they were bowling pins. Another screech sounded from the stairwell. Then the last gunman stopped shooting, his whole body shaking before he collapsed to the ground.

Laney peered from around her shield. The man was down, two prongs in his back. Ezekiel was sprawled across the doorway at the top of the stairs.

What the . . .

Bas stepped over Ezekiel and into view. "To quote one of the best movie lines ever, come with me if you want to live."

CHAPTER 31

Shock rippled through Laney as she let her guy drop. "Bas? What are you doing here?"

The last time she had seen Bas had been on the estate the night before she'd left. He'd never mentioned that he was heading back to Rome.

Bas glanced behind him. "I'll explain later. There are more coming."

Before Laney could blink, Drake had Bas by the throat, holding him against the wall. "Explain *now*."

Laney expected Bas to panic, grabbing for Drake's hands. But he didn't. He slammed the side of his hand into Drake's Adam's apple, then wrapped his other hand around Drake's arm, breaking his hold and forcing him to bend at the waist before shoving him away. "We *don't* have time."

Shouts sounded from upstairs. Bas turned his eyes to Laney. "Please."

Laney stared at Drake before nodding at Bas. "Lead the way."

Bas rubbed his throat, hurrying down the stairs past Drake. Laney stepped to the side, her hands ready in case Bas tried anything. But he sprinted past her to a door in the corner beyond the cells. "This way, quickly."

Footsteps sounded on the stairs. Laney exchanged a look with Drake before following Bas. Drake was right behind her, pulling the door closed behind him. Bas hurried ahead through what looked like a storage room which emptied out into another hallway with a stairwell at the end. He sprinted up the stairwell, stopping at the landing. "Hurry."

Laney reached the landing, and Bas led them down a long hall before stepping into a large room. The ceiling was at least twenty feet above them. Giant pillars held up the roof. About a dozen old wooden produce crates were scattered haphazardly along the walls, but otherwise it was empty.

Dust rose around Bas as he sprinted down the middle of the room. Laney exchanged a confused look with Drake. The back of the room was a solid wall. There was no exit. What was Bas thinking? Was he trying to trap them?

Laney put out a hand, stopping Drake as Bas reached the back wall. He reached for one of the ancient pillars and stretched up on his toes, pushing against the stone. A small door, hidden in the wall, cracked open an inch.

Bas ran for it, working his fingertips in and pulling it open fully. He glanced nervously at the doorway beyond them. "Come on! Hurry."

"I don't trust him," Drake said.

"Neither do I. But between him and the guys trying to kill us, I choose him." She ran across the room and slipped into the opening.

Drake stopped at the doorway, his gaze focused on Bas. "After you."

Bas rolled his eyes. "Oh, for goodness sake." He hurried in, flicking on a flashlight he pulled from his pocket. Drake stepped in, pulling the door closed behind him. The tunnel went dark, only the dim light of Bas's flashlight offering any illumination.

Bas made his way down the tunnel. The tunnel had been hewn from the ground, reinforced with an ancient wooden frame.

"Where are we?" Drake asked.

"This tunnel leads from the Castle of the Holy Angel into the city."

"Is this the tunnel that Pope Clement VII used to escape the Roman army?"

Bas shook his head. "No. That one is well known. A few visitors are even allowed to walk along it every year."

"And this one?" Laney asked.

"It is known to very few."

"So who told you about it?" Drake asked.

"The woman who raised me."

An interesting choice of words. Not mother, but the woman who raised me.

"Well, being we have some time, perhaps you could explain how a group of priests just turned into a bunch of ninjas and tried to kill us." Drake's tone made it clear it was not a question he was asking.

"Were they even priests?" Laney asked.

"Oh, they are priests all right. They belong to a special order. The Brotherhood of the Eclipse of the Sun."

"I've never heard of them," Laney said.

"Very few have. You only know of them if you are a member or you are a target. And those who are a target do not live long enough to tell anyone."

Drake grunted. "So, the Vatican has a hit squad. How special."

Even in the dim light, Laney could see Bas's wince. "It's not a hit squad. They are charged with protecting the papacy."

"I thought that was the court jester's job," Drake said.

"The Swiss Guards *do* guard the Pope and Vatican City. But the Brotherhood are more specialized," Bas said.

"They're the Vatican's black ops," Laney said.

Bas's gaze flicked to her for a moment before he nodded. "That would be a fair interpretation. Although they have a very strict mission statement."

"Which is?"

"They are to make sure that the papacy survives."

"And Drake and I are somehow a threat to that?"

"There are people who believe you are indeed."

Laney threw up her hands, frustration punctuating her words. "Why on Earth would they think that? I mean, I know I haven't exactly been to church in a while, but I hardly think that qualifies as a threat to the papacy."

"When the world first learned of your abilities, there were two camps, one who thought you were a hero, a saint. And then on the other side . . ." Bas's voice drifted off.

"They thought I was the antichrist." The arguments for Laney being the antichrist had all come from Elisabeta's efforts to destroy her. *That woman is dead and still making my life hell.*

"This brotherhood, this Eclipse of the Sun, they believe I'm the antichrist?"

Bas nodded. "Yes. And they believe you are the fulfillment of a prophecy that will destroy the Roman Catholic Church, if not the whole world."

CHAPTER 32

You are the fulfillment of a prophecy that will destroy the Roman Catholic Church, if not the whole world. The words hung in the dark air. Laney was trying really hard not to grab Bas by the throat like Drake had done and demand answers from him. Lucky for him, a banging sounded from the tunnel behind them, reminding her why that was not the best call right now.

"They've found the door," Drake said.

"Yes. But not the way to open it. We need to hurry." Bas picked up his pace, all but running through the dark tunnel. Laney and Drake kept pace with him easily.

Next to her, Drake pulled out his phone, switching on the flashlight. The light was dimmer than Bas's flashlight. He handed it to Laney. "Here."

"What are you—"

Drake blurred.

"Hey!" Bas yelled as the flashlight was wrenched from his hand. Drake disappeared from view. Laney smiled. She had been thinking of doing the same thing.

"What is he doing?"

"Checking the way." Laney held up the phone to light the tunnel as best she could. "Apparently he doesn't trust you."

"And do you?"

"No. What are you doing back in Rome? How did you know we were in trouble? You are keeping secrets. Those secrets are endangering me and the people I care about."

She felt Bas's gaze on her but didn't turn. "You're right," he said. "I will tell you everything. But first we need to get safe."

A dark thought crossed her mind, making her go still. "What about my uncle? Will these men, this brotherhood, go after him as well?"

Bas smiled. "Don't worry about Patrick. I have a friend watching over him. He'll keep him safe."

CHAPTER 33

The dull headache that had begun between Patrick's eyes an hour ago had now shifted across his entire skull. He took a sip of water, fatigue weighing him down. Under the best of circumstances, this interrogation would be taxing. But given his current state of health, he was fading fast.

He leaned his elbows on the table in front of him. There were empty seats on either side of him. A semicircle table sat across from him, where six members of the Vatican's Enhanced Individuals Council sat. He'd been answering their questions for ninety minutes. This was the first break he'd had and that was due to a phone call for the head of the council, Cardinal Francisco.

Patrick reached for the glass of water near him. Lifting it, he realized it was empty.

"Allow me, Father." The American representative appeared next to him, filling his water glass. The man had appeared just before the session began. The members of the council had not looked happy at his appearance, but the man had ignored them and simply sat in one of the seats behind Patrick. Patrick hadn't caught his name when it had been offered at the beginning of the session.

"Thank you." Patrick took another long drink. All this speaking had left his throat and mouth dry. The representative placed the pitcher on the table within reach of Patrick.

"Do you mind?" He indicated the chair next to Patrick.

"By all means."

As the man took his seat, Patrick struggled to remember his name. Was it Daniel? David?

The man extended his hand. "I'm David Okafur."

"Patrick Delaney."

"It's a pleasure, Father."

Patrick studied the younger man next to him. He had strong hands, the veins standing out, and sharp cheekbones that told him the man watched what he ate. He was dressed in a pale pink shirt and light gray suit with a slim tie. He would have looked at home on a Paris runway.

But the calluses on his hands told him this was no up-and-coming bureaucrat. Patrick placed his glass on the table. "So tell me, why is the United States government sending an intelligence operative to the Vatican under the guise of a diplomatic officer?"

A slow smile spread across David's face. "My hands, right?"

Patrick nodded. "Your knuckles, the callus on the outer right-hand side. My niece has the same hands."

"Perhaps I study martial arts just as she does."

"I think we both know those type of calluses don't come from simply studying martial arts. They can only come into being by putting that studying into practice. So again, what is the United States' interest in this?"

David scanned the room. The cardinal was in discussion with his aides in the back corner. The others had not returned to the room. "The United States government has a vested interest on all matters relating to Delaney McPhearson."

"A lot of countries do. But I don't see their representatives here."

"Well, the United States and the Vatican see eye to eye on certain endeavors providing them a closer relationship."

Patrick couldn't for the life of him interpret that double speak. A cell phone rang out across the hall. The cardinal glanced at the screen and answered quickly. His eyes narrowed. He barked something into the phone before disconnecting the call and quickly dialing another number. He met Patrick's gaze for a moment before he shifted his gaze away.

Uh-oh. Patrick did not like that look. He pushed himself back from the table. "If you'll excuse me, I think I'll use the facilities before we reconvene."

David stood, placing his hand on the bars of Patrick's wheelchair. "Let me help you, Father."

Without waiting for Patrick's approval, David began to push him toward the door. The cardinal waved at two of his aides, who quickly hustled over. "The cardinal requests that—"

David did not stop as he spoke. "The father needs to use the facilities. I'm sure you understand."

"But—"

David ignored them, pushing Patrick's chair into the hall and picking up the pace once they were outside.

Patrick swallowed. Something was wrong. Two priests appeared at the end of the hall. They stood for a moment, their eyes narrowing before marching toward Patrick.

David leaned down. "Friends of yours?"

"No."

He sighed. "I thought as much." His phone beeped. He paused their forward momentum to glance at his watch, reading the text there. "Wonderful."

Once again, he started pushing Patrick, aiming for the two priests. "David?"

"Just one second, Father."

The first of the priests reached them. "Father Patrick, we are going to have to ask you to—"

David punched the man in the chin. His eyes rolled back in his head before he dropped. The second priest threw a round kick at David, who stepped at a forty-five-degree angle toward the man while catching his leg. David's forearm slammed into the man's knee, resulting in an audible snap. Switching the hand that held the priest's leg, David whirled around, landing an elbow on the priest's chin before sweeping his other leg. The priest crashed to the floor.

The cardinal's aides gasped at the end of the hall. Two more priests rushed from the other side of the hall. A glint of metal flashed from under their jackets as they ran.

David grabbed the handlebars of the wheelchair and began to run. "Time to go, Father."

CHAPTER 34

WASHINGTON, D.C.

The files on the desk in front of Shremp held no interest for him. He pushed aside the latest report on farm subsidies in the Midwest. He was meeting with a panel in the morning to discuss shoring up some of the subsidies for some of the smaller farms. The farmers were a strong voting bloc, but right now he couldn't care less about them.

Because he still couldn't find Delaney McPhearson.

He'd received a report from a source inside the Vatican that McPhearson and her boy toy had been taken for a tour of the Castel Sant'Angelo and then had disappeared. They'd been allowed in before the crowds but had not been seen coming out. He'd had his intelligence people pore over all feeds around the ancient mausoleum, but they had caught no whiff of them. He growled, shoving aside the files and grabbing the receiver of his desk phone. He punched in the number from memory.

His head analyst, Sheila Lyles, answered. "Yes, sir."

"Where is she?"

"There's been no sign of her yet."

"How's that possible?"

"We don't know, sir. It's possible she slipped through with a group and we were unable to pick up on her."

"I thought you were good."

"*I am*. But this is Delaney McPhearson, not some normal person. She escaped a plane that blew up in midair. It doesn't exactly stretch the imagination that she might figure out a way to leave a tourist site undetected . . . sir."

Shremp grunted. Shelia was getting a little testy. "Find her. Call me as soon as you do." He hung up the phone.

Damn it. He stood up, glaring at the reports on his desk before striding across the room. *Forget it. I need to eat something.*

His assistant hurried into the room just as Shremp was reaching for the door handle. He had to jump back to avoid getting hit. "Damn it, Tony."

"Sir, sorry, sir, but the President has asked to see you in her office."

"Fine, fine. Call my—"

"Sir, she sent a car for you." Tony stepped aside, and Shremp got a look at the two large Secret Service agents waiting for him.

Well, this doesn't look good.

Twenty minutes later, Shremp was being ushered into the Oval Office. The President was pacing over by the fireplace. She stopped as Shremp walked in, nodding at her aide, who closed the door behind Shremp.

Shremp inclined his head. "Madame President."

"What have you heard from Rome?"

"Uh, well, McPhearson has disappeared, it seems."

"And what of her uncle?"

Shremp frowned. Her uncle? Why on Earth was he important? "I have not checked up on her uncle."

"Well, I have. He was last seen in a meeting with the Vatican council. He went for a bathroom break and never returned."

Shremp frowned. "The man's in a wheelchair. I can't imagine he could get very far."

"Not on his own."

A feeling of dread crawled up Shremp's spine.

"It appears Mr. Okafur was also at the meeting. He helped Father Patrick from the room and did not return either. You wouldn't be working a separate mission, would you, Senator?"

Sweat began to trickle down his back. What was David up to? "No, Madame President, of course not. I have no interest in Patrick Delaney."

She studied him a long time before finally nodding. "Very well. I need to know as soon as Mr. Okafur makes contact, is that clear?"

"Yes, of course, Madame President."

"You're excused."

He bowed. "Thank you, Madame President."

He let himself out the door. He nodded at the aide, but his mind was not on where he was. No, it was focused on David. David had taken the priest. Why? Was he working for the United States or against it? Who was pulling his strings? It was possible it was Bruce, but while he did not like Bruce, he had no doubts about the man's loyalty. But David, he had not been born in the United States. Who knew where his loyalty lay?

As he stepped outside, he saw his car was waiting. He'd arranged for it to follow him to the White House. He hurried over, his driver opening the door for him as he approached. Shremp slipped into the back seat, pulling out his phone and punching in Sheila's number.

"Yes, sir."

"I need you to get me everything you can find on David Okafur."

"Sir?"

"He's a CIA agent. Find me everything you have on him and *find him.*"

"Is he a higher priority than McPhearson?"

"No, McPhearson is still the main priority. But I believe Okafur might be somehow related to her disappearance. So find him and get me everything you have on him."

"Yes, sir."

Shremp disconnected the call. He could feel it in the air. Everything was about to break. All his carefully laid plans were about to come to fruition. McPhearson going missing was a problem, but she was still too far away to stop anything. David was also a problem but a human one, easily dealt with. Neither of them could interfere with his plans.

He glanced back over his shoulder at the White House. Soon he'd be the one summoning people to *his* Oval Office. He just needed one more piece to slip into place.

CHAPTER 35

ROME, ITALY

Bas had been leading Laney and Drake through the dark for the last twenty minutes. Laney was not surprised that there were so many tunnels underneath Rome. It seemed every time someone dug into the earth, they bumped into another piece of history. The tunnels dated back to the beginning of Rome itself and had been used on and off since then. They'd been used as catacombs, World War II bomb shelters, unofficial sewers, and even for mushroom farming. She was, however, surprised at Bas's familiarity with them.

He stopped now at a tunnel that crossed with theirs. Laney flicked a glance above the tunnel. It had the sign of the cross scratched into the rock. She'd noticed different scratching at each of the tunnel openings.

"This leads back to the Vatican." Bas pressed a piece of paper into Laney's hands, wrapped around a flashlight. "The tunnels are extensive. These are the directions. Follow them carefully. I warn you, some spots will be difficult to get through."

"Where are you going?"

"To throw them off your scent. Now go." Bas stepped into the dark, his footsteps barely audible.

Laney looked up at Drake. "What on earth is going on?"

"I have no idea. Do you want to follow untrustworthy him or follow his untrustworthy map?"

Laney gave a rueful chuckle. It was true she didn't trust Bas. The fact that he was back in Rome *and* that he'd shown up when they needed him could only mean one thing: He was part of the Brotherhood. But following him seemed unwise if he was going back to the Vatican. Laney was less worried about the Brotherhood or even the Swiss Guard than she was the cameras everywhere in the Vatican. She had learned the hard way how video could be manipulated to tell the wrong story.

"Untrustworthy map. But if we find an earlier way out, we take it."

Flashing the light around, she couldn't see any structural supports for the tunnel ahead of them. It was dirt, which meant no wooden structures to keep the earth from burying them. It also looked narrower and less well traveled.

Drake laughed as he looked ahead.

"You find this funny?"

"Well, I had been hoping to have some time alone with you. This seems to be the personification of 'be careful what you wish for.' But I'll take what I can get." He took her hand.

Laney squeezed his hand back as they began to walk. But within a few feet, she had to let go of his hand. The tunnel narrowed, making it impossible to walk side by side. And she was right. It was definitely less used than the other tunnels they'd been in. She'd lost count of the number of spiderwebs she'd walked into and the times she had to crawl to get through the narrow passages.

Behind her, Drake wasn't doing much better. "I take it back. I won't just take what I can get. This is horrible."

Laney muffled a laugh. "What? Spending time with me in a dark, dank, cobweb-filled tunnel is not exciting enough for you?"

"Exciting? No. Disturbingly gross? Yes. How long have we been walking?"

"About forty-five minutes." Laney squinted, trying to make out something in the distance. "Is that light?"

"Oh, thank the gods." He pushed past Laney, striding forward. This time Laney did laugh. It was good to know the all-powerful archangel had some kryptonite: spooky tunnels.

But as much as Drake's antics amused her, she had to admit, she too wanted out of this tunnel. Not just because of the spiderwebs, but because she got no service down here. She needed to reach her uncle. She hated leaving him behind, but she couldn't exactly go storming through the Vatican looking for him. She just hoped *he* wasn't getting farther and farther away from her while she scrounged around in the dark.

The light down the tunnel brightened as Drake pushed up on an opening in the ceiling. He grabbed the edge and hoisted himself through.

Laney jogged forward as Drake put a hand down. Laney jumped, grabbing hold, and Drake pulled her up. She stumbled as her feet touched the ground, falling into Drake, who pulled her close. He pulled a cobweb from her hair. "That's better."

She wiped some dirt from his cheek. "Same."

He kissed her. Like every other time, a little thrill danced through her body as his lips met hers. She would love to lose herself in the feel of him, but the reality of what was spreading around them had her stepping back and taking her first good look at their surroundings. It appeared to be an abandoned building. The room was large with stained and cracked wood floors. Plaster walls in need of repair surrounded them with arched doorways leading to other rooms. She listened intently but didn't hear anyone in the building, although she could make out sounds of light traffic outside. Nothing to set off any alarm bells.

"Any idea where we are?" she asked.

"I believe we are somewhere east of the castle. The water we heard before, I think that tunnel went under the Tiber."

Laney had examined a map of Rome on the plane, but she had not memorized it. She'd just gotten the basic lay of the land. She frowned. "So we're heading toward the Trevi Fountain?"

Drake shrugged. "That direction at least. Where did Bas want us to meet him?"

Laney pulled out the piece of paper. "Somewhere in Ludovisi, the address is on Via Belisario. Any ideas?"

"Not a clue." Drake pulled out his phone. "Mine's dead."

Laney checked hers. "Mine's close, and I can't get a signal. Let's head out and see what we can find."

They made their way through the building to the front door. It seemed to be a home that had been abandoned long ago. They stepped out onto a residential street.

Laney pulled out her phone but still had no signal. "How in this day and age can there be a place in a city without a signal?"

Drake offered her his arm. "Let's take a stroll, my dear. I'm sure we'll find a signal soon."

Laney linked her arm through his, and Drake led her down the street. A few cars went by, none of them looking too closely at Laney or Drake. Pedestrian traffic was also light. A few kids whipped by on bikes, laughing as they called to one another. An older woman with a scarf over her head bustled by, going in the opposite direction pulling a grocery cart on wheels. But other than that, the whole area was quiet. Laney checked her phone again only to find that it too had died.

They crossed one road then another before Drake pulled her to a stop. "Look." She glanced up at the street sign: Belisario.

A quick glance at the numbers on a few of the buildings let them know they needed to go right. Laney hustled down the street. The buildings became a little larger with more that had been abandoned. Ahead, a large white wall surrounded a three-story building. She frowned, staring at it.

"I think that's it."

Drake stopped just down the street from it. "Are you sure?"

Laney double-checked the address, then looked back at the sign hanging next to the gates. 378 was clearly written there, right underneath a sign proclaiming the building to be the School of the Holy Mother and Home for Children.

Bas had sent them to an orphanage.

CHAPTER 36

WASHINGTON, D.C.

The A/C wall unit in Senator Shremp's office was buzzing, distracting him, and it wasn't the only thing. There'd still been no sightings of McPhearson, her boy toy, or Okafur. He needed to set things in motion before she popped back up. He just needed to make sure his ass was covered before he did so.

Sweat rolled down his back. He glared at the A/C, even as he pulled on his jacket. It wouldn't do to be seen sweating through his dress shirt.

The senator had to have the air conditioner on because the heating was also broken and would not go below seventy-four degrees. Maintenance had promised to get it fixed. But that had been three weeks ago.

"Senator? He's here," Adam called through the intercom.

Finally. Shremp punched the intercom button. "Send him in."

Shremp glared at the offending wall unit before offering his hand to the tall, well-suited man who had just entered his office. "Edwin, good to see you."

"You as well, Senator." Edwin Kincaid III laid his overcoat over the second chair in front of Shremp's desk while taking a seat in the other one. "First let me say what an honor it is for Rowling, Kincaid, Baxter, and Associates to have received your call last week. We are well versed in national security law and have brought to bear all the resources our office has to offer."

"Yes, yes. Your firm is well regarded in these halls."

Edwin smiled, his teeth blindingly white. "Our reputation is very important to us. I hope you will speak just as well of us."

"That depends on what you have for me."

Edwin's smile didn't dim. "Of course. I think you will be very happy." Edwin pulled a folder from his briefcase and slid it across the desk toward Shremp. "This is a five-page report detailing our legal interpretation. Would you like me to summarize it for you?"

"Please." Shremp pushed the folder to the side, resting his hands on his paunch.

"As per your question, the extent of your legal power regarding the Fallen, you are allowed to incarcerate any Fallen, without exception."

"No crimes need to have been committed?"

"The executive order does not stipulate that, and therefore it is allowed. In addition, the term 'physical examination' is not defined and therefore is left at the discretion of the individual issuing the order."

It was an effort to keep the smile from Shremp's face at that news.

"I should warn you, however, that six civil suits have been filed contending that the executive order is unconstitutional and seeking an injunction."

"What are their chances of succeeding?"

"Good. The Fallen as a group have not demonstrated that they are a danger, even though individual members have. Stripping an entire demographic of their civil rights is rarely, if ever, successful."

"But until those suits are settled?"

"Until then, the executive order stands. The interpretation we just discussed does as well."

"How long?"

"I would say two days at most."

Not much time. He'd need to move quickly, but that meant one more issue needed to be addressed. "And the question regarding the autonomy of my position as head of the CEI?"

"As it stands, you are under the auspices of the External Threat Task Force within Homeland Security. The ETF has always enjoyed a great deal of independence. While you are answerable to the head of Homeland, and of course the President, you are not required to notify them of the actions you are going to take, nor ask their permission. You are the sole decision maker regarding the direction and actions of the CEI."

Well, this just keeps getting better and better.

"Of course, if the President is unhappy with your actions, she can remove you from the position. That removal, however, would need to be approved by Congress."

Ah, but by then it will be too late. I will have all the cards. He stood, extending his hand across the desk. "It has truly been a pleasure, Edwin. I will be providing your name should anyone ask for a reference."

Standing, Edwin shook his head. "Thank you, Senator. I am glad you are pleased."

Shremp watched him exit the office. *Oh, I am more than pleased.*

He picked up the phone on his desk. "Adam, put me through to the CEI Retrieval Force."

CHAPTER 37

BALTIMORE, MARYLAND

Jen jogged from the bomb shelter up to Henry's house. Through the windows, she could see Henry on the phone in his office. The sight warmed her despite the turmoil surrounding them. She let herself in the front door and stepped into his office just as he was disconnecting the call.

The scowl disappeared from his face as soon as he caught sight of her, replaced by a soft smile. He moved around the desk and pulled her into a hug. "Hey."

"Hey," she said, leaning against him. Henry was a billionaire, a powerful Nephilim, and a brilliant man. But none of those characteristics were the reason why she loved him. She loved him because no matter how much the world was falling down around them, he made sure that she knew they were in this together. And that whatever life threw at them, he would be right by her side.

When she'd lost the baby, both of them had been spun out as they dealt with the grief. But instead of it pushing them apart to lick their wounds alone, they'd grieved together. Their baby had brought them closer together. She squeezed him tighter.

"How are the kids?" he asked.

"Scared." Jen had been organizing everyone for the move, although "move" sounded pleasant. They were sending all the kids into hiding. They had complied with the law and had each of the kids register. But neither of them planned on allowing anyone to know where the kids were, not until they were certain the kids would be safe.

"Are the hideouts ready?"

"Yeah. That was the last of the arrangements. Mark and Dylan agreed to go with them, along with a handful of others."

Jen nodded. "Did Yoni and Sascha get to Arizona all right?"

"Yeah. Although Yoni keeps saying he can be back here if we need him."

"No. Sascha's due to give birth in a few weeks. He needs to focus on her, Dov, and Max and keep them safe. He can't be anywhere near this."

"I know, but he's struggling a little bit with that order."

Jen sighed. "I know. He cares about those kids as much as anyone. Standing back when they might be in trouble can't be easy for him or Sascha, but they need to put their little ones first right now." A shiver of grief pierced through her chest, picturing a little girl with Henry's eyes and her own features. Tears pressed against her eyes. These moments of grief seemed to come out of nowhere.

Henry pulled back, tipping her chin up as a tear escaped her lashes. He kissed it away. "I love you, Jen. And we will have a family one day."

"I know. I just wish . . ." She sighed, leaning back against him.

Henry rested his chin on top of her head. "Me too."

Jen was content to stay in Henry's arms as long as the world let them. But it was only a few seconds later when Henry's phone rang.

"Sorry." He extricated himself from Jen and reached over to his desk, grabbing his phone. He frowned as he answered it. "Matt?"

Even without her extra abilities, Jen would have been able to hear Matt clearly. "Get them out, Henry. The CEI is coming for them."

"For who?"

"All of the kids, and for you and Jen as well. You need to run. Run now."

CHAPTER 38

Jen bolted from Henry's house before he even had a chance to say anything. She was standing in front of Dom's first blast door mere seconds later. She punched the code in while pulling out her phone.

Mark Fricano, one of the guards who'd been left with the kids when Jen had headed to Henry's, answered. "Jen, did you miss us al—"

"The government's coming for the kids. Get them out the back entrance."

Mark didn't even respond to her. "I need everyone to grab their packs and get to the back entrance now!" he yelled before disconnecting the call.

Jen let out a shaky breath. Henry's staff was all former military. Jen truly appreciated their willingness to follow orders without asking a bunch of useless questions.

Jen sprinted through the halls, but each of the blast doors took a little time to get through. It took three minutes to get downstairs. Jen sprinted into the bomb shelter, nearly crashing into Dylan Jenkins, who was grabbing a pack from the closet in the front hall.

"Report," Jen said.

"We're doing a final head count. Then we'll be out."

Jen strode past him, her long-legged stride eating up the floor as she made her way to the group of kids at the back of the room. A dozen faces turned to her, all looking too young for this kind of stress. One older face also looked unworthy of this stress. Dom stood anxiously ringing his hands on a dish towel, looking like he didn't know what to do.

Frowning, Mark turned around as Jen approached.

"What?" Jen asked.

"The count's off. We're missing two."

"Who's not here?" Jen demanded.

Danny pushed to the front. "Molly and Theresa. They went to their mom's with Shaun and Joe."

"I'll get them." Jen turned to Dylan. "Get the rest of them out. We'll catch up."

Dylan nodded.

Lou, Rolly, and Danny headed for Jen as everyone else made their way to the back entrance.

"What are you guys doing? Get going."

"We can help," Lou said.

"You can." Jen nodded back toward the group in the main room. "Keep them together."

"What about Nyssa and Cain?" Lou asked.

"What about them?"

"Cain's probably on the recordings from the Fallen prison," Danny said quietly. "And what if they know about Nyssa? What if Elisabeta told them about her when she told everyone about the Omni?"

Jen's mouth fell open. Crap. She hadn't thought about that. But the government couldn't be interested in them. Of course, if they knew Cain had been at the SIA facility . . . Damn it. She couldn't take the chance.

"Okay. Rolly and Lou, grab Cain and Nyssa. Tell Molly and Theresa they need to get down here as well. Go."

With a quick look at Danny, they blurred from the room.

Jen looked at Danny. "You need to get going."

He nodded but stayed where he was.

"You don't have to go," she said softly. "It's the Fallen and Nephilim they're after. You can stay with Dom."

"No. I need to go. I need to run electronic interference and keep everyone hidden." He paused. "You and Henry will be coming too, though, right?"

Jen nodded. "We're right behind you. Now go."

Danny started to go, then turned and threw his arms around Jen. "I love you, Jen."

Jen wrapped her arms around him. "Love you too. Now go."

Danny disappeared down the hall. Jen wasted no time sprinting back up the stairs. She'd just stepped outside when her phone beeped, signaling a text.

Government's at the gate.

CHAPTER 39

Mary Jane ran a hand over Nyssa's hair and then Susie's as they slept side by side. Nyssa looked like she could be a McAdams. She looked so much like the rest of the kids—all redheads with blue eyes. Billy's coloring wasn't evident in any of them. He used to joke that the redhead gene was simply too strong in the McAdams line. But now she had a feeling he was happy they didn't look like him, that there was no tie that made their connection obvious. He'd also insisted Mary Jane keep her maiden name and the kids all take hers.

At the time, she'd loved how feminist it made him seem. But now, now she didn't know what to think.

Laughter drifted up the stairs. Molly, Theresa, and the boys were all downstairs in the kitchen helping Cain pull lunch together. Cain was a really amazing cook.

Tomorrow, Molly was going into hiding along with the rest of the kids from the school. It was tearing Mary Jane up. At the same time, she knew it was the safest option. But it killed her that there were forces out there that looked at her beautiful little girl and saw a monster. Molly had the biggest heart. She'd never even killed a bug. She'd release them outside instead. How could anyone actually think she was a threat?

But if that horrible video was indicative of how the government thought they could treat Fallen, Mary Jane had no choice. But she was not splitting up her family. Molly would go tomorrow, but in a few days she, Joe, Shaun, Susie, and Jake would follow. The boys had actually been the ones to insist. Their little sister might be super-powered, but she was still their little sister. And they were not letting her go anywhere without them.

Mary Jane had been so proud of them. And so terrified. But there were moments in life where there were no good options. Letting her daughter go off alone was unimaginable, as was placing her other children in danger. But that was where they were. No good options.

The floorboard creaked behind her. She turned around, unsurprised to see Jake there. She stepped out of the room, closing the door but leaving it open a crack.

"They asleep?" Jake asked.

Mary Jane nodded. "Yeah. They have no idea all this stuff is swirling around them."

"How are you?"

"Absolutely terrified."

Jake hugged her. "It will be all right, Mary Jane. Somehow it will be all right."

"I hope so, Jake." She leaned against him, breaking apart as Joe bounded up the stairs. "Lunch is—" He winced, looking at the girls' bedroom door, and lowered his voice. "Ready."

Mary Jane wiped her eyes. "Okay. I'm coming. It smells delicious."

"It does," Joe said. "It's cauliflower pizza."

Mary Jane looked at Jake with raised eyebrows.

"It's actually pretty good."

"O-kay." She followed her son down the stairs. As she stepped into the kitchen, Cain, with floral oven mitts on, was placing the last of six pizzas on the kitchen island.

He smiled. "Just in time."

"Wow, this looks great." Different toppings and different scents mixed together to rival any pizza shop. "You really need to tell me where you learned to cook so well."

Cain exchanged a quick grin with Jake. "I've just picked up a few things through my travels."

The back door flew open. Jake had his weapon cleared of the holster as Lou and Rolly blurred into the room.

Lou swept the room, her gaze stopping on Molly and Theresa. "We need to go. The government's coming."

Jake's phone beeped. "They're already at the gates."

Panic welled through Mary Jane. No, it wasn't supposed to be like this. She was supposed to have tonight with all her children under one roof.

Rolly stepped forward. "We need to go." He nodded at Cain. "You and Nyssa need to come too."

"I'll grab Nyssa." Lou disappeared up the stairs before anyone could say anything.

Molly stood, a tremor running through her body. "Mom?"

Mary Jane pulled Molly to her, crushing her to her chest. "Be careful. Stay with the group and do what they say. And remember, no matter what happens, I love you. I love you so much."

"Mom . . ." Molly's shoulders shook.

Lou reappeared, both girls in her arms. "In the dark, I couldn't tell which was Nyssa, so I just grabbed them both."

Mary Jane turned. Both girls looked almost identical, even in the light. She gasped, floored by the realization of what she had to do.

Cain looked at her and nodded. "I'll watch over her."

"Mom?" Joe asked.

"Susie has to go. The government won't take our word she's not Nyssa. They'll take her if Nyssa's not here."

Jake's phone beeped again. "We're out of time. They're in the gates."

Molly took Susie, holding her tight. Tires squealed outside.

Mary Jane grabbed Theresa and Molly's arms, pushing them toward the back door. "Go. Go!"

CHAPTER 40

Jen was almost at Mary Jane's when the teenagers came spilling out the back door. Cain was unceremoniously draped across Rolly's shoulders as they all sprinted for the shelter.

Jen didn't say anything, just shifted direction to lead them away, seeing the headlights from the corner of her eyes as two large SUVs squealed onto Sharecroppers Lane. She stopped at the edge of the woods, making sure none of the government agents caught sight of the kids before sprinting after them.

Ahead, the first of the kids burst into the shelter door. Jen had left it open so as to not slow them down. She was the last through, yanking each door shut behind her as she blew through. She burst into the foyer and through Dom's main room right behind Rolly. He dropped Cain on the floor outside the tunnel.

Cain grabbed onto the wall as he swayed. "That's a horrible way to travel."

Jen did a quick head count, then did it again, her heart pounding. "Molly. Where's Molly?"

Theresa clasped Susie to her. "She gave me Susie. She went to get Zane."

Jen whirled around. Oh my God. The cats. She'd completely forgotten about them.

"Where's Zane?"

"He went for a run with Cleo and Tiger."

"Get into the tunnel," Jen called as she pulled her phone and dialed Henry. *Come on. Pick up. Pick up.*

"Jen?"

"Molly's still on the estate."

"What happened?"

Terror raced through Jen. "She went for the cats. We forgot about the cats."

CHAPTER 41

Outside, tires squealed to a stop a few cottages down from Mary Jane's, followed by the slamming of doors and yelling... lots of yelling.

Mary Jane's heart pounded. She had never been so scared in her life. *Please, please keep everyone safe*, she begged silently.

A man's voice over a bullhorn sounded. "Attention, attention, everyone in the houses. Step outside with your hands raised. No sudden movements."

"Jake, what do we do?" Joe asked.

"We do what they say." He placed his gun in the holster on the counter.

"I thought you said we were going to fight," Shaun demanded.

"We are. But we fight smart. We are outnumbered, outgunned, out resourced. We do not give them a chance to provoke us to do something that they can arrest us for. There are different ways to fight Shaun. And sometimes the most effective ways don't involve fists." Jake clapped him on the shoulder. "Now let's go."

Jake led the way, followed by Shaun, then Joe and Mary Jane brought up the rear. Jake paused at the door, hand on the knob. "Everybody ready?"

"Yeah," Joe said while Shaun nodded.

Mary Jane wasn't sure what she did, but Jake must have taken it as an affirmation. He opened the door a crack.

"We're coming out!" he yelled. "We are not armed!"

Mary Jane's chest tensed. Part of her couldn't believe this was happening. How could this be happening?

Jake pushed open the door. The once idyllic street now looked terrifying. Armed men were everywhere. A helicopter flew overhead, scanning the street. Heavily armed individuals swept into a house across the street after kicking in the door.

Six soldiers knelt in front of Mary Jane's house, their weapons trained over the rock wall on Jake and then each person as they exited the cottage. One man separated from the six, his weapon pointed at Jake—the rest kept their focus on Mary Jane and her boys. She had never felt so powerless in her life. With the flick of a finger, someone could end the lives of her boys and Jake. The only comforting thought was that Molly and Susie weren't there.

"Down! Get down on the ground!"

Mary Jane paused.

"Get down on the ground!"

Jake started to lower himself, his hands still up. The boys did the same. Mary Jane was a little slower to catch on but started to lower herself as well. Apparently the soldiers along the wall didn't think they were moving fast enough. Four of them vaulted up, surging forward to kick each of them in the back.

Mary Jane cried out as her face slammed into the dirt. Her arms were wrenched behind her back, her sleeve pushed up. Pain lanced up through her arm and she screamed. Next to her, the boys yelled as well.

Her hands were held tightly behind her for another two minutes. She didn't dare move or speak.

"They're clear."

The pressure on her hands immediately eased. A strong arm

gripped her by the upper arm and pulled her up. "Name," the man in front of her barked.

"M-Mary Jane McAdams."

"Put your hands in front of you."

Mary Jane did. The man quickly wrapped zip ties around them, pulling the wire tight.

Her boys received the same treatment next to her, as did Jake. "What's going on?" she asked.

The man ignored her question, just pushed her toward the street. "These four are cleared."

The soldiers led them to the edge of the street and had them sit on the curb. Mary Jane sat between her boys, wanting more than anything to hold them tight, but that wasn't an option. She frowned, realizing her arm felt wet. She glanced down. A red cut, blood still seeping, was now on her forearm. A quick glance at her boys showed they had been cut as well. "Why did they *cut* us?"

"To see if we would heal," Jake said. "They're looking for Fallen."

"That's . . . that can't be legal," Joe said.

"I think we are beyond that point now," Jake said quietly as another group was led to the curb and unceremoniously dumped there. Mary Jane recognized them. They worked in the kitchen at the main house.

A roar sounded from down the street. Mary Jane's blood went cold. *Oh my God.*

Gunfire burst out from the same location as the roar. Mary Jane craned forward to see what was happening. She could just make out a pale shadow slinking into the trees.

"It's Zane," Joe said, starting to stand.

Jake grabbed him, keeping him in place. "No. Stay down."

Joe tried to shake him off. "Let me go."

A soldier stormed over. "You were told to sit." He jammed the end of his rifle into Joe's face. Joe collapsed, blood dripping from his mouth.

"No!" Mary Jane screamed, reaching for Joe as Jake leaped to his feet, burying his shoulder into the soldier's hip as he raised his weapon to strike Joe again. The two of them went down in a flurry of feet.

Soldiers streamed over to them. Two of them yanked Jake off the soldier. Mary Jane hunched over Joe. "Joe, Joe!"

Shaun started to get up but was unceremoniously yanked down by another soldier. "Stay down!" A gun was aimed at his face.

Joe lay still, but his chest moved up and down. His nose was broken, blood running down into his mouth.

"That's his mother!" Jake yelled as a soldier grabbed her arm, pulling her back.

"No! Joe! Let me help him! I'm a nurse!" Tears streaming down her cheeks, Mary Jane scrambled, trying to get back to Joe as two soldiers grabbed him under the arms and started to pull him away.

"Stop fighting!" the soldier ordered, slamming the butt of his gun into the back of her head. She crashed to the ground, her bound hands coming to her face as her vision faded in and out. Her thoughts slowed down. The soldier raised the weapon again.

Mary Jane could do nothing but watch.

Then the soldier was flying through the air, landing in a heap on the porch.

"Mom!" Molly crouched next to her.

Mary Jane blinked hard, dark circles appearing at the edge of her vision. "No, no. You have to go. Run."

"Not without you." Mary Jane felt herself lifted in the air.

A gunshot rang out. Molly stumbled, Mary Jane dropped, holding on to Molly. Blood seeped from her arm. "No!"

Soldiers approached from behind. Mary Jane yanked Molly behind her. "Leave her alone. She's just a child!"

Moving swiftly across the ground, two shadows separated from the trees. They landed on the two men trying to pull Joe away. The men screamed. Shaun bolted to his feet and grabbed Joe, dragging him away from the men as Cleo and Tiger flung the men away.

Soldiers opened fire.

"Cleo! Get out of here!" Jake yelled.

Cleo sprinted for the trees, Tiger on her tail.

A third shadow landed on the soldiers in front of Mary Jane. Zane bowled right into them, swiping their guns away, baring his teeth.

Shots rang out. Molly grunted. Mary Jane whirled around in time to catch her. "No!"

Jake roared, but three soldiers kept him on the ground.

Mary Jane threw herself over Molly as soldiers encircled them. "No! No!"

Two other convoys screeched to halt, soldiers pouring out of them. Zane roared before the sound was cut off as gunfire rang out.

Shaun sat holding Joe in his arms, tears rolling down his cheeks, his eyes wide in horror as he looked at Mary Jane.

Then a blur materialized next to him. Henry knelt down, meeting Mary Jane's gaze between the shapes of the soldiers encircling her as she covered Molly, whose blood was seeping into the ground from a stomach wound.

"Get them out of here!" she yelled.

Henry grabbed the boys. In a flash, they were gone. No one even noticed. The circle around Mary Jane and Molly tightened. Mary Jane looked down at her beautiful little girl. Her eyes were closed, and there were so many gunshot wounds dotting her chest that Mary Jane couldn't even count them in a glance. Molly would heal but not anytime soon from that many wounds. More than anything Mary Jane wanted to pull Molly to her, protect her from everything swirling around them. But with her bound hands, she couldn't even reach out and stroke her cheek. "I love you, Molly. Do you hear me? I love you."

A soldier reached down and pulled her away.

"No! Let me stay with her. No!"

Jake roared once more. He flung a soldier off him and charged to his feet. An electric charge rammed through Mary Jane's system, and she crashed to the ground. She felt the soldier step behind her. From the corner of her eye, she saw him raise his weapon. But she kept her gaze level with her daughter's much-too-young face. Then pain exploded across the back of her head, and her world went black.

CHAPTER 42

Mustafa took the corner way too fast, half the truck coming up on two wheels. But he didn't slow down. He glanced in his rearview mirror. Matt's SUV took the corner just as fast and just missed sideswiping a tree. He didn't slow down either.

Mustafa pressed down on the accelerator. He had already been on the way to Chandler Headquarters when Matt called him to let him know they were raiding the place. Mustafa could not believe it had come to this. He'd been helping arrange the transport for the kids tomorrow. He'd just gotten off the phone with Gerard. The cats were loaded up from the reserve, and Noriko and Gerard, along with a phalanx of guards, were already escorting them to a spot in South Dakota.

He had felt good, thinking they were ahead of the government. He never thought they'd go after the headquarters. The kids at the estate ranged in age from six to eighteen. Hardly national security threats. But the President needed to prove she was on top of the Fallen issue, and apparently taking a bunch of children into custody was her way.

Mustafa yanked the wheel to the side, so lost in his feelings of anger that he'd nearly missed the turnoff. He raced down the road, praying for everyone on the estate. An empty field appeared ahead. He didn't even slow as he crossed into it, his SUV bucking under the uneven surface. Kids. They were going after kids.

He screeched to a halt near an old well, slamming the truck into park before vaulting from the driver's seat. He sprinted for the well and yanked on the bushes next to it.

Matt brought his SUV to a halt next to Mustafa's. A puff of wind, and Matt was at his side. "Move."

Mustafa shifted to the side as Matt wrenched the three remaining bushes out of the way, revealing a door. A padlock with a chain was on the outside. Matt grabbed it and yanked it off, pulling the chain through the handles.

"Step back," Matt ordered.

Mustafa scrambled back as Matt placed both hands on one of the doors. Bracing his legs, he pulled the whole door off.

A cry sounded from inside the door. Mustafa scrambled past Matt and peered in. His heart nearly split in two at the sight. Over two dozen kids stood there, their faces smudged with dirt, their eyes wide. More than a few had red eyes shining brightly with tears.

Jen stepped forward, a six-year-old in her arms. "Mustafa. Thank God."

He nodded. "It's all right. Come on."

He reached out a hand and pulled the first child up. Matt grabbed another one. Quickly, they got all the kids out, instructing them to pile into the SUVs.

They were three miles from the estate. After the Day of Reckoning, Mustafa had helped Jake, Matt, and Henry create a tunnel leading from Dom's to this field. Only the four of them and Dom knew of its existence. The other tunnels leading from Dom's had been too well known to trust that they could use them again.

Jen led all the kids toward the SUVs, splitting them up between the cars.

Cain stepped out from the hole, holding Nyssa. "Thank you, Mustafa. That's everyone for now." He gripped Mustafa's hand. "Have you heard anything from the estate?"

"Not yet. Let's get everyone moving, then we'll see what we can find out."

A sound made Mustafa freeze as he stepped from the doorway. He had his weapon pulled. Cain shoved Nyssa at Danny, who was only a few feet away. "Take her."

He stepped next to Mustafa.

A dark shadow appeared in the entryway. Lou and Rolly appeared at Mustafa and Cain's side. "It's a Nephilim," Lou said.

Henry stepped through the doorway, a body draped over his shoulder. Shaun appeared from behind him, his face unnaturally pale.

Cain rushed forward, pulling Shaun toward him before he dropped. "What happened?"

"The feds weren't exactly concerned with keeping everyone safe." Henry carried Joe toward the SUV. Even in the dim light, Mustafa could make out the damage to the boy's face.

Lou grabbed Shaun's sleeve. "What about your mom? And Molly?"

It took Shaun much longer than it should have for him to understand the question. "They . . . they shot Molly. Mom threw herself in front of her as the soldiers advanced on her. I don't know what happened then. Henry yanked us out of there."

Lou met Rolly's gaze. He nodded. They both stepped toward the doorway. Mustafa jumped in front of him, his hands out. "No."

Lou glared at him. "They *shot* Molly."

"I know. And if you two go up there, they will shoot you as well. Do you really think that if there was a way to get Molly and her mother out, that Henry would have left them there? Do you really think he and Jen wouldn't be leading the charge back? The estate is lost. We regroup. We make a plan. And then we go after our people."

"What if they're already dead?" Lou demanded.

Jen blurred in front of them. "Then you getting killed won't change that."

"We need to be smart about this. Not emotional," Mustafa said.

Cain nodded. "Mustafa's right, as much as I hate to admit it. We all thought the war was with Samyaza. But it wasn't. This is the true war. And tonight is just a battle. Do not sacrifice yourself unnecessarily."

"We need to go. You can't protect Molly or her mom, but there are two dozen kids in these cars you *can* protect." Mustafa waited, knowing there was no way he could stop the two teenagers in front of him if they decided to go. They could bowl through him in less than a second, and he wouldn't even know they'd moved until he hit the ground.

"I need you to help me protect the kids," Jen said. She and Lou had an unspoken conversation for a long few seconds before Lou's shoulders dropped. "Okay." She and Rolly turned for the SUVs. Jen draped an arm over Lou, pulling her close. Mustafa let out a breath.

"Well done," Cain said quietly before following them.

It was a tight squeeze in the SUVs for everyone, but no one complained. Mustafa hopped in the driver's seat.

Cain sat behind them, Nyssa once again wrapped in his arms. Shaun sat on his other side, Susie in his arms, while Lou held on to Joe, who was blinking and looking around in confusion.

Jen sat in the passenger seat, her face tight. "We need to go. They have choppers in the air."

"Yes, we do." Mustafa put the car into gear and quickly turned out of the field. Matt was right behind him in the other SUV.

They reached the end of the road, and Mustafa turned right. In the rearview mirror, he watched Matt go left. That was part of the plan. They couldn't escape together. And this way, one of them would have a better chance of getting to safety. He watched Matt's taillights disappear.

Good luck, my friend.

CHAPTER 43

Laney did not sense any Fallen or Nephilim inside the walls, or anywhere nearby, for that matter. But she and Drake still did a little recon. The grounds of the school were entirely enclosed by the ten-foot white wall. They jumped onto the top of the wall along the side where they were hidden by trees on the property. The three-story building was the largest building on the property, but there were two other buildings as well. One was an old stable. The other was a single-story flat building that had been obviously created more recently than the other two buildings. In the back of that building was a small playground, where children ranging in age from five to twelve played.

"It really is a school," Laney said.

"Either that or those are some very short and compelling spies. Shall we try the front door now?"

Laney nodded, not sure what to make of it. Cain had mentioned that the copy of the tome Patrick had gotten in the mail had come from a school in Rome. It seemed too much of a stretch that this was not the same place. Did that mean these guys were allies?

They made their way back to the metal gates at the front. The gates were locked, and there was a bell, an actual old-fashioned bell, next to it. Drake pulled the cord, and they waited.

Two minutes passed. Laney was reaching for the cord again when the front door opened. A nun in a white habit with a white wimple stepped out of the building. A large dark rosary hung around her neck and swung with her movements as she hurried to the gate.

Her movements were of a young, energetic woman, but as she approached, Laney could see the lines in her olive complexion and wrinkles around her eyes. Her hands were curled from arthritis but still slim and strong, although her skin had taken on a parchmentlike quality. Laney would be shocked if she were any younger than sixty, although she was probably closer to seventy, maybe even eighty. The nun stepped to the gate, peering up at them.

"Can I help you?" she asked in a thick accent that took a moment for Laney to place because it wasn't Italian. Spanish, maybe.

"Good afternoon," Laney said. "We were asked to meet our friend Father Sebastian Gante here."

A smile burst across the woman's face. "Bas. Oh, how wonderful. We did not know he was back in the country. Come in, come in." She opened the gate, waving them forward. "I am Sister Cristela."

"This is Drake, and I'm Delaney McPhearson."

The woman gaped, her hand flying to her throat. "Oh my. I'm so sorry. I didn't recognize you. I left my glasses inside."

"That's all right. It's a pleasure to meet you."

"Oh, and you as well. Please follow me." She hustled toward the building, and Laney had to practically jog to keep up with her.

Sister Cristela moved much faster than a woman her age

should. Laney recalled an article she'd read about aging nuns. A study of almost 700 nuns, ages 75–102, followed over a period of thirty years, found that nuns often were able to stave off the effects of Alzheimer's if they had what was called idea density—a great number of thoughts packed into a writing sample. Nuns with positive outlooks lived significantly longer than those with less positive outlooks. The nuns in general lived longer than most women. The nuns who read more and intellectually stimulated themselves seemed to do a better job of staving off dementia. After their death, it was found that these nuns had all the physical signs of Alzheimer's in their brains but had demonstrated no symptoms.

Sister Cristela certainly seemed to live up to the study's findings. "Is there a phone we can use? Our cell phones died."

Cristela stopped, taking Laney's hands. "Oh, of course, your brother. You must be so worried."

Laney stared down at the small woman, dread coiling in her stomach. "What do you mean?"

"I just saw it on the news. Your brother's home—it was raided by the government. Warrants have been put out for all of them." She paused. "And for you as well."

CHAPTER 44

BALTIMORE, MARYLAND

The dream was strange. Everything was covered in a low-hanging, thick fog. Mary Jane kept running, but she couldn't see anything or anyone. Just more and more fog. Where was everybody? She ran faster, but it made no difference. There was nothing. Her foot caught on something. She tripped, flying forward. She braced her hands but knew the impact was going to be—

Mary Jane's eyes flew open. She reared up, her arm pulling painfully. A metal cuff was wrapped around her wrist, the other half around the metal bars of a hospital bed. She stared at it, trying for a moment to figure out some medical reason for a handcuff to be around her wrist because she could not fathom the reason she normally saw people cuffed to their hospital beds being applied to her. As a nurse, she knew unruly patients often had to be restrained, but those cuffs were padded to keep the patient from hurting themselves. This cuff was metal, and that was only used by law enforcement. Why would—

Her gaze caught the bandage on her other arm, where the

soldier had cut her to see how quickly she would heal. And just like that, everything that had happened came rushing back to her. The soldiers, the zip ties, Joe getting hurt, Jake trying to protect them, and Molly.

Oh my God, where is Molly?

The door opened. Mary Jane's gaze snapped to a silver-haired man walking in. He wore a dark gray suit and had a coat slung over the arm that also carried a briefcase. He looked more like a lawyer than a doctor or soldier.

The man placed his briefcase and coat in a chair and walked to the side of the bed. "Mary Jane McAdams, I'm Brett Hanover. I run the legal department of the Chandler Group."

Mary Jane said nothing, studying the man. He looked like a lawyer, and she'd heard his name before, but her trust was nonexistent at this point. She'd trusted the government, and they'd beaten her, her son, Jake, and shot Molly. She crossed her arms over her chest. "Prove it."

He smiled. "Jake suggested you would not believe me. He wanted me to tell you that Shaun cheats at checkers, and something about a racist sundae?"

Mary Jane's shoulders slumped with relief. Shaun did cheat at checkers, and the racist sundae was a joke about Mary Jane's boring sundae choice: vanilla ice cream, marshmallow topping, whipped cream, no cherry. "How's Jake? And the boys? And Molly? Have you seen Molly?"

Brett pulled up a chair, sitting next to the bed. "I've seen Jake. He's fine aside from some bumps and bruises. The boys are not in custody. Jake suggested that Henry may have had something to do with that, but I have not had any word on them, or Henry, for that matter."

"And Molly?"

Brett's mouth turned down. "I have no information on your daughter, I'm afraid. I have been able to get in to see you and Jake because you are not Fallen."

"Not Fallen? Why does that make a difference?"

"The President's executive order removed the constitutional protections guaranteed to all American citizens if they are proven to be Fallen. Similar to how the PATRIOT Act removed protections for individuals accused of terrorism, individuals identified as Fallen do not have the right to an attorney, and the government can refuse to divulge any and all information regarding where they are being held. They don't even have to admit they are holding her."

"But she's only thirteen."

"I know. And I believe this order is unconstitutional. I submitted a case against the government, as did a few other civil rights groups. The case will be heard tomorrow by the Fifth Circuit Court in D.C."

"Tomorrow?" She glanced at the window. The sun looked like it had barely been up. "So they can just hold my daughter, torture my daughter, for at least one full day, and there's nothing we can do?"

"I'm afraid right now, that is true. The Chandler Group is trying to find out where they took Molly and Zane, but so far they've had no luck."

Mary Jane couldn't absorb what he was saying. She was locked in a nightmare, and she was powerless to do anything.

"I have managed to get you and Jake released."

But not Molly. Mary Jane couldn't get the image of Molly falling out of her mind.

"The government is digging in its heels about Molly, but I think they will be changing their tune soon."

"Why? They hold all the cards."

"Not all of them." Brett glanced at his watch, then pulled out his phone. His fingers danced over the screen as he spoke. "Jake wanted me to remind you that he said they were going to fight them with everything they had. And that one of the first weapons they were going to use was truth."

"What does that mean?"

Brett looked up and smiled. "Henry prepared in many ways for the siege. One was making sure that every inch of the estate was being recorded. He caught everything the government did last night on camera. And this morning, it was released to the media. I'm just waiting on word for who's going to show it first."

"You think that will help?"

"Oh, I can guarantee no one involved in last night's raid is going to be happy."

CHAPTER 45

ROME, ITALY

"Come in, come in." Sister Cristela waved Laney and Drake in through the large metal doors before leading them across a marble floor, cracks showing its age. Ahead, a large four-foot statue of a Pope stood in an alcove. The walls were plaster, showing attempts at patching them over the years. But otherwise, the space was spotless. A small waiting room sat off the foyer. Sister Cristela turned on the TV, switching it to an American news channel.

Laney's eyes focused on the TV and the armed soldiers guarding the Chandler gate. She barely heard Sister Cristela as she spoke. "There's a phone there if you need to call anyone."

"Thank you." Drake headed for the phone, but Laney couldn't pull her gaze from the TV.

She slumped into a chair, staring in horror at the sight of the estate looking like a militarized zone. What had happened? On screen, the anchor recounted the raid.

Drake came and sat next to her.

"Did you reach anyone?"

Drake shook his head. "No. Henry, Jake, Jen, Cain, Lou—no one's answering."

A different anchorperson appeared on the screen, reading a statement about the raid. "Last night's raid was conducted by the Committee on Enhanced Individuals Retrieval Force. A dangerous Fallen who was hiding at the Chandler Estate was apprehended and is now in government custody. We do not know at this time who the individual is—all the government would say was that the Fallen was a danger to society. We now go to our—"

Laney sprang to her feet. Who did they take? All the possible candidates flew through her mind. "It had to be an adult, right? They wouldn't take one of the kids, would they?"

"I don't know, Laney," Drake said softly before crossing the room and turning off the TV.

Laney jumped forward, reaching for the controls. "What are you doing?"

"You are tying yourself in knots. You can do nothing about what is happening there. So let's figure out how we're going to get back there and what exactly Bas has been up to."

Laney felt her anger deflate. "You're right. I can't do anything from here."

"No, you can't. But there's another mystery for you to solve. Come take a look." Drake walked to the alcove built into the wall directly across from the main doors and led her to the statue of the Pope. The Pope held a book and a child.

Laney studied the statue. It was very well crafted, but she couldn't understand why it was important. It was just a statue of a Pope. She'd seen dozens if not more of them since coming to Rome. "I don't get it. What am I looking for?"

"What do you see?"

She glanced at the name at its base but couldn't quite make it out. "John Anglicus. I don't recognize him. Is he one of the early ones?"

"Indeed, *she* was one of the early ones."

Laney started. "She?"

"Look closer, Laney."

She turned back to the statue, inspecting it a little more closely this time. The features on the face were soft, almost feminine, but the same could be said for many statues. But closer examination of the body revealed a swell of breasts.

Her gaze flew back to the face and the long lashes on the eyes before they turned to the child in her arms. "It's Pope Joan."

Pope Joan had been a Pope sometime around the ninth century, although debate raged as to when or if she even existed. Her legend dogged the Church for centuries before Pope Clement finally declared that she had never existed.

But all traces of her were harder to remove. She had been killed by a crowd when she gave birth to a child on her way from St. Peter's to the Pope's residence at Lateran Palace. For a century, the papal processions avoided the street where it occurred, even though it was the most direct route from the church to the residence.

Her legacy had endured in other ways as well. In ancient tarot cards, the card for hidden knowledge depicted a female Pope. At the basilica in St. Peter's Square, Bernini, one of the most famous artists of the 17th century, carved eight images of a woman wearing a papal crown. The images seemed to tell the story of a woman giving birth.

"Why would they place a statue of her here?" Laney asked.

Drake shrugged. "This is the School of the Holy Mother. Perhaps it is a different mother they revere."

Steps hurried down the hall toward them. Laney turned, expecting to see Sister Cristela. But it was a different, more familiar face that made their way down the hall to them. "Bas?"

Bas smiled. "I am glad to see you made it, Laney. And you as well." He nodded at Drake.

"What are we doing here?" Laney demanded.

Bas indicated the building with a sweep of his hand. "This is my home. I grew up here."

Laney stared at him, stunned. Bas grew up here? And then he showed up in the United States.

"There is much to explain"—he nodded to the statue—"for what her death began."

Laney growled, she was so annoyed. "I don't care about a long-dead Pope. Do you know what is happening in the States? I need to get back. I don't have time for a history lesson. Now where is my uncle?"

"He'll be here."

"If the Brotherhood is targeting Laney, they would be smart to target him as well. Would you know if they had him?" Drake asked.

"Not immediately. But—"

Laney headed for the door.

"Laney, wait." Bas darted in front of her.

Clouds blocked the sun. Thunder rumbled. The first traces of fear dashed across Bas's face.

Laney locked eyes with him. "I suggest you get out of my way."

He put up his hands. "Laney, I am trying to help. I swear, I am on your side."

The clanging of a bell sounded outside.

"That's the front gate," said Bas.

Drake headed for the door. He didn't slow down as he approached Bas. Bas wisely leaped out of the way just in time, because Laney was pretty sure Drake was going to go right through him. Laney was right behind him. She blurred out the door to the gate. Sister Cristela shrieked as wind blew her skirt as she came around the side of the building.

Laney did not stop to apologize. Through the gate, she could see her uncle sitting in his wheelchair. She stumbled to a run, bending over and gulping in breath.

He's okay. He's okay. The fear she had been holding at bay crashed into her with the force of a semitruck. Ever since they had entered the tunnel, she had forced herself not to think of her uncle. Short of storming the Vatican and creating a huge international incident, there was nothing she could do. But the fear had been a constant. She had nearly lost him a few months ago. Ever since then, his mortality and the fact that one day she would lose him had been the thought constantly taking up residence in the back of her mind.

Drake put an arm around her, helping her straighten. "He's all right, ring bearer. He's all right," he whispered before hurrying to the gate.

Laney followed behind him, trying to get her emotions under control. The last thing she wanted to do was worry her uncle. Drake had the gate open by the time she reached it.

Laney hurried through, throwing her arms around her uncle. "Thank God. I was so worried."

Her uncle patted her back. "It's been a bit of an adventure. Luckily, I had some help, although I'm not exactly sure how he fits into everything."

Laney studied the tall, dark-skinned man next to her uncle. He smiled. "It is a pleasure to finally meet you, Dr. McPhearson. I am David Okafur." He extended his hand.

She took it. "Thank you."

He smiled again, inclining his head. "Now I believe I have lost any attempts to follow us, but perhaps we could move this conversation inside just in case?"

Laney placed her hands on the handlebars of her uncle's chair. She gave David a pointed look. "Yes. I think we need to chat."

David inclined his head in agreement. As David stepped through the gate, Sister Cristela gave a happy little cry. David hurried over to her, lifting the tiny nun up and twirling her around.

He placed her down, smiling down at her. "I believe you have shrunk since I last saw you."

She whacked his stomach with the back of her hand with a grump, although her eyes still sparkled. "Always with the insults, this one."

David offered her his arm. She tucked her ancient arm through his. "Sister Cristela, you know you are my favorite Salvadorian nun."

"And *you* know your flattery does not work with me," she replied even as she held his arm a little tighter.

Laney watched the exchange in confusion. She leaned down to her uncle. "Who exactly is he?"

"I was introduced to him as the United States representative at the Vatican."

"*He's* a U.S. envoy?" Drake asked.

"That's what I was told. But when some priests tried to abduct me, he defended me and got me out of the Vatican. I would not have been able to do it on my own."

Laney's hands tightened on the wheelchair. "I'm sorry, Uncle. I never should have let you go in there alone. I should've—"

He reached up and patted her hand. "You couldn't have known. I still don't truly know what any of this is about."

Ahead, Bas stepped out of the front door, a smile crossing his face at the sight of David. David extricated himself from Sister Cristela and quickly hurried over to Bas. Their hug was filled with warmth and familiarity. These two weren't just casual friends. They were family.

Drake nodded toward the two men. "I believe the answers to those questions lie with those two men."

Laney gripped her uncle's chair tightly. "Well, then let's go get some answers."

CHAPTER 46

Photos lined the walls of the hallways that Bas led them down. Children at play smiled out at them from the black-and-white to the colored shots, a progression of faces through time. Laney paused halfway down one hall, inspecting a photo of three smiling children around ten years old. The little boy and girl were identical, from their dark hair to their dark eyes and their bright smiles. Both had their arms around the waist of a darker-skinned boy whose smile lit up the shot.

Drake peered at the shot as well. "What is it?"

She nodded to the boys. "Bas and David," she said before heading toward Bas. He had disappeared in a doorway at the end of the hall.

The doorway Bas had entered opened up into a large, bright kitchen. A tall woman with large muscular arms and curly dark hair sprinkled with gray looked up from where she was rolling dough at a large kitchen island. She let out a happy cry, dropping the rolling pin and hurriedly wiping her hands on her apron. David strode over to her, and she threw her arms around him. She spoke quickly in Italian. David responded in kind. The two chatted back and forth before the woman glanced at Laney, Patrick, and Drake. Her mouth fell open.

She quickly shifted to English. "Oh my. Oh, forgive me, how rude. You, you are the ring bearer."

Laney inclined her head, not sure how exactly to respond to the woman's wide-eyed look.

That wide-eyed look only grew wider as she took in Drake. She turned to Bas. He shook his head slightly, making Laney frown. What was he warning her about?

"Sylvia, may I please introduce Delaney McPhearson, her uncle, Patrick Delaney, and Drake."

Sylvia curtsied, using her apron as a skirt. "It's an absolute pleasure to meet you. It's an honor. It's—"

Bas cut her off, for which Laney was glad, because she was pretty sure the woman was going to curtsy again. "Sylvia, we are going to speak in the den. Maybe some snacks?"

"Oh, of course. I have some lemon bars I just made, and—"

David put an arm around her. "Why don't I help you set up a tray, and we can catch up?"

"It was nice meeting you," Laney said, politeness overriding her misgivings of Bas and David.

Sylvia beamed at her. "Yes, yes, you as well."

Laney followed Bas down yet another hallway. The place was huge. He led them to a large den at the end of the hall. Commercial carpet covered the floor. One wall was lined with bookcases only two shelves high, filled with books and board games. Pictures created by what could only be years of children filled the walls above them.

Five different couches and a dozen chairs were scattered into different seating areas. None of the furniture matched. There were five different rugs for each of the sitting areas as well. Yet there was something incredibly welcoming about the space.

The wall opposite the bookshelves was lined with old windows. Sunlight streamed in from them along with the sounds of children. Laney pushed Patrick toward them, the squeals and laughter of children too enticing to avoid. The windows overlooked a courtyard, where a group of five children were bouncing a large ball between themselves.

"I never tire of that sound," Patrick said, looking out.

Bas walked over to stand next to them. "It is a good place to grow up."

"You grew up here?" Patrick asked.

"My sister and I arrived here when we were only four years old. I remember just being so scared. And then I remember sitting in Sylvia's kitchen with a giant glass of milk, an afghan over our shoulders that Sister Cristela had knitted, and a giant plate of sugar cookies in front of us. We spent the first year sitting in Sylvia's kitchen. She never minded. She would let us help with her baking, although I'm sure at that age we were more of a nuisance than a help. But she never made us feel that way."

"It sounds like you found a home," Laney said.

"We did. All the children here do."

"That we do," David said as he walked in carrying a tray.

Laney turned. "Your accent isn't Italian."

"Ah, no. I spent my first seven years in England. The accent never left, even when my parents returned to Italy. They passed away in a car accident a year later."

"I'm sorry," Patrick said.

David shrugged. "I suppose it was their time."

"Then you ended up here," Laney said.

David placed the tray on a coffee table and began to unload mugs. He poured tea into each of them. "Yes. And I am very grateful I did. It gave me a family again."

Laney looked between the two men. "So you two have known each other for what, two decades?"

"Almost three, actually," Bas said.

"And you are some sort of government bureaucrat," Drake said, looking at David then turning to Bas. "While you went into the priesthood, becoming a member of some secret violent group of priests. Seems you went down different paths."

David took a seat, lifting a cup of tea and twirling a spoon through it. "Our paths are not as dissimilar as they appear. My government work is slightly more active than my current title would suggest."

Laney studied the man. He had the confidence of a man who knew he could handle himself. She doubted there were many situations David Okafur found himself uncomfortable in. He smiled.

"So how did you come to help my uncle?" Laney asked. "Did you just happen to end up the liaison in this case?"

Bas shook his head, taking a lemon bar from the tray. "No. We have spent years putting things into place so that we would be ready when we were called."

"Called? Called to do what?" Laney asked.

David took a sip of tea. "Why, help you, ring bearer. You are the culmination of our life's work."

CHAPTER 47

"What do you mean they have escaped?" John Moretti yelled.

Ezekiel cringed, hunching his shoulders as if waiting for the blow. "I-I do not know what to say, sir. We followed the plan exactly. But they escaped the cell before our brothers were even in the room. And they took them down with ease."

"Yes, but how did they escape the castle?"

"I-I—we had all the exits covered. All the tunnels. But they knew of one that we did not even know about."

John narrowed his eyes. "What?"

"It leads out from one of the old storage rooms. Our brothers broke through the wall and followed them through the tunnel, but it branches off in multiple directions. They lost them."

"How did they know it was there? Did they have inside help?"

"Not that we know of, but the security cameras went down during the escape, so we cannot rule out that possibility."

John seethed. He should have taken the inner council's warnings more seriously. Apparently McPhearson was more dangerous than they thought. Or more likely, it was God's soldier.

They needed to get to him, remind him of who he was. They needed him helping *them*, not unwittingly helping the antichrist.

"Very well. Make sure Father Patrick is taken to—"

"Sir, he has gone missing."

"*Missing?*"

"Yes, Your Eminence. Our men moved in to intercept him, but the U.S. envoy defended him and took down our brothers. Then the two of them escaped."

"Escaped? This is the Vatican! We control every camera, every exit. How did they escape?"

"Um, once again, the cameras went down."

John glared at him. "And you don't think someone on the inside helped them either?"

"Sir, our people are loyal to the Vatican, to the Church. They would never betray us."

John studied him. Ezekiel believed what he said, but that did not make it true. He was completely loyal to the Church and could not conceive of another member of the priesthood who did not have the same level of loyalty.

But John had heard rumors of another group within the Church. A group whose goal was not to fulfill the wants of the Church but were to make the Divine Feminine the equal of God. He had written them off years ago. After all, in all his time in the Church and in all of the Church's history, there'd been no sign of them.

Except perhaps in the tenth century. Pope Joan, the only female Pope. She had been stricken from the books, but John did not doubt her existence. He was, after all, a practical man. He could admit she had existed. Just as he could admit that she could never be publicly recognized.

But supporting Delaney McPhearson, another woman trying to take a place she did not deserve, trying to usurp the real power of the male Pope, that could not be allowed. And she had slipped through their fingers. But the moment was gone. He could not dwell on it. He needed to focus on next steps.

"Where is Bas? Has he returned?"

"I believe he went to visit his sister."

John nodded. Father Bas was extremely close to his sister, who ran an orphanage in Rome. She was a good nun, dedicated to her charges and the Church. "Very well. Contact all the members of the High Council. We will need to meet to discuss next steps."

"Yes, sir. Of course." Ezekiel hurried from the room.

John turned and stared out the window, watching the heavy traffic in the streets of Rome below. Delaney McPhearson had slipped from their grasp and the net they had placed around her. But she would be destroyed. It was only a matter of time.

He took a breath. This wasn't even the first battle. This was a sparring match. They'd thrown some light punches just to see what she could do. And now they knew. She protected herself and those she cared about. They could use that. They *would* use that.

The Church and the Brotherhood had existed through the ages. Delaney McPhearson was no match for them. It would take time, but they would succeed. After all, many others had tried to destroy the Church and they themselves had paid the ultimate price. She would be no different.

CHAPTER 48

Laney looked between Bas and David. The two could not be physically more different, yet the expressions on their faces were identical.

Patrick rolled his chair over. "What do you mean the culmination of your life's work?"

Bas gestured to the chairs. "Why doesn't everyone take a seat, and we can discuss it?"

Drake shrugged, his gaze on Laney. "Your call." He cracked his knuckles. "Listen or not, either way, I'm game."

The threat was clear, and both men suddenly looked ill at ease.

"I, for one, would like to know," said Patrick. "David did help me out of what could have been a very difficult situation."

"All right." Laney took a seat near Patrick, automatically reaching for the tea and handing him a cup after pouring in milk and sugar. "So, tell me, how do two orphans from Italy end up involved in whatever the heck is going on now?"

David shook his head. "It's not just two orphans. There have been dozens, hundreds even, over the years."

"And who calls the shots?"

"I do." A tall woman with dark hair strode into the room.

David jumped to his feet to hug her. The woman smiled as her arms slid around him. She wore a long white habit with her dark hair pulled back. She was striking even without any makeup to accentuate her dark eyes.

Laney turned to Bas. "Your sister?"

Bas nodded.

"Mine as well," David said as he escorted the woman over to join them. "Unofficially, of course."

Bas stood. "Laney, this is Sister Angelica Gante. She runs the school."

Laney extended her hand. "Sister."

The sister took Laney's hand in both of hers. "Please, please call me Angelica. It is an honor to have the ring bearer pay us a visit."

"And this is Drake," Bas said as Drake stepped forward.

Angelica gasped, her eyes growing large. "It's you."

Drake took her hand, bringing it to his lips. "Ah, you've seen my show."

Angelica aimed a frown at Bas. "Your show?"

Now it was Laney's turn to frown.

Bas stepped forward, drawing their attention. "Angelica has never met a fallen angel before. She saw you on TV at the coronation."

"Yes, it was quite an event," Patrick muttered.

Angelica gestured to the couch. "Please, sit, sit." She smiled at David. "We have missed you. How is Rahim?"

"He's good. Working away, saving more innocent souls."

"You should have brought him."

"Next time. I had a feeling this time would be a little more action oriented than he would appreciate."

Angelica studied Patrick, Delaney, and Drake. "It appears that is the case. I just received a report from Carlos."

"Carlos works in the Vatican," David explained. "He's a custodian. He helped Father Patrick and I get out."

"Is he all right?" Patrick asked.

Angelica smiled. "Yes, he is fine. No one knows he was involved. But the Vatican security was still in an uproar when I spoke with him. They are examining every exit. Every tourist."

"Are they all in on it?" Patrick asked.

Angelica shook her head. "No, no. But the Brotherhood, they have their tentacles everywhere. They are not questioned by the Vatican security. Security responds to their directives as if they were ordered by the Pope himself. I believe they may even think that is the case. They believe they are doing the right thing."

"Is the Pope part of the Brotherhood?" Patrick asked.

"No," Angelica said quickly. "He is a good man. He knows nothing of their work or their mission beyond the official group that is charged with seeing to the papacy's protection. He has no idea the lengths they have gone to or will go to in order to protect him."

"How have they been able to get such control, such power?" Laney asked.

Angelica sank into the couch, sitting between Bas and David. The affection between the three of them was obvious. David handed her a lemon bar on a plate while Bas arranged her tea. She took a sip and a bite of lemon bar, smiling her thanks at each of her brothers. "Delicious. Well, the Brotherhood goes back decades, to the death of Pope John Paul I."

Laney frowned. "Only decades?"

"Officially decades," Angelica said. "Unofficially, they have existed for much longer than that. They go back to the first millennium of the Church. To an incident that, had it been allowed to be known, they believe would have rocked the Church to its very core."

Patrick frowned, his hand going to his chin. "During the first millennium?"

Laney knew he was wracking his brain, rifling through hundreds of years of Church history, looking for an event that would have spawned such a group. Laney didn't need to go through quite as many mental calculations. She just needed to recall the statue of the Pope in the front foyer of the orphanage. "Pope Joan."

Angelica studied Laney over the rim of her cup, her eyebrows raised. "Yes. I should have known the ring bearer would make the connection."

"When you say ring bearer, it's as if you have known her for years," Drake said.

"No, not years," Angelica replied. "Millennium. We have studied you and the Great Mother."

"You have the tome," Patrick said.

"No. We've never actually had it," Bas said. "But the Brotherhood has one."

"How did you send me a copy, then?" Patrick asked.

Angelica patted Bas's knee. "That was thanks to Bas. He has been secretly scanning the Tome page by page for years."

"It's one of the reasons I joined the Brotherhood."

"Why not just steal it back?" Drake said.

"Because it would let the Brotherhood know we existed. And it is better if we continue to work in the shadows," Angelica said.

Patrick made a small sound. Laney turned to him, concerned, but he was smiling. "You're Followers."

Angelica nodded. "Yes."

"Followers?" Drake asked. "Followers of what?"

"The Great Mother," Laney said softly. "How long does your line go back?"

"To the very beginning," Angelica said softly.

CHAPTER 49

Laney looked at the three people in front of her. Were they really followers of the Great Mother? Had they somehow orchestrated all of this to help Laney?

"What do the Followers have to do with the Brotherhood?" she asked.

"For centuries, nothing, although Joan was one of us. But we existed along parallel tracks. It wasn't until the death of Pope John Paul I that our lives intersected."

"Ah," Patrick said,

"'Ah?' Why 'ah?'" Drake asked.

"Pope John Paul I, who was known as the Smiling Pope, was only in office for thirty-three days before his death," Patrick said.

Laney had to admit she did not know much about the history of the Popes. "Thirty-three days? That's awfully short. Was he extremely old?"

"No. He was only sixty-six at the time of his death," Angelica said.

"How'd he die?" Drake asked.

"Officially, a heart attack," David said. "But unofficially, there were rumors that he had actually been murdered."

"A Pope murdered? That's—" Laney was going to say crazy, but then she flashed on the statue of Joan from the entryway and shut her mouth. Maybe it wasn't so crazy.

Bas clasped his hands on the table. "Allegedly, the night before he died, he asked for the Vatican Bank to be investigated."

Laney knew the Vatican Bank had been a problem for the Church's image for years. Scandals wracked the financial arm of the Vatican's empire involving issues from Mafia links to insurance benefits involving Jews from the Holocaust, covering up abuses of Vatican spending, and even laundering money for the underworld and Italian elites.

"But John Paul had made other enemies," Bas said, continuing. "He had claimed that God was not only the Heavenly Father but the Heavenly Mother as well. He was viewed as a supporter of women's rights and even agreed to meet with a delegation from the United States who was arguing that the Church should rethink its views on banning birth control."

"That's awfully progressive," Laney said.

"Perhaps too progressive," her uncle said. "After John Paul's death, he was quickly embalmed and cremated."

Laney's head snapped up. "Cremated? The Church doesn't cremate."

"Technically, you can cremate. It's been allowed since 1963. But he's the only Pope who's been cremated," Patrick said.

"Okay, a potential murder of a Pope what, forty years ago?" said Drake. "Very unfortunate. But what does that have to do with what happened today? Or the Followers?"

"There are some who say that Pope John Paul's death was foretold," Bas said.

"Nostradamus," Patrick said quietly.

Bas nodded, quoting the ancient seer:

"When the sepulcher of the great Roman is found
The day after will be elected a Pope
By his Senate he will not be approved

Poisoned is his blood by the sacred chalice

HE WHO WILL HAVE *government of the great Cape*
Will be led to take action
The twelve Red Ones will come to spoil the cover
Under murder, murder will come to be done."

The room was quiet as the words of the long-dead seer hung in the air. "The Church began to take prophecies very seriously at that point," said Bas.

"Not just because of that, though," Patrick said, his gaze on Bas. "But because of the prophecies regarding the lines of the Popes."

"The lines of the Popes?" Laney asked.

Angelica nodded. "There are three separate prophets who have argued that the lines of Popes will end with the 112th Pope after Pope Clementine. And that that time will also coincide with the end of the world."

"And what Pope are we at now?" Drake asked.

Angelica looked at each of them. "One hundred twelve."

CHAPTER 50

Bas took over the story as the shock from Angelica's words faded. "The Brotherhood of the Eclipse of the Sun was created to keep the prophecies from being fulfilled. John Paul II was ordained after John Paul I. There were two assassination attempts on his life, which the Brotherhood thwarted."

"Were those prophesized?"

"Yes."

"But John Paul II didn't die. He lived. So that right there must demonstrate that the prophecy has been thwarted," Laney said.

"There are some who say that," Angelica said. "But the Brotherhood, they are highly conservative in their interpretation of the prophecies. They believe that each individual prophecy can be avoided by diligence, but it does not change the prophecy that follows. So the only chance the world has is for them to stay vigilant and act when the signs that the prophecy may be coming true appear."

"But what does that have to do with me? I mean, to state the obvious, I am not a Pope," Laney said.

Bas nodded to her ring. "No, but you do bear the mark of God. You are also his chosen representative on Earth. If the prophecy of the last Pope is to come true, you are the only one capable of fulfilling it."

"What is the last prophecy?" Drake asked.

"They all generally say the same thing," Bas said, "but Malachy is perhaps the most succinct: '"Rome, the seat of the Vatican, will be destroyed, and the dreadful Judge will judge the people."'

Laney frowned. "But that's not me. If anything, that's what would have happened if Samyaza had come into power. But by stopping her, we avoided that happening."

"I agree with you," Angelica said. "If the prophecy was going to come true, it would have been at the hand of Samyaza. But the truth is, you still could level Rome if you chose."

Laney frowned. "Technically, I could. But any country could. The Vatican's a two-square-mile country. Any country that wanted to could take it over or destroy it. It does not require my powers to make it happen."

"That may be," Patrick mused, "but I believe it is the third secret of Fátima that the Brotherhood is perhaps most concerned with."

Laney frowned. "The third secret of Fátima? That refers to the assassination of John Paul II? Or at least the attempted assassination?"

"That is what the Church says," Patrick said.

"But . . ." Laney prodded.

Patrick frowned. "There are many parties that are not satisfied with that translation. When Sister Lúcia sealed the third secret, she said it could not be opened until 1960. But it wasn't publicly revealed until 2000, although the Church had opened it earlier. But there are some who claim that what the Church revealed was actually a fake. That the real secret is still hidden in the Vatican vaults."

Laney studied Bas, who shifted in his seat, his gaze darting away from Laney's. "You've read it, the real one."

Bas met her gaze for only a moment before looking away. "As a member of the Brotherhood, I was given access to it once I reached the inner council. Learning the third secret was one of my primary directives."

"And?" Drake asked. "Don't keep us in suspense."

"It speaks of a wicked council and the rise of the abomination of abominations."

"The Fallen," Laney said softly.

"Here." Angelica stepped forward, handing Laney her phone. It was a translation of the "original" document:

There will be a wicked council planned and prepared that will change the countenance of the Church. Many will lose the Faith; confusion will reign everywhere. The sheep will search for their shepherds in vain.

A schism will tear apart the holy tunic of My Son. This will be the end of times, foretold in the Holy Scriptures and recalled to memory by Me in many places. The abomination of abominations will reach its peak and it will bring the chastisement announced at La Salette. My Son's arm, which I will not be able to hold back anymore, will punish this poor world, which must expiate its crimes.

One will only speak about wars and revolutions. The elements of nature will be unchained and will cause anguish even among the best (the most courageous). The Church will bleed from all Her wounds. Happy are they who will persevere and search for refuge in My Heart, because in the end My Immaculate Heart will triumph."

Laney handed the phone back. "I guess I don't have to ask how they interpret that."

Angelica slipped the phone back into her pocket. "They believe you and your followers are the wicked council. That you will usher in the end of times."

"That I'm the antichrist while they are the ones who will shepherd the people to the righteous path," Laney said.

Bas nodded slowly.

Drake snorted. "Please. It sounds like this brotherhood of

yours is more likely the 'wicked council' than Laney and her group."

"I agree," said Bas. "The Brotherhood, they are so adamant about protecting the papacy that I don't think they see how they are creating the very thing they are trying to prevent."

David frowned. "How?"

Patrick folded his hands in his lap. "The Fallen, like all humans, have a choice in who they become. The Church could use this example to support their message: that humans are good and made in God's image. They could take the time to speak with Laney, not interrogate, but speak and learn what she can do and what she has done. Instead, they fear what they don't know and try to hide it away. The Church's track record for banishing knowledge appears to continue unbroken."

Laney knew what he meant. The Church had rebuked Galileo for his heliocentric argument that the Sun did not revolve around the Earth but that the Earth revolved around the Sun. It took over a hundred years before they could accept Darwin's idea of evolution. Now, it was their refusal to condone stem cell research that marked their anti-science bias. They had a long habit of accepting things well after the rest of the world had.

And if that's the case, I'll be dead and buried before they realize I'm not the bad guy.

"But what can they actually do?" Drake asked. "The days of the Vatican being the stronghold of power are long past."

David raised an eyebrow. "Moretti arranged for you to be out of the country when the President of the United States issued her executive order. You are now not allowed back in the United States. And if they had succeeded in abducting you, I do not think the United States would be rushing to help secure your release. So it seems like they still have a little bit of power."

Laney turned to Bas. "Could you do something to convince them?"

"My voice does not hold much sway on the order." Bas grimaced. "And now I'm sure it holds none."

"Why risk that now?" Drake asked. "You've been with the Brotherhood for years."

"True, but the Brotherhood was never my primary directive. I am a Follower before a brother."

"I still don't understand that. How are you Followers?" Patrick asked.

David leaned forward. "In the seventeenth century, the Followers were based in Spain. But they were found. The leader at that time, a woman named Marguerite, knew they would be found. She sent a group ahead, forbidding them from telling her where they were going. Some went on to the New World. They were rooted out in the Salem Witch Trials."

"And another group went to Italy," said Patrick, "or should I say back to Italy. They folded themselves within the ranks of the Church."

Bas nodded.

Laney frowned. "But that must have been dangerous. The Church is not known for embracing the role of any women, never mind the idea of a Great Mother."

"That is true. But by working from the inside, we have been able to spread our influence and be in important locations. And we have gotten very close to getting the Great Mother acknowledged."

"Pope John Paul I. He was a Follower," Patrick said.

"Yes."

Laney turned to her uncle. "How do you know that?"

A light glowed from inside Patrick, and for the first time in a long time, he looked like his old self. She should have known a history lesson would be the thing to bring him back. "His reference to both the Holy Father and the Holy Mother. At the time, scholars believed he was referring to God as male and female. But he wasn't. He was referring to the Great Mother."

"Yes. Very good, Father." Angelica beamed.

"But how does the idea of a Great Mother reconcile with the Church's idea of God?" Laney asked.

"It's not different from its view of Jesus, Moses, Noah, or any other Biblical figure. The only difference is the gender of the subject. Recognizing the Great Mother does not negate any of the greatness of God. But the Church, since its early days, cannot and will not acknowledge the role of women as being anything other than subordinate."

Laney knew that was true. Mary Magdalene had been a critical disciple in the Church. And yet Peter made sure women did not have a large role in the running of the Church. Each successive Pope further diminished the role, pointing to the "fact" that all of Jesus's apostles were male. The role of Mary Magdalene, who unlike her male counterparts, stood with Jesus right up until his crucifixion, was relegated to a footnote in history. She was just another Mary. Or a prostitute, in Pope Gregory the Great's reimagining of history.

Patrick nodded. "I have a great deal of difficulty accepting the Church's view of the role of women. Pope John Paul II is considered to be the most recent and most definitive answer on the issue when he wrote the ecclesiastical letter, the Ordinatio Sacerdotalis that 'the Church has no authority whatsoever to confer priestly ordination on women.'"

Drake's gaze ran over Father Bas and Sister Angelica on the couch. "So how can you two have pledged your life to the Church?"

"It allows us to do God's work, to do good," Angelica said. "And to protect those that need to be protected. Our job would be much more difficult if we were on the outside."

Bas took her hand. "Besides, we truly believe our vows. Our duty is to serve God. The Church is part of how we do that. But being a Follower is the larger part of how we do that."

David leaned back. "I am less self-sacrificing. I like having things and sex."

Angelica nearly choked on her tea. She quickly put the teacup down as David pounded her back with his hand. She glared at him when she could finally speak. "You did that on purpose."

"Yes. You have become entirely too serious in your old age."

"I am two weeks older than you!"

"Still older."

Laney frowned, watching him. "So what do *you* do? You said you're not just a bureaucrat."

Drake spoke before David had a chance. "No. He's a contract killer for the U.S. government."

David eyed Drake, speaking slowly. "I prefer to think of myself as a secret soldier of patriotism. But it's true. I freelance between different agencies—CIA, NSA, even your SIA a few times."

Laney frowned. "Wait. But why would they send you as the representative to the Vatican? That doesn't make any sense."

"Sure it does." Drake was up and across the room in a flash, holding David by the throat. "Because he's been sent to kill you."

CHAPTER 51

Laney bolted to her feet. "Drake!"
Bas pulled his sister behind him.
But David showed no reaction. He simply raised an eyebrow.
"Do you deny it?" Drake demanded.
David grimaced. "No," he managed to squeak out.
Laney pulled on Drake's arm. "Drake, let him go. Now."
With a growl, Drake released him.
Angelica stared at Laney and Drake as David dropped to the ground, gasping for breath. "You can control him?"
Laney frowned, then looked at Drake. "Drake? No."
"But then why did he—"
"Because I asked him to, not because I *ordered* him to." She was about to tell them she couldn't control any Fallen, not since she'd taken the Omni, but something made her hold that little fact back.
Patrick inched his chair forward. "Well, I'm going to hold back my judgment as to whether or not it's a good thing Drake didn't kill him until he explains what his mission is."
David put one hand on the edge of the couch, pulling himself up. Angelica moved toward him, but David waved her away. "It's all right. I'm fine."

Angelica whirled toward Laney, Patrick, and Drake. "I will not stand for any more violence."

Drake crossed his arms over his chest, not retaking his seat. "Then I suggest your 'brother' start speaking. Quickly."

David took a drink of tea, rubbing his neck. "Well, that was a novel experience."

"Speak," Drake ordered.

David resumed his seat. "As I was explaining, my skills are in demand within the U.S. government. Not to toot my own horn, but I am one of the best at what I do."

Drake snorted. "*One* of the best?"

"I said I was *trying* not to toot my own horn. But if you'd like me to toot, then I *am* the best at what I do. The U.S. government has sent me after individuals that no one else could touch, both legally and physically. Individuals who were monsters, destroying all they touched. On my last mission, I killed an overlord. He created an army of four hundred child soldiers. He pulled them from their families, got them addicted to drugs, and had them kill their mothers as a test of their loyalty. Most of them were so addicted that they did it without even thinking about it. But no one could get to him. He surrounded himself with his 'soldiers' and 'wives,' the sisters of his soldiers."

"I heard about that case. He was found hanging from a tree. There was very little left of him after the animals had gotten to him," Patrick said.

David's eyes turned almost black, and Laney read the conviction there. And the darkness. "It was the least he deserved. I don't pretend to be a good man. I've had a dark side since I was young. But I have tried to channel that darkness into acts that, if not in and of themselves are good, can lead to good."

Drake wasn't moved. "And what about Laney?"

"I was called to a special meeting shortly after the Day of Reckoning. It was held in the bunker beneath the White House. Some members of the President's cabinet were there along with heads of various agencies. And me. The topic of the meeting was what to do with the threat of the Fallen. But the question was also raised about what to do about you."

"Me?" Laney asked.

"The government is worried about the amount of power you possess. If you chose to turn against the government, they aren't sure they would be able to stop you."

Laney sat back, the news hitting her hard. She knew there were members of the government that were nervous about what she could do, what the Fallen could do. But the idea that the President was actively looking into how to take her out was more than a little disturbing.

Patrick took her hand. "But that is just a precaution, right? The same way the government has precautions for different countries in case they launch a missile or attack an American holding, right?"

"True..." David said.

"But?" Laney demanded.

"You're talking about more than the registration," Drake said.

"Yes." David paused. "They recovered one of your cats after the Day of Reckoning."

Laney blanched. Thunder had gone missing. They had thought he was dead. She had never considered that he could have been taken. "Where is he?"

"I'm afraid he's dead now. There's a doctor. She's been appointed by the President to look into his anatomy, trying to replicate it. My understanding is she tried to use the cat to breed but was not successful."

Horror crawled through Laney. Most people she knew looked at the leopards as merely animals. But Laney knew they were so much more. Their intelligence was on par with humans. They had empathy, feelings, even a sense of humor. And they could communicate with one another as easily as humans did. And Laney could communicate with them. Experimenting on them was no less horrific than the idea of experimenting on humans, which led her to another disturbing thought.

She looked at David. "Do you know what their plans are for the Fallen?"

He shook his head. "No. Elisabeta threw a wrench in that particular avenue anyway. They have none in custody. One of the conditions of Elisabeta's coronation was that all Fallen being held anywhere in the world must be released. And everyone let them go. But they *want* to find a way to make more Fallen. That is priority number one. Priority number two is to figure out what weaknesses the Fallen may have. Without a test subject, though, none of that matters."

Laney swallowed. "Apparently you haven't seen the news lately."

"No," David said slowly. "What's happened?"

"They have a Fallen. They took someone during the raid."

Patrick's head snapped toward her. "What? Who? What raid?"

"It happened while we were at the castle and you were at the Vatican."

Drake's gaze was full of meaning as he looked at her. "You mean, while we were all being targeted."

Laney's head whipped toward him. Was there any possible way that was a coincidence? But even as she thought it, she knew how low the chances of that being true were. The U.S. was working with someone in the Vatican. The weight on her shoulders grew even heavier.

"You said they took someone?" Patrick asked.

"I don't know who. They haven't released the name. We tried to call, but we couldn't reach anyone, so you know they've all ditched their phones." Laney frowned. "Actually, Dom should have found a way to contact us by now."

"If they've taken someone . . ." David went silent.

"What?" Laney demanded.

David's voice was quiet. "I suggest you start praying."

CHAPTER 52

SOMEWHERE IN VIRGINIA

The last few hours had been a haze of pain, blood, and fear. Molly had no idea where she was or who the people around her were. After she'd been shot, she'd been cuffed. She'd come to long enough to see her mom get dragged into a waiting SUV. Then she'd passed out.

When she'd woken up, she was in a dim concrete cell, chained to the wall. The chains had been so tight she hadn't even been able to stand. She'd passed out again, although she thought that might have been more from fear than pain.

When she'd woken up, the chains had been loosened a little so she could sit up, and a cot had been brought in, although she couldn't reach it. Then gas had filtered through the air and she was in the black again.

All things considered, she would have preferred to have stayed there.

She awoke on an operating table. Her arms had been cut, as had her legs, some shallow, some so deep she couldn't even scream as the pain roared through her. She yanked on the straps, but they were too strong for her. Then a doctor stepped forward and cut her more. Blood dripped from her arms and legs into buckets and yet still he cut. The pain was blinding. Her whole body felt like it was on fire.

"No more. Please no more."

The doctor smiled, the eyes crinkling at the corners above his medical mask. "Oh, we're just getting started."

HOURS PASSED. Molly dropped in and out of consciousness. And each time she woke she begged them to stop. They never did. She began to pray for the darkness to sweep her away. In the dark, she was safe. In the dark, her mom held her and told her everything was all right. In the dark, no one hated her or tried to hurt her.

After what felt like days, the doctor stepped back from the table. "All right, that's enough for today. Tomorrow we'll move on to the chemical responses."

Molly rolled to her side, dry heaving.

"Note the response," the doctor ordered, not an ounce of compassion in his face or voice as he left the room.

A guard pushed her stretcher into the hall. She closed her eyes, breathing shallowly, waiting for the pain to lessen. And sure enough, it did.

"Still awake, little girl?" the guard asked, his voice cruel.

Her eyes flicked open.

The guard had dark hair and light eyes as he glared down at her. "My brother died on the Day of Reckoning. One of your kind killed him. You make me sick." He spit at her. It landed on her cheek before sliding down to her ear.

"Hope you've been enjoying yourself because this morning was just the warm-up. When they start up again, it's poison and bleach. They're going to see how you react to all of it. You know what happens to a person's trachea when they drink bleach? It rots away, scorching its way down to the stomach. Think you can survive that?"

He shook his head, not waiting for her response. "I don't think you can. You abominations have weaknesses. We're going to find them. And you're going to help us." The guard stopped the stretcher in front of her cell. He glanced back out into the hall. "I'm supposed to give you a sedative to knock you out and get you locked up. But you know what? I have a better plan."

His fist slammed into Molly's cheek. Her face exploded with pain, two of her teeth loosening. But he was as good as his word, and she slipped into the darkness.

CHAPTER 53

WASHINGTON, D.C.

Shremp walked through the halls of the West Wing with confidence, his chest puffed out while people scurried out of his way. The morning raid had been a success. Chandler's entire estate was now being picked over with a fine-tooth comb. Plus, they had one of the Fallen in custody and one of the cats as well. Sure, some had escaped, but they would be caught soon. It was only a matter of time.

Shremp smiled at Neil Jakub as he stepped into the President's outer office. Neil leaped to his feet. "This way, Senator Shremp. The President wanted you to be shown in as soon as you arrived."

Shremp straightened his tie. "Thank you."

Neil opened the door, and Shremp strode past him, his shoulders back. "Madame President, what an honor to be asked—"

President Rigley speared him with her gaze. "*What* happened last night?" she demanded through gritted teeth.

Shremp's steps faltered. "Madame President?"

"What *happened* last night?" she repeated.

Shremp walked slowly to her desk and began to take a seat.

The President's voice whipped out. "I did *not* invite you to sit."

Shremp halted halfway down to the chair before straightening. "I'm not sure what you've heard, but last night was a success. We have a Fallen in custody, as well as a cat. And we have removed a sanctuary for the Fallen as well. It was a huge success."

She took a deep breath. "Tell me, Senator, is this dangerous Fallen you have in custody a thirteen-year-old girl?"

"Um, well, yes, but she's still a—"

"And this Fallen sanctuary you removed, was it offering sanctuary to *children?*"

"I believe some of them were at least eighteen years of age."

The President drummed her fingers on the desk. "Tell me, would the public at large have any issues with how this raid was conducted?"

Shremp straightened his shoulders. "Absolutely not. It was the height of professionalism—"

The President raised her hand, stopping him. "The height of professionalism?" She grabbed the remote from her desk and hit a button. The screen at the far side of the room sprang to life. It must have been paused, because he hadn't even noticed it when he walked in.

The President stalked toward the screen. Shremp followed, squinting at the screen as the President raised the volume.

Onscreen, a soldier rammed the butt of his rifle into the face of a teenage boy with his arms bound. The boy fell back, and a woman dropped to his side, screaming. Two more soldiers grabbed her, pulling her away.

Meanwhile, the man who'd been next to the boy tackled the soldier to the ground. Two other soldiers yanked the man away while the woman stayed hunched over the boy, screaming his name.

The third teenager tried to get up, obviously trying to get to the boy, but he was yanked down, a gun aimed at his face.

Shremp cringed when Jake Rogan, who he finally recognized,

yelled "That's his mother!" as the men started to pull the woman away. Even with the poor lighting, it was easy to see how she was desperately trying to get back to the boy. One of the soldiers slammed the butt of his gun into the back of her head. She collapsed to the ground. The soldier stepped forward, his weapon raised as if he was going to strike her again.

Then it looked like a disturbance in the tape, but a girl appeared out of nowhere, flinging the man away.

Shremp smiled. Now they were getting somewhere. That "child" had just assaulted a federal agent.

"Mom!" The girl's cry could be heard clearly as she knelt down to her mother.

The mother's attempts to get the girl to leave could also be heard. Then the girl lifted her mother as if to take her away. Shremp smiled more broadly. Perfect. Failing to follow the instructions of a federal officer. A bullet slammed into the girl, and she stumbled, dropping the woman, who managed to gain her feet in order to catch her daughter. Soldiers appeared, and the woman pulled the girl behind her, begging them to leave her child alone. Okay, Shremp could admit that looked bad. But still . . .

The soldiers opened fire, and the mother whirled around, her scream drowning out the gunfire as she caught her daughter. She lowered her to the ground as the soldiers approached. The woman fell on top of her daughter, covering her with her body, trying to protect her. Then subtitles appeared at the bottom of the screen.

"I love you, Molly. Do you hear me? I love you."

A soldier yanked her way as the mother begged to be allowed to stay with her daughter. Then she was Tased and dropped to the ground, and a soldier slammed the butt of his gun into the back of her head. Soldiers approached the daughter and put restraints on her arms and legs as her blood ran into the street.

The President pressed pause and turned to Shremp. "Well?"

"I think this does an excellent job of demonstrating the danger the Fallen present to society at large. That girl flung a U.S. federal agent like he was—"

The President's voice was incredulous. "You think this makes us look *good*? Do you know what I saw? I saw a girl trying to protect her mother after her brother was knocked unconscious by a federal agent for no good reason. I think this demonstrated the ruthlessness of the people trying to track down the Fallen while the 'dangerous Fallen' apparently was only interested in protecting her family. She tried to leave with her mother, to protect her mother. From *us*."

Shremp shook his head. "I don't see that at all. I think any rational person who views this would see the danger that—"

"Any rational person who does not have a heart!"

"None of this matters. This won't be released to the public. So why does—"

The President's teeth were gritted again. "This is *not* our recording. Chandler apparently recorded the entire incident last night and released it to the media as well as sent us a copy."

"But still, no one who views this could argue we behaved outside the law. It's not a problem."

"Not a problem? *Not a problem?*"

The President switched over to a twenty-four-hour news channel. An anchor was in the middle of a broadcast.

"—disturbing video which shows an excessive use of force against an American family not, I repeat, not accused of committing any crimes."

Shremp pointed at the screen. "Yeah, but that's—"

The President switched to another news channel. "Is this who we as a country have become? I know the Fallen are dangerous, but was this little girl really so dangerous that it justified any of these actions? And to be honest, I'm not sure I would have reacted differently if someone was trying to hurt my mother or brother."

The President switched through channel after channel.

And Shremp simply could not believe what he was hearing.

How could these people look at this recording and not see the danger he clearly saw?

The President glared at Shremp. "This Molly McAdams, where is she?"

"She is in custody."

"In good health?"

"I believe so, yes."

"You *believe* so?" The President curled her hands into fists. "I want a full reporting on where she is being held and a full accounting of her health. Is that understood?"

"Madame President, it would perhaps be politically better if you were kept out of certain aspects of the ongoing—"

"You think anyone will accept an 'I was not aware' defense? I am the President of the United States." She pointed to the screen. "This was done on my watch. You will get me that accounting."

"Yes, Madame President."

"And, Senator, if this blows back on me, I will be using you as a shield. Do you understand?"

"Yes, Madame President. Of course, Madame President."

Shremp bowed before hastening to the door. He stepped out of the office and hustled down the hall. Spying an empty conference room, he ducked inside, pulling out his phone and dialing quickly.

Dr. Paul Highland answered. "Yeah?"

"What is the status of the McAdams girl?"

"We have finished the first round of testing." He chuckled, the sound sending ice through Shremp's veins. "She was a little worse for wear, so we stopped to allow her to heal before the second round. We should be able to begin in another hour or so."

God damn it. "You need to stop immediately."

"Why? That was the whole point of getting her."

"I know, but apparently the country is losing their mind over her. The raid last night was recorded."

"So what? These things are a national security threat. Honestly, they're not even human."

"I know that, but the optics look bad."

Paul sighed. "Fine. What do you want me to do?"

Shremp paced the room, trying to figure out the best approach. If the girl were ever released, she would undoubtedly explain what had been done to her. But they also couldn't hold her indefinitely. If she were killed, then the problem would be solved. She would be unable to say anything. They could control the narrative. And after paying out a settlement to her family, she would simply be forgotten.

Shremp moved to the back wall, as far from the door as possible. He could not be overheard. "Make the problem go away."

"We'll have to start over," Paul warned.

Shremp paused. "How did the morning experiments go?"

"Well, we've got a good picture of the healing abilities, and they managed to take a lot of blood." He chuckled again. "Which also let us know how much blood loss they can sustain and still survive. It was incredibly educational. For phase two, we were planning on beginning the chemical experimentation. I believe that will probably be more effective in fighting the Fallen than the traditional law enforcement approaches."

Shremp sat in a chair, his leg jiggling as he figured out the best way forward. If Paul was speaking honestly, the morning's experimentation had been highly successful, and the next round could provide even more successful insights into the weaknesses of the Fallen. The President wanted the situation handled, but if he came up with effective ways to eliminate the Fallen, well, then the President would be the one who would be grateful, wouldn't she? And besides, the girl had already been through one round of investigation. It seemed wasteful to not complete the process.

"Fine, fine. Complete the chemical examination, but then take care of her."

"Of course, sir. You know best. Now, what about the cat?"

"No one cares about the cat. Continue the experiments on it."

"Yes, sir. As for the other problem, how do you want it handled? Accident?"

"No, then we'll look incompetent. Make it look like she tried to overpower the guards. You'll need to injure some of them. But make sure she does not get out of that facility alive."

"Yes, sir. I'll get it done."

Shremp disconnected the call, shoving the phone into his pocket. Damn that Chandler. He was not going to let the fate of some inhuman girl affect his chances of being President. The people of the United States deserved more than that. They deserved a Shremp Presidency and the greatness that would come from it.

CHAPTER 54

ROME, ITALY

They had called a break to eat dinner. Not because anyone was hungry, but the kids needed to be fed, and Sylvia couldn't do it alone. Laney hadn't been hungry, her mind too full. A group of priests thought she was going to bring down the papacy and the world. She really didn't know what to do with that. And right now, she didn't have the time to focus on it.

Laney had eaten quickly, then tried again to reach anyone from the estate. The only person she had been able to reach was Yoni, and that was because she had forgotten he had headed out west with Sascha, Dov, and Max. But Yoni hadn't been able to reach anyone either besides Brett, who had no information on where anyone had disappeared to. He had to wait until they reached out to him. He'd promised to call Yoni if he reached anyone. And Yoni promised to reach out to Laney. She'd hung up the phone, hating being out of the loop.

On a hunch, she'd checked one of the email accounts Dom had set up for her when she'd gone on the run, and there'd been a message from Dom with the coordinates of the safe house. So now at least she had a destination in mind. But getting there was the problem. Any airport she flew into, she'd be recognized. She was okay with taking a risk for herself, but innocents could also get hurt. She needed a better way, a more under-the-radar way, to get home.

So now she stood at the window in the rec room, trying to think of some other avenue to get back home, but she was distracted by her view of the courtyard below. A group of children were running around Drake, who had a handkerchief tied over his face. He walked with arms outstretched, trying to tag as many children as possible. He was being intentionally horrible at catching them. Children squealed and ducked out of the way. Laney smiled, watching the scene. Who knew Drake was so good with kids?

For a moment, she pictured the two of them with their own little one. She started at the image. Ever since she'd learned she was the ring bearer, she had not spent much time thinking about her future. It wasn't a conscious decision, but somewhere along the way, she had just stopped. Her life was duty. She was sure she would be defending people against the Fallen for the rest of her life. And she didn't need to picture that because she lived that. But Drake, he made her want things that she wasn't sure she could ever have. And at the same time, he made her feel like they were completely possible.

Drake pulled off the handkerchief, his gaze going straight to Laney. He smiled. She felt the warmth of that smile all the way to her toes. She placed a hand on the glass in front of her, returning the smile. God, she loved that man. He was infuriating, arrogant, obnoxious, loyal, funny, irreverent, tender, and everything she never knew she needed.

Drake whirled around as a little boy snuck up on him. With a cry, he lifted the boy into the air. Three other kids charged him. Drake's face crumpled in mock agony as he sank to his knees. The kids piled on him, and soon Drake was hidden under a pile of small laughing bodies.

A laugh burst out of Laney. Her hand flew to her mouth. And this was why she loved him. The world was falling down around them, and he still gave her these small moments of joy.

"He is good with children."

Laney turned to David, who appeared beside her. "You move awfully quietly."

He smiled. "A trick of the trade."

"Hm." She turned back to the window.

"So he's the Las Vegas magician."

"Illusionist," Laney said automatically.

"Of course. But he is so much more than that."

She felt his eyes on her. "What do you know about him?"

"Quite a bit. He's mentioned in the Tome."

Laney frowned. Drake was in the Tome? Of course, he was one of the guardians of the tree, so she supposed he could be mentioned in reference to that duty. Or maybe his time as Achilles. She was sure that time was rather well documented. "What does it say about him?"

"You haven't read it?"

"I've been a little busy."

David gave a soft chuckle. "I'm sure you have. Well, I read what I could when I was in college. And I was taught more by Sister Sophia. She ran the orphanage when I first arrived. I remember thinking she was the oldest person I had ever seen. I knew she had to be at least ninety."

David's smile was contagious, despite her concerns about the man. "And how old was she?"

"Fifty-two. She passed away three years ago. That's when Angelica took over. I still miss her."

Laney studied the man. He was not easy to figure out. He clearly cared deeply for Bas, Angelica, and everyone associated with the orphanage. And yet his day job. . .

He raised an eyebrow. "Trying to figure me out?"

"You are a bit of a riddle."

"Really? I think you and I are quite a bit alike."

Laney wasn't sure she liked being compared to a contract killer.

"I see I've offended you. That was not my intent. I realize what I do, it is not everyone's taste. But everyone I killed was someone who did massive damage. And who the world could not and would not restrain. I do not regret what I did, much like I do not think you regret taking Samyaza's life."

"I do not regret taking her life. But I do regret that there was no other way."

"See? Another thing we have in common."

Outside, Drake had the children line up in two rows facing each other on either side of the courtyard. Laney frowned, trying to figure out what game he was teaching them. Then she realized it Red Rover. Where on earth had Drake learned that?

David followed her gaze. "I must admit, *he* is not what I expected."

"What did you expect?"

"Someone focused, militant, serious."

An image of Remiel and Ralph flitted through her mind. "There are some archangels like that. But Drake, he's a little different from the rest."

Now it was David's turn to frown. "You know he is *very* different from the rest, don't you?"

Laney studied his face, the crease in between his eyes. "What do you mean?"

Bas hustled into the room. "Laney, the TV. You need to come."

Laney met David's gaze for a moment before hurrying toward Bas. Bas didn't wait for her. He just sprinted out of the room. Laney held her breath.

Oh God, now what?

CHAPTER 55

INEZ, KENTUCKY

Lou lay staring at the ceiling. They had made it to the safe house. She had helped get all the kids settled in and done a shift at guard duty. Now she was supposed to get some sleep.

She was in one of the bedrooms on the second floor. There were four bedrooms up here, along with an office. All were filled with kids. Lou had had to step over three bodies sprawled on sleeping bags on the floor to reach her spot by the window. Everyone was sleeping. The only sound in the room was the deep, even breaths of the other six kids. Lou knew she should sleep too. She should be able to. Her whole body ached with fatigue.

But she couldn't. Every time she closed her eyes she saw a member of the McAdams family and the devastated looks on their faces. Joe had a concussion and a broken nose. The other three members weren't hurt, but you would never know that by looking at them. Mary Jane and Jake had arrived an hour ago. Molly's mom couldn't seem to stop shaking. Jen had finally given her a sedative to help her sleep. Shaun and Joe sat by her bed, holding her hands, barely able to form sentences. Even Susie was more subdued than usual. Cain was keeping her with Nyssa.

Then there was Molly. Lou's gut tightened as she pictured her.

She was good kid. A really good kid. She was quieter than her brothers and even a little shy. But it was obvious how much her brothers adored her. Even Lou had started to look at her as a little sister. It was hard not to feel protective of her, even though Lou knew she had the same abilities that Lou had.

An image of a robed figure standing over Lou shot through her brain. Lou's pulse raced, and she took a shaky breath. What she had experienced at the hands of the Katzes in their bid to rid the world of anything associated with the Fallen had left her scarred. It had taken months for the nightmares to not be a daily occurrence. And it had taken even longer for her to stop jumping at shadows.

Then Zach's death had brought all those nightmares back to the forefront. He'd been another good kid, like Molly. But unlike Molly, he'd had a horrible family, and he had always felt like he had to prove he was worthy. But he had been worthy, more than worthy—worthy of kindness, worthy of friendship, worthy of love. And Lou prayed each night that he had understood at least that much before he died.

A tear slipped from the corner of her eye, and she wiped it away. She couldn't take another death. Zach had been hard. Jen's baby had been hard. But Molly? Sweet, innocent Molly? No, she couldn't handle that. She knew herself, and if Molly died while she lay here doing nothing, it would send her to a really dark place. And she didn't think she'd ever be able to crawl her way out of that.

The dark was always a part of Lou's not-so-easy life. Losing her mother, her grandmother, her sister. Truthfully, drugs had taken her sister long before death had. She'd seen a lot of horrible stuff, experienced a lot of horrible stuff. All those experiences should have toughened her up for what happened with the Katzes. She should have been able to, if not shrug it off, shove it into a corner and ignore it. God knew, she had enough practice shoving other horrors into the corners of her mind, never to be visited again. But she was still struggling.

And if she was still struggling with what had happened to her, how was a sweet kid like Molly going to be able to cope? Molly was one of those kids who laughed when a puppy licked her and still picked flowers. She was *good*. And Lou knew just being ripped away from her family would be traumatic for her. But she also knew that the government was not going to simply throw Molly in a cell and leave her. They were going to see what her abilities allowed her to do. They were going to push Molly to the breaking point and probably past it.

Lou could not just sit here and wait until they tracked Molly down. She needed to *do* something.

Lou sat up quietly, trying not to wake any of the other kids in the room. She grabbed her boots and crept across the floor, stepping over bodies in sleeping bags. Nearest the door, she stepped over Theresa, who lay with her younger sister wrapped in her arms, tears dried onto her cheeks.

Lou quietly slid out the door, pulling it gently shut behind her. Quickly donning her boots, she crept down the hall to where the boys were sleeping. The door was ajar. She peeked her head in but didn't see Rolly or Danny.

Frowning, she headed down the stairs. Henry and Jen were talking quietly in the kitchen. Lou avoided them by slipping down the hall. She jolted at the sight of Rolly, who stood silently by the front door. He put his finger to his lips, then pointed outside.

Lou nodded, following him as he silently opened the front door. They made it only a few steps from the door when a flashlight speared them.

"Where are you two going?" Mustafa asked.

"Uh," Lou said, scrambling for an explanation.

But Rolly pulled a can of soda and a protein bar from his pocket. "Nutritional supplies for Danny. He's pulling an all-nighter trying to track down where they took Molly."

Mustafa's voice softened. "Okay. Just try to convince him to get some sleep."

"Will do." Rolly took off toward the large shed Danny had set up his computers in. Lou hustled behind him.

A space heater working in the corner had warmed the place up nicely, but there was nothing that could be done for the smell of old grease.

Danny looked up from his monitors as Lou and Rolly stepped in. "About time." He pushed away from the desk and rolled over to a metal box behind him. Opening the lid, he began to rummage inside.

Lou stepped forward. "About time? What are you two up to?"

Rolly sighed. "Well, I've been spending the last hour standing by the front door trying not to look weird, not an easy task."

"But why?"

"Waiting for you. We knew you'd come looking for us," Rolly said.

"Why?"

Danny turned around. "Because you want to get Molly back as much as we do." He held his hands out. There was a disc no larger than the end of a pencil and small syringe.

"What's that?" Lou asked.

Danny smiled. "These are part of the plan."

The door to the shed slid open. Jake stepped in. "And what exactly are you three up to?"

Danny shoved his hands in his pockets, hiding the objects from view. "Uh, just talking. I've pinpointed possible locations to within fifty miles of the estate."

"That's good." Jake strolled over. "Now why don't you tell me what you plan on doing about getting Molly back?"

Rolly let out a nervous laugh. "What? That would be crazy. We'd—"

Jake put up a hand. "I'm not here to stop you. I'm here to help you. So tell me what the plan is."

CHAPTER 56

ROME, ITALY

The kitchen, which still smelled of the delicious pesto and pasta dinner Sylvia had created, now stood silent. And yet there were six adults crowded around the large metal island. No one said a word. While Bas had been running for Laney, Angelica had retrieved Drake from the courtyard. Sylvia and her husband Rosario took his place, keeping an eye on the children outside, and more importantly making sure they did not come inside.

Now Laney sat with her hand wrapped in Patrick's. Drake sat on her other side, his arm warm around her shoulder, but still she felt cold. Angelica, David, and Bas all sat near them, their gazes all fixed on the old TV that Rosario had dragged over to the island with the aid of an extension cord.

The TV was tuned to CNN International, and they had been covering only one topic for the last hour: the raid of Chandler Headquarters by the CEI. The recording hadn't been made by the government. No, this recording had been made by Henry. Laney recognized the camera angles.

Laney gasped as the attack on the McAdams family replayed

on the screen. She closed her eyes. No, she couldn't watch this again. She stood up. "I think I need some air."

Without waiting for a reply from anyone, she headed for the front door, not wanting to go through the door at the back of the kitchen and run into all the children.

She stepped outside, breathing in the fresh air. The children's laughter sounded in the background. They sounded so happy, so full of life, so carefree. Meanwhile, the Chandler kids were running for their lives.

The broadcaster said only that Jake, Molly, and Mary Jane had been taken into custody. Which meant Molly was the "dangerous Fallen" the government had apprehended. What little dinner Laney had eaten threatened to reappear as she pictured the bullets crashing into Molly's chest. She was just a child.

Everyone else had escaped. No mention was made of the cats. Laney prayed they were all right. Although with the information David had shared, she knew that the government would not hesitate to grab one of them or kill one of them. She closed her eyes.

Please, God, not Cleo.

And what about Cain? If they saw him, saw his eyes . . . She put her hand to her mouth. Then there was Nyssa, Henry, Jen, Lou—the list of people she was worried about went on and on. And here she was thousands of miles away. She felt so useless.

She felt him before she heard him. "What do you need?"

She turned. "We need to get home. I can't help them from here."

"That might be a little difficult. Right after you left, a new report came in. The U.S. government has closed all small private airports. All planes must land at a major airport and are subject to inspection."

"Why?"

"They are saying it's just a new counter-terrorism approach. But I think we both know what they are really looking for or trying to prevent."

"They don't want me back there." The truth of it was staggering. She had risked her life for the United States. She had just saved them and the rest of the world, and now this. "How can this be happening? I . . . I no longer have a home."

Drake opened his arms. "You always have a home."

She fled to the safety of his arms. "Thank you."

He leaned his chin on the top of her head. "You never have to thank me for loving you."

She closed her eyes. For this one little moment, she felt at peace. She felt safe. But what about the people who weren't? Her heart ached for Mary Jane, for Molly, for all the McAdamses. To do that to a child. She shook her head. How could the United States sink so low?

"I never should have left. I knew something was wrong. Why did I leave?"

Drake tightened his arms around her. "You can't be everywhere, Laney. None of this is your fault." He paused. "What do you want to do about the Brotherhood?"

She closed her eyes in frustration. Honestly, right now they were a small pesky annoyance. She knew that they had somehow managed to get her out of the country. David had mentioned seeing the leader with the President. But that was a problem for another day.

"They'll have to wait. They are low on my list of priorities right now, even though I'm high up on theirs."

"They've demonstrated quite a bit of power, being they were able to maneuver you out of the country."

"I know. But I can only face one problem at a time. Or, at least, problems on one continent at a time. And right now, North America wins. The Brotherhood we'll deal with once we get everyone safe."

"So what do you want to do?"

"I want to go home."

A throat cleared behind them.

"Go away," Drake growled.

David chuckled. "I would be happy to, but I think you may need my help."

Laney released Drake, and as soon as she stepped away from his embrace, she felt cold. She wanted to tell David to go away too, but she also wanted to know what he was talking about.

"How can you help?"

"Part of my job allows me access to certain technology that is beyond the range of most individuals."

Laney wanted to tear out her hair. "English, David. Pretend I'm stupid."

"There's a plane. It's a Lockheed SR-72."

Laney frowned. "A 72? I thought it was an SR-71."

David smiled. "As far as the public knows, the SR-71 *was* the last reconnaissance jet used by the U.S. The 72 is the replacement, and I'm violating quite a few laws by admitting it even exists. But it will suit our purposes. It cannot be seen by radar as it incorporates stealth technology, and it flies really, really high."

"Can't we just take a regular stealth jet?" Drake asked.

David shook his head. "Too small for what we need and not as fast."

Laney frowned. "You said it flies really high. How high exactly is really high?"

"Ninety thousand miles." David smiled. "So, exactly how indestructible do you two think you are?"

CHAPTER 57

SOMEWHERE IN VIRGINIA

The air was cold as if the air conditioner was up too high. Molly shivered, her eyes still closed, but it was no use. She was no longer asleep. God, she wanted to sleep. She wanted to pretend none of this was happening.

But the cold wouldn't let her drift off again. Her eyes were crusted from the tears that had dried there. Or maybe it was blood. She reached up and wiped at them. Peering at her hand, she saw that the crustiness was partly dark.

Images swam in her head. She crushed her eyes closed, curling into a ball, trying to shut them out, but they were insistent on replaying. The slices, the bullet wounds, the taunts, the powerlessness. Tears rolled down her cheeks. Why was this happening to her?

She'd always been a good kid. Doing the wrong thing made her tense up inside until she felt like she was going to be sick. She was the one the teachers relied on, that parents felt relieved when they learned she would be somewhere with their kids. Other kids had even teased her about being a Goody Two-shoes, but she didn't care. It was just who she was. She had spent her life being the "good one," and now here she was being tortured. They called her an abomination. A man had even spit on her.

That action, for some reason, had cut even deeper than some of the actual cuts by the knives.

And Zane was here somewhere too. He was no doubt receiving the same treatment. But she didn't think he could heal as quickly as she could. She took stock and knew her injuries had all healed. Physically, she was back to perfect condition. But she felt so tired, so beaten down. It was like her thoughts had to swim through molasses to get out.

The window covering of her cell door slid open. "Rise and shine, buttercup. It's time for you to start round two."

Molly wanted to fight. She wanted to show them she wouldn't go along with them. But her whole body began to shake, images of what was to come dancing through her brain.

I can't do this again. She scrounged back against the wall, a whimper escaping her throat.

Two men stepped into Molly's cell with rifles aimed right at her. Molly tried to inch farther back into the wall, but the concrete would not give.

The guard from earlier smiled as he followed them in. "Now, if you cooperate, we won't have to shoot you. If you don't, we'll shoot you and then do what we need to do. But you'll just be making it harder for yourself."

Once again, Molly thought she should fight. But what was the point? She was on her own. Even if she took down these three, there were dozens more throughout the building.

And she wasn't a fighter. She'd never actually thrown a punch in her life. The chances of her succeeding at an escape on her own were pretty much zero.

"So what's it going to be?"

The other guards raised their weapons slightly higher.

With a cringe, Molly put up her hands. "I'll cooperate."

"Of course you will." He walked to the end of the bed and unlocked the chain from the wall. He tossed it on the bed. "Carry it," he ordered.

Molly gathered the thick heavy chain. It was easily a hundred pounds. But it wasn't much of a strain to carry it. She stepped off the bed and shuffled forward. Her legs were in shackles that didn't have enough give, forcing her to take tiny steps.

As she reached the hallway, the guard shoved her. "Hurry up. We don't have all day."

She pitched forward, slamming onto her knees. A dull roar came from down the hall. Molly's head snapped up.

The guard laughed. "Apparently your little pet doesn't like the testing any more than you do."

Zane was nearby. They were abusing him the way they did her. Anger rolled through her. She might not be able to fight for herself, but she had always been good at standing up for others. She rolled her hands into fists.

A door clanged at the end of the hallway, stopping her motions. Two guards appeared, dragging a girl with dark hair between them. The girl's head hung low, obscuring her face, but there was something familiar about her.

"What are you doing with her?" the guard yelled.

"We were told to drop her in one of these cells."

Molly's head snapped to the guard who'd spoken. She'd been so focused on the girl that she'd barely even glanced at the guards. Jake didn't show any sign of recognition as his gaze slid past her. A tingle ran over Molly as they came closer. Rolly was the other guard. And although the girl didn't look up, Molly knew it was Lou. Hope pierced through her.

They came for me.

Paul grunted. "You were supposed to get permission upstairs."

"You want us to take her back up there? We night need to dose her again." Jake was closer now. He'd been walking toward them ever since they appeared at the end of the hall.

"Fine," Paul growled. "Put her in here for now." He nodded toward Molly's cell.

Jake's gaze flicked toward Molly. He gave her the smallest of nods. It was all the encouragement Molly needed. She yanked on each of the guards' shirts, crashing their faces together.

Paul leaped back. "What the—"

But Jake grabbed him, slamming his fist into his face before running him into the wall, knocking him out.

Rolly and Lou each took a guard, pitching their faces into the ground. Then they stopped making any noise.

Jake knelt by Molly, pushing her hair out of her face. "You okay, honey?"

Molly burst into tears and flung herself at Jake. He held her tight as she sobbed. She barely noticed as Lou and Rolly unlocked her chains.

Jake stood up, slipping his arm under Molly's legs and carrying her. "Let's get you out of here."

Molly shook her head, squirming out of Jake's arms. "No. Zane. He's here too." Before any of them could respond, she sprinted down the hall. Lou and Rolly were at her sides in less than a second. Neither tried to stop her. They just kept pace with her.

"He's around here somewhere," Molly said as she slowed, peering in a doorway. The room held a bunch of cages, and a white-coated woman stood with her back to the door, making notes on a clipboard.

Lou and Rolly spread out, taking different doorways. Rolly waved at them from the second doorway he checked. Lou and Molly blurred over. Rolly held up three fingers. Molly nodded.

Lou nodded to the door. "How do you want to—"

Molly yanked the door open and dashed inside, sending the guard near the door into the wall. Lou caught the scientist across the room with a clothesline as he whipped around.

Rolly tackled the third man, slamming him into the wall. "Glad to see we thought our entrance through carefully."

Molly hurried to the table in the middle of the room. Her heart pounded and her throat felt tight. Zane lay strapped down, and tubes led to buckets of blood on the floor. Large swaths of his skin were missing.

Molly ran a trembling hand over his head. "What did they do to you?"

Zane's eyes opened, looking into Molly's face. His gaze was so tired, so full of pain. Tears ran down her cheeks. "I'm so sorry, Zane."

He licked her hand before his eyes closed. His chest moved slowly before it stopped moving altogether. The heart monitor attached to him gave a long beep.

Molly gasped. "No."

But Zane didn't stir. He lay perfectly still. "Zane, no." Tears dripped down Molly's cheeks onto Zane's fur. She laid her head on his chest. "No."

Rolly put a hand on Molly's shoulder. "Molly, we need to go."

"I'm not leaving him here. They don't get to have him."

Lou shook her head. "Molly, we don't have—"

"She's right." Jake walked in. "We're not leaving him. Get those straps off him. Rolly, can you carry him?"

"Of course." He started to unstrap him.

Jake leaned down, grabbed a container of blood, then walked over to the nearest sink. He dumped the container, running the water to wash it all away.

"What are you doing?" Lou asked.

"They don't get to use any part of Zane." Jake grabbed another container. Molly grabbed two others and dumped them as well. Jake walked over to a specimen container. He grabbed each specimen and dropped them in a metal wastebasket. Then he pulled out a lighter and set it on fire.

Lou poured bleach down each of the drains they used. "We need to go."

Molly took the last strap off Zane before Rolly draped him over his shoulders. "Be careful with him."

Rolly met her gaze with a nod. "I will."

Jake moved to the door, touching a mic at his neck that Molly hadn't noticed before. "We clear, Danny?"

"Yeah. Take the southwest stairwell. I'll be there with the car."

"You ready, Molly?" Jake asked.

She nodded, looking at Zane. "Yeah. I want to go home."

CHAPTER 58

INEZ, KENTUCKY

Mary Jane paced along the yard. When she'd woken up this morning, Jake had been gone. But she didn't have time to focus on it too much because all she could think about was Molly. All night, she'd replayed images of Molly being shot, over and over again. The moment had lasted mere seconds, and yet for Mary Jane that moment had never ended. She lived there now.

And when she wasn't reliving that moment, she was imagining all-new horrors that the United States government was inflicting upon her daughter. How had it come to this?

The front door opened. Joe and Shaun bolted out, searching the yard.

Mary Jane hurried up the steps. "Boys? What's wrong?"

"Danny called," Shaun said, his voice rushed.

Joe cut in. "He, Jake, Rolly, and Lou are coming back. And they said they have Molly."

Mary Jane gripped Joe's hand. *"What?"*

"They said they have Molly," Shaun said. "She's all right."

Mary Jane's mouth fell open, and she couldn't seem to form a word. Jen and Henry stepped outside as well. Mary Jane's gaze snapped to Jen, who nodded back at her. "It's true."

Relief nearly sent her to her knees. Jen and Henry's heads snapped toward the driveway. Mary Jane whipped around as a black SUV came into view. Tears pressed against her eyes, and her chest ached at the sight. Then she was running, stumbling over the ground. The vehicle stopped, and a small figure with bright red hair blurred. Molly slammed into Mary Jane. Henry had run behind and managed to grab the two of them before they hit the ground. Mary Jane hugged her daughter, tears streaming down her cheeks, her chest heaving. Molly seemed so tiny, so fragile as she sobbed.

"Mom."

"It's okay, baby. You're safe. You're home."

Joe and Shaun piled onto the hug. Mary Jane knew they deserved to hug her solo, but she could not get herself to back away. She could not let her daughter go. She wasn't sure if she would ever be able to let her daughter go again.

Over her children's shoulders, she saw Lou, Rolly, Danny and Jake get out of the car. She met each of their gazes, hoping they could read the thanks in her eyes because words were beyond her at this moment.

Rolly smiled, putting an arm around Lou. Henry walked over and hugged Danny. Jen hugged Jake.

But then Jake said something to Henry, and his smiled faded. He looked back at Mary Jane.

Shaun and Joe stepped back. Molly kept her hand clasped in Mary Jane's and turned to the SUV. Jake and Henry disappeared around the back. Then Henry reappeared, Zane in his arms.

Mary Jane gasped. "No."

Molly surged forward. "No! You can't take him!"

Henry stopped, looking at Mary Jane, not sure what to do.

"No! You can't have him!" Molly yelled, grabbing Henry's arm.

Jake whispered in Henry's ear. Henry lowered Zane to the

ground. And it was as if the cord holding Molly up had been snapped. She crumpled to the ground, throwing her arms over Zane and sobbing.

Mary Jane sank to the ground next to her, not knowing how to help her little girl. So she just stayed with her, rubbing her back as she sobbed. And she sobbed right along with her, once again feeling completely helpless.

CHAPTER 59

Molly had stayed with Zane for an hour, not letting anyone but Mary Jane and the boys near him. Finally, exhaustion won out. Molly let Henry take Zane, and Jake had carried Molly into the house and placed her gently in bed. Mary Jane, Shaun, Joe, and Theresa had taken up vigil around her, and none had moved. That had been five hours ago.

The covers shifted, and Mary Jane's eyes flew open. She launched herself up as Molly stirred, muttering in her sleep. "No."

Mary Jane tensed, not sure if she should wake her, guaranteeing she'd remember whatever was plaguing her sleep, or wait and hope she fell back to sleep, letting the dream disappear into her mind, never to be recalled.

A tear slipped from under Molly's lashes. "No," she begged.

"Mom?" Joe sat up from the end of the bed.

Mary Jane turned. "She's dreaming."

"No!" Molly sat straight up, her arms flinging wide. Mary Jane reared back, just managing to avoid getting hit. The lamp on the side table did not fare as well. It crashed into the wall, leaving a dent before dropping to the ground in pieces.

"Wha—" Shaun's head appeared from over the side of the bed.

Molly scrambled back against the headboard, her knees at her chin, her arms wrapped around her legs as she looked around widely.

"Molly, honey, it's Mom. It's Mom, baby." Mary Jane stretched out her arm.

Molly just stared at her.

"Molly?" Joe asked quietly.

Her head turned, and recognition returned. Her head whipped back to Mary Jane. Her face crumbled. "Mom."

Mary Jane had her in her arms in a flash. "It's okay, baby. It's okay. You're safe." But Molly just cried harder. Mary Jane hugged her tight, rocking back and forth. She kept repeating the same phrases. "It's all right. You're safe. The bad men can't get you now."

But her words didn't help. Molly just cried as if her world would never be the same again. And down deep, Mary Jane knew it wouldn't. Mary Jane had shed her own share of tears, but they weren't all of sorrow. More than a few were tears of rage. She had never been a violent woman. She never saw violence as the solution to problems. But in this situation, she wanted to kill every last person that had touched her daughter. And not because she thought it would solve anything, but because they deserved to die.

The depth of her anger stunned her but also strengthened her. She would not let anyone hurt her daughter again. Whatever she had to do, she would keep her safe.

The boys and Theresa slipped out of the room after a little while. Mary Jane hoped they would eat something. But she knew each of them would find a spot to cry in private first. She'd seen the tears in their eyes. She knew how much they ached at seeing Molly's pain.

And even as she sat there holding Molly, she knew she would have to find a way to help her get past this, help them all get past this.

Molly gripped her Mom's hands. "Mom." There was so much

in that one little word: fear, confusion, desperation, and loneliness.

Mary Jane shifted Molly so she was facing her. "Look at me, Molly."

Molly's head lifted. Her blue eyes, rimmed in red, met Mary Jane's gaze. There was so much pain in her face that Mary Jane struggled to keep back her own tears. She took a shaky breath. "You are safe. You are loved. What happened to you, you did not deserve. And what happened to you says nothing bad about you. But it says horrible things about the people who did them."

"No, I'm an abomination. I'm—"

"*Never* say that again. You are my daughter. You are perfect. You are exactly as you should be. You were made this way for a reason. And knowing you, I know it is for a good purpose."

Molly dropped her gaze. "You don't know what they did. If you did—"

"It doesn't matter. It doesn't change who you are."

Molly shook her head, her voice whisper soft. "No, it does change who I am."

And Mary Jane had no answer for that. Because she was right. What had happened to Molly had changed her. It had changed all of them. So she just hugged her daughter to her and prayed the men who did this died a horrible death.

CHAPTER 60

Mary Jane jolted awake, her eyes flying open. The room was dark, but the small light from the hallway provided enough to see by. She had fallen asleep sitting up against the old wooden headboard of the queen-sized bed. Molly stirred next to her but settled right back down. Mary Jane said a silent prayer of thanks.

Mary Jane had prayed that she would continue to sleep, that it would give her daughter some respite from the grief tugging at her. But sleep offered her daughter no solace. She would jolt awake screaming or crying, usually both. And her screams painted a picture Mary Jane didn't want to see.

No, please, no more.
It hurts. Please stop. It hurts.
Mommy!

Each plea was a dagger to Mary Jane's heart. Jen had finally had Molly sedated. She needed to sleep, and her mind wouldn't let her. Mary Jane worried the sedation would trap Molly in her nightmares, but the sedation should have worn off hours ago, and still Molly slept. Mary Jane had barely closed her eyes. She ran a hand over her daughter's hair.

What did they do to my baby?

At the end of the bed, Shaun rolled over, his arm falling over the side of the bed and onto Joe's chest. Her boys had refused to leave Molly's side, even though Mary Jane knew they were hurting just as much as she was.

A shadow appeared in the doorway. Mary Jane stood up and quickly hurried to the doorway, stopping to pull the blanket over Theresa, who slept on the couch in the room.

Cain stepped back to let Mary Jane out. "How is she?"

"Sleeping, finally. And Susie?"

"She's fine. She doesn't realize anything has happened. Her and Nyssa are curled up together."

Mary Jane nodded. "Good, good. I should get back to—"

Cain put a hand on her shoulder. "When was the last time you ate something?"

"Ate? I'm not hungry."

"When did you last eat?" he asked again.

"Uh . . ." She ran through the events of the last few days. "I don't know."

"That's what I thought. I made some stew. It's on the stove. You need to go have a bowl."

"No, Molly needs—"

"You not to get sick. She is sleeping, and she will need you when she awakens. But you also need to take care of yourself. You can't take care of everyone else and neglect yourself."

She looked back into the room, where three of her children slept. "They hurt my baby." A tear rolled down her cheek. She'd thought she'd run out of those.

"I know. She did not deserve anything she has gone through." Cain pulled her into his arms. "But your family is strong. Together, you will all get through this."

She nodded into his chest. They would. The world might be falling down around them, but they had each other. And an ever-expanding group of people that were quickly becoming family.

She pushed back, wiping at her eyes. "I could probably eat something."

"I will sit out here, and I will come get you immediately if Molly awakens." Cain smiled. For the first time since she'd met him, he wasn't wearing his glasses, and in the dark, his eyes looked almost completely black.

Must be a trick of the light.

"Thank you. I won't be long." She headed for the stairs, pausing at the top. Just the idea of walking down them seemed insurmountable. She could not remember a time when she had felt so tired. The closest she could remember was when Billy died.

She made her way down the stairs slowly, her hand firmly clasped on the bannister. She felt a small tingle of victory when she reached the first floor without incident. She had been convinced she was going to pitch forward halfway down and break her neck. Right now she would take those small little victories. She made her way into the kitchen, the smell of the stew making her stomach rumble.

"Hey," Jake said, quietly entering the kitchen from the other side of the room.

"Hey. Cain said I should eat."

"He's right. Sit. I'll grab you a bowl."

Mary Jane slunk into a chair, not capable of arguing. Jake placed a bowl of steaming stew in front of her. She took a tentative spoonful, her mouth watering. Then she quickly finished bowl. Jake didn't say anything, just grabbed her bowl and refilled it. He placed a large glass of juice next to it. Mary Jane finished both, her mind feeling much clearer than it had before. She pushed the bowl back.

"Another?" Jake asked.

"No. I'm good." She looked around the kitchen. "Where is everybody?"

"Asleep." He nodded toward the clock. It was four in the morning.

"Oh, I didn't realize. Why are you up?"

"Danny's been working on a few things. I wanted to check on him."

Mary Jane nodded absentmindedly. Danny always seemed to be working on something. She looked over at Jake. In the dim light, the angles of his face were sharper, making him look tougher. And he was tough. But he was also tender. And he had risked his life to save her daughter. She took his hand.

"I never said thank you for bringing Molly back."

"You don't have to say thank you."

And she knew he was telling the truth. He wasn't a man that expected thanks. He was a man who saw people in trouble and helped. It was who he was. He was a good man. And she was so grateful he was in their lives. "How did you find her? I thought Danny hadn't been able to track them down."

Jake smiled. "He knew the CEI had tried multiple times over the last day to nab Fallen, but they weren't having any luck. He had it down to about a ten-mile radius, and then he found the facility. But getting in was the problem. That's when he and Rolly came up with a plan."

~

"THIS IS A HORRIBLE PLAN," *Rolly groused from the second row of the green Subaru.*

"You didn't think it was so horrible when we came up with it back at the house," Lou replied from where she sat next to him.

Rolly crossed his arms over his chest. "Yeah, well, that was when I was bait. You being bait makes it a horrible plan."

As Jake watched them from the driver's seat, he couldn't disagree with Rolly. He liked the plan as much as anyone can like a plan that revolves around putting a teenager in harm's way. But he felt better with it being Lou. And it wasn't just him being sexist—although he was introspective enough to acknowledge that it did play a role—he knew how much of a toll Lou being abducted by the Katzes had taken on her. She'd lost a lot of herself on that day, and she hadn't fully returned to who she once was. He hated the idea of this plan adding to her psychological burden. But he also recognized that this was something she needed to do.

"Look, I appreciate you guys worrying about me, but I know better than you guys what Molly's feeling right now. And I need to do this, okay?"

Rolly studied Lou for a long moment before he finally nodded. "Okay. But if you get into any trouble—"

"I will call for help . . . loudly," Lou said.

"You know how that plunger works?" Danny asked.

"Yup. You made me show you six times. I have not forgotten in the last ten minutes," Lou said dryly.

"Go, Lou," Jake said.

Without a word, Lou opened the car door and hopped out. She jogged down the street. Halfway down the block, she began to feign a limp.

Jake waited until she was half a block away before he dialed his phone.

"Nine-one-one, what's your emergency?"

"There's, there's one of those Fallen. She's on the street. I just saw her on TV."

"Where are you?"

Jake rattled off their address.

"Is she armed?"

Lou crossed the street, disappearing into the alley in between a restaurant and a rundown apartment building.

"I—I couldn't see. But she ducked into an alley. I think she's hurt."

"Sir, stay on the line. Do not approach the subject."

"Are you sending someone?"

"A special unit is already on the way." Jake disconnected the call.

They had intentionally chosen this street, knowing how close it was to the facility that held Molly. They figured they'd take any Fallen directly there, which would be their way in. But being they were trying to do this quietly, busting down the door was not going to work. They needed something a little subtler.

"Danny?" Jake asked.

Danny's hands flew over the keyboard. "They're checking out the cameras in the area. I inserted the feed we created earlier."

"I'm getting into position." Before Jake or Danny could say a word, Rolly had blurred out of the car and up the fire escape of the apartment building. He'd watch the alley from up there.

Jake watched him go, concerned about how worried Rolly seemed.

Danny caught his gaze. "He'll be all right. Lou's his family. He's really protective of her."

Jake thought he might be trying to convince himself as well. "I understand that."

Danny tensed. "They're coming."

Jake slipped from the car and moved casually down the street, keeping the visor of his baseball cap down low over his face.

An SUV swung onto the road behind him with a squeal of tires. His head jerked up as another swung onto the road ahead of him. He had to keep from shaking his head at their foolishness. If Lou were actually trying to get away, the squeal of their tires would be like a starter pistol. No wonder they hadn't managed to catch any Fallen.

Jake rolled his eyes. What a bunch of hot dogs. He tapped his mic. "Danny?"

"I've got all their communications blocked. They won't be able to call in help."

"Good. Lou?"

"Ready."

"Rolly?"

"Good to go."

Jake tensed. A million things could go wrong right now. *Come on, God, we just need one little break.*

As Jake turned the corner, the two SUVs screeched to a halt in front of the alley, pulling their cars into a turn so they blocked the road. The *doors to the SUVs flew open. Four agents burst from the car, rifles pulled into their shoulders as they advanced on the alley.*

Jake picked up his pace. He'd just reached the alley when the first shots rang out.

CHAPTER 61

Jake's heart nearly stopped as the rapid fire started and then died away.

"Got her!" one of the agents yelled, his voice ringing with triumph. "Grab the sedative."

"Hold," Jake said quietly into his mic, knowing how hard it was for him to not rush into that alley, never mind how hard it would be for Rolly. As horrible as it was, this was part of the plan.

An agent went to the back of one of the SUVs and pulled out a long rifle. Jake recognized it. It held the sedative. The agent moved to the end of the alley, dropped to one knee, and fired.

Rolly's growl could be heard clearly through Jake's earpiece. "Danny?"

"Lou was getting up, and then she was hit with the sedative. She's lying flat."

None of the agents moved for thirty seconds. Then one yelled. "Clear. Move."

They hustled into the alley. Jake sprinted across the street as Rolly jumped from the roof of the apartment complex, landing on two of the agents. Lou reached up, grabbing the wrist of the one who'd tried to pull her up and breaking it. He screamed. She stood and threw him into the wall. One of the agents turned to run, but Jake was right in front of him. He kicked out the man's knee before elbowing him in the chin. An uppercut turned off the lights for him.

Danny sprinted into the alley. "Lou?"

"I'm good." She stood. Her legs were spotted with blood, as was her chest.

"Oh my God." Rolly blurred over to her. "How many times did you get shot? How are you still standing?"

"I managed to dodge most of the shots. I only got hit once. I had to do a little acting. The blood packets helped with that."

She pulled up her shirt and pulled off the blood packets that had been attached to her chest with masking tape. She winced as she rolled up her sleeve and pulled the syringe that had been filled with adrenaline from her arm. "Getting shot really hurts."

"Yes, it does," Jake agreed before grinning at Danny. "I guess you were right. The adrenaline does counteract the sedative."

Rolly looked down at Lou. "Are you sure you're okay?"

"Yeah." Lou glared at the men lying in the alley. "Now let's go get Molly."

∽

MARY JANE SAT DUMBFOUNDED. "You all . . . you did that, for Molly? Lou let herself be shot?"

"Her and Rolly kept arguing over who got to be the target. Lou won."

"But they're just kids themselves."

"Pretty special ones."

"I owe them so much. They risked their lives."

"It's kind of what they do. Like I said, they're pretty remarkable kids. And Danny, he planned it all out. He controlled all the cameras in the area, all the communications. We took one of the CEI's SUVs, and once we got to the facility he controlled all those cameras as well. He got us in and out, and they didn't even know we were there."

When Billy had died, part of the reason it had been so hard was that she knew no one would love her kids as much as she did, as much as Billy did. As a parent, you would risk your life gladly if it meant saving your child's. And yet here she had found an entire group of people that hadn't just talked the talk, they'd walked the walk. They had risked their lives to save Molly, just like months ago they'd done the same to save Susie. She did not even know what to say to express how thankful she was to each and every one of them. But she promised herself she would find a way to show them.

"Uh, Jake?" Danny stood in the doorway, shifting from foot to foot.

Mary Jane got to her feet and strode over to him, wrapping him in a hug. "Thank you, Danny. Thank you."

Danny didn't react for a moment, but then his arms wrapped around her. "You're welcome."

Mary Jane pulled away, smiling at the young genius as she wiped her eyes. "I just can't get over how amazing you all are."

"I'm not like them. I just—"

"No. Do not *ever* tell me you are not amazing. You saved my daughter's life. Both of them. You are not a Fallen, but your abilities are just as important. Don't ever doubt that, Danny."

He nodded, ducking his head. "Yes, ma'am."

Mary Jane gave a watery chuckle before kissing his forehead. "All right. Well, I will leave you two to speak."

She stepped past Danny and started for the stairs. But as she reached the bottom step she realized she could use some coffee. She turned around.

Reaching the kitchen doorway, she paused as Danny's words reached her. "I managed to recover the video from Molly's time at the facility. It's not good, Jake."

"Let me see it," Jake said.

Mary Jane stepped into the room. "Me too."

Danny whirled around, shaking his head. "Mary Jane, you don't want to see this. It's—"

"My daughter. She is traumatized because of what they did to her. And I need to know what that was if I am going to help her."

Danny looked at Jake, his voice pleading. "Jake."

Jake took Mary Jane by the arms. "Do you realize what you are asking? She was tortured, Mary Jane. Do you want those images in your head?"

She didn't. She wanted to run upstairs, pull the blankets over her head and never, ever look at what had been done to her daughter. But if she was going to help Molly, she needed to know what happened. If she was going to find a way to help her live with those memories, she needed to know how bad they were. And together they would share that pain. She couldn't ask her daughter to move past something she was too scared to even look at.

"I need to see it," Mary Jane said quietly. "For Molly's sake, I need to see."

CHAPTER 62

Mary Jane stopped back up at the room where her kids slept to tell Cain where she would be if he needed her.

He frowned when she explained what she would be doing. "Are you sure you want to do that?"

"Want? No." She glanced into the room where Molly lay with her arms wrapped around a pillow like it was a teddy bear. "But I need to. I need to know what she went through so I can help her the rest of the way."

"And you have people around you that will help both of you."

"I know." She turned to head down the stairs, then stopped to hug Cain. "Thank you, Cain. These last couple of days, you have been such a sense of comfort, of home. It would have been much more difficult without you here."

Cain slowly wrapped his arms around her. "Thank you for letting me help you."

It seemed an odd thing to say. But Cain was odd. Even though he looked to be about her age, his demeanor was very paternal. She pulled away. "You'll let me know if they need me?"

"Without a doubt."

She headed back down the stairs to where Danny and Jake

were waiting for her. She had expected them to head to the living room, but Danny walked right past the opening and headed out the front door. She glanced at Jake, who answered her unasked question. "Danny has everything set up in a shed out back. He tends to get lost in his work and has found it works better if people aren't walking in and out."

Mary Jane nodded as she followed Danny across the quiet yard. She knew there were guards patrolling the area, but she couldn't see any of them. Everything was quiet, peaceful. Pink was just beginning to break along the horizon.

Danny pulled open the metal shed door with a screech before slipping inside. Light spilled out into the yard from the open doorway. Mary Jane's heart began to race, and she hadn't even stepped inside yet.

"You don't have to do this," Jake said.

She walked around him. "Yes, I do."

Some old farm equipment had been pushed against a far wall. Another wall had been completely cleared out and lined with Danny's equipment. Mary Jane wondered how they'd even managed to get it all here. Did he have stashes of computer equipment stored around the country in case they needed to hide?

"Actually, yeah," Danny said. And Mary Jane realized she'd asked out loud.

"All the safe houses have electronics. In this day and age, it's impossible to get by without them." He pulled some binders off a chair and gestured to it. "You can sit here."

Mary Jane nodded and walked over on trembling legs. She sat down, but it really was more of a collapse. She scanned the monitors; there were four of them. "Which one?"

Danny pointed to the one directly in front of her. "This one."

She nudged her chair back a little farther from the screen, and when she realized what she was doing, stopped. She needed to see this through.

Danny looked at her. "Are you ready?"

Her heart leaped, and she gripped the sides of the chair, shaking her head. "No. But go ahead."

The screen in front of her flickered to life.

∼

MARY JANE THREW UP. All that lovely stew that had warmed her when she and Jake had sat in the kitchen burned her throat as it came back up. Danny had wanted to stop the tape, but Mary Jane wouldn't let them. She'd sat there in horror, in terror, in anger, in tears, as she watched grown men torture her little girl.

The screen had been blank for minutes now, and still Mary Jane could not stop shaking. Even without the images on the monitor, she could still see them. She closed her eyes, more tears being pushed out.

"Mary Jane?" Jake asked quietly.

She shook her head. She wasn't ready to talk. She couldn't talk. If she opened her mouth, she was going to start screaming and would never be able to stop. What they had done to Molly . . . How could anyone be that cruel?

All she could think was how that had been similar to Mengele's experiments during the Holocaust. When she'd been in school and studied the Holocaust, the teacher had assured them all that nothing like that could happen in the United States. We had too many laws, too many people willing to stand up for others. But where were those people, those protections, when her daughter had needed them? This wasn't some crazy person off the street who'd grabbed her and tortured her. This was government-ordained torture.

How was this legal? How could anyone think this was okay? And what kind of person could look at Molly and think she deserved any of this? Where were their consciences? Where were their hearts?

But she knew the answer to that. They had no heart, no

conscience. In their minds, they had stripped Molly of her humanity. She wasn't a person. She was a thing to them. And you can abuse a thing.

Next to her, Danny wiped at the tears on his own cheeks. He had sat next to her, tears streaming down his face. But he didn't leave her side. She knew he felt guilty for showing her. She hated that he now had these images in his head.

He looked at her, his eyes swimming in tears. "How could they do that?"

He sounded so young then. And he was. With his intellect and responsibilities, it was easy to think of him as a full-fledged adult. But he wasn't. He was the same age as her boys. She couldn't imagine them being able to watch that. But Danny had stayed.

Danny's bottom lip trembled. "I shouldn't have let you watch it. I shouldn't have—"

Mary Jane took his hand. "Thank you, Danny."

"What? Why are you thanking me? I never should have told you that I found the recordings."

"You didn't, remember? But now I know what she went through. Now *she* doesn't have to tell me for me to understand. That is a gift you gave both of us. Thank you."

Danny shook his head. But Mary Jane just leaned forward and kissed his forehead. "Images, they have power, Danny." Mary Jane stood up, her knees buckling for a moment.

Jake grabbed her before she could fall. "I've got you."

She held on to him. "I know." He nodded at Danny over her head and led Mary Jane to the door. *Images have power*, she repeated to herself, then she went still.

"Mary Jane?" Jake asked.

She turned to Danny, an idea forming in the back of her mind. "Can you take still images from that footage?"

Danny nodded slowly. "Yeah, but why would I want to?"

"To help Molly. To help all of them."

CHAPTER 63

ROME, ITALY

It took David a full day to arrange a safe way to sneak Laney and Drake over to Germany. The jet they would be taking was in a hangar at Ramstein Air Force Base. David would be able to get to the plane without an issue. It was getting Laney and Drake on it that would prove problematic.

They made it most of the way without incident. Drake fell asleep in the back of the car. But Laney kept checking the newsfeed for any new developments. The recordings from the raid were playing over and over again. Laney tortured herself by watching them.

Laney felt sick watching the people she cared about being hunted like that. But what happened to the McAdamses, that was beyond any piece of human dignity. Even after she shut off the recording, she could hear Mary Jane's agonized screams.

And I wasn't there. I wasn't there for them.

She turned and looked at David, who'd sat silently as the recording had played out in the car. He was part of the government. He was allegedly on their side, but wasn't that what spooks were good at? Convincing you of one thing while doing another? The longer she studied the man, the more her anger began to boil. All those people on the run, the McAdams family torn apart, a little girl being terrorized, and Laney couldn't reach any of them. Her voice was low when she spoke.

"Did you know?"

"Laney, I—"

"*Did you know?*" she yelled. Wind slammed into the side of the car, sending it sliding across the road.

"What the hell!" Drake bolted upright, instantly awake.

David wrestled with the wheel, sweat breaking out on his forehead. "No, no! It had to have been Shremp. He's grabbing power, using the Day of Reckoning as a stepping stone to the White House. But he and I, we are not exactly friends."

"And if you had known?"

David glanced at her, his Adam's apple bobbing nervously. "I don't know. I'd like to think if I had known that was going to happen, I would have warned them."

She studied him, not sure what to believe. "I'd like to think that too."

She looked away from him, taking a deep breath. She needed to calm down. She needed to trust David, at least to a certain point. Her anger was just going to make things more difficult. She closed her eyes, breathing deep. Drake, for once, decided to stay silent, perhaps recognizing how precarious her emotions were right now.

No one said anything for the last twenty minutes of the trip. Laney managed to work her anger down. She needed to focus on what was right in front of them. One step at a time.

David pulled to the side of the road two miles from the Air Force base. He turned to look at Laney and Drake, his eyes almost lost in the car's dark interior. "You two understand the plan, yes?"

Laney tried not to be insulted. She knew David did not really know them. She knew he was risking a lot. But honestly, it was not exactly a difficult plan.

"You mean the 'jump over the fence and run to the plane' plan?" Drake asked. "Yes, I believe we can recall it."

"No one can see you, at least not until after I have the plane."

"We got it. Stay quiet. Stay down. Run like the wind when you roll out of the hangar," Laney said.

"I'll text you the code for the plane door as soon as I'm in the cockpit. That'll be your two-minute warning."

"We've got it, David. Now how about you go get us a plane?" Drake stepped out of the car. He leaned back in. "And remember, if you are betraying us, I will pull you apart limb by limb." He smiled, shutting the door.

Laney shook her head at him.

David raised his eyebrows. "He's not serious, right?"

"Oh, he's serious all right. But as long as you don't betray us, you have nothing to worry about, do you?"

"Where's the trust?" David grouched.

"Back in Rome. Look at it from our perspective: You work for the United States government, who has attacked all the people I care about. You led us hundreds of miles from the people *you* care about to a heavily fortified, highly populated military base. Now you are about to walk in there, where you can raise the alarm and have dozens of soldiers ready to take us down when we hop the fence. Or you can wait until we're on the plane. We open up the door, then boom, no more Laney or Drake."

"Ah, but bombing planes doesn't seem to be able stop you either. I'd probably need a better plan than that."

All civility dropped from Laney's tone. "Yes, you would."

The smile dropped from David's face as well. "I'm not here to betray you. I know who's in the right here. Be prepared. It should take me about ten, fifteen minutes once I'm on the base."

"We'll be waiting." Laney stepped out of the car.

Laney watched the taillights of David's car until they disappeared from view.

"He's probably setting a trap," Drake said.

Laney pictured David with Bas and Angelica. She shrugged. "It's possible. But I say we give the man a chance. He's risking a lot for us."

Drake picked up her hand, bringing it to his lips. "Your wish is my command."

Laney raised an eyebrow. "Really?"

"As much as is possible." His lips traced the back of her knuckles. "But if he does betray us, I will make sure he has a very short time to regret it."

But David was as good as his word, and fifteen minutes later, Laney and Drake were buckling into the SR-72 as David took off from the runway.

David grinned back at them. "See? Piece of cake. We'll be crossing into U.S. airspace in only a few hours. You two might want to get some sleep, especially if you want to *hit the ground running.*"

Laney groaned at the joke attempt.

After all, the plan was for them to parachute from the plane at an altitude humans probably wouldn't survive while David landed a few states away.

"Don't give up your day job," Drake said.

"Not sure that's an option." David turned back to the console.

"You *should* try and get some sleep," Drake said to her.

"I know. But every time I close my eyes, I see Molly."

"We can't help her at this moment. The best we can do is prepare ourselves for when we arrive."

"Look at you, being all mature and rational."

He smiled. "Like I've told you many times before, I am a man of hidden depths."

She smiled, but then it dropped from her face. "Tell me it's going to be all right, Drake."

He took her hand and kissed the back of it. "I can't tell you that. But what I can promise you is that I will be right by your side helping you through it."

She squeezed his hand. "Right now, I'll take it."

CHAPTER 64

INEZ, KENTUCKY

Molly lay wrapped in Mary Jane's arms. She seemed to be in deep. Mary Jane hated to leave her. But there was something she needed to do.

The door pushed open softly. Jake stood in the doorway. She nodded. "I'll be right down."

She ran her hand through Molly's hair. She needed to go. She knew that. But she could not seem to make herself step away from her daughter. Those images kept lurking in the back of her mind, reminding her that she had not protected her daughter before. How could she leave her now?

The door opened again. She looked up, expecting to see Jake. But Cain stepped in. The bed shifted as he sat on the other side of Molly. "Are you all right?"

Mary Jane started to nod but then shook her head. "No. Not at all."

"Jake told me what you are planning. I think it is very brave."

She ran her hand over Molly's curls. "No. I'm not the brave one."

"I think it may run in the family." He paused. "I'll stay with her. I'll make sure nothing happens to her."

She nodded, her gaze on Molly as her heart broke yet again as she pictured what had been done. Her voice shook as she spoke. "They hurt my baby."

"The world can be a cold place. In my life, I have seen the best and the worst humanity can do. And the people here in this house, they are amongst the best. None of us will let any further harm come to Molly."

"Will you stay with her? Until I get back? It will be a while."

"I will not leave her side. I have already arranged for Lou and Rolly to look after Susie and Nyssa. Molly will be my sole focus."

Mary Jane nodded, knowing Cain would keep his word. She trusted him. But still she couldn't make herself step away. "I don't understand why any of this is happening. I don't understand why my daughter has these abilities. I don't understand why Laney can do what she can. I don't even understand why Elisabeta wanted Nyssa."

Cain took her hand. "And you deserve to understand. When you return, you and I will sit down, and I will answer all of your questions. If there is anyone who can answer them, I can."

She looked into his face, his dark glasses still hiding his eyes. "Why do you wear those glasses even in the dark?"

"That is part of the explanation. When you return, I'll explain it all. Now, I think you need to get going."

She glanced at the clock. They had a long drive ahead of them. She leaned down and kissed Molly's cheek. "I love you, little girl. I always have, and I always will." She stood up.

"I'll keep her safe. Now go."

Mary Jane turned her back to the bed and walked quickly from the room before she could change her mind. But as she stepped outside the room, her back straightened. She needed to do this for Molly. She headed down the stairs.

Danny stood waiting for her. He handed her a flash drive. "Everything is on there. You just need to plug it in."

She gripped it. "Thank you, Danny."

"I could go with you, if you need me to." His big eyes looked up at her. Another young one who had been through too much in a short life.

She squeezed his arm. "I appreciate that, but they need you here. But thank you, Danny, for everything you've done."

"I wish it was more."

She sighed. "I think we all wish we could do more."

Jake stepped out of the kitchen, a thermos of coffee in his hands. "Mustafa's already in the car. You ready?"

She nodded. "Yes. Let's go."

CHAPTER 65

WASHINGTON, D.C.

The phone rang, jerking Shremp into wakefulness. He blinked hard, staring at the clock on the table next to his couch. Seven p.m. He'd been lying on his stomach and his back ached. Drool had pooled on his pillow, and he wiped at his mouth as he scrambled for the phone, knocking over his tumbler with the last remnants of his third nightcap.

"Yeah?" His voice was scratchy from lack of use. He cleared it. "Who is this?"

"It's Sheila, sir."

Shremp rubbed his forehead, trying to work away the effects of the alcohol. He'd had his staff cancel all his afternoon meetings and then headed for home. Just as he'd stepped inside, Sheila had sent him some preliminary information on Okafur. The information within had made what little hair he had left stand on end.

David Okafur had been orphaned at the age of ten. He'd spent the next seven years in an orphanage in Italy. Then he'd gone on to Oxford University before moving on to graduate work at MIT. The CIA had recruited him while he was in grad school. He'd shown an incredible proficiency at all types of spy craft from hand-to-hand to espionage to strategy to even technological warfare. He was a master spy. His missions had been classified. It would take time for Shremp to work through that. None of that was what concerned him, though. It was his personal life.

Okafur lived with a man. A man who had lived his entire life in Iran until seven years ago when Okafur had arranged for him to get a visa and move to the United States. Shremp had started drinking then.

Okafur was obviously compromised. Who knew what type of influence this Rahim had exerted over him? They knew countries across the world were looking into ways to incorporate the abilities of the Fallen into their military forces. The country who was able to create Fallen first would win. And Delaney McPhearson, she was the lynchpin to make that all happen.

What would happen if David turned her over to the Iranians, a religious despot's regime with no interest in human rights? It would be a nightmare. If that happened, Shremp would personally make sure that Bruce Heller was charged with treason. He had handpicked David from MIT and mentored him throughout his career. If David had turned, it was Bruce's fault.

"What do you have?" Shremp asked.

"One of Okafur's aliases was used a few hours ago."

"Hours?"

"It took time to put traces on all of them. He has a lot of them."

"Fine, fine. Where was he?"

"Germany. At Ramstein."

Shremp frowned. "A military base? What was he doing?"

"He borrowed a jet."

"A jet?" He pictured Okafur with a military jet loaded with tactical nukes.

"Yes, sir. It's a high-altitude plane. It's used for covert surveillance. It travels at Mach 3.3, making it virtually untraceable for radar."

"But you can trace it?"

"Yes, sir."

"Good. Let me know when you figure out where—"

"That's why I am calling, sir. We *have* found it. It is about to enter U.S. airspace outside Maine."

Shremp paused. He was coming back to the U.S. "Was he given permission to enter U.S. air space?"

"No, sir. No one but us even knows he's there."

Shremp's mind whirled frantically. What was Okafur up to? Why come back to the United States without letting anyone know? Unless he was bringing back someone or something that he was trying to keep hidden from the United States. And Shremp couldn't allow that to happen.

"Connect me with Air Force Strategic Command. Immediately."

CHAPTER 66

OFF THE EASTERN COAST OF THE UNITED STATES

The flight had been uneventful. Laney had even fallen asleep, although she'd done it sitting upright in a jump seat, so it hadn't been the most restful of sleeps. But she'd take what she could get these days.

"Ah, Sleeping Beauty awakes." Drake turned around and smiled at her from the co-pilot seat.

"Hey." She wiped at the side of her mouth self-consciously. "Where are we?"

"Just entered U.S. airspace," David said. "We'll be over the jump site in only a few minutes."

Laney undid the straps of her restraint and stretched, trying to work out the kinks in her back and neck. "So no problems?"

"Smooth sailing," Drake said. "Perhaps—"

An alarm sounded, accompanied by a blinking red light on the console.

"What is that?" Drake demanded.

David ignored him, his hands flicking switching and buttons.

A radar screen appeared on his right-hand side. "We've been spotted."

"I thought this thing was supposed to be able to avoid that," Laney said.

"It is! Unless someone's looking for it."

"And did you tell someone to look for it?" Drake asked, his voice low.

"I'm on the plane too! If it gets hit, I don't have any superpowers to keep me alive. So no, I did not tell anyone to shoot down this plane."

Drake growled. "If you—"

Laney put a hand on his chest, cutting him off. "What do we do?"

"Strap in. This is going to get dicey."

Laney retook her seat, securing the five-point harness. Drake moved to sit across from her in the other jump seat.

David's hands flew over the console. Then his head jerked to the radar screen as a beeping began.

Drake glared at the back of David's head. "That sounds bad."

"Incoming missile," David said as the whole plane jerked to the right. "Hold on."

Even over the roar of the plane she could hear the decoy flares being deployed and exploding behind them. The missile wasn't fooled, though.

"Damn it. Damn it. Damn it," David mumbled. He jerked the stick to the left.

Laney grabbed the straps of her harness as they practically turned on their side. Her eyes grew large as the missiles flew past ahead of them.

She swallowed. "Are we—"

"Not yet," David barked, putting them into a steep dive just as Laney saw the missiles start to curve back toward them.

Laney's stomach felt like it hit the floor as her feet tried to rise from it.

"I'm going to be sick," Drake mumbled, looking more than a little green.

The skin on Laney's face felt like it was trying to reach the back of her head. She wasn't sure how much more of this she could handle before she blacked out. Then the plane leveled out, but Laney could still feel the g-force pull. They hadn't slowed down, which meant they weren't out of danger.

"This is going to be close," David said, although Laney was pretty sure it wasn't her or Drake he was talking to. She managed to turn her head and saw a mountaintop ahead of her. They were aiming right for it.

CHAPTER 67

LEXINGTON, KENTUCKY

The reflection in the Holiday Express mirror looked ten years older than when Mary Jane had seen it just a few days ago. Her left eye was black, her cheeks sunken. A cut on her forehead had required four stitches. She didn't remember that injury.

I guess I got that when they Tased me.

She gripped the edge of the sink, the words shocking her to her core. She had been Tased by federal officers then knocked out. They had knocked Joe unconscious, attacked Jake when he tried to defend them, and Molly . . . Tears flooded her eyes. She couldn't think of Molly. She'd never be able to do what she needed to do if she thought of what they had done to Molly. She needed to stay strong. She could not help her any other way.

Mary Jane ran a brush through her hair, but that was all she did to improve her appearance. She wore no makeup, and she had turned down Brett's offer to get her new clothes. Her clothes were stained with Molly's blood, even a little of Joe's on her sleeve. She wanted the world to see what had been done to her family. She would not sugarcoat any of the harm.

A soft knock sounded at the door. "Mary Jane?" Jake called softly.

She took a breath. "Be right out."

She stared at her reflection for a few more moments, praying for strength she didn't think she had.

Please, God, help me. Give me the strength to do what needs to be done. She closed her eyes and, shaking her head, opened them. She straightened her shoulders. *Okay.*

She unlocked the door and stepped out. Jake stepped toward her, but she held out a hand. "If you hug me, I will lose it."

He shoved his hands into his pockets. "Okay. Whatever you need."

"Have you heard from Henry?"

"Everybody's fine."

"Even Molly?"

"She's all right. Cain's staying by her side."

She wanted nothing more than to rush back to her, throw her arms around her, and tell her everything was all right.

But that was a lie. Nothing was all right. Her daughter had been tortured by the U.S. government, and Mary Jane hadn't been able to do anything to stop it.

But she could do this. And the sooner she got this over with, the sooner she could get back to Molly. "Let's go."

∽

THE CROWD of reporters shuffled and chatted on the other side of the doors. Mary Jane had never in her life spoken in public like this. The last time she spoke to a room full of people was junior year of high school, when she did a report for her history class on the founding fathers. Half the class had focused on the rainstorm out the window, completely ignoring her.

She could not let this group ignore her. They needed to listen. They needed to *help*. Her hands shook, picturing Molly curled up and sobbing. Tears threatened to break again, but she willed them back.

You can cry for a week straight once you get through this, she promised herself. *But for now, the last thing you are allowed to do is cry, do you hear me?*

"You've got this," Jake said, staring down at her.

"I hope so."

He took her by the shoulders, and she looked up into his eyes. *"You've got this,"* he said. "Because you love those children of yours. And you will do anything in your power to protect them. We don't have any special abilities, but this is something we can do. Take that love you feel for your kids and make them feel it. And make them feel your fear. You are the perfect person for this."

She took a shaky breath and nodded. "Let's go."

He squeezed her arm gently as Mustafa opened the door. Mary Jane walked through the narrow aisle in the middle of the room, rows of chairs on either side. All talking stopped for a moment as she stepped in. Then everyone seemed to be talking at once. Questions were shouted at her from all the reporters. Mustafa and Jake walked on either side of her, keeping them back. She looked neither left nor right, just kept her gaze on the small stage at the front of the room.

Brett stepped from the front of the room so she could see him. He would be next to her. He would step in if it became necessary and answer any questions. Flashbulbs popped and cameras whirled, but Mary Jane blocked it all, focusing on getting to the front of the room, one foot in front of the other.

Before she knew it, she was climbing the three short steps to the stage. A podium was set up off to the right, and a large screen took up the back of the stage. Jake and Mustafa took position in front of the stage, scanning the crowd. Brett nodded at her, taking a seat to the back and side of the podium. The lights dimmed, and a spotlight shone on her, making her blink.

But as soon as the light came on, a sense of calmness came

over Mary Jane. The screen flickered to life, and a picture of Molly appeared. It had been taken after soccer practice one fall day. Her hair was wild, her cheeks rosy, her blue eyes shining. And her smile—it was impossible not to smile back at that smile. So Mary Jane smiled at her beautiful daughter. As she turned to face the audience, she saw more than a few people smiling at her daughter's picture as well.

Taking a breath, Mary Jane looked out into the audience and began to speak. "Thank you for coming here today. My name is Mary Jane McAdams, and this is my daughter Molly. Molly is smart, quiet, sweet, and a ferocious soccer player. She is thirteen and caught between the world of a teenager and she's also a kid. She likes to have sleepovers with her friends but still has her collection of stuffed animals. And when there is a thunderstorm, she still crawls into my bed." Mary Jane paused.

"Molly is also a Nephilim. We only learned of her status last year. Her father was a Fallen. I never knew that. He never used his abilities. He never had to. He was a good man. He provided for us, loved us, and as far as we were concerned, he was exactly like us. But he wasn't. He was taken from us in a car accident. Molly was in the car. A good friend believes that is when Molly's abilities awakened."

The crowd was leaning forward, taking notes, engaged. Mary Jane plowed on. "I was terrified when I learned about Molly's abilities. Her brothers were jealous. In their words, they wanted to be superheroes too."

A smattering of chuckles drifted through the hall.

"But I was terrified. I worried about what it would mean for her, of the danger it could place her in. Because out of my children, Molly, she's my quiet one, she is my thoughtful one. And I worried it would be more than she could bear. But as we parents often learn, our kids often know more than we do."

"When the Day of Reckoning came, Molly wanted to go out and help. I told her no. She was too young. She was not trained.

But she argued that God gave her these gifts and He wanted her to use them." Mary Jane smiled. "It stinks when your kids use your own logic against you." Another smattering of chuckles.

"Molly stayed with us as we watched the news reports and the horror began to unfold. We were all in my living room—myself, my children, my two brothers, and their families. All of us were glued to what was happening on the screen, the horror playing out. None of us could look away. None of us, except for Molly.

"Unbeknownst to us, somewhere during those broadcasts, she snuck out. She went to go help people in our neighborhood by herself." Mary Jane looked over her shoulder at Molly's picture. "This beautiful, timid thirteen-year-old girl went to help when the rest of us couldn't even look up from the TV. And she did help. She helped save dozens of people that day. She went into burning homes. She pulled impossibly large trees off people so others could drag them to safety. Again and again she used her abilities to save and protect those around her."

Tears sprang to Mary Jane's eyes. "I could not have been more proud of her. She *was* a Godsend that day."

Her smile dimmed as she remembered what came next. "And yet, when school began again, people began to whisper, people began to write cruel things on her locker and online, calling her all types of horrible things. I asked her how she felt about all of it, and she told me she knew what she could do was scary to people who didn't understand her abilities. And *she* understood that. She said it would take people some time, but they would understand she was still the same person and everything would go back to normal.

"Who wouldn't be proud of a daughter like that? She had no anger for those that scorned her. She understood their fear and forgave them the moment they did something. That is a completely different kind of strength. She is an amazing girl.

"But then as time wore on and people didn't change, I saw the pressure taking a toll on her. She was becoming more withdrawn, quieter. She was sad. So we moved to the Chandler Headquarters to give Molly a chance to be around kids like herself.

"To give her a chance to be normal."

Mary Jane blinked, tears of pride and sorrow burning at the back of her eyes. She took one last look at her daughter's smiling face and then turned her back, nodding at Brett. The light flickered as the image on the screen behind her changed. "This picture was taken three days ago at the Chandler Headquarters. We had just finished a delicious dinner and were in the middle of a brutal Scrabble marathon.

"One day later, the U.S. government came to arrest my daughter. In the process, they broke the nose of my fourteen-year-old son, who was not resisting them."

The image shifted behind her, and she knew it was a close-up of the soldier slamming the butt of his rifle into Joe's face. The audience gasped.

"I tried to help my son. I leaned down to him." The image shifted again behind her.

"I was pulled away and then kicked in the back by a soldier." Another image.

"The soldier went to kick me again, but Molly, she wouldn't let him. And they shot her." Another image.

Mary Jane told herself not to look, but she couldn't stop herself. She glanced over her shoulder. On the large screen, she caught Molly as she fell, her scream practically audible. No one in the room made a sound.

Mary Jane turned back, tears pressing against the back of her eyes. "My daughter was then taken into custody. We were not told where she was taken. She was not allowed access to a lawyer. My beautiful, sweet child went from a little girl to an enemy of the state. And her crime? Abilities she never asked for and had only used to help people."

Her breath hitched as she pictured Molly's devastated face. Jake glanced over his shoulder at her. She took strength from his look and faced the crowd once again. "Molly was a prisoner of the CEI. The agency wanted to determine the weaknesses of the Fallen. And they had no compunction about experimenting on a thirteen-year-old child who still sleeps with a teddy bear."

The light flickered behind her, but Mary Jane just gripped the podium, her knuckles turned white as the crowd gasped before starting to mumble. But as image after image played, the crowd went silent, horror in the air.

"My daughter was stabbed, shot, cut, and tortured, all in the name of the United States government. Over and over again, they tortured her. For hours." Mary Jane took a breath. "But they weren't done. The afternoon of the second day they had her, they pulled her out of her cell to begin the next phase of experimentation: chemical attacks. She was saved before they could commence those attacks."

Mary Jane reached a shaky hand for the glass of water on the shelf under the podium. She took a drink to quench her thirst and to give her a moment to shove those horrible images from her mind. "My daughter is in hiding, in more ways than one. My beautiful, sweet little girl is traumatized. She cannot be left alone. She has a power that as children we dreamed of. And yet she is just a terrified child. And it is *our* government that has done this to her. She did not ask for these abilities. But she felt a duty to use them to help others. In return for that selflessness, the United States government named her an enemy of the state and tortured her. They tortured a *child*."

Mary Jane took a breath. "I am not standing here today to tell you that all Fallen and Nephilim are good. We all know that is not true. But they are not all evil. Like all of us, there are good and there are bad. We cannot declare them all evil, any more than we could declare any other ethnic group entirely evil. Our government is wrong in this. This is not the America people have fought and died for.

"The Fallen are not the only ones with extra abilities. Anyone who owns a gun has an unfair advantage in any confrontation. We do not remove their rights. In fact, we adamantly defend them. Men have a physical advantage over females in almost any confrontation. We do not remove their rights. This is a country that embraces freedom, that is a symbol of human dignity." She waved her hand toward the screen. "Where is the dignity in these actions? And if we cannot protect our children, then what right have we to call ourselves the land of the good?

"We need to protect ourselves, yes, but not at this cost. Torturing a child? Who among you can defend that? Who among you could look themselves in the mirror and be proud of a government that ordained this? This country is the greatest in the world. It is a beacon of freedom and democracy. What was done to my daughter is a dark stain on that history. And anyone who considers themselves a true American, a good person, cannot allow it to happen to anyone else.

"I'm not a fighter. I'm not a public speaker. But how can I stay silent when a government feels entitled to torture children in the name of national security? How can you? When the history books are written about this time, which side will you be on? The side that history demonizes and struggles to understand how they could have allowed such cruelty? Or will you be on the side of the heroes? Will you be the person that future generations look back upon and point to as the type of person we all should strive to be?"

She paused, her gaze scanning the room. "Who do *you* want to be: the hero or the villain?" She stepped back from the podium.

No one said a word. No one even moved. Mary Jane wasn't sure how to interpret that.

Brett tapped her arm. "Nicely done," he whispered before turning to the audience. "Are there any questions?"

Everyone in the audience launched themselves to their feet, hands in the air, questions ringing out.

CHAPTER 68

OVER THE EASTERN PORTION OF THE UNITED STATES

The mountaintop grew larger in the windshield of the jet. Laney tensed. If they hit it at this speed, well, she didn't think even her ability would allow her to heal from that.

She looked over at Drake. He stared intently back. "Guess we're going out with a bang."

She tried to smile in response, but she couldn't quite manage it. They were almost at the giant rock face. It now took up the entire windshield, no sky visible beyond it.

"Hold on!" David yanked on the stick.

If Laney thought the pull was bad during the dive, it was nothing compared to now. Her very brain felt like it was pushing against the back of her skull. If she could raise her hands, she would have placed them there to keep it from leaking out. At the same time, it felt like an anvil was pushing against her chest. Drawing a breath proved almost impossible.

The plane jolted.

"Yes!" David yelled, moving the stick so they were still going up but at a less painful angle.

"It hit the mountaintop?" Laney asked after checking to make sure none of her teeth had been dislodged.

"Yeah. The people of West Virginia will be less than thrilled but better than having us splashed all over their countryside. You two need to put those suits on." He nodded toward a small cabinet built into the side of the plane, only a foot away from where Drake sat.

With trembling hands, she loosened her harness. She stood, stumbling a moment as her knees buckled. "You do this a lot?"

David grinned, not seeming to be at all affected by the wild ride. "More than I can legally admit."

Laney shook her head with a smile, making her way over to the cabinet. Drake was still trying to undo his harness. She patted his shoulder as she opened the cabinet door. "You okay?"

"I hate this guy."

She laughed. "I kind of like him."

"I like you too, Laney," David called over his shoulder.

Drake just glared. Laney tossed a jumpsuit at him and started to climb into a second one.

"Grab the helmets too," David said. Laney reached in and pulled out two helmets. This time she laughed out loud.

"What's so funny?" David asked.

"We're familiar with these helmets." They were the same brand as the ones they'd used when they bailed out of Gerard's plane.

"Good. The chutes are in the cabinet by the door."

"I'll get them." Drake blurred to the back. He was standing next to Laney in seconds, handing her a chute.

"That really never gets old." David grinned. "Okay, well, I was hoping to carefully take you through an explanation of what you need to do, but we no longer have time for that. They will already be sending a second missile."

Laney shrugged the pack onto her back and snapped the locks across her chest. "I've skydived before."

"Me too," Drake said.

"Good. Well, you are going to need to freefall for, well, a while. Pull the red cord when you reach about three thousand feet. That blue cord is what you pull if the red cord doesn't work. Got it?"

"Okay," Laney said.

"On the cuff of your suit is a console. Turn it on."

Laney did. The small screen popped to life. A countdown was on it, the numbers increasing.

"That's your altitude. We're at about 87,000 right now, so you'll need to freefall a good long ways. Those suits were designed for that, and they should keep out most of the cold. Don't forget the gloves."

"Okay." Laney pulled on the gloves in her pocket. "What about you?"

"Well, I'm going to make sure the next missile has something to chase."

"What?"

"No auto-pilot, or at least, not this high up, and we do still need to get you guys out. I'll lead them away, drop altitude, and then bail. When they check out the wreckage, it will be states away from you."

"I don't like that."

David shrugged. "It's the best plan."

The alarm sounded again. All three of their heads whipped toward the radar screen. "Go. Now!" David yelled.

Drake grabbed Laney's arm and pulled her to the door. He punched it open. The wind tried to rip her out, but Laney met David's gaze one more time. He nodded at her.

She lowered the shield on her helmet and dove out the door.

CHAPTER 69

BALTIMORE, MARYLAND

This is not a good idea.

Yoni drove slowly by the back of the Chandler Estate. He had taken Sascha, Dov, and Max out to Arizona to stay with Sascha's parents, and they had planned on staying there until at least a few weeks after Sascha gave birth.

But then he'd seen those images on the screen. Sascha had been unable to stop crying for hours. Yoni had struggled to hold it together himself. He still could not imagine that his government, the government he had sworn to defend as a Navy SEAL and readily did so for years, would treat a family like that. They'd offered no threat. Not even Molly with all her abilities.

He had wanted to come back. He had wanted to help immediately, but he couldn't leave Sascha. She was the one who pushed him to go. She promised not to give birth until he got back.

But it was Max who cinched it for him. Max had looked him in the eye, the old soul speaking, not the young boy. "You need to go, Yoni. There's someone waiting for you. They need your help."

Yoni had no idea who it was. The entire estate had been

emptied, at least to his knowledge. The only person he could think of was Dom. Dom never left the estate. Not in the nearly two decades he had lived there. Yoni figured he might be the one who could need his help. Yoni tried to call him, but all the estate's communications were down, so he needed to go check personally.

The problem, though, was going to be getting to the bomb shelter. The government had pulled out most of its forces, but it had left a group to guard the estate. No one was being allowed in. He'd seen Brett get turned away at the front gate as he'd attempted to enter with a dozen members of Henry's staff. Ahead, the road was barricaded. Yoni made a left and drove a mile away to the empty field that had once been used as an exit for runaway slaves. Laney had used it when she'd disappeared. A Hummer sat with the motor running at the edge of the field. Yoni felt eyes on him as he drove past. He wasn't getting in that way.

Damn it. As far as he could tell, they had all the entrances blocked and at least two patrols inside on foot. He made the next left, bringing him back toward the estate. He took another side road that dead-ended and pulled his car along the side of the road. He grabbed his black backpack from the back seat, pulling a black knit cap from the front pocket and slipping it over his bald head. Bald might be beautiful, but it also shone like a spotlight if hit just right. He disabled the interior light before he slipped out the door.

Hitching the pack over his shoulders, he began to jog back toward the estate. He was just going to have to go over the side. Physically, he wasn't worried about the climb. He just really hoped the alarms on the fence had been disabled. And that he'd figured out the timing of the patrols correctly. Otherwise he was not sure how he was going to explain his all-black ensemble. He didn't think with his age and tanned complexion, they'd believe he was Goth.

He waited across the road from the estate, crouching low behind a series of tall, dense yews. After thirty minutes, his knees began to ache a little. He shifted, trying to get more comfortable, when he noticed the flashlight of one of the patrols appear. He tensed, lowering himself and keeping still. Two-man patrol. Their flashlights drifted back and forth as they walked, but they didn't stop. Yoni watched as they disappeared around the bend in the fence. He counted to two hundred and then rose from his hiding place.

Checking to make sure the road was clear as well as the grounds behind the fence, he hurried over. He looked up with a sigh. Up and over. He reached up to grab the metal when someone grabbed him by the back of the shirt and yanked him to the ground.

CHAPTER 70

SOMEWHERE ABOVE PENNSYLVANIA

Air whipped past Laney, rustling her suit. She was pointed down at a seventy-degree angle, trying to put as much distance between her and the plane as possible. She knew she was traveling incredibly fast, and yet it didn't feel like that because there was nothing to judge herself against. Just empty sky.

Drake appeared in her peripheral vision. A light appeared on her other side. The missile was high above them. She turned her head to watch the plane as it sped away, the missile catching up fast.

Come on, David. Go. The plane pulled into a dive. The missile compensated.

But then it was out of view, too far away to see what was happening in the dark sky.

Laney glanced at her sleeve. Another forty thousand feet and they could safely deploy the chutes. A mushroom cloud of fire erupted from the direction of the plane.

Her head snapped to the left as she gasped. *No.* That was too soon. David couldn't have escaped that quickly. Guilt dogged her for suspecting him.

Oh, David, I'm so sorry. Yet another person dying while trying to help. There was too much death.

She opened her eyes, resolve replacing her anger. He would not have died in vain. He'd sacrificed himself to protect the people being victimized in the United States. People like Molly. Laney was going to make sure that never happened again. She deepened her dive. She needed to go faster. Too much was happening. Too many people were getting hurt, and she was not going to let that happen.

Not anymore.

CHAPTER 71

BALTIMORE, MARYLAND

Yoni's fist was already moving as he hit the ground, but it stopped mere inches before the face looming over him. "Cleo?"

She licked his face in response.

Yoni chuckled as she buried her head in his chest. "Yeah, I missed you too, girl. I'm glad to see you got out."

A second head appeared on Yoni's another side.

"Moxy?" Danny's black chow shepherd mix licked the other side of his face, her tail wagging like mad. A third shadow loomed behind the other two. Tiger stood quietly back, Rolly's dachshund, Princess, perched on his back.

"Hey, guys." Yoni pushed Moxy and Cleo back as he sat up. Moxy was a bundle of nervous energy next to him, bouncing around. "Well, it's good to see you guys, but I need to get inside. Wait here. I'll be back."

He went to grab the metal again. Cleo batted his arm away, standing between him and the fence. Yoni frowned. "What's going on, Cleo?"

She looked at the fence, then Yoni, and shook her head.

"Cleo, I appreciate the concern. But I need to check—" She head-butted him in the chest as she walked by.

Yoni grunted, rubbing the spot where she'd made contact.

She looked over her shoulder at him pointedly, then started to walk again. Tiger fell in step with her, Princess still sitting on his back like a little furry cowboy. Moxy sat on the ground next to him, looking up at him with her tail wagging.

"I guess that means they want me to follow them, huh?"

Moxy tilted her head, her eyes wide.

Yoni rolled his eyes. "Great. Not only am I taking orders from giant house cats, I am now looking for confirmation from an average canine."

Moxy gave a small whimper.

Yoni reached down and rubbed her head. "Sorry, buddy. You're not average. All right, let's follow your friends."

CHAPTER 72

MATAMORAS, OHIO

Laney and Drake landed in an empty field. She'd hit the ground at a run and then rolled as her head tipped forward, a large rock digging into her ribs as she rolled over it. Drake, however, stayed on his feet, landing like a professional only a hundred feet away. Rolling up her chute, she stashed it in a shed at the edge of the field.

Drake dropped his in next to hers before tugging on her arm. "Come on. We need to be away from here."

They ran for a full ten minutes before they stopped. Laney scanned the sky and the ground, but no one seemed to have noticed them.

"I think we're good," Drake said.

She glanced back where she'd seen the fireball. "Do you think—"

Drake's voice was quiet. "He couldn't have made it, Laney."

Laney took a trembling breath. "I can't stand this. Why do people have to keep dying? What are we doing that is so wrong? We *help* people. But that's not why any of the governments of the world want these abilities. They want to keep people in line. They want to dominate others."

"It's human nature. You may use your powers to help others, but not all do. Like Samyaza, they seem to want to get as much as they can from them."

She knew he was right, and she hated it. She also knew that if any government uncovered the formula for the Omni, it wouldn't be long until it made it into the private world and the criminal one. Like guns, the Omni would attract those most interested in doing harm. And her job, fighting back that tide, would get that much harder.

"Don't go there, Laney."

"How do you know what I am thinking?"

"Because I know you. And I know every expression on your face. Don't go off the deep end worrying about things in the future. There is plenty for you to worry about in the here and now. So let's focus on that. Let's go find our friends. Then together, we'll figure out the next steps."

Laney smiled. "I'm still trying to figure out when you became the level-headed one in this relationship."

"Hey, even ten-thousand-year-old archangels can learn."

Laney balked. "Ten thousand years? You're ten thousand years old?"

"Actually, I'm a little older than that. But that seemed a less sensational number."

Laney just stared at him.

He shifted his feet, looking uncomfortable. "What?"

"I just, I don't know. I just suddenly feel very, very young."

"Perhaps, but your soul is very, very old."

Laney raised an eyebrow. "Really?"

He winced. "Yeah, that sounded a lot better in my head."

She laughed. "Well, come on, Casanova, before you bowl me over with more romantic words about my elderly personality."

He kissed her forehead. "Old, young, the world keeps turning, and we keep finding each other. That is all that truly matters."

Laney smiled. "See? Now that was much better." She leaned up to kiss him, then pulled away with a sigh.

"You're thinking about the future again, aren't you?"

She nodded. "Yup."

Drake sighed heavily. "Apparently we've reached the point in our relationship where my kisses cannot distract you from the world outside. Perhaps we should try a romantic weekend getaway."

"Been reading couples magazines?"

"Just the headlines."

"Well, as soon as the world calms down, you, me, some tiny little hut on an abandoned island."

"Now *that* is a plan I can get behind."

CHAPTER 73

BALTIMORE, MARYLAND

Yoni jogged behind Cleo and Tiger for three miles. If he didn't know better, he'd think they were just trying to make sure he got some exercise. But each time a car approached, they disappeared into the trees before Yoni even heard the engine. As soon as the car had passed, they'd slip right back onto the road and continue forward.

Soon, they left the few houses around the estate behind and entered another field. Cleo and Tiger jogged across the field, lengthening their stride and putting more distance between Yoni and them. Moxy kept pace with him.

The two cats headed right for a group of bushes off to the side of the field. Yoni frowned. What were they up to?

Cleo reached the series of bushes first. Her teeth clamped around the base of one, and with two giant tugs, she yanked it from the ground. Tiger did the same to the one next to it. Then they dropped the bushes a few feet away before repeating the process with another two bushes.

Yoni jogged to a stop. "Uh, you guys dragged me out here to do some midnight landscaping?"

Mouth full of spruce, Cleo could only give him what he interpreted as an annoyed look. He put up his hands. "Sorry."

Cleo began to dig at the dirt. Tiger and Moxy joined in to help. Yoni shifted from foot to foot, wondering what the hell he was doing here. He should have ignored the cats. He knew they were smart, but they couldn't possibly know what he was planning. He should head back and see—

Cleo's nails scraped metal. Yoni's head snapped up. He hurried forward, helping push the remaining dirt out of the way. "Holy crap. It's another entrance."

He felt a little angry that no one had mentioned it to him but gave them a pass being everyone's lives had been tossed up in the air in the last few days. Pulling his flashlight from his pack first, he yanked open one of the doors, stumbling as it came off its hinges and slammed to the ground. He winced, glancing around.

Damn, that was loud. But it didn't seem to have attracted any attention. He flashed his light inside. A tunnel had been burrowed from the dirt. "Okay, I'll—"

Cleo slipped inside, followed by Tiger with Princess, then Moxy.

"I'll apparently bring up the rear," he grumbled, following them in. He picked up the door and secured it in place behind him before hurrying to keep up with the rest of his pack.

The tunnel made a straight line back to the estate. Yoni guessed it was maybe a mile long, cutting under a bunch of other properties that Henry didn't own. Yoni was pretty sure those owners would not be thrilled to know what was happening under their backyards.

Ahead, a single metal door led to what Yoni hoped was Dom's and that Cleo hadn't led them to an opening that would have them stepping out of the fountain in front of the main house and no doubt a couple dozen soldiers.

Cleo sat down to the side of the door. Yoni frowned, trying to figure out why. He smiled, whispering, "Oh, big genius cat can't manage a door that slides open."

He started to move past her. Cleo shot out a paw. Yoni tripped over it, barely managing to not faceplant into the door. She gave a huff that sounded suspiciously like a laugh.

Yoni grunted as he unlatched the lock. He waited a few seconds, but he couldn't hear anything on the other side of the door. He slid it open a few inches. It led into the back of the guest room at Dom's, where Patrick had stayed for a short time while he was recuperating.

He leaned out and listened, but he couldn't hear anything. He glanced down at Cleo, who nodded before sliding the door open farther and trotting inside.

Well, I guess that means the coast is clear. Yoni was tempted to pull his weapon, but he didn't want to shoot anyone unless it was life and death. And he also didn't want to be shot, so he figured unarmed was the best call.

Yoni slipped out after Cleo with Tiger, Princess, and Moxy following him. As they reached the doorway, the cats split off, heading toward the main area while Yoni checked Dom's bedroom. The room had been tossed. Clothes, books, and papers were scattered. Dom was a bit of a slob at times, but this was way beyond his normal level. The government had been looking for something.

He quickly checked the other rooms in this part of the shelter. All the rooms had received the same treatment. He stopped in the storage room and grabbed one of the radios and burner phones. He also went to the back wall and, pushing on the third wall tile from the bottom, reached into the hidden compartment there. He pulled out the code that would let him know what safe house they were using. To anyone else it looked like a random assortment of pictures, numbers, and Greek letters. Dom had designed the code in case they all got separated. Everyone was taught the code, and the numbers were changed weekly.

He frowned as he stepped into the main room. But where was Dom? With all the cameras he had in the place, he must know Yoni was here. A quick scan of the main room revealed no Dom, but the cats had opened the fridge and were helping themselves and the dogs to whatever they could find. Cleo turned on the faucet and took a long drink. Tiger grabbed Princess by the scruff and lifted her to the counter so she could reach the water as well. They were quite a little team.

Yoni made a beeline for Dom's lab. If the government had been here, Dom no doubt had locked himself in there as soon as they left. He was probably terrified.

"Dom?" he yelled. "Dom, it's Yoni." His foot hit something, sending it sliding across the floor.

Yoni went still. *No, no, no.* He scurried down on his hands and knees and reached under the table to retrieve the object. *Please let me be wrong. Please let me be wrong.*

But as his hands wrapped around the object, he knew he'd identified it correctly in those few seconds. He pulled the eyeglasses out, the masking tape still holding the edge of the glass in. Dom's glasses.

But where the hell was Dom?

CHAPTER 74

OVER WESTERN WEST VIRGINIA

The cold air blew on David's face. He knew that wasn't right. Why would the air be blowing so hard? There was something tickling at the back of his brain. Something important he was supposed to remember. He sunk a little farther into the darkness. He didn't want to remember. The wind was biting, but inside his mind he was warm. Rahim smiled at him. "Open your eyes, David."

"No. It's cold out there."

"I know. But you need to open your eyes."

He snuggled deeper into the dark. "No. This is good."

"Open your eyes!" Rahim yelled.

David's eyelids flew open. Air rushed past him as he fell toward Earth. The plane. He'd managed to wrestle himself into a parachute harness after setting the controls, slamming in the last buckle as he leapt from the plane. He'd just gotten clear when the missile hit. The concussive blast had sent him flying head over heels, knocking him out.

His head still felt woozy, only in part due to the lower level of oxygen in his first few minutes of flight. God, he was cold. He felt like his thoughts had to push through a swamp before he could understand them.

Below him, he could almost make out trees. He frowned. The AAD should have released by now.

Too close. I'm too close. He grabbed for the ripcord and yanked. The parachute unfurled. His head snapped back as he shot straight back up in the air. His vision tunneled as spots appeared at the edges.

He fought the darkness now, but it was slowly creeping over him. He needed to stay awake long enough to get his feet under him. He was going to hit hard. There was no avoiding that. But if he could get his feet under him and tuck into a roll, he could offset at least some of the damage. If he didn't, he'd break just about every bone in his body.

He forced his eyelids open, flashing back to church when he'd be struggling to stay awake during a boring homily.

Come on, David. You can do this. You can do this.

But it was no use. The dark would not be held at bay. He saw the ground clearly before his eyes shut. He knew he needed to prepare, get into position for landing, but his body didn't seem to be responding to any of his commands. Rahim flashed across his mind, and pain lanced through his heart.

I should have taken the time you wanted. I should have told you every day how much I loved you. I'm sorry. Please forgive me.

His mind tensed, but his body just dropped, as unresponsive as a crash test dummy's. He would not survive this. In his mind, he said goodbye to Bas and Angelica. But it was the image of Rahim he clung to.

"It will be all right," Rahim whispered. "Whatever happens, it will be all right."

He waited for the pain, knowing it would start with his ankles snapping as he landed, or maybe his shins. But the first hit didn't come from beneath him. It came from the side. Something slammed into him. Then he was rolling and rolling before the darkness took over.

CHAPTER 75

INEZ, KENTUCKY

The large farmhouse sat quietly in the night. A porch light was on, and another dim light shone weakly through the window. It was close to four a.m. Laney wasn't surprised that everyone was sleeping. She was actually happy. With everything that had happened, if anyone could sleep, that was a good thing.

She and Drake had caught a replay of Mary Jane's press conference when they'd stopped at a coffee shop. It had been a risk, but they'd overheard people speaking about the conference, and Laney needed to know what was happening. No one in the shop had even glanced at them, their horrified gazes focused on the screen. Drake had had to pull Laney away. She, too, had been unable to look away.

On the good side, she knew Molly was safe, but those images . . . Laney knew it would take a long time for Molly to get over what had happened to her. When Henry had been tortured, it had taken him time. But a kid as young and innocent as Molly? Laney wasn't sure she'd ever be able to get past it.

Drake moved a little closer to Laney, his arm brushing against hers. "Is there a reason we are not announcing ourselves?"

Laney shrugged. They had slipped past the security of the farmhouse. There had been over a dozen guards, both Fallen and non. The Fallen couldn't sense either Laney or Drake, making it relatively easy to slip past them. No one else would have much luck in the same attempt.

Now they stood at the edge of the trees. They'd been here for two minutes, just watching the house.

"Are we waiting for something in particular?" Drake asked.

"No," she said but didn't move.

"The guards will be along any minute."

Laney nodded but still stayed where she was.

"Laney."

She didn't take her eyes from the farmhouse. "I keep trying to figure out how I could have changed all this. What I could have done. All these people, their lives have been completely upended. All these children are now being hunted. Did it have to come to this?" Tears pressed against the back of her eyes. "Was there something else I could have done to spare them?"

Gently, Drake turned her chin toward him. He wiped a tear from her cheek with his thumb. "No one could have done more, Laney. In each moment, you did what you thought was best, without consideration for what was best for you."

Laney shook her head. "But we're still here. Maybe if I had gotten to Samyaza sooner or had explained to the government sooner..."

"None of this would have changed. There was no way to get to Samyaza earlier than you did. And if you had told the government sooner, all of this would have simply happened sooner. Governments, they don't see the individual. They see the threat. Whenever they learned of the Fallen, this would have happened. It was unavoidable."

"But what they did to Molly..."

Drake winced. "That was beyond cruel. And I know you blame yourself for allowing that to happen. But every bad thing in the world is not your responsibility. You need to stop taking on unnecessary blame."

"I know. I just wish I could have helped her. I wish I could have spared her that."

"You are not alone in that feeling." Drake nodded toward the farmhouse. "I am sure that house is full of people who feel the same. And I believe that the world is full of people who feel the same as well."

Laney took a shaky breath. "I hope that's true."

"I have lived a long time, Laney. And there are two things that have been proven over and over again: Those in charge always try to maximize power. And most people are basically good."

She looked up at him in surprise. "You really believe that?"

"I do. But the good tend to be quieter than the bad, more easily cowed. But they will always outnumber the bad. Humans, you are complex and confusing, but the large majority of you are good. Don't forget that."

She studied him. "Who are you? Where is the arrogant illusionist I first met?"

He leaned forward, placing a kiss on her forehead. "He is here if you need him. But right now, I think this is the Drake you need."

"How many Drakes are there?"

"As many as you need."

She leaned forward, and he wrapped his arms around her. She closed her eyes, breathing in his warmth, his strength. "Thank you."

"No need to thank me." His voice shifted, taking on a lecherous tone. "Not when you can show me."

She pushed him away with a laugh. "And the moment is ruined."

"I thought you missed Vegas Drake?"

"I didn't say I *missed* him. I was just curious as to where he had gone."

"Ah, my mistake, then." He extended his arm to her. "Shall we?"

She nodded, taking his arm. They stepped out from the trees and started toward the farmhouse. They had only gone a dozen feet when Laney stopped.

Drake frowned down at her. "Laney?"

She smiled, slipping her hand from his as the door opened. Tingles ran over Laney's skin. The lights in the house flashed on. Henry stepped out onto the porch, his eyes scanning the darkness before falling on Laney. A smile broke across his face.

"Laney's back!" he yelled into the house before running for her. Laney met him halfway. He wrapped her in a hug, twirling her around. Jen appeared, pulling Laney into her own hug. And she realized this was what life was. Caring about people, connecting with them.

She met Drake's gaze over Jen's shoulder. He nodded at her. And she smiled. He was right. People were basically good, if given the chance. And these people here were all proof of that. And she would find a way for them to live normal lives again.

She would.

CHAPTER 76

The kitchen was packed with people. Laney sat at the table with Nyssa snuggled in her lap. Cain was doling out pancakes, eggs, bacon, coffee, and everything else he could make as fast as he could make it. He'd already sent food to the other building for the rest of the kids and guards. Henry, Jen, Danny, Lou, Rolly with Susie in his lap, Matt, and Jordan Witt were all around the table, catching Laney up on what was happening.

Cain filled up another tray with plates before nodding at Lou and Rolly. "I'm going to run this up to Molly and the boys. Could you two bring the girls? I think it would do Mary Jane and Molly some good to see them."

Rolly stood, hugging Susie to him. "Happy to." He started to follow Cain from the room.

Laney stood, holding Nyssa. "I'll be right back," she said to everyone before walking with Lou from the room. She stopped Lou at the bottom of the stairs. "So how are you?"

Lou didn't meet her eyes. "I'm good."

"Lou," Laney said quietly. "I know how hard going after Molly must have been. I am so proud of you."

Lou darted a glance at Laney before staring back at the bannister. "I couldn't leave her there. What I went through was bad, but what she went through . . ." Her bottom lip trembled. "You should have seen her, Laney. She was just so scared. And then when Zane —" Lou cut off, taking a deep breath.

Laney hugged Lou tight with one arm, a dozing Nyssa in the other.

Lou's shoulders shook. "She didn't deserve that."

"No, she didn't. And neither did you." They stayed there for a little while, just sharing the pain. And Laney wanted nothing more than to take Lou's from her. But that was not one of her abilities.

Finally Lou pulled back, wiping at her eyes. "I'm sorry."

"Don't you ever apologize for crying. Crying's not a weakness, Lou. It's a sign of how strong you care. And that is not a bad thing. Emotions, how much we care for others, that's what moves us forward when we want to pull back. It's why you went after Molly even though it must have scared the heck out of you."

"I guess."

Laney ran a hand through her hair. "You're stronger than you know, Lou."

Lou gave her a small smile and then took Nyssa from her arms. "I'll take her up, and then I'll stay with Molly, just in case."

Laney squeezed Lou's hand as she stepped on the first step of the staircase.

Lou paused, looking down at Laney. "I'm really glad you're back. We all are."

"I am too."

Lou headed up the stairs, and Laney watched her go. What she'd said was true: There was a core of steel in Lou. She had been through so much, and yet she still loved with all her heart. And as scared as she was, she had gone after Molly. It took strength to do that. And not everyone was that strong. Lou would be okay. Helping Molly, it would actually help Lou as well.

Henry, Matt, and Drake stepped from the kitchen before Laney could reenter it. The looks on their faces were not happy. Dread coursed through Laney. "What?"

Henry nodded to the door. "One of the perimeter guards just contacted us. We have visitors."

CHAPTER 77

Laney stood in the middle of the open space in front of the farmhouse. Headlights appeared in the distance, making their way toward her. Tingles ran over her skin.

"Two," she said to Matt, who stood next to her.

He nodded but didn't reply. Jen and Jordan were with the kids in the other building. They would get them out if things turned sideways. Cain, Lou, and Rolly were upstairs with the McAdamses.

The headlights shifted closer. This guest had not been expected. And had not been given their address. Not that Laney supposed she should be surprised he'd found them.

The Range Rover came to a stop twenty feet away. The driver stepped out, but the headlights made it difficult to make out more than their general shape. Then the driver stepped in front of the lights.

"It's good to see you again, Dr. McPhearson," Bruce Heller said.

Laney crossed her arms over her chest. "It still remains to be seen if the feeling is mutual."

Bruce smiled. "I can understand that."

The back door of the car opened, and another man stepped

forward. Laney tensed. There was something familiar about his shape. It almost looked like—

She gasped as David stepped into the light. He kept a hand on his ribs, and it looked like one of his eyes was closed, but he was somehow standing in front of them.

"How?" she asked.

He tried to smile as he nodded back toward the SUV. "A little divine intervention, I think. I managed to get out of the plane with a good three seconds to spare. But I would have been road-kill if someone hadn't intercepted my fall."

"Speaking of which, why don't the two Fallen who are with you step out of the car?" Laney asked.

Bruce grinned wider. "I've never seen that ability of yours. You really can sense them. Amazing." He shifted his head back toward the car. "Come on out."

Both passenger side doors opened. The first woman who stepped into the light Laney had never seen before. At first she'd thought she was in her forties. She had a slim athletic build with a short brown pixie cut, but as she stepped closer, Laney realized she had misjudged her age by at least two decades. She had to be close to sixty, but she held herself with a quiet physical confidence.

The second woman stepped forward and nodded at Laney. "Good to see you again."

Laney couldn't help but smile. "Maldonado. Good to see you too."

"I took your advice. On the Day of Reckoning."

Laney knew immediately what she was referring to. When Maldonado had dropped her off at the estate after the disastrous meeting with the External Threats Task Force, she had asked Laney what she should do if Elisabeta's threats came true. Laney had told her to save as many as she could. "And how did that go?"

"Very well. And it felt good."

Laney nodded. "I know what you mean."

Bruce frowned, obviously not understanding what they were discussing. Laney saw no need to clue him in.

"And you are?" Laney asked the other woman.

The woman stepped forward offering her hand. "Susan, Susan Jacobs."

Laney shook her hand. "Jacobs. Interesting last name."

Susan smiled, keeping her gaze on Laney. "It's got a long, rich history. My family were some of the earliest settlers in the country. My line settled in Salem."

Laney jolted.

The woman nodded. "Yes, I'm one of those Jacobs."

The Tome of the Great Mother had been buried in the grave of George Jacobs, buried in 1692, one of the victims of the Salem Witch Trials. He'd been identified as a witch by his granddaughter, Meg, who later recanted her testimony against both her grandfather and a Reverend Burroughs. But her recantation came too late. But she recanted anyway, even though by doing so she was signing her own death warrant. She sat in jail in Salem awaiting her own death when the trials were brought to an end by the governor.

Bruce cleared his throat. The woman rolled her eyes. "Yes, yes. *We* are part of those Jacobs."

Laney looked between Susan and Bruce. "'We?'"

Bruce cleared his throat. "As I was about to say, I'd like you to meet Susan Jacobs, the head of the American branch of the Followers of the Great Mother." He paused. "And my mother."

CHAPTER 78

"Your *mother?*"

With every possible variation of this conversation that had run through Laney's head, none had wandered down this particular road.

David winced. "Not to be demanding, but any chance we could move this conversation inside? Where perhaps there might be some coffee and a really soft surface to lie down on?"

Laney realized just how bad off David must be to ask. She glanced at Matt, who nodded back at her. "Of course. Do you need help, David?"

"I would not be adverse to a shoulder to hang on to."

Laney started forward.

David grinned. "Don't suppose Drake is around?"

Laney laughed at the mischievous smile on his face. "Sorry. I'll have to do."

"Any other tall, muscular men that could offer some aid?"

Laney slipped an arm around his waist. "How hard did you hit your head?"

"I think it's the oxygen deprivation. I'm feeling a little loopy." David stumbled as they began to walk.

"I can't believe you made it out of the plane. When we saw it explode, I—" Her words cut off as the fear and grief she felt replayed in her mind.

"I'm all right, Laney. Just a little banged up. I'll be good as new in a few days."

"Thank you for everything. I don't know how we would have gotten back without you."

"You would have found a way. From what I can tell, you always do."

Drake appeared on David's other side. "Look who's returned from the dead."

David sighed with a smile. "Perfect timing." He pitched forward in a dead faint.

Laney gripped him, keeping him from hitting the ground before Drake swept him up in his arms. "I'll put him on the couch."

Drake carried David up the porch stairs as Laney held the door open. Laney smiled, thinking loopy David was going to be annoyed that he had missed out on being carried over the threshold.

Drake laid him on the couch, and Jordan was already there with a blanket to pull over him. He nodded at Laney. "I've got this. Jen went for the first aid kit. We'll keep an eye on him. You go speak with your guests. I'm going to take a trip around the perimeter and make sure they didn't bring any additional friends with them."

My guests. Right. Laney turned for the kitchen and stepped in as Cain was pouring coffee for the deputy director of the CIA.

And his mother.

Bruce took a sip of coffee, his gaze meeting Laney's over the rim of the cup. "I suppose you would like an explanation."

Laney looked from Bruce to Maldonado to Susan. "Yes, I think that is well overdue."

CHAPTER 79

WASHINGTON, D.C.

This time, Shremp had been ready when the President had tried to call him on the carpet.

The President glared at him over the Resolute desk. "And I hear you ordered a strike on a military plane?"

Shremp straightened his shoulders. "I did. I believe Delaney McPhearson was being smuggled back into the country, and I took decisive action."

"You shot down a plane over the United States. Who gave you the authority—"

"*You* did. When you made me the head if the CEI. You should have paid a little more attention to the fine print."

"I will have you removed—"

"You can't. Not without a full hearing by Congress, and they do tend to drag their heels on these things. Besides, it won't exactly make you look like you have a firm grasp on the reins if you admit you knew nothing of it."

The President narrowed her eyes. "Who exactly do you think you are talking to?"

"A soon to be former President." Then he turned on his heel and headed out of her office and the White House. Even as he kept his shoulders straight, his gaze straight ahead, he smoldered.

The air had cooled since Shremp had entered the White House. As he stomped back outside, it felt like a slap in the face. *Another* slap in the face. He waved for his driver to open his door. Without a word to the man, he slid into his seat.

How dare she? He could feel the heat still in his cheeks. He had not been scolded like that since he was a student at St. Mary's. His ears still felt blistered from the tongue-lashing he'd just received. The President had been furious after Mary Jane McAdams's press conference. She'd actually been furious before it, but the press event had sent it to all-new heights.

The driver got behind the wheel and turned to him. "Sir?"

"The facility."

"Yes, sir." The driver started the car, not needing any more instructions than that.

Shremp stewed in the back seat as they pulled through the exit, leaving the grounds of the White House. The first time he'd ever set foot in the White House, he had felt the power the building contained. And he'd felt like a part of it.

Now, though, he did not feel the same. Oh, he had power, but not enough. The President, she had power. And with an army of Fallen, she would have even more. The United States would be unstoppable. *She* would be unstoppable.

He settled back in his seat, calm settling over him. Which was why he planned on making sure she never attained the Omni. He had known his methods would cause some difficulties. Of course, he'd thought he would be able to complete the testing with the subject before he was found out. The first round had only been the healing aspect of the Fallen's skills. It was the later rounds that would have really yielded benefits.

If my people hadn't let her be taken. He curled his fist. The rescue of the girl had delayed his plans. He could not even blame her rescue on that arrogant McPhearson. She'd been in Italy at the time. But blowing her out of the sky, well, that had been rewarding. At least he'd nipped that little problem in the bud.

And the testing had not been a total loss. It was possible that the blood taken from the subject could offer some insight into their abilities, and more importantly, how to reproduce them.

He picked up the phone and dialed. His aide Adam picked up quickly. "Yes, sir?"

"How did the press conference play?"

Adam hesitated. "Our initial polling indicates a great deal of sympathy for the McAdams family and by extension the Fallen. The images of Molly—"

Shremp cut in with a growl. "You mean the Fallen."

"Yes, of course. The images of the Fallen have stirred a great deal of public conversation. The majority of the conversations seem to fall on the side of the Fallen, at least young Fallen. And the treatment. People are struggling, it seems, to accept the idea that it is justified."

"There must be some who support it."

"Of course, of course. Unfortunately, those individuals tend to be rather extreme in their views: white nationalists, anti-immigration groups, anti-feminist men's rights groups. Generally, not groups that appeal to the larger demographic."

Shremp closed his eyes. Damn it. Groups that did not appeal to the larger demographic was a nice way of putting it. Those groups were soundly rejected by the larger population. Anything they supported tended to be automatically and actively rejected by the larger community of people. This was not good.

"We need to find a way to change the narrative. We need to remind people of the horror of the Fallen, remind them how much damage they can do to them and their families. How is the news segment on Samyaza coming?"

"Good. It will actually run tonight. It will highlight the damage she did during her reign and the deaths that are believed to be attributable to her. There is also a segment on the history of Samyaza and the fallen angels that will run on one of the history channels."

Shremp grunted. It was better than nothing but not by much. "Contact the Pegasus Group. Have them create a campaign that will remind people why we need to control the Fallen."

"That's going to cost."

The Pegasus Group was a public relations firm. They had a way of turning water into wine. Or if necessary, wine back into water. And Adam was right, they did not come cheap. "I know. But we need to change the conversation."

"How do you want me to pay for it?"

"Take it out of my personal account. But set up an LLC in Delaware. I don't want anyone tracing it back to me."

Delaware's LLC rules were notoriously lax. They did not require the names of the LLC to be publicly available. In fact, individuals could place a lawyer or agent as the face of the company to further lengthen the distance between owner and public acknowledgment.

"Yes, sir."

"Let me know when you have it set up." Shremp disconnected the call.

He settled back in his seat, watching the scenery fly by. He was taking risks both politically and financially, but it would all pay off in the end. After all, it was the big risks that resulted in the big rewards.

CHAPTER 80

INEZ, KENTUCKY

Susan Jacobs sat across from Laney, calmly sipping her coffee. Laney looked between her and Bruce. To be honest, she could not see any resemblance. Bruce had brown eyes, Susan bright blue. Bruce's hair was a light brown bordering on blonde while Susan's was a rich brown, although that could as easily be the result of a good colorist as much as Mother Nature.

But he was on the short side while she was tall and statuesque. And if she was his mother, she had to be at least seventy, which meant the woman looked incredible for her age. Even their skin tones were different, with Bruce's being a little darker and more olive than his mother's.

Bruce took a last bite of pancakes before he pushed away his plate. "Thank you. That was delicious." He turned to Cain, who stood leaning against the counter. "You are one great chef."

Laney did not like the speculative look in Bruce's eyes. But Cain merely raised his own coffee mug, accepting the compliment without words.

"All right, now perhaps you two can start explaining," Laney said, wanting Bruce's attention to be anywhere but on Cain.

"All right. Where would you like us to start?" Bruce asked.

"How about how you found us?" Henry said. "And have you told anyone else?"

"No. No one else knows. Only the four of us who were in the car," Bruce said.

"And how you found us?" Jake asked.

"I'm afraid that was David. He put a small radioactive tracer on you in Italy. He wanted to make sure he could find you if you got separated. Once we found him, we simply followed the tracer here."

Laney wanted to be mad at him, but he had risked his life to get them here, so she supposed she would give him a pass. At least this time. "How did you find him? Did he contact you?"

Bruce shook his head. "No. In fact, I had no clue as to his whereabouts since he left the Vatican with your uncle. He was not instructed to do that. I have, however, been keeping track of Shremp's activities. When I heard he had ordered a Blackbird to be blown from the skies, I knew it was David bringing you back into the country."

"Wait, that was *Shremp*? He tried to kill us?" Laney asked.

"So it appears. To be honest, I'm surprised. He's ambitious, immoral, and greedy, but that was a bold move. He must think he's got something that will protect him politically."

"Any idea what that is?"

"No."

"But even with that, how'd you know it was David, Laney, and Drake on the plane?" Jake asked.

Bruce shrugged. "There are only a few people who have access to that plane. A quick check showed there were no scheduled flights for it. And that it took off from Ramstein. It wasn't hard to deduce that David had led you over the border."

"Why didn't you stop Shremp from shooting it down?" Henry asked.

"Because then he would know I was watching him. And besides, that is not as simple to do as one would expect, even for me. So we tracked the plane. When it was shot down, we were quite a distance away. My mother and Maldonado immediately ran for the site after we calculated where any survivors would land." He nodded to his mother. "My mother was able to grab David before he hit, managing to spare him most of the damage that he would have sustained without her aid."

Laney raised her eyebrows at that. Susan smiled in response. "I'm spry for my age."

"So it seems." Laney looked between her and Bruce. "So how exactly does the son of the leader of the Followers end up being one of the heads of the CIA?"

Bruce started to answer, but Susan put a hand on his, and he automatically went quiet.

Interesting.

"I came into my powers when I was seventeen. At the time, I thought I was the Devil incarnate. You see, I was raised by Followers. We revered the Great Mother and her good deeds. We emulated them where we could. I dedicated myself early on to furthering her mission, and I was being groomed to take over the Followers one day. And then I learned I was a Fallen."

Susan gripped her mug. "I was devastated. I was terrified. All I knew of Fallen were that they were constantly trying to destroy the good work the Great Mother had tried to build up."

"They're not all bad," Laney said.

Susan smiled. "I know that now. But at the time, we no longer had access to the book. All we had were the stories that came down to us. And in them there was one common theme—the Fallen were the bad guys."

"So what did you do?" Henry asked.

"I did what anyone in my position would do—I joined the Church. I began the process to become a nun."

Laney didn't think she could be more shocked.

Susan shrugged. "I figured if there was any organization that could help me restrain my dark side, it would be the Church, plus I would be able to work for the Followers through the Church."

"But you didn't become a nun," Jake said.

She smiled. "No. A fateful trip to Rome helped me understand more about my nature. I met a group of nuns over there. Incredibly kind, smart women who opened my eyes to the true nature of the Fallen."

Laney met her gaze.

Susan nodded in response. "Yes. I learned about the European branch of the Followers."

Bruce's head snapped up. Apparently, this information was new to him.

"They taught me that being a Fallen did not destine me to be evil. That Fallen, like everyone else, were given the chance to choose every step of their lives, whether to use their gifts for good or evil. With Fallen, though, the temptation to do evil is greater because the rewards can be so much richer, quite literally.

"After my time in Rome, I realized the life of a nun was not for me, but my commitment to the Followers had only deepened. I dedicated my life to spreading her message and working behind the scenes to put people in positions so that one day, if needed, we could aid you."

Laney looked to Bruce. "Are you a Follower as well?"

He nodded. "Since I was a child. When I came to live with my mother, she began teaching me about the Great Mother."

"'Came to live with'?" Henry asked.

Bruce nodded. "I bounced around foster care for the first six years of my life before my mom found me."

Susan gave his hand a little squeeze. He held on to it as she spoke. "I worried about having my own children, about passing my abilities on. What if I could not keep them from giving in to the temptation? What if they unleashed evil on this world? I couldn't take the chance, so I never had any biological children." She smiled. "I have never regretted that choice. As it turns out, my children were already out in the world, just waiting for me to find them."

Bruce Heller of the CIA had come from a loving family. Laney didn't know why, but that truly shocked her. She had to admit to having a bias against people who chose that kind of work.

Jordan appeared in the doorway. "More guests are arriving."

Laney stood up. "Who?"

"Yoni. And—"

Laney.

Laney's heart leapt, and she blurred from the room and out the front door. Yoni was just stepping out of a black Yukon. Cleo nearly knocked him over in her haste to get out behind him.

"Hey, hey!" Yoni yelled as he grabbed on to the door to keep from falling.

But Cleo bolted past him. She sprinted for Laney. Laney blurred toward Cleo, tackling her and rolling with her on the ground. Cleo nuzzled the side of Laney's neck as she laughed. "Oh, I missed you so much."

Moxy and Princess barked, jumping around Laney and Cleo before running excitedly for the porch. Tiger approached, nuzzling Laney from the other side. Laney wrapped her arms around both of them as she sat up. A picture of Nyssa appeared in Laney's mind. She nodded at Tiger. "She's all right. She's upstairs. Go on."

Tiger sprinted for the house, stopping at the door to rub against Cain, who held the door open for him. Susan and Bruce watched the scene.

Susan's mouth was slightly open. "I had heard about this ability, but to see it . . ."

"Hey, Lanes." Yoni walked up.

Laney got to her feet and hugged him tightly. "What are you doing here? I thought you were in Arizona."

"I was, but when I heard about the estate I thought I'd come back and check on Dom. I ran into these guys when I was about to climb over the gate. They showed me a back way in."

"Thank you for finding them. How's Dom?"

Yoni's gaze snapped to her, his smile dropping from his face. "You don't know?"

"Know? Know what?"

"Dom wasn't there."

"Wasn't there? But he never—"

Yoni shook his head. "I—I went over his security tapes. They . . . the government. They took him, Laney. I thought you guys knew. I thought you already had a plan to get him back."

Oh my God. Laney's hand flew to her mouth. She'd never imagined they would do that. Dom never left the estate. They thought he'd be safe.

"Where? Where did they take him?"

"I don't know, Laney. But, Laney, how they treated him . . ." His words drifted off.

Laney felt light-headed. This was her fault. Dom had made the Omni, the Mortus. What if they knew? What if that was why they took him? Her stomach rolled, and she knew she was going to be sick. "We have to find him."

Bruce stepped forward. "I may be able to help with that."

CHAPTER 81

BLUEFIELD, VIRGINIA

The man towered over Dom as he lay curled up on the cold floor. "The Omni, Doctor. We know you made it for McPhearson."

Dom blocked the man's voice out. He closed his eyes, the events on the estate playing out like a movie in his mind.

Dom paced the large room of the bomb shelter. His hands shook. He could not seem to stop shaking. He had made sure that Henry's security feeds stayed up all over the estate, making sure they recorded every single thing the agents did when they were on Chandler property. But that meant he saw everything they did to the McAdamses.

He took a shaky breath, wiping at a tear. He still couldn't believe they had shot Molly. Besides Danny, Molly was the other child that he thought he understood. She was like him. Quiet, shy, but always watching. She was just a sweet, sweet kid. And those agents had shot her down like she was a rabid dog.

Mary Jane's screams ran through his mind again, and his pulse raced. It was all falling apart. He knew it would.

Henry and Jen had led the kids through the tunnel. Mustafa and Matt were supposed to pick them up. Henry had wanted him to go too. But Dom said no. He couldn't. He looked at the screen where the agents were trying to get through his blast door at the surface. He had not stepped off the Chandler Estate in decades. And it wasn't that he wouldn't like to see the rest of the world. There were many things out there he wanted to see.

But he couldn't. The only time he had even left the bunker was when Henry had gone missing. And it had taken all of his courage to get himself to the main house. But leaving the estate? Going out into that world? No, he couldn't do it. The world outside was filled with dangers he was not equipped to handle. Even the thought of it made him feel off-kilter, as if the walls were moving in.

He paused to look at the security screens. A smaller man stepped up to the camera, a small device held in his hands. He attached wires to the lock. A few seconds later, it popped open. Dom opened and closed his fists. What do I do? What do I do? They're going to get in. I can't stop them.

He watched the screens. They were through the second blast door. They'd be here any minute. He could lock himself in the laboratory, but it wouldn't help. If they could get through the blast doors, they could get through the lock on his lab door with no problem.

He glanced at the back hall. He'd covered the opening where Henry and all the kids had escaped. For a split second he considered following them. But even the idea of walking down that dark tunnel made him dizzy. He wouldn't make it. He would collapse before he got more than a few feet.

And he hated it. He hated that he couldn't go out in the world. But he had learned early on how horrible the world could be. His parents had died in a car crash, along with Dom's brother and sister. He'd been fifteen. The world had been a cold place after that, even though he had an aunt who took him in and loved him. But when he turned twenty-

two, she had been killed. Just a random mugging. The perpetrator had never been caught, not that it truly would have mattered if he had been. It wouldn't bring her back.

He'd retreated from the world at that point. Henry had offered him a place, inspired by his research. First he'd lived on the estate in one of the houses. But then he'd had a complete breakdown after 9/11. He couldn't function. Henry had gotten him the best psychiatrists, but Henry was the one that finally realized what Dom needed—a safe place. He'd had the bomb shelter built for him.

Dom looked around. He'd called this place home for years. It had been a safe place. He'd found happiness here. He'd found a family here. He'd never thought he'd have that. And no one looked at him funny because he couldn't leave. They just moved things down here or even brought him along via FaceTime.

And now, now the outside world was finally coming for him.

The alarm at the front door went off. Dom covered his ears as the red lights flashed. They were through the front door. Unknown feet rushed toward him. Dom's eyes watered, and he couldn't make out faces. It was as if a group of faceless humanoids was swarming toward him.

The loud buzzing that had started in the back of his mind drowned out all other sounds. One of the faceless humanoids raised his arm. Was he saying something? What did they want?

Something slammed into Dom's back, and he pitched forward onto his knees. His glasses flew off. He reached for them, but large black boots kicked them away. His arms were yanked behind his back. Dom thought he cried out, but he couldn't be sure. It all felt so unreal.

A man crouched down. This close, he could almost make out his features. But the buzzing... he couldn't hear anything the man said. He shook his head, feeling his tears roll off his chin.

The man leaned forward, his mouth angry, spittle flying into Dom's face. The man brought the back of his hand across Dom's cheek. Pain exploded across it as he toppled to the side.

Dom curled his knees to his chest, ducking his head down. No one *touched him, but he wouldn't have even noticed. He'd shrunk far into his mind, repeating a single phrase over and over again.*

Nowhere is safe. Nowhere is safe. Nowhere is safe.

∼

DOM'S BREATH HITCHED, and he pulled his arms over his chest, feeling the panic all over again. "Nowhere is safe. Nowhere is safe. Nowhere is safe."

"Guy's losing it again," someone called. Dom wasn't sure who spoke. Pain lanced through his arm, and his vision dimmed.

"Nowhere is safe. Nowhere is safe. Nowhere is . . ."

CHAPTER 82

INEZ, KENTUCKY

The shed was more than a little crowded. Henry, Jen, Laney, Yoni, Cleo, and Bruce all hovered over Danny as his hands flew over the keyboard. Drake had taken one look at them all crowded in there and decided to do a security sweep.

Bruce leaned forward, his hand on the back of Danny's chair. "Okay, so to get into the Department of Defense, you'll need my password. It's—"

"I'm already in," Danny said. "I'm going to black ops, right?"

Bruce stared down at him. "How did you— You know what, doesn't matter. But when this is done, you and I, young man, need to discuss your job opportunities in intelligence work."

Henry crossed his arms over his chest, his voice deep and brooking no argument. "No, you don't."

Laney bit back a smile as Bruce jumped. She had a feeling he didn't scare easily. But a seven-foot-two Nephilim sounding like the voice of God with the unmistakable hint of violence in his voice would make anyone jump.

"There should be a file in there labeled SD-132," Bruce said.

Danny didn't say anything, but the screen flashed as he scoured through screen after screen. Finally, he nodded. "Got it."

A spreadsheet appeared on the monitor. Laney peered over Danny's shoulder. "What is this?"

"A list of all locations Shremp has visited since he became the head of the CEI. Can I get in there?" Bruce asked. Danny scooted over, and Bruce pulled up a chair. He grabbed the mouse and began scrolling through the file.

"The Department of Defense keeps that close an eye on him?" Laney asked.

Bruce smiled but kept his gaze on the screen. "Not intentionally. I may have had one of my people add a tracker to his car that automatically updates every twenty minutes."

"Because you knew what he was planning?" Jen asked.

"Because my job is to gather information. So I gather it on everyone that could be important." Bruce stopped scrolling, highlighting one cell. "There."

It was an address in western Virginia. "What's there?" Henry asked.

Danny's fingers flew over the keyboard for a few seconds before he answered. "According to the IRS, a government warehouse that stores old IRS files."

"And according to reality?" Jen asked.

"Oh, it *is* a government warehouse that stores old IRS files." Bruce paused. "It also contains three levels under the building that are used for secret government testing. It's a biological weapons manufacturing site."

Laney's jaw dropped. "You're kidding."

"I'm afraid not. It's been in operation since 9/11."

Laney shook her head in disbelief, even though it made sense. In 1975, the Biological Weapons Convention treaty was ratified, making it the first multilateral disarmament treaty banning the development, production, and stockpiling of an entire category of weapons of mass destruction. But a few decades later, the U.S.

determined that testing non-lethal biological agents did not violate the spirit of the treaty. And after 9/11, all sorts of activities previously considered off limits became fair game.

Bruce shrugged. "Well, not to sound like a petulant teenager, but everybody's doing it."

"How do you know Dom's there?" Henry asked.

"I don't for sure. But being your friend is a scientist, and given the list of places Shremp has visited, this makes the most sense. I can contact my team and get satellite footage that can confirm he's there. It might take a little—"

"Got it." Danny hit a button, and satellite images of the facility flashed onto the screen.

Bruce looked at him, shaking his head. "Seriously, kid, if you ever want a job—"

"He doesn't. *Ever*," Henry said.

On screen, a large white warehouse with a flat roof and a ten-foot chain-link fence surrounding it came into view. There was a guardhouse at the gate with two guards and another two guards patrolling the area, one with a large German shepherd.

A large SUV pulled up to the gate, and after a short conversation the SUV was waved through. It pulled to a stop in front of the door. Danny zoomed in as Shremp stepped out. Danny fast-forwarded until Shremp exited the building. Laney glanced at the clock. He'd been inside for less than an hour, and he did not look happy.

"Well, somebody's a little upset," Jen murmured.

"I'm going to go back to just after the attack on the estate." The image on the screen shifted as Danny backtracked to the day before. A few cars had come and gone, but they appeared to just be people who worked at the facility.

"Hold on," Laney said as a Humvee appeared on the screen. The Humvee idled by the gate while the driver spoke with the guard.

Danny's hands flew over the keyboard, an image appearing in

one of the other monitors. "It's a government plate. It's being used by the CEI."

Laney nodded but said nothing as the Humvee was waved through. It pulled up to the front of the building. Four soldiers stepped out of the Humvee, looking around.

"What are they doing?" Danny asked.

"Making sure there are no witnesses," Jen said quietly.

Finally, the driver nodded. Danny zoomed in as they opened the back of the truck. A man was pulled out. Two soldiers grabbed him under the arms and started to carry him into the building.

Danny gave a strangled cry. Even with the black-and-white picture and his eyes closed, the damage to Dom's left eye was clear. It was swollen. A dark substance, which Laney assumed was blood, had dropped onto his shirt. He gave no sign that he knew where he was.

"Is he—"

"He's alive," Bruce said quickly. "They wouldn't bother bringing him there otherwise."

Henry stepped forward. "We need to get him out of there. Dom, he's not equipped to deal with the outside world. A drive outside the estate would stress him to the point of a breakdown. This—" Henry's hand shook as he pointed at the screen. "I don't know how bad the damage something like this could do to him."

"Is there surveillance inside the facility?" Jen asked.

"Yes, but it's contained onsite. There's no way to access it from outside," Bruce said.

Her throat feeling tight, Laney watched as they dragged Dom inside and he disappeared behind the door. She'd set him up for this. She'd asked him to make the Omni. The government wanted the Omni, and now in their minds they had a way to get it. They didn't care that they would destroy a man to do it.

"If he gives them what they want, he'll be fine," Bruce said.

Laney shook her head, wiping as a tear tried to escape the corner of her eye. "He won't give them the formula. Dom is many things, but what he is above all else is loyal. He won't tell them."

Dom had been the one who had helped her go on the run. And he never told a soul how to find her, even as Henry and Jake scoured the world looking for her. He had kept everyone safe by not revealing what he knew.

"They have ways to make people comply," Bruce said quietly.

"Laney's right." Henry placed his hand on Laney's shoulder. She reached up and held on to it, needing the support. "Dom won't tell them. With his psychological state, even if he wanted to, I'm not sure he would be able to communicate with them."

Danny looked up at Henry, horror in his eyes. "He's been with them for days."

Laney swallowed. Dom had been out of his bunker for days, surrounded by unfriendly faces. She felt light-headed, imagining the terror, the horror he must be experiencing. And if the treatment of Molly was any indication, then they were not going to be going at him with kid gloves.

"So what's the plan?" Bruce asked.

"We're going in. We're getting Dom," Laney said.

Henry and Jen nodded back at her.

Bruce looked at each of them. "Understand that if you do this, if you go get Dom out, you will have to hurt American soldiers. There is no way around that. You will be declaring war on the U.S. government."

Laney wanted to deny what Bruce was saying. She wanted to find another argument, a way to spin this that was not a declaration of war. But he was right. If they took this step, that was exactly what they would be doing. When she had taken out Samyaza, she had hoped that was the end of the war. But it turned out that was just the beginning.

"We already took down American soldiers when we got Molly out," Jake said.

Bruce turned to look at him. "You were saving a child. And

they were part of the External Threats Task Force. That can be spun. But this? This is different. Dom is a material witness. You will be attacking a federal facility, a *top-secret* federal facility. So make no mistake, if you go after him, you *are* declaring war on the U.S. government."

Laney looked at the faces of each of the people in the room. They all nodded back at her. She shook her head. "No. We're not declaring war. The U.S. government already declared war on us. We're getting Dom back."

CHAPTER 83

Bruce had gotten them all the information he could on the facility. Danny had downloaded the schematics, and Bruce was filling in the gaps. Everyone else was either getting ready for the rescue or preparing to move the kids again.

Laney had taken the time to grab a quick shower, being it had been days, and she managed to call her uncle on a phone Danny assured her couldn't be traced as long as she kept her conversation short. He assured her he was fine, and he sounded more worried about her. She couldn't tell him much, because she didn't trust that someone wasn't overhearing their conversation, but when she got off the phone, she promised herself she'd figure out a way to get him back with all of them.

A few minutes later, when she stepped out onto the porch, Susan was the only one out there, sitting quietly in a rocker.

She walked over and joined Laney at the railing. "It's quite a group of people you have here."

"They are the best."

Susan looked over her shoulder, and Laney followed her gaze. Cain was heading up the stairs with a pot of coffee, no doubt for Mary Jane.

"He's Cain, isn't he?"

Laney jolted, looking for Bruce, but there was no one within earshot. "What makes you say that?"

"The book was buried with my great-great-great-grandfather. But the stories and traditions remain. He looks just like the description: Hair dark as an ebony stone, and eyes as dark as night." Susan raised her eyebrow.

Laney did not indicate any response to the words. "I don't know what you are referring to."

Susan smiled. "When I saw him on the coronation dais with you, I wondered. When I saw him leap in front of you, taking the shot, I thought for sure I must be wrong. After all, Cain, *the* Cain, would never make such a sacrifice for anyone, would he? But then the agents who shot at you dropped themselves. Somehow you got the world's first murderer on your side. Any doubts I had about whether or not you were the real deal were put to rest."

Laney studied Susan for a long moment. "What about your son? Does he have doubts?"

"Bruce has spent his professional life figuring people out. He can read people within minutes of meeting them. It's how he knew Maldonado was hiding something. It's how he knew at that meeting that you were the most powerful person in that room."

Laney raised an eyebrow. "I thought that meeting was classified."

"My son does not reveal state secrets, but he knows that certain obligations supersede political ones. But I want you to know, we are both on your side."

"Even though the two of you keep information from each other."

"We both play roles in our lives that require us to hold secrets close to the chest."

"Like the fact that you knew about the European Followers."

Susan nodded. "Yes, and I know I walked in here with the king of spooks and a convenient story to explain why, even though we are mother and son, and we look nothing alike. And a claim to a group that you are not even sure exists anymore. You do not trust me. I do not blame you for that. But I hope one day you realize I am an ally is this fight, as all my ancestors have been. And that when you need my help and that of the others, that we stand ready to aid you."

"Others?"

"There are three dozen of us. Followers all. And if you need us, we stand willing to help."

Laney studied her, her mind whirling.

"What is it?" Susan asked.

Laney gave her a small smile. "If you are telling the truth, my uncle Patrick would really love to talk to you." Mentioning him gave her a pang of regret. She wished he was here.

"I've heard a great deal about him. I hope we get the chance to meet him someday."

"Me too."

"I have some connections. I will let people who want to go underground know where to go. I'll hide them until I can get them to you."

Laney hesitated.

"You have no reason to trust me. But I hope you can find it in yourself to do it anyway. I want to help."

Drake's words drifted through her mind. *People are basically good*. Logic told her not to trust her because Susan was right: All her explanations were perfect. But there was something about her that made Laney *want* to trust her. And truth was, she needed help.

She nodded. "Okay. Find the ones you can. I'll contact you when I have a place arranged to hide them."

"My people are already putting out feelers to the Fallen community."

"There's a community?"

"After the Day of Reckoning, the Fallen came out of the woodwork. Some to help, some not. But those that helped, they've struggled with going back to their normal lives. People look at them differently. So online, they speak with one another, sometimes meet up at community centers. Under different banners, of course. But they're starting to connect. The government is keeping track of them, of course, but we have ways to get around that. If someone wants or needs to run, we'll provide an escape route."

Laney nodded. "Good. Thank you, Susan."

Susan glanced down the hall, lowering her voice. "Bruce does not know about the Fallen community, at least not through me. I think we should keep it that way."

"You don't trust him?"

"I do. But he is in a difficult position. He will get information that can help us before any of us can. But he also must answer to some higher-ups. I prefer not to add to that burden by making him keep more hidden away."

"It must make it difficult for you two."

Susan shook her head. "No. We both just try to protect the other one as much as we can. It's what you do when you love someone, as you well know."

Laney looked down the hall where Jen, Jake, Henry, and Lou were packing food into bags. "Yeah."

"I'm going to make some phone calls. When Bruce is finished, we'll take our leave. It has been a great pleasure to meet you, Delaney. I look forward to working with you in the future." Susan held out her hand.

Laney shook it. "And I you."

Susan gave her a smile before stepping off the porch and heading toward the SUV where Maldonado waited.

Laney slipped into the house as Jake and Henry walked down the hall toward her.

Jake glanced out the door to where Susan stood. "Can we trust her?"

"I think so."

"That's not very convincing," Henry said.

She sighed. "No. It's not. But sometimes you just need to take a leap."

Laney looked at the men in front of her. They were living proof of the good in this world. Five years ago, she hadn't known either of them. Now, they had each saved each other's lives dozens of times.

"Thank you," she said quietly, "for always being there. I couldn't have done half of what I've done without you two in my corner."

"Hey, that's what triads are for."

Laney startled at that. She'd almost forgotten. The ring bearer always came as a package deal with two other people. For her, they were Henry and Jake. But their circle had expanded so much, it was easy to forget that destiny and prophecy often only spoke of the three of them.

Henry nodded back to the kitchen. "We'll be ready to go in another few minutes. We've figured out who's going with the exception of Drake. Is he coming?"

Laney frowned. "Probably, but actually, I haven't seen him since the shed. Have either of you?"

Both men shook their heads.

"I'm going to go scout around for him. Don't leave without me, okay?"

"Wouldn't dream of it." Henry kissed her cheek before heading outside.

"I'm going to check on the McAdams." Jake headed up the stairs.

Laney pulled out her phone and called Drake but got no reply. She frowned.

Drake, where are you?

CHAPTER 84

BLUEFIELD, VIRGINIA

"Sir."

Shremp's eyes flew open. He looked around, seeing the tall chain-link fence ahead.

"We're almost here, sir."

"Yes, yes, fine." Shremp wiped the side of his mouth while trying to clear his mind of cobwebs. He opened a bottle of water, taking a long drink as the driver pulled up to the guardhouse.

The window next to him lowered. The guard nodded at him. "Senator."

"How's it been this morning?"

"Quiet. It's always quiet."

"That's what I want to hear."

"Yes, sir."

Shremp rolled the window back up as the driver headed forward. There was a large building inside the ten-foot chain-link fence. It was a white three-story-high warehouse with a flat roof. If not for the fence and the guards, the location would be completely unremarkable.

The SUV pulled to a stop. Shremp straightened his tie, running his hands down the front of his suit jacket to work out any wrinkles. His driver opened the door. He stepped out, buttoning his suit jacket as he looked around. A light wind blew, rustling the leaves on the other side of the fence. There were no buildings in sight, just trees. The sight of them made Shremp uneasy. He'd grown up in Manhattan, on the Upper East Side. The only trees he'd seen growing up were in cement squares along the edges of some streets. Occasionally his family's driver would go through Central Park. Shremp had always looked at it with distaste. Why anyone would want to spend time outdoors when the indoors were so much cleaner, so much more civilized, was completely beyond him.

He turned from the fence. "Wait here," he instructed the driver without looking at him.

Two guards stood at the door. One opened it. "Senator Shremp, if you'll follow me."

Shremp followed the man into the building. Rows and rows of file cabinets lined the place. The other two floors had the same setup: no offices, just aisles and aisles of files. There must be millions of pieces of paper in the space.

But Shremp wasn't interested in any of that. The soldier led him to a large freight elevator in the back.

"You have your key, sir?"

Shremp pulled the key from his pocket.

"Very good." The soldier opened the gates of the elevator. Shremp stepped in and placed his key in the slot on the elevator panel, which only listed three floors. Shremp turned the key to the left when the soldier had secured the gate. The elevator shuddered and then began to descend. The floors underneath the facility could only be accessed with the key. He pulled the key from the panel, slipping it back into his pocket as the elevator came to a stop.

A different soldier opened the gates. "Senator."

He strode past the man. A man and woman in suits stood waiting for him, Agents Barbara Frankel and Roger Hennessey of the External Threats Task Force and now part of the CEI.

Frankel nodded. "Good afternoon, Senator."

Shremp ignored the greeting. "What have you learned?"

"Nothing," Hennessey said.

Shremp narrowed his eyes, his anger spiking. "What? You've had him for days."

"The subject is psychologically fragile," Frankel said.

Shremp glared at her. "Psychologically fragile? Why the hell do I care about that? The goal is to break him. If he's 'psychologically fragile,' half your job should already be done."

Hennessey grunted, his lips tightening as he glared back at Shremp.

"You have something to say?" Shremp demanded.

Barbara put a hand up in front of Hennessey. "We have called in a specialist, but it would probably be easier if we just showed you what the problem is. If you'll follow me?"

Shremp strode forward, ignoring the Neanderthal Hennessey. He hated his type. Tall, strong, they always thought they held all the power. Well, Shremp was going to teach them all what real power was. Brawn was a weapon, but intelligence, that was where the true power was. And Roger looked like the type to struggle with simple instructions.

Frankel stopped at a door midway down the hall. "This is an observation room. The subject will not be able to see or hear you, but you will be able to both see and hear him."

"Fine, fine. Open the door." Shremp gestured to the door.

Frankel stepped inside. A large observation window dominated one side of the room. Shremp strode over to it, peering into the room on the other side. The room was bare bones. The only furniture in the room was a cot, a toilet, and a small sink. And its one occupant wasn't making use of any of it. Instead, he was sitting on the ground, his knees pulled up to his chest, rocking back and forth in the corner of the room.

Shremp frowned, trying to figure out if the man was faking. "How long has he been like this?"

"Since he was brought in."

Shremp studied the man. Tears stained his face, although every once in a while one would cascade down his cheek. He was shaking and sitting in a pool of water. Or at least Shremp hoped it was a pool of water. He watched him for a few minutes, looking for any sign the man was faking. But he never wavered.

He grunted. "Psychologically fragile" may have undersold the man's state. "When will the specialist arrive?"

"Two hours."

Shremp nodded. He wasn't happy with the delay, but even he could tell questioning the man would be useless. He wasn't sure there was any way they could get any information out of him.

The man's lips were moving, but Shremp couldn't make it out. "What is he saying?"

Frankel walked over to a panel on the wall and turned up the microphone in the room. The man's words became clear. He repeated the same phrase over and over again.

"Nowhere is safe. Nowhere is safe. Nowhere is safe."

CHAPTER 85

INEZ, KENTUCKY

Laney called Drake a few more times and couldn't reach him. She did a quick run of the perimeter and even a few miles out but got no sense of him. She stopped now on the edge of the woods, watching people load crates into the back of the SUVs.

Images of Dom flitted through her mind along with feelings of panic. What if they were too late and irreparable damage had already been done?

Why didn't I check on him sooner?

She stepped back into the woods, not wanting anyone to see the panic coursing through her. *My God, they took Dom. Dom.* He was harmless.

It's your fault. They took him because of you. The voices had been stirring at the back of her mind ever since she had learned about his capture.

Laney sat at the base of a tall tree, leaning her head back and closing her eyes. Laney had to admit, she was scared. Dom was not like the rest of them. His brain, in multiple ways, worked differently. He could not handle all the stimuli of the outside world. Henry had created a world where he could live, where he could thrive. And Laney had seen him really come out of his shell in the last few years. But now she worried that when they got him back he would be a shell of his former self.

A sensation rolled over her.

Here.

She called silently to Cleo's request. Cleo slipped through the trees to Laney's right, her footfalls barely audible. A picture of Zane flowed through her mind. Laney felt the weight of that death too.

I'm sorry, Cleo.

Cleo lay down next to her, resting her head on Laney's thighs with a sigh.

Okay?

Laney thought about lying, but Cleo would know. *No. I'm worried about Dom. About all the kids. About all of us. The government is coming for us. I don't know how to protect everyone against that.*

Cats safe?

For now. Gerard and Noriko got to the other site without running into any problems.

What now?

What now? That was the question she had been discussing inside with Henry, Jen, Mustafa, Matt, and anybody else who wanted to chime in. They had a plan in place for getting Dom out. They'd leave within the hour. But the bigger question still needed to be answered: then what?

They would get Dom out and they would all still be in hiding. It would only be a matter of time before the government found them. When she'd been on the run, it had been easier. She only had to worry about herself. She could move easily from place to place. But now they had over three dozen people, not to mention the cats.

Henry was trying to find somewhere they could go. But where was safe? As far as Laney could tell, every government on the

Earth was targeting Fallen. They could not trust any of them. So where did that leave them? They could move from place to place, but with a group their size, that would attract attention.

Where Drake? Cleo asked silently.

Actually, I don't know.

She ran her hand through Cleo's fur, the rhythm of the action calming her. The connection between the two of them was deep and real. Being away from Cleo never felt right. Even now, when everything was dark, Cleo's presence was soothing.

Cleo lifted her head.

"What is it?"

Drake back. Looking for you. Cleo stood, stretching.

Laney frowned, not sure how Cleo knew that but trusted her impression. They made their way back to the farmhouse. And sure enough, Drake's familiar shape was the first body she picked out of the lineup on the porch. And as always, her heart ticked up a beat at the sight of him.

In a blur, he was in front of her. "There you are."

"Here I am. But where were you?"

"Looking for a place to hide your little group of rebels." He smiled.

Hope sprang inside of her. "And?"

"I've got one. You should all be safe there."

"Where is it? Is it secure?"

"Very secure. I will have Henry help me make arrangements while you go take care of Dom."

"You're not coming?"

"No. I will be needed here to make sure everything goes smoothly. I will escort the first group. And I have no doubt you will be able to extricate your unusual friend without my aid."

While Laney knew he was right, she still would have preferred to have him by her side. He must have read her emotions on her face.

He reached up, trailing his fingers across her cheek. "I would prefer to be with you as well, but this requires my personal touch, I'm afraid." Drake paused. "Do you want me to go get your uncle?"

Laney looked up into Drake's face and knew if she said yes, he would find a way to get to her uncle and get him back here. She shook her head. "No. I believe Bas will keep him safe. And right now, we need to make sure we can all get to this spot."

"I do believe Bas and Angelica will keep him safe, but you should call him, tell him you're all right."

Laney smiled. "Already did. Now where are we going? Where is this hiding spot?"

He leaned forward and kissed her gently on the lips. "Bolivia. I'm taking them to a former hiding spot for the Tree."

The image of a giant willow appeared in her mind. "That's brilliant."

He bowed. "It is indeed. But they will not be able to enter without me. I will have to accompany them. It hasn't been used in thousands of years."

"Sounds homey."

Drake laughed. "It will be. The hiding spot takes on the appearance the archangel wishes it to be."

"Wait, you mean Remiel chose a dark cave with a bottomless pit?"

Drake nodded. "He's a somber fellow."

Laney groaned. "Please tell me you're not going to make it look like the Vegas strip."

Drake flashed her a wicked grin. "Complete with topless bars and neon as far as the eye can see."

Laney dropped her head. "That's it. I'm turning myself in."

Drake chuckled, tipping up her chin. "Just kidding. You'll love it."

Laney nodded, her mind whirling. "Will cell phones work inside?"

"No. Someone will have to exit the location to call or even receive calls."

She nodded. "All right."

Drake frowned. "What are you planning?"

"Susan mentioned something about a community of Fallen, if they need to go into hiding, I'll need to find a way to contact her."

Drake's eyebrows rose. "I see. I'll need to increase the size, then."

"Is that a problem?"

"Not for me."

Jake walked off the porch, directing people to the SUVs.

"I believe that is your cue."

Laney nodded, watching the group of people loading into the vans. Jen, Mustafa, Yoni, Matt, Hanz, and Jordan she expected. But her heart skipped a beat at the sight of Lou, Rolly, and Danny climbing in.

"What are they doing?"

"They insisted," Drake said.

Laney started toward them. "No, absolutely not."

Drake stepped in front of her, blocking her way. "Laney, Dom is their friend."

"But they're children."

"Not anymore. Besides, Danny is needed to access the building's security and copy their feeds. Matt wants to make sure that Dom's treatment is documented."

Laney's shoulders slumped. "God, I hate this."

"I know. But you'll have Dom back shortly, and then we'll all be safely hidden away. This will be over soon."

Laney shook her head, because only the first two parts of his statement were correct. They would get Dom back then they would be hidden away. But she knew that it would be a long, long time before this was all over.

CHAPTER 86

BLUEFIELD, VIRGINIA

Dom's heart raced. He knew if it kept beating so hard he'd pass out, maybe have a heart attack. He'd passed out on the car ride here. That had been good. Unconscious was better than conscious right now.

Without his glasses, he could only see vague shapes. Movement from the corner of his eyes told him the bad woman was back. Dom could see her, he could almost hear her, but the buzzing was still growing, blocking all sounds out. And that was okay. That was good. Because it made it easier to not be here.

He closed his eyes. In his mind, he wasn't here. He was at his kitchen table with everyone sitting around him, eating dinner. He'd had to get a bigger table last year. There were too many people now coming to his Sunday dinners. He'd had twenty-two one Sunday night. He smiled as Lou swatted at Rolly. Danny caught his gaze and smiled at him. He loved these dinners.

These last few years had been the happiest of his life. When he'd met Danny, his life had improved more than he ever thought possible. Danny was another lost soul like him. But then Laney had arrived. And she'd brought with her Jake, Lou, Rolly, Jen, Cleo, Max, Patrick. All of a sudden his tiny, lonely little world had exploded with people. And he hadn't been scared. He'd embraced them. All of them.

Slowly he felt the change inside him. The recognition that maybe, just maybe, the world was better than he remembered. And even though he'd never told anyone, he thought that maybe he could start joining in again. He wasn't planning anything big. Maybe having dinner one night at Patrick and Cain's or walking around the estate with Cleo. Just small little journeys that for him a few years ago would have been the equivalent of manning his own rocket to the Moon.

But then Elisabeta had begun her reign of terror. Dom could read the winds of change. He didn't need Max's abilities to see what was coming. He could tell the governments would want more once the Fallen were discovered. They would want the Omni.

He didn't regret making it for Laney. She had brought so much into his life. He could see now how empty, how quiet it had been before. She had given him a chance to be important, to make a real difference. He had helped her protect people, people he didn't know and would never meet and people he would die to protect. When Mustafa had arrived with the request, he'd immediately known that the government would one day come for him. Part of him had thought that Laney and Henry would be able to keep him safe, but he knew that more likely than not, one day, they would get to him. But he still would have made the same choice.

He knew the formula for the Omni. He forgot nothing. And like so many other facts, that information was locked away in his mind. But he would never tell them. He would never betray Laney's trust. It was the least he owed her for all she'd brought into his life. So he would lock it away, just like he'd locked himself away from the world.

He'd lock it away. Lock himself away. Away from the pain, away from the hurt. The buzzing grew louder as he pulled his knees to his chest and rocked back and forth.

Lock it away. Lock it away. Lock it away.

CHAPTER 87

Shremp had booked a hotel near the facility. He didn't want to make the long trip back to D.C. only to have to turn around and return, because he wanted to be there when the man finally gave up the information he was looking for.

Agent Frankel had asked him to hold off returning until later. She wanted to give the doctor a chance to work and allow the techniques he employed the time they needed to be effective. But with the condition the guy had been in, Shremp wasn't sure it would ever work. And that was not acceptable. He had lost the McAdams girl, so this little scientist was going to have to make up for that loss.

But now as the elevator took him to the lower levels, he worried this might just be a great big waste of time. Frankel stood waiting for him as the doors opened. She smiled.

"Good morning, Senator."

"Agent Frankel. Any progress?"

"Actually, yes. The doctor asked to speak with you before you go in."

Shremp frowned. "Fine. Where is he?"

"This way." She led him past the door they had entered yesterday. She knocked. "Come in," came the muffled reply.

The agent opened the door, stepping aside to allow the senator in. "Major Gina Carstairs of the United States Marine Corps, this is Senator Bart Shremp." Frankel didn't wait for a response, she simply closed the door behind him.

The African American doctor looked up from the desk, her dark hair pulled back in a ponytail.

"You're young," Shremp said, taken aback.

"And you're not." Carstairs didn't smile. She gestured to a chair in front of her desk. "Take a seat."

He bristled at her tone. "See here, I am a United States senator, not one of your patients. And I will be shown respect."

The doctor studied him, her gaze making him uncomfortable. "*You* see here. I have taken an oath to do no harm. And I am not completely convinced that what you want falls under that umbrella."

"You have been ordered to make the subject comfortable. Surely you can manage that."

"Do you *know* who you have in that cell?"

"That is of no concern to you."

The woman's eyes blazed. "Of no concern? *That* is Dr. Dominic Radcliffe, one of the greatest minds of our time. And a very delicate mind at that."

Shremp waved away her concerns. "Please. He was removed from his home for failing to comply with—"

"He suffers from agoraphobia. He has not *left* his home in close to two decades. And you yanked him out without concern for his mental state. I have medicated him to help his emotional state, but let me be clear, I did that for him, not you."

Shremp narrowed his eyes. "Let me remind you, you are under the command of the CEI as well as being under a strict nondisclosure agreement. You cannot speak of any of your activities here."

"That's not entirely accurate. You mean I cannot speak without penalty. I can speak if I am willing to accept the *cost* of those words." She met Shremp's gaze without a flinch.

He swallowed.

Finally, she broke off her gaze. She stood and strode past him for the door. "I will take you to the patient. But you are not to upset him. I am going to check on him, and you may observe, quietly and unobtrusively, but you are not allowed to speak with him until I give you permission. Is that clear?"

Shremp glared at her back. Obviously Frankel had chosen the wrong specialist for this particular assignment. He'd have to have to her watched.

Shremp expected Carstairs to head to the same room as yesterday, but instead she headed down the hall. Shremp glanced at Frankel, who fell in step with him. "He was moved?"

"Yes, the doctor believed the other room held too many bad memories. She thought a fresh start might help him recover."

He shook his head. For God's sake, they were talking about a man, not a child.

The doctor stopped at the end of the hall. Hennessey was standing guard outside the door. Carstairs glared at Shremp, warning him without words to behave before opening the door.

He glowered. That woman really needed to learn the pecking order around here, and she was way below him. But before he could inform her of this, she stepped into the room.

Shremp stopped in the doorway. This room was much nicer than the other one. A door in the corner led into a private bath. A real bed, not a cot, was pushed against the wall. A table to its left held a pitcher of water and some plastic cups. And there were even flowers, yellow daisies, on the table.

The doctor was kneeling down next to the bed. "Dr. Radcliffe? It's Dr. Carstairs."

The man on the bed flickered open his eyes.

Carstairs smiled. "Good morning."

His eyes grew wide.

"No, no, it's all right. No one will hurt you. I'm Dr. Carstairs. We met yesterday. Do you remember?"

Radcliffe nodded, some of the tension draining from his face.

"How are you feeling?"

Radcliffe started to shake. "Th-thirsty."

"Of course." Carstairs quickly walked to the table and returned with a glass of water. "Let me help you." She gently helped Radcliffe sit up. He took the glass with two hands, the way a child would.

Shremp tamped down his annoyance.

Greatest mind of our time. Please. The man had soiled himself yesterday. He was hardly a great mind. He stepped in. "All right, we need some answers."

Carstairs whipped around. "He is *not* taking questions right now. He needs to eat. He needs to take his meds. Your questions will have to wait."

Frankel stepped in, touching Shremp's arm. "Perhaps we should let the doctor complete her work. I have a breakfast set up for you down the hall."

Shremp glared at the doctor and then at Frankel, who smiled at the man on the bed. He turned on his heel and strode down the hall. Frankel hurried to catch up with him.

He glared. "Perhaps you are not as up for this task as I thought."

"Don't doubt my dedication, Senator." She glanced over her shoulder at her partner down the hall. "Ever heard of good cop, bad cop? Well, Roger is horrible at good cop. And this particular subject may need kid gloves to get any information from him. But I assure you, if the gloves need to come off, I will happily remove them."

He read the commitment in her eyes. "Good. Now what are we having for breakfast?"

Breakfast had been all right, just egg sandwiches. Then Shremp had been shown to an office down the hall where he had worked for three hours, mostly on the phone with Adam. Frankel had brought in BBQ takeout for lunch, which had more than made up for the sad little breakfast.

He wiped the last remnants of sauce from his face. "That was good." He glanced up at Frankel, who had joined him for lunch. "And as enjoyable as your company may be, I think it's time we spoke with the good doctor."

Frankel nodded. "I spoke with her before I went to get lunch. She should be ready. I thought you might want to read her preliminary report." She slid a manila folder toward him.

He opened it, quickly reading the two-page report inside. He glanced at the comments—high empathy and strong protective qualities. He laughed. "Strong protective qualities? She can't be serious."

"I believe she is. There are different ways to protect people. But if she is correct, and he feels the answers to our questions will harm those he cares about, he will shut down. He won't answer them."

Shremp dropped the file on the table. "Then how the hell are we going to get the answers out of him?"

Frankel smiled, reminding him of a shark. "You brought the doctor in to make him capable of answering questions. You brought *me* in to make sure he answers them. Have a little faith, Senator. Now, shall we go see what Dr. Radcliffe has to say?"

CHAPTER 88

Hennessey was standing outside yet another door. Frankel strode right up to him. "Well?"

"The doctor's been in with him since this morning. They just finished lunch. And then I had them brought here."

"And how are they getting along?" Frankel asked.

Hennessey smiled. "Extremely well."

"Excellent." She turned to Shremp. "Senator, I'm going to ask you to observe from the room next door. It is the same setup as the other observation room."

"Very well." Shremp opened the door in front of him and stepped in. The ceiling lights were a low wattage, casting a shadowy light across the space. A coffee machine sat in the corner. Shremp made his way over, pouring himself a cup. He walked back to the window, blowing on the coffee. Taking a seat on one of the chairs set up in front of the window, he placed his coffee on the table next to it.

In the room, Carstairs sat at a table with Radcliffe. Her hand held his as he shook his head. Shremp walked over to the panel he'd seen Frankel use and turned up the volume.

"—all right. I'll be right here the whole time."

"I want to go home." Radcliffe's voice was soft.

"I know, Dom. Just a little longer, and I'll make sure you get home, okay?"

Apparently the doctor was the one who was suffering from a protective complex. He worried she might interfere with the questioning. He should have picked a man. They would have been less likely to sympathize with Radcliffe.

But after reading Carstairs's file this morning, he could see why Frankel had chosen her. She had an incredible record of getting through to difficult patients and in some incredibly difficult situations. She'd once talked down a soldier who held a live grenade in the middle of a forward base in Afghanistan. He threatened to blow himself and everyone else up. Command had wanted to evacuate the base, but it wasn't possible due to a report about snipers in the area. Carstairs had stayed with the man for three hours, even as the camp suffered a mortar attack. She finally got the soldier to hand over the grenade and the rest of his weapons, saving dozens of lives in the camp.

In the other room, the door opened. Frankel walked in, smiling as she nodded at Radcliffe. "Good afternoon, Dr. Radcliffe."

He didn't respond but shrank back in his chair as Hennessey followed Frankel in. After closing the door, he leaned against it with his arms crossed.

Frankel moved forward. "I'm not sure if you remember me, but we met yesterday. I'm Agent Frankel, and this is my partner Agent Hennessey."

Dr. Radcliffe spoke to the table. "With the CEI."

"Yes, that's correct." Frankel beamed at him like he was a star pupil before glancing back at Hennessey. "I told you he'd remember, didn't I?"

Hennessey just grunted in response.

Frankel took a seat across from the two doctors, placing her hands on the table in front of her. "Now, Dr. Radcliffe I need to ask you a few questions. On behalf of your government." She looked at Dom, but he said nothing, just stared at the tabletop.

"The government knows you have been working for the Chandler Group for, oh my goodness, seventeen years. That is a long time." She smiled.

Radcliffe continued to stare at the table.

"We know you are very close with Henry Chandler, Danny Wartowski, Jake Rogan, his head of security, and of course, Delaney McPhearson."

Radcliffe's eyes darted up at Frankel before he shifted his attention back to the table. But Shremp could see his trembling had increased.

"I have seen the news coverage of Delaney McPhearson. It is hard to believe all the things she can do. I've heard she can control the weather, is that true?"

Radcliffe's gaze seemed locked on the table in front of him.

"That's not a hard question, is it, Doctor? Can McPhearson control the weather?"

Carstairs rubbed his arm.

Radcliffe nodded. "Yes."

Frankel sat back, acting stunned. "My goodness. That must be something to see. And animals? She can control them too?" She stared at Radcliffe expectantly.

Radcliffe shook his head. "No."

This time, even Shremp could tell her surprise was genuine. "She *can't* control animals?"

Radcliffe shook his head, his voice quiet. Shremp leaned forward to hear him better. "No. She doesn't control them. She only communicates with them."

Frankel frowned. "So why do they do what she asks?"

Radcliffe looked up. "Because they want to."

"Huh. I did not know that." Frankel sat back in her chair, her hand at her chin. "And the cats, are they normal leopards?"

Radcliffe didn't look up.

Frankel leaned forward. "We know about Ruggio Labs and the experiments."

"Then you don't need Dr. Radcliffe's input." Carstairs stared daggers at Frankel.

Frankel smiled. "Dr. Carstairs, you are allowed to be here as an aid to Dr. Radcliffe. However, if you interrupt me again, I'm afraid you will have to leave."

Carstairs nodded, but her look stayed angry.

"Now, Dr. Carstairs is right. We do know all about the cats. Honestly, I did not know something like that was possible. But it has gotten the government thinking about what else is possible. Because we know, actually the whole world knows, that Delaney McPhearson's powers have expanded. That she now has the same powers as the Fallen, the speed, the healing, the strength."

Radcliffe's chair began to rattle as his shaking increased.

Frankel spoke louder to be heard over the vibrating metal. "And we know that she gained those powers through a substance called the Omni. But someone had to make it for her. Someone she trusted. Someone incredibly smart. We think that someone is you."

She stared at the man.

"I didn't hear a question in there," Carstairs said.

Frankel smiled. "True. There was no question. So here it is: Did you make the substance known as the Omni for Delaney McPhearson?"

Radcliffe shook his head, beginning to hum.

"Is that a no, you didn't make it or no, you refuse to answer?"

Carstairs leaned closer to him. "Dom? Are you all right?"

Frankel stood up, pulling a slim plastic case about the size of a pencil case from her jacket pocket. She opened it and pulled out a syringe. "Dr. Radcliffe, you are not cooperating."

Carstairs leapt to her feet, placing herself in front of Radcliffe, who now sat rocking back and forth. "What are you doing? What is that? I will not allow you to inject him with anything."

Frankel's voice was ice-cold. "You are obstructing my interrogation, Doctor. Hennessey."

Hennessey sprang from the wall, grabbing the doctor's jacket. Carstairs reached up, grabbing the fist that held her and twisted it. Hennessey yelled, his knees buckling. Carstairs twisted his arm, slamming the large agent's head into the table.

"Don't touch me," she growled. Then she went still before she started to shake.

Shremp gasped. *What the?* That's when he noticed the small device in Frankel's hand and the wires extending from it to Carstairs. A Taser. Hennessey leaped to his feet, this time slamming Carstairs's face into the table and holding her there.

Radcliffe had fallen off his chair and was scurrying away. Frankel walked around the other side of the table toward him, reminding him of a predator going after its prey. "Look at me, Dr. Radcliffe. Look at me!"

Radcliffe kept shaking, but his gaze darted to her before returning to Carstairs. "Good. Now you need to listen. The U.S. government has sent me to retrieve the formula for the Omni, and I will do my duty, by whatever means are necessary."

Hennessey pushed his forearm against Carstairs's neck. She grunted, gritting her teeth.

"L-let her go," Radcliffe begged.

"Well, that's up to you. I will let her go as soon as you tell me the formula."

Radcliffe shook his head.

"Don't tell them, Dom," Carstairs spit out. Hennessey slammed a huge fist into her kidneys. She cried out.

"Well, that is your choice, of course. But remember, if you choose not to answer my simple little questions, I have to figure out more creative ways to make you talk." She pulled the trigger again, and Carstairs jolted as more volts rushed through her.

Tears streaming down his cheeks, Radcliffe pushed back from the table. "No, no. Stop!"

Frankel's voice was frighteningly pleasant. "I can stop, Dr. Radcliffe. But what will you do for me in exchange?"

Radcliffe's shoulders slumped. "I-I'll tell you."

Frankel smiled as she pushed a legal pad and pen toward him. "Excellent."

CHAPTER 89

Shremp stared at the list in front of him. The doctor's handwriting was difficult to make out, and to be perfectly honest, he wasn't sure half these words were real. But if they were...

Frankel turned from the computer with a smile. "They all check out. Everything on that list exists."

Shremp grinned. Finally. He'd had Frankel check each substance on the list just to be sure the doctor hadn't been lying to them. Not that he'd really thought he was. The man was too terrified to lie to them.

"Send that list to this address." He scribbled an email address on the top of the legal pad and handed it to her.

Frankel turned back to the computer. A few keystrokes later, and she turned back. "Done."

He smiled. "You did well. I didn't think he was going to tell us anything."

"Psychological profiles always help. His protective nature was the key. I had heard how close he was with the people in the Chandler Group and that he may have helped McPhearson when she was on the run. But I needed the psychiatrist to confirm it."

"Carstairs was a smart choice. You brought the psychiatrist in knowing that would be the case?"

Frankel shrugged. "I played a hunch. She is known for being a fierce advocate for her patients, as well as being highly regarded. Plus, she reminds me a little of McPhearson—strong, no nonsense. If Radcliffe was going to try to protect anyone, she seemed like the most likely candidate."

"Speaking of Carstairs, what exactly is the plan with her?"

"She's in a cell down the hall. We'll hold on to her until we are sure that Radcliffe's formula actually works."

Shremp nodded. "Good. And then what do we do with her?"

"Depends." Frankel met his gaze. "Do you want anyone here to tell the world what happened here?"

Shremp didn't hesitate and didn't pull his gaze. "No."

Frankel nodded. "Then we'll make sure no one hears from her. And we'll do the same for Radcliffe."

"I knew you were perfect for this job." He stood. "I'm heading back to D.C. You have everything handled here?"

"Yes, Senator. You have nothing to worry about."

He turned for the door. *Nothing to worry about and everything to hope for. You're welcome, United States. I have just made sure you remain the greatest country on the planet.*

CHAPTER 90

All three rows of the Suburban were filled with Chandler and SIA operatives. Laney and Cleo sat in the last row. With Laney's face being so well known and Cleo being Cleo, it made more sense for both of them to be in the back of the darkened van rather than up front where a random person driving by might see them. She absentmindedly ran a hand through Cleo's fur while she thought of Dom.

When she'd met him years ago, he'd been the stereotypical absent-minded professor. His brain raced with so many thoughts that the everyday aspects of life often fell through the cracks. He almost always had the buttons on his sweater-vest and oxford mismatched. She wasn't sure she'd ever seen him when his glasses weren't sitting at a slight angle, with his hair some sort of wild halo around his face. But none of that mattered. Dom was a good man, a good friend. When Laney had gone on the run, he'd helped her. She had trusted him, and he had paid her back by keeping her secret.

And now, his trust in me is why he is in this situation. She had known when she'd asked Dom to make the Omni for her that she was putting him in danger. But she never thought it would come to this. She never thought it would be her government that would take him. She rolled her hand into a fist. *And I left him alone.*

Guilt rolled through her. She had left him on his own. She should have warned Henry or Jake. Told them the government might target him. But she had never honestly thought they would.

God, I was so stupid, so naive.

Cleo huffed as she lay half on the floor and half on the bench next to her. She watched the traffic go by on the highway outside the window. A minivan pulled up next to them. Cleo's head perked up. She leaned her snout against the black glass, leaving a ring of condensation as she exhaled. There was a little kid in the back of the minivan eating goldfish from a snack cup. Cleo stared at him, willing him to look her way.

Laney patted Cleo's back. "He can't see you, honey."

Cleo sighed as the minivan pulled away without the child even glancing over.

Mustafa turned from the row in front of her. "She likes kids, huh?"

"Loves them. Honestly, her idea of heaven would be a schoolyard at an elementary school during recess."

"I wish she could do that."

"Me too."

Mustafa paused. "We'll get him back, Laney."

"Yes, we will," she said, looking back out the window. She knew Mustafa was right. They would get him back. The real question was what kind of shape would he be in when they got him back?

Jake pulled off the exit, then made two turns before pulling to a stop behind a foreclosed restaurant. The second SUV pulled in as well. Everyone piled out. Jake went to the back of the van. Pulling the doors open, he started handing out gear.

"Anyone you see you assume is a bad guy. Tasers and nonlethal force unless there is absolutely no other option. We do not want the government to tag us any more than they have to for this."

Laney met Jake's gaze. It probably wouldn't matter if they walked in without hurting a soul or just blew the whole damn place up. The government was going to want their heads after this. Laney looked at Lou, Rolly, and Danny. "You guys are in and out no matter what you hear. Your job is only to get Danny to the security room, get the intel, and get right back out."

Rolly smiled. "We've got this. It's not like it's our first time."

"No, but you do tend to take side trips on these little missions," Laney said.

"One time," Rolly argued.

"More like five," Danny grumbled.

Rolly threw up his hands. "Fine, five times. We've changed."

Laney shook her head, catching Lou's gaze. "In and out, Laney. I promise," Lou said.

Laney nodded back at her. She wanted to ask Lou if she was sure she wanted to do this. But she was here, which meant she was.

Jake closed the back of the SUV. "All right, everyone put your earpieces in. From this point forward, we are on mission. The facility is only ten minutes from here. Does everyone know their role?"

Everyone nodded back at him. Cleo sat on the ground, leaning against Laney. Laney placed her hand on Cleo's head, needing the extra contact.

Jake's gaze scanned the group in its entirety before he nodded. "Good. Then let's load up and go get Dom."

CHAPTER 91

The plan was to hit the facility before they even realized they were at the gate. Jen, Matt, and Hanz lined up next to Laney down the street from the facility. The SUVs were running behind them, everyone inside them. Matt nodded. "Ready."

"Then let's go." Laney sprinted forward, reveling in the strength that flowed through her limbs as her legs ate up the distance. In a blur, the four of them crashed into the gate, sending it flying. Matt and Hanz stopped momentarily to handle the guards at the gate, but Laney and Jen didn't. They blurred toward the main building. Two guards whirled around, their eyes widening at the gate and the sound of two SUVs racing down the drive.

Laney slammed into one, sending him crashing into the wall. Jen grabbed a leg of the other, yanking him off his feet. Neither man even had time to scream before they were out cold. Neither Laney nor Jen paused, they just burst through the open door. Laney didn't look back. Their job was to get inside. Those coming after them would take care of restraining whomever they came across.

A man in fatigues rounded a corner, a sandwich in his hand.

Jen flew toward him, her knee catching him in the groin so hard that even Laney winced. An uppercut to the jaw sent him falling to the floor.

Rows and rows of towering shelves filled with files greeted them. Outside, one of the SUVs halted, and running feet sounded behind her.

"I'll take the upstairs," Jen said.

"Try not to make the next guy incapable of reproducing."

"I make no promises," Jen said before disappearing into the aisles.

Jake stepped through the doorway. Behind him, Matt and Hanz were tying the guards' hands and feet with zip ties after removing their weapons. Jake stopped at her elbow, weapon in hand, scanning the room. "Well?"

"I don't sense any Fallen." She frowned. "This seems like its only storage."

Cleo trotted up.

Laney looked down at her. *Find Dom.*

Without a word, Cleo slipped into the warehouse. Laney met Jake's gaze.

"After you."

She rolled her eyes. "Such a gentleman."

He chuckled. "Hey, you're the one who heals quickly. Any gunfire, and I'm using you as my shield."

"You damn well better," Laney said as she headed inside. "I'm going to run some laps."

"Happy hunting." Jake moved down the first aisle. Laney zipped through each aisle on the first floor. There was one guard at the back of the room. Laney knocked him against the wall. "Guard down, back of the room."

"On our way," Matt said.

Jen's voice came through Laney's earpiece. "Second and third floors cleared."

Laney, Cleo called.

On my way. Sensing where Cleo was, she hurried to the back of the building, where Cleo sat in front of an old freight elevator. Jake was inside, examining the panel. He looked up as she arrived. "It only goes up."

"Let's see about that." She tapped her mic. "I need Danny."

Seconds later, Lou and Rolly appeared with Danny between them. They released him, and he stumbled, grabbing on to Rolly to keep from hitting the ground. He glared at his friends, speaking through gritted teeth. "I'm pretty sure I could have just *jogged* here."

Rolly clapped him on the shoulder. "That would have taken too long."

"In here, Danny," Jake said.

With another glare at Lou and Rolly, Danny stepped inside and studied the panel. In a few seconds, he'd pulled the face of it off. The ancient face gave way to a much sleeker control panel underneath. Danny pulled that face off as well and started attaching wires. "This definitely goes down."

"We need a breach team," Jake said into his mic.

Matt and Hanz arrived along with Yoni, Jen, and Jordan. They all loaded into the elevator, including Cleo.

Laney turned to the teenagers. "When we give the all-clear, you grab whatever tapes you can find and get back to the vans. Right now, you stay against the wall. Your job is to keep Danny safe, understood?"

Rolly snapped his heels together and initiated a crisp salute. "Yes, Mein Heir."

Laney narrowed her eyes.

Lou grabbed Rolly's arm. "Ignore him. He's an idiot. We'll get Danny down and then out as quickly as, well, inhumanly possible."

"Good." Laney turned back to the panel. "Okay, Danny, let's see what's underneath this place."

CHAPTER 92

HEADING TO BOLIVIA

Mary Jane looked around the plane in disbelief. She could not believe she was sitting in an old cargo plane, surrounded by people she didn't even know a month ago, heading to some mysterious hiding spot that only Drake could get them into.

The plane was loud. Boxes of supplies were stacked high, taking up half the plane, with small narrow paths between them. Molly was sitting with Susie in her lap, Joe and Shaun on either side. Theresa was sitting next to Molly, holding her hand.

Cain unbuckled himself once Nyssa slipped off to sleep and walked over to Mary Jane. "How are you?"

She shook her head. "I don't know. Everything is happening so fast."

He gave her a sympathetic smile. "Do you still want to have our conversation?"

Mary Jane didn't hesitate. "Yes."

Things were happening fast, but she needed to know why.

Maybe it would help her, and more importantly, Molly, understand how they came to be here.

Twenty minutes later, Mary Jane was still trying to accept everything he had shared during that time. "So Atlantis was real? And Lemuria too?"

Cain nodded. "Yes. But much like the world right now, they became focused on material gains rather than spiritual ones. It led to their destruction. They didn't listen to the warnings. They thought they were untouchable."

Church had been a large part of Mary Jane's life. She had gone to Catholic school from kindergarten through high school. She'd even attended a Catholic college. That was in addition to church every weekend, Bible school, and youth group. Yet as Cain spoke, the more she struggled to comprehend. It was all so different from what she had been taught.

She gestured around the plane. "And all this, it dates back to then?"

"It dates back even earlier. To the very first people."

"Adam and Eve?"

Cain shook his head. "They weren't the first." He explained about the first people arriving and being immortal. That they were led by two people, Adam and Lilith.

"But she's evil, isn't she?"

"No. In fact, she was the only one who held on to the old ways, the ways of goodness. She tried to get people to come back to the path, but they felt they knew better. And then she made us mortal."

Mary Jane watched Cain. It was strange. When he spoke, he made the history come alive. *Almost as if he were a witness to it rather than just a teacher of it.* Mary Jane shook her head, shaking off that thought. "And what about you? How did you get involved in all this?"

"I knew Laney's biological mother. And I tried to keep her from doing something that would result in her death."

Mary Jane started. "You tried to save her?"

"Yes and no. Because by saving Victoria, I would have doomed others. But I didn't care about that. I just wanted her to stay with me."

"She died?"

"She did." He glanced over at Nyssa and smiled.

"And your glasses? You said you'd explain why you always wear them."

"I did." He paused. "I know all of this is difficult to believe, but it is true." He went quiet.

She leaned forward, sensing he was worried for some reason about revealing his secret. "It's all right. Whatever it is, it's all right."

He patted her hand. "You are a good person, Mary Jane. I hope we can still be friends after I tell you. You will actually be the first person I have told this to in a very long time."

"I'm honored."

He gave her a nervous smile before picking at a loose thread in his pants. "Tell me, what do you know about Cain from the Bible?"

She frowned. "I suppose what everyone else knows. He killed his brother, and as a result, he was punished by God to roam the Earth forever. He's the world's first murderer."

Cain nodded. "All true. Do you remember how he was supposed to bear a mark that would warn people to stay away from him, lest they suffer God's wrath?"

A chill slipped up her spine. He couldn't. No. "Whoever harmed him would receive sixfold the injury they intended."

"Sevenfold, actually." He looked down, sliding his glasses off. "I have lived a very long time, Mary Jane. A very long time." He looked up.

Mary Jane gasped. His eyes were black, completely black. She inched back. "I-I don't understand."

"Yes, you do. Your mind is just taking a minute to catch up with the facts. I am not *a* Cain. I am *the* Cain."

She stared at him, shaking her head. It wasn't possible. Cain, if he even lived, had died thousands and thousands of years ago. There was no way the man standing in front of her was the Cain from the Bible. That man had been arrogant, selfish. He was a *murderer*. This man was kind, generous, considerate.

"No. I don't know why you think that, but you are not the Biblical Cain. You are a good man. That Cain died forever ago."

"You don't believe me because you don't want to believe me. But tell me, before your daughter, did you believe in reincarnated angels? Nephilim? Did you believe a person like Laney with all her abilities could exist? With everything you have seen, and while looking in my eyes, can you honestly say I am not telling the truth?"

Mary Jane wanted to tell him he was wrong, mistaken. But there was no hesitation in his words. The way he spoke about history... "Your... your eyes are the mark?"

He nodded. "It has kept me relatively safe for my life. For millennium, they were viewed as a sign of my demonic nature. Most people gave me a wide berth as a result, although a few would tempt fate, much to their detriment. As people grew more educated, as societies became more civilized, I started to hide them. But that, in my long lifespan, is a very short time period, only the last two hundred years. Before that, my eyes were a large part of my power."

Mary Jane could see that. Even knowing him, she felt a trickle of fear when she looked at him. As a nurse, she'd never seen anything like it. She'd never heard of anything like it. The closest medical condition she could think of was primary acquired melanosis, which caused brown spots to appear in the sclera. But this was not that. This was something unique. "You... you killed your brother."

"I did." He looked away. "I have not always been a good man.

But my time with Laney, Patrick, Nyssa, they have let me be who I am meant to be, not the monster I thought I was."

Mary Jane's gaze strayed to Nyssa, who sat playing with Susie. And it all clicked into place. "Susie. Elisabeta took her and all those other children because she thought she was Lilith."

Cain nodded. "Yes."

"*Is* Nyssa Lilith?"

"Yes. But she will remember nothing until she turns thirteen. Until then, she will be just an ordinary child. And I intend to give her a wonderfully ordinary childhood."

Mary Jane sat back, stunned. "You, she—" She couldn't seem to form a sentence.

Cain stood. "I realize this may change how you feel about me. But I did not want to keep this from you any longer. You have become dear to me, and I consider you a friend. I hope one day you will accept me for the man I am, not the one I was." He walked away, slipping through the crates and out of her view.

Mary Jane watched him go. She had been taught all her life that Cain was evil. And yet he had done nothing but offer friendship to her and her family. She had trusted him from the moment she had met him. She had sensed an old soul, but she could never have guessed just how old.

"Mary Jane?" Henry sat down next to her.

"Hey, hi."

"Just wanted to see how you're doing."

"I'm all right. Any word from Jake . . . and everybody else?"

"They reached the facility. First group got in. But don't worry. They are all very good at what they do."

Mary Jane kept staring at the space where Cain had disappeared.

"Something wrong?"

"What? No, um, just . . . did you know about Cain?" She paused, horrified that she had just almost betrayed Cain's confidence.

"You mean that he is *the* actual Cain?"

Mary Jane nodded.

"I've known since before I met him. But how did you learn about that?"

"He told me."

Henry let out a low whistle. "That is the first time he's done that to my knowledge."

"So it's true?"

Henry nodded. "Yes."

A simple little word and yet earth shattering in so many ways. "Is he . . . is he a good man?"

"When I first met him, he wasn't. To be honest, I hated him and would have killed him in a heartbeat. He was trying to take my mom. But Laney helped me see through his eyes. He was desperate to keep Victoria from dying. She was the only family he had. And once she died, there was no guarantee he would be able to find her again. I can't imagine living for so long with so little connection. He kept himself away from people. No one could really understand what he had been through except Victoria. He *needed* that connection."

"And now?"

"And now, Laney saw the good in him. The good I don't think he even saw. She treated him like that man, rather than the evil man everyone else saw him as. And it changed him."

"You trust him?"

Henry paused, then gave a little laugh. "Actually, I do. He loves Laney, Patrick, Nyssa. He stood next to Laney on that dais, even though he didn't have to. He has billions hidden away. He could have disappeared if he wanted to. But he didn't. He's here with all of us. Not because he has to be, but because he wants to be. He's standing up, and I respect him for it."

"I don't know what to think."

"I won't tell you what to think, but I will tell you to trust your gut." He paused. "So what does your gut tell you?"

Mary Jane stood up, kissing Henry on the cheek. "Thank you."

She hurried down the path through the boxes that Cain had disappeared into. She found him a few rows back, checking boxes off on an inventory list. "Hi."

He looked up, the light glinting off his black eyes for a moment.

Mary Jane had to stop herself from stepping back. His eyes really were frightening. She forced herself to step forward. "I thought you might need some help."

He stopped for a moment before handing her the checklist. "I'd appreciate that."

She smiled, taking the clipboard from him. "What are friends for?"

CHAPTER 93

BLUEFIELD, VIRGINIA

As soon as the elevator doors opened, bullets roared into the car. Laney could tell Matt was about to blur. She grabbed him, holding him back. "Wait."

Closing her eyes, she summoned the wind. It barreled through the hallway in front of them. Two screams sounded, followed by thuds. Laney, Matt, and Hanz were moving before the last thud had faded. A soldier was sprawled across the hall only a few feet from the elevator. A man and a woman were farther down the hall. Jordan tied up the soldier while Matt reached the woman first, quickly zip tying her hands. Hanz did the same for the man.

Laney scanned the hall and turned back to Cleo. *Any more?*

Two. Behind doors. One's Dom. Cleo padded out of the elevator and trotted to the end of the hall. Laney followed her, seeing Lou, Rolly, and Danny slip out and go down the other hallway. Laney's gut tightened. But then Jordan and Jen slipped out after them, easing some of Laney's fear.

Cleo stopped at a doorway at the end of the hall. She scratched at it.

Step back. Laney slammed her boot into the door, wincing as the bottom hinge tore loose and the door flung open.

She hadn't meant to hit it so hard. A cry sounded from inside the room. Laney stepped in, cautiously. At first she didn't see him. The bed was empty. But then she caught movement in the corner of the room, hidden by the bed. Laney walked forward slowly. "Dom?"

A whimper sounded.

She rounded the bed, and her heart broke at the sight. Dom cowered against the back wall, his hands over his head as he crouched low.

She knelt down in front of him, reaching out to touch his arm, but he jerked away with a cry. "Dom, Dom. It's me. It's Laney."

What did they do to you? What did I do?

Cleo nudged her aside, laying her head on Dom's arm. Dom went still, but he didn't push her away. He lifted up his head, his eyes unfocused, as if he couldn't understand what was in front of him. He reached up tentatively and touched her. "Cleo?"

Cleo licked him in response.

"Cleo!" Tears flowed from Dom's eyes. He wrapped his arms around her, his shoulders shaking. Then Dom looked up through tear-drenched eyes. "Laney?"

She smiled, feeling tears press against the back of her eyes. She spoke softly. "Hey, Dom. How about we get you out of here?"

Yoni spoke as he crossed the room toward them. Laney hadn't even heard him arrive. "I brought you something." He held out Dom's glasses. Dom reached up and took them, placing them on his face. Like usual, they sat at a slight angle.

Laney took one of Dom's arms while Yoni grabbed the other. "Come on, Doc. We've got you."

Between the two of them, they got Dom to the door and into the hall. He reared back as he saw the two agents on the floor. "They, they—"

Laney stepped in front of him, blocking his view. "They won't hurt you. I promise."

"Come on, Doc. We need to get you out of here," Yoni said.

Dom shook his head, starting to shake. "No, no. I-I can't. I don't want to go out—"

Yoni slipped his arm around his waist. "Doc, we need to—"

Jen blurred into view, plunging a needle into Dom's arm without a word. Dom's eyes rolled back in his head. Yoni stumbled under the sudden weight, but Jen propped Dom up before he could fall.

"What did you do?" Yoni's face was stricken as he tried to push Jen's hands away and take Dom.

Jen placed a hand on Yoni's arm, her voice soft. "He hasn't been in the outside world in years, Yoni. It's better if he's not awake for this next part."

Yoni opened his mouth, then shut it, his shoulders falling. "Yeah, I guess that's probably true." He took a deep breath. "But let me take him, okay?"

Jen nodded, transferring him to Yoni's arms.

"I'll get him to the van." Yoni headed down the hall. Laney watched them go, her heart feeling heavy and her throat tight. Dom looked so helpless in his arms.

Jen stepped next to her, her shoulder touching Laney's, which let Laney feel the tremor run though her. "It'll be okay, Lanes. We have him now."

"Yeah." But she knew neither of them believed Jen's words. It was going to be a tough road back for Dom.

A loud screech of metal sounded from down the hall where the teenagers had disappeared. Laney and Jen exchanged a look. "I better go see what they're up to." Jen blurred down the hall and around the corner.

Here. Cleo stopped in front of another closed door.

Laney had forgotten about the other person.

"What is it?" Jake asked as he approached.

"Someone's inside."

Jake hefted his gun. "Good or bad?"

"Only one way to find out." Laney kicked the door open. She stepped inside and barely managed to duck the punch aimed at her head from the side. She turned, grabbing the woman's outstretched fist, putting her into an armbar and pushing her up against the wall. "Hey."

The woman struggled against Laney's hold. "God damn it. Let me go."

"Who are you?" Laney demanded.

"Shouldn't you know?" the woman sneered.

Jake stepped into the woman's line of sight. "What is your name?"

The woman stopped struggling, surprise flitting across her face as she studied Jake's face. "You're Jake Rogan."

He nodded.

Laney felt the fight flow out of her. Carefully, Laney released her, stepping out of range. The woman turned around, rubbing her elbow, her eyes going wide at the sight of Laney. "You're Delaney McPhearson."

Laney nodded. "And you are?"

"Major Gina Carstairs, United States Marine Corps, board certified psychiatrist." She paused, her head snapping to the doorway. "You're friends with Dr. Radcliffe. He's here. You have to—"

"We've got him."

The woman's shoulders sagged. "Thank God."

"I take it you're not part of this little circus," Laney said.

"I was drafted, but I didn't agree with their methods." She gestured to her swollen eye.

Laney met Jake's gaze. She could read the skepticism there. "Well, I guess we can work that out later."

The major frowned. "What do you me—"

Laney shot her with a tranq dart.

The major's eyes bulged before she reached for Laney. Laney caught her as her eyes closed.

"Well, what the hell are we going to do with her?" Jake asked.

Laney picked the woman up. "Find out what she knows. But not here."

Jake shook his head but just stepped out into the hall. "Okay."

Laney hefted the woman over her shoulder and followed him just as more banging sounded. "What is that?"

Jake shook his head. "You're kind of going to have to see it for yourself."

Adjusting the woman on her shoulder so her belt wasn't cutting into her skin, Laney hurried toward the elevator as Jen appeared, carrying an old computer tower.

Laney stopped short. "Uh, Jen? What are you doing?"

Jen placed the tower on the ground only to be joined by Lou and Rolly each carrying their own towers while Danny and Jordan carried one between them. "Danny said it would take too long to transfer the data. According to him, these are the computers the dinosaurs used, so he suggested we bring the entire system with us."

Laney's mouth dropped open, and she shook her head. "Well, sure, why not?"

CHAPTER 94

WASHINGTON, D.C.

Senator Bart Shremp could not keep his leg from jiggling underneath the table. The senator from Illinois was droning on about corn subsidies. He'd been talking for twenty minutes now, and Shremp honestly couldn't recall a word of what he'd said. He couldn't even say for sure if the senator was arguing for or against the subsidies. He was attending the meeting on agricultural subsidies because he was required to. But while his body might physically be sitting in the conference room of the Hart Building, his mind was most definitely not confined within the room or even the building.

No, he was imagining how he was going to roll out his information. Once he received verification from the lab that the substance was in fact the Omni, he would have to carefully plan who he let know and how. As the head of the CEI, he had access to a large budget. He could go ahead and initiate a test program to see how effective the serum was on a handpicked crew of subjects. Perhaps he could borrow some candidates from the military, individuals who were used to taking orders and were patriotic. Then he would have a group under his command that were more powerful than any other group with the U.S. military.

Not that he was planning a coup. No, if he played this right, a coup would not be necessary. If he played this right, he was practically guaranteed the White House on a silver platter. He would be the one who brought the greatness back to the United States. He smiled.

Perhaps I'll even take a little sample of the Omni myself. It would be good to feel that kind of power running through my veins.

"Senator Shremp, do you have a vote?"

Shremp looked up. The rest of the committee was staring back at him. He shook his head. "I abstain."

The committee head nodded, and the secretary jotted down his vote. "Very well. The initiative passes. I think this would be a good time to break for lunch. We'll see everyone back here at one o'clock."

The senators and their aides began to gather their things. Shremp stood and stretched, his lower back aching. Damned chairs. He waved at his papers on the table. "Take care of that, would you, Adam?"

"Yes, sir."

Shremp strolled out of the room. A few senators called out to him. He gave them a wave, tossing in a few good-natured "Hey, how you doings" as he headed for the elevator. He pressed the button, and the doors slid open.

"Hold the elevator," Senator Mitch Roberts called, hurrying forward. Shremp pretended not to hear him and hit the button to shut the doors. A few minutes later he was stepping out into the brisk fall air. The temperature had dropped a few degrees since he'd been inside.

Should've grabbed my coat, he thought as he headed down the steps. His phone rang, and he pulled it out quickly. It was Frankel. "Hello?"

"Senator Shremp?"

"Agent Frankel." He glanced around, making sure no one could overhear his conversation. "I thought we agreed you were not to call me on my cell unless there was an emergency."

"That is *why* I am calling."

"What's happened?"

She spit out the words. "Delaney McPhearson."

Dread flowed through Shremp.

"She attacked the facility. Radcliffe is gone. So is Carstairs."

"Damn it! How could you let this happen?"

"How could I let this happen? I told you we needed better security. But you were worried about raising red flags."

"Immaterial."

His mind whirled. McPhearson had led an attack against a government facility. He could use this. She'd attacked and killed government soldiers. The public would eat it up. The one thing the public wouldn't stand for was someone attacking American soldiers doing their jobs.

"Actually, this is good, good. Get me profiles on each of the soldiers that were killed. I want stuff that makes them look like American heroes. Also—"

"No guards were killed."

"*What?*"

The man running the coffee stand by the curb looked up at Shremp. Shremp turned his back on him and picked up his pace. "What do you mean no guards were killed? You just said she attacked the facility."

"Like I said, she attacked the facility, but no one was killed. They used Tasers, tranq guns, and non-lethal force. There are some broken bones, concussions, but everyone will live."

"They didn't kill anyone?"

"No."

God damn it. That wasn't going to sell.

"There's another problem."

"What?"

"They have a copy of the security tapes."

"*What?*" he shrilled.

"The system is internally controlled. It can't be hacked into. They didn't have time to make a copy, so they just took the whole system."

"Are you kidding?"

"No, sir. They have video of everything that was done at that facility. *Everything.*"

This was just getting worse and worse. Prior to housing Radcliffe, they'd had a few other "guests." Their treatments would not exactly endear them to the public. "We need to get out ahead of this."

"What do you want me to do?"

"Nothing. I think you've done enough." He disconnected the call and immediately called Adam. As soon as Adam answered, Shremp started barking orders. "Find me everything you can on a Major Gina Carstairs. I want every 'I' she failed to dot and every 'T' she failed to cross, and I want it yesterday. And—"

"Sir, the lab has been trying to reach you."

Yes! "Good, what do they—"

"It's not the Omni."

"What?"

"The ingredients are all real, but they don't make the Omni."

"Well, then what do they make?"

"Um, Rootin'-Tootin' Raspberry drink. Like Kool-Aid."

Shremp's mouth fell open. "What?"

"Rootin'-Tootin' Ras—"

"I heard you!" He seethed. That basketcase had played him. He had given him the wrong formula.

"Sir, what do you—" Shremp disconnected the call.

He stood up, pacing the room. No, no. This was all going wrong. He took a few breaths, trying to control his breathing. He had been in Washington for close to twenty years. He was not going to let anything stop him from achieving his dream of the presidency. Not when he was so close. He just needed to figure out the right angle to spin this.

Because if his time in Washington had taught him anything, it was that there was always an angle to play.

Always.

He dialed Frankel's number, speaking as soon as she answered. "Here's what you are going to do."

CHAPTER 95

BLUEFIELD, VIRGINIA

Laney sent everyone but Jen to the airfield. Jake had just sent a text saying that they had made it all right and they were in the air. The last plane would leave in an hour. Laney really hoped she and Jen made that plane, because the only way she could see Jen and her getting down to South America was through a really long run.

But that was an issue for another time. Right now the issue was what they were going to do with Major Carstairs.

They had taken the major to the foreclosed restaurant they'd stopped at on the way. They'd propped her against the wall of a booth, waiting for the sedative to wear off so they could question her.

Laney had had Danny run a quick search on the woman. From her official record, this appeared to be the first time she had ever worked with Senator Shremp. She had a stellar military record, and in fact, had spent the majority of her time over the last ten years in Afghanistan, Iraq, and Germany.

The German station had given Laney pause. After all, Carstairs had been at the same base that David had managed to get in and out of without a problem. She'd contacted Bruce and David, and they denied any knowledge of the woman, but Laney wasn't sure she believed them.

"How long do you think it will be before she wakes up?" Jen asked.

Laney pulled out a chair at a table across from the booth that the major was propped up in. "Oh, she's already awake. She's just hoping we don't notice. Isn't that right, Major Carstairs?"

The major's eyes squinted open. "Maybe."

Laney smiled. "I would have done the same thing."

"Me too." Jen took a seat on the table of the booth next to the major, her gaze on the woman.

The major grimaced, stretching her back as she straightened. "What did you guys give me?"

"Just a little sedative."

The major looked around. "Where are we? And what do you want?"

"We are somewhere where we will not be disturbed. And we want to know if you're a good guy or a bad guy." Jen leaned forward, the leashed violence clear in her tone and posture. Apparently Jen wanted to play bad cop.

The major raised an eyebrow, eyeing Jen. "And how exactly are you planning on doing that?"

Time for good cop. Laney sat back, crossing her feet at the ankles. "Through conversation. Major, why don't you explain to us how you ended up working with the CEI?"

The major cringed, sitting a little straighter. She looked between Laney and Jen. Laney worried for a moment that she was going to stay silent. But then she shook her head, blowing out a breath. "Following orders. I've only been back on the mainland for two months. My last station was Kandahar. Anyway, apparently one of my superiors was not happy when I turned a fellow soldier in for sexual harassment and sent me to work with the senator."

Jen raised an eyebrow. The major caught the look and glared back at her in response. "Look, I have not spent the better part of my adult life serving this country to allow some little asshole to think he's entitled to make comments about my sex life, my anatomy, or my potential."

Laney put up her hands. "Hey, preaching to the choir here."

The major nodded. "Anyway, the officer is being investigated, but I am now persona non grata. So when the CEI requested a psychiatrist, my command leapt at the chance to throw me in."

"What were you told?" Laney asked.

"That there was an enemy combatant with a serious psychological disorder who needed to be questioned."

"An enemy combatant?" Jen demanded.

The major eyed her. "That's what I was told. Imagine my surprise when I arrived to find it was Dr. Dominic Radcliffe, renowned intellectual and friend of Delaney McPhearson. I knew of Dr. Radcliffe's condition, his agoraphobia. I was not happy when I learned of how they'd gotten him there. But I figured being he was there, I could at least try to help calm him down, stabilize him. So I did."

"And then?" Laney asked.

The woman looked like she was ready to spit. "And then they 'interrogated' him. I insisted on being in the room. It was fine at first. Standard stuff, but then they tried to drug him to get responses."

"You allowed that?" Laney asked.

"No." She nodded to her darkening eye. "That's how I got this little souvenir and how I ended up locked in that room. They used me to get Dr. Radcliffe to provide them with some sort of formula."

Laney's heart raced as she sprang to her feet. "He gave it to them?"

The major's head snapped to Laney, and she backed away. "To protect me, he gave it to them. I don't think he would have any other way."

Laney turned her back on the woman. The government had the formula for the Omni.

Oh my God. By now, Shremp could have shared it with dozens of people. *What the hell am I going to do?*

Behind her, the major spoke quietly. "How is he? Dr. Radcliffe?"

Laney turned around as Jen answered. "He's with people who care about him. We sedated him. We thought it would be best until we get him somewhere safe."

"That is probably best." The major crossed her arms over her chest. "Now what are you planning on doing with me?"

"That is the question." Laney took a seat back in her chair, pushing the thoughts of the Omni aside. Yet again, that was a problem for another time. Right now, they needed to deal with the immediate problem, which was what to do with the major. Laney had never taken a prisoner. Well, at least not one who wasn't destined for an SIA prison cell. And she really had no interest in going down that road. Besides, Danny had managed to bring up the video from Dom's interrogation, and the major was at least telling the truth about that.

But then again, *it's possible she was a plant.* Of course, that would require Shremp having the foresight to know that Laney would take the woman with them, which seemed like a bit of a stretch. God, the world of "what ifs" was going to eat her alive if she let it.

She sighed, feeling very tired. "I'm inclined to just to let you go."

The major's head snapped up. "Seriously? After all this?"

"Well, I wanted to see what you knew. And to learn if you harmed Dom," Laney said.

"And if I had?"

"I would have turned you over to the police," Laney said.

"I would have punched you a little first," Jen muttered.

Laney rolled her eyes at her.

"What?" Jen said. "I would have."

Laney's phone beeped, and she answered it. "Hey. We're about to start heading back."

"Do you still have Carstairs?" Jordan asked.

"Yeah. We were about to let her go."

"Well, you might want to warn her that she's been made a big part of the story."

"What?"

"I sent you a news link. You need to watch it."

"Okay." Laney disconnected the call and immediately clicked open the link Jordan had sent.

"What's going on?" Jen moved over to peer at Laney's phone.

"Apparently Dr. Carstairs is in the news."

"What?" Carstairs exclaimed.

After a moment's hesitation, Laney propped her phone up so that Carstairs could see as well. She hit play. It was a clip from CNN.

"Breaking news at this hour. We have learned that a major in the United States Marine Corps has apparently led an assault in conjunction with Delaney McPhearson and her people on a secret military base that was on the front lines of the battle to defend against the Fallen."

Carstairs mouth fell open. "*Led* the assault?"

Carstairs growled as a man in uniform appeared on screen. "I would like to say I am surprised by this admission, but unfortunately I am not. Carstairs has had a difficult transition since returning home. To be honest, I was waiting for something like this. She definitely has a problem with authority."

"That's the asshole I put the complaint in about!" Carstairs yelled.

The anchor went on to detail how a secret facility had been

investigating Fallen abilities had been attacked, all the guards killed. Laney paused the recording, feeling numb.

Carstairs reared back. "Did you—"

Laney frowned, looking at Jen, her mind whirling. "No. Everyone was alive. I mean, a little banged up or tranqed, but not a single one was killed."

Jen kept her gaze glued on Laney. "Which means if they are dead, and we didn't kill them . . ."

"Then the government did."

"Why would they do that?" Carstairs asked.

"To make it look like we declared war on the United States. To turn the public against us," Jen said.

Laney shook her head. "But Danny must have gotten footage from the attack. He could—"

Jen's voice was somber. "We took their security system with us. We won't have any footage from after that point. We could get some satellite footage, but it won't show anything from inside the building."

Laney put her hand to her face. Jen was right. They had nothing to counter the government's argument. "We need to find out what happened."

"I'm sure Danny's already on it." Jen nodded to the phone. "Let's see what else they have to say and how Carstairs fits into all of this."

Laney nodded, hitting the play button, but feeling adrift. Was it possible the government would sacrifice its own people just to set Laney and her friends up? I mean, if they had the Omni, why take this step? Laney barely listened to the rest of the recording. It detailed Carstairs's history, all of which countered what Danny had already dug up on the woman. But Laney had a feeling those records had already been changed. The recording ended, and no one spoke. The only sound was the drip of the leaky sink from behind the counter.

Carstairs looked pale, and there was now a noticeable tremor in her hands. "They made me sound like an unstable woman. I've dedicated my adult life to this country, and in one fell swoop they wiped all my hard work away."

Laney took a seat in the booth across from her. "I'm sorry you got caught up in this. But I promise we will try everything in our power to get your name cleared."

Carstairs stared at her. "Why? You're not responsible for this."

Jen gave a small laugh as she pulled a chair up to the end of the table. "That is Delaney McPhearson's true superpower. Her ability to feel responsibility and guilt for any actions that might even be tangentially related to her."

Laney rolled her eyes. "I'm just saying, the major helped Dom, and now she's being hung out to dry. The least we can do is help clear her name."

Carstairs raised an eyebrow. "The least you could do is walk away. Clearing my name is a bit more involved."

Jen shrugged. "It's what we do."

Carstairs looked between the two of them. "Neither of you is what I expected."

Jen nodded toward Laney's phone. "Well, you can't always believe what the government says about people."

"Yeah, I see that." The major blew out a breath. "Well, what the hell am I supposed to do now?"

"Do you have some people you can stay with?" Laney asked.

The major shook her head. "I don't want to bring this to anyone's doorstep. I have some money stowed away. I'll lay low, hire a lawyer—"

Jen shook her head. "They've probably frozen your accounts. And I don't think on your own you can lie low enough for them to not find you."

Carstairs dropped her head into her hands. "I cannot believe this is happening."

"We know how that feels." Laney glanced at Jen and raised her eyebrows. Jen looked at Carstairs before nodding. "You could come with us," Laney said.

Carstairs's head snapped up. "What?"

"Look, you're wanted. You're going to need a place to hide out. We are in the same situation. So you're welcome to come hide with us."

"But you guys don't even know me."

"No. But you protected Dom when no one else did. That counts for something," Laney said.

"What if I'm a plant? I could trade in your location for my own safety."

Jen smiled. "Then I'll break every bone in your body, wait until they heal, and then do it again."

Carstairs gave a nervous laugh. "She's kidding, right?"

Jen raised an eyebrow, and Laney shook her head. "Nope. She's serious. So if you have any intention of trying to use us, it will go badly for you. People have tried to take us down before. It hasn't gone well for them."

The major looked between the two of them. "But if I keep your confidence, I have your word you'll help me hide until I can get my name cleared?"

"And we'll help you clear it," Laney said.

"Well, I guess you have a deal."

Laney extended her hand. "Welcome to the club, Major."

The major took her hand. "You should probably call me Gina."

EPILOGUE

WASHINGTON, D.C.

The President walked down the hall toward the apartment of the bunker. Since the coronation, she'd spent her nights down here as much as she could stand. She hated being underground. But the Secret Service seemed to be issuing threats on the hour that landed her here. It became easier to simply stay down here, although she knew people thought she was the one demanding she stay down here.

But that was her decision too. She'd rather look nervous than have the country know how many times the Fallen had come close to breaching the White House defenses.

The Secret Service agent opened her door, nodding as she passed. "Good evening, Madame President."

"Good evening, Felicia." She stepped through, waiting for Felicia to close the door before she kicked off her shoes. She slipped into the slippers she kept by the door. She wanted to throw on her pajamas and curl up on the couch, but she wasn't quite done for the night.

She poured herself a scotch and took a sip before topping her glass back off and pouring another in a second glass. She carried both to the coffee table, placing them down as a knock sounded.

"Come in," she called as she sat in the large chair facing the door.

Vice President Eric Brisbane stepped in. He smiled at the Secret Service agent, waiting until the door was closed to speak. "Well, Shremp sure has mucked things up."

The President nodded toward the other glass. "True, but he'll take the fall, and our hands are clean. And now we know that Dr. Radcliffe won't break."

It had been a risk putting Shremp in charge of the CEI. He was ambitious. He was stubborn, and he was not particularly politically adept. He also believed himself to be much smarter than he was.

Eric unbuttoned his suit jacket as he took a seat on the couch, grabbing the other tumbler. "You were right, though. He did get us answers quicker than we would have otherwise been able to manage."

The President smiled grimly. She was not happy about the events of the last few days. Taking Molly McAdams, that had been unforeseen. And what happened to her, Shremp would have to pay for that. But those actions did provide insight into what the Fallen were capable of, what they could withstand.

And even though Molly was only a child, she had withstood quite a lot. So as much as the President disliked—hated, in fact—what had been done to her, it was a necessary evil. Because if Molly at her young age could withstand that much pain and injury and recover, well, her scientists suggested an adult could withstand almost double.

Which meant the United States and the world had a huge problem. A problem they were no closer to solving.

"You've had the lab's results verified?"

"Dr. Radcliffe lied. And the blood from the subjects was useless. They could not detect any difference in them from non-enhanced individuals. The animal research is demonstrating a difference, but that's years out."

"And that's cats. We need human soldiers." The President sipped her scotch. Delaney McPhearson was on the run, wanted for murder. She had taken her little Fallen friends with her. Wherever she had gone, it was outside the U.S. They were able to verify that much.

"Do you think she did it?" Eric asked.

"Did what?"

"Killed those soldiers in Bluefield."

The President pictured Delaney McPhearson on coronation day. She had been focused and ruthless when dealing with Samyaza but careful to make sure no innocents were harmed. She could have taken out every single agent who tried to arrest her. Yet she didn't. She'd let herself be arrested.

She shook her head. "No. That was Shremp."

Eric did a double take. "Are you sure?"

"Yes. But as far as the public knows, it was McPhearson. Until we figure out a way to neuter her, put her on a leash, or create a weapon that can defeat her, she will be publicly held responsible."

"And what about Shremp?"

"His political life is over. He's not a man who can handle public shame."

"But he killed people."

"And once McPhearson is taken care of, he will be held accountable. Until then, McPhearson will be held accountable in the public's eyes for Shremp's actions."

"I understand."

"And do you agree?"

"Reluctantly, yes. Any word on the Omni? Any other lines of investigation?"

The President took a deep drink, the alcohol burning its way down her throat. "No."

And if they never found a way to neutralize McPhearson or defend against the Fallen, the President didn't know what was to come of the world. She could foresee the world breaking into two camps: enhanced and non-enhanced. And the enhanced would have no use for the non-enhanced. She gripped her tumbler to her chest.

And it is my job to keep that from happening.

"What about Moretti and the Vatican?"

"I haven't returned his phone calls."

"Are you planning on returning them?"

"Not sure. They're guided by some apocalyptic prophecies."

"You don't believe them?"

She shrugged. "I think Delaney McPhearson has the potential to cause an apocalypse. I'm just not certain some long-dead psychics are the experts we should be turning to right now. But I'll keep Moretti in the wings. He could prove useful again."

It was why she had agreed to help the Vatican get McPhearson out of the country. She had wanted to clear the board for whatever actions Shremp was going to take. If they had somehow managed to take her out, her hands would be clean, and at least one of her problems would be gone. But they had failed. Now that problem remained.

"Do you think anyone will figure out a way to create the Fallen?"

"Of course. And whoever figures it out will be the most powerful country in the world." Her eyes cut to him. "And we need to make sure it's us."

The idea of anyone else having that power was unimaginable. The U.S. was a symbol of democracy, freedom, and all that was decent in this world. They deserved to be on top.

She lifted her tumbler to Eric in salute. "After all, we're the good guys."

Delaney McPhearson's journey continues in The Belial Sacrifice. Now available on Amazon

FACT OR FICTION?

Thank you for reading *The Belial Fall*. It's bittersweet to be finishing up the Belial Series, but I am very happy with where we are headed. There is one more book in the series, *The Belial Sacrifice*. If you enjoyed *The Belial Fall*, please leave a **review** so other people can find the series. Now enough with all that, on to everyone's favorite part: the facts!

Prophesies. The prophesies mentioned in *The Belial Fall* are real. A s to whether they have been accurately translated as applied to the current church is a matter of opinion. First, both Nostradamus and Malachy predicted the line of Popes would end with the 112th. (In fact, a third seer, the Monk of Padua who lived in the eighteenth century also predicted the same line of Popes.

The quote attributed to Nostradamus in *The Belial Fall* is also real. He did predict that the Cardinal would murder a Pope, just as Malachy predicts that the Rome will be destroyed and there will be a judgment. And the current Pope is in fact the 112th.

There is debate about the third secret of Fatima. As mentioned in *The Belial Fall*, Sister Lucia did write a third secret and said it should not be opened until 1960. The Church opened it at that time but did not reveal its contents until 2000. In fact at one point they said they would never reveal it. In response, a man named Laurence Downey hijacked a plane in 1981 demanding the secret be revealed. The Church however, did not relent until 2000. The revelation left many disappointed and wondering why the Church had refused to reveal it.

Some even argued that what the Church revealed was false and that the true prophesy is what can be found inside *The Belial Fall*. For more information, click here.

Pope Joan. The Catholic Church denies that there was ever a female Pope. As mentioned in *The Belial Fall*, the time during which Pope Joan was alleged to have risen to the head of the Catholic Church was a time where hygiene was not a critical factor of everyday life. As a result, it would be possible for a woman to hide her gender even while living with men.

According to reports, the direct route between St. Peter's and the Pope's residence was avoided for close to a century following Pope Joan's death. There are statues of female Pope's within the Vatican and the tarot card for secret knowledge did indeed depict a female Pope.

The Great Schism. The Great Schism mentioned in the Prologue that split the Roman Catholic Church from its more orthodox members is true. It is a few decades after that that Pope Joan is alleged to have been Pope.

Iran's treatment of gay people. Sadly, everything in *The Belial Fall* depicting Iran's treatment of homosexuals is accurate. They can face death if their status becomes known.

The Vatican as a Country. The Vatican is in fact a full fledged country in its own right. The Vatican is the world's smallest country at only two square miles. Officially, it has only 600 citizens, although millions visit it annually. It also has its own television and radio stations, post office, banking and postal system, and newspaper. It even had its own police and security force.

The difficulties plaguing the Vatican bank are also true. Scandals wracked the financial arm of the Vatican's empire involving issues from Mafia links to insurance benefits involving Jews from the Holocaust, covering up abuses of Vatican spending, and even laundering money for the underworld and Italian elites.

The Obelisk at the Vatican. The obelisk that sits in St. Peter's square did in fact travel from Egypt. It was also at one point in the possession of both Caligula and Nero.

Underneath the Vatican. The Vatican had been built on the site of St. Peter's grave, although construction on the Church did not begin until the fourth century A.D. There are sections underneath the Vatican that are completely off limits to the public, the site of Peter's grave being one of them.

Women and the Church. Well, this is a slightly controversial subject. I have largely stayed away from any storylines involving the church because I did not wish to offend anyone in any way. But as we were moving along, I realized there was no way to avoid talking about the Church and it's view of women.

As with many people, after I read *The Da Vinci Code*, I became fascinated by the early church. As referenced in *The Da Vinci Code*, there is a great deal of research supporting the idea that Mary Magdalene was indeed the wife of Jesus and two that he intended for her to be the head of his church after his death.

St. Peter. The stories attributed to Peter are true, at least according to the Bible. He was not a fan of women or Mary Magdalene in particular. And the Vatican is believed to be built over his grave.

Pope John Paul I. There have been rumors that Pope John Paul I was murdered by the church. He was only in office for fifty-five days when he died. Pope John Paul I did claim that God was not only the Heavenly Father but also the Heavenly Mother. He supported women's rights and agreed to meet with a US delegation to discuss birth control

The night before his death he also allegedly asked for an investigation into the Vatican bank. He was found dead the next

FACT OR FICTION?

morning and his body was quickly embalmed and cremated. He is the only Pope to be cremated.

Castle San Angelo. The Castle is of course real. And the history depicted in The Belial Fall is real as well. It has at times been a home, a fortress, a prison, and a museum. There is also a tunnel leading from the Vatican to the castle through which at least one Pope had to escape.

Mary Magdalene. Mary Magdalene was never a prostitute. Pope Gregory the Great decided to link the two together even though there is nothing to suggest Mary was in fact the woman of ill-repute who bathed Jesus's feet. There is however a great deal to suggest that Mary was a wealthy woman and one who was viewed by Jesus as his equal. And of course, there is the argument that she was in fact his wife.

Brotherhood of the Eclipse of the Sun. The Brotherhood of the Eclipse of the Sun is completely fictitious.

Nuns and Aging. A study was done on nuns and aging. According to the researchers, the most significant factor helping stave off the effects of Alzheimer's was the intellectual activity level of the subject. Nuns who were more engaged intellectually with pursuits did not demonstrate behavior associated with the disease even though after death, it was clear they had the signs of the disease all over their brains. (Click here for a summary of the research or simply do a search for 'nuns and dementia study'.)

So what should we take from that? We all need to read more, think more, and eat our greens! (Greens were not specifically mentioned in this study, but ever other study on longer lifespans mentions it!)

Thank you again for reading *The Belial Fall*. I hope you have been enjoying reading about Laney's journey as much as I am enjoying writing it. And if you get a chance, I would appreciate it if you could leave a **review**. The pre-order page is also available for the last book in the series, *The Belial Sacrifice.*

If you'd like to hear about upcoming publications, gain access to exclusive content, and receive my monthly newsletter, sign up for my mailing list.

Thank you again.

Until next time,
R.D.

CHARACTERS OF THE BELIAL FALL

The Triad
Delaney McPhearson: Ring bearer with the power to control the weather, the Fallen, and animals
Jake Rogan: Former Navy SEAL, Laney's former love, Henry's best friend
Henry Chandler: Nephilim, Laney's brother

Laney's Allies
Yoni Benjamin: former Navy SEAL, Israeli born, married to Sascha Benjamin with whom he has a young son named Dov
Cain: the biblical Cain, who has been alive for thousands of years, anyone who harms him receives an injury seven times their intent.
Patrick Delaney: Laney's uncle, Roman Catholic priest, raised her since she was eight, born in Scotland
Drake: Las Vegas's Entertainer of the Year ten years running also archangel on sabbatical; was Achilles in the one life he lived as a human and he loved Helen of Troy (Laney) passionately
Rolly Escabi: teenage nephilim
Mustafa Massari: head SIA agent

Noriko: Jen's half sister, has visions and can communicate with animals, direct descendant of Lemurians

Lou Thomas: teenage Fallen

Gerard Thompson: formerly Elisabeta's right hand man until Victoria opened his eyes to his past lives. She helped him recall the time after the Fall when he had a family that Samyaza killed; formerly, Barnabus, close friend of Achilles and Helen of Troy

Danny Wartowski: teenage genius, started working at Chandler at age ten, head analyst, unofficial adopted son of Henry Chandler

Matt Clark: Fallen, Director of the Special Investigative Agency (SIA), under the auspices of the Department of Defense tasked with tracking and containing Fallen,

Jennifer Witt: Love of Henry Chandler, best friend of Delaney McPhearson, sister of Noriko, nephilim

Jordan Witt: Jen's brother, served with Jake in SEALs, operative with Chandler, Mike's twin

Mike Witt: brother of Jen, twin of Jordan, FBI agent

The Bad Guys

Elisabeta Roccorio: reincarnation of Samyaza

US Government

Nancy Harrigan: United States Secretary of State

Margaret Rigley: President of U.S.

Bruce Heller: Deputy Director of CIA

Moses Seward: former head of the Homeland Security's External Task Force, tortured Cain

David Okafor - CIA agent

Rahim Nabavi - David's partner

Stanton Calloway III - overseer of the Chandler group on behalf of the US government

Bart Shremp senator from Minnesota and chairman of the SEA

Chang Kim - David's assistant

Barbara Frankel - AEI agent on loan from Homeland Security

CHARACTERS OF THE BELIAL FALL

Roger Hennessy - AEI agent on loan from Homeland Security
Eric Brisbane - Vice President of the United States

The Church

Pope John Anglicus: tenth century Pope

Lucia: Pope John's servant

Ignatius: Pope John's main guard

Father Sebastian Gante (Bas): Priest sent by the Vatican to question Patrick

Sister Angelica Gante: Head of the Holy Order of Maternal Love

Sister Cristela: seventy-year old nun from El Salvador,

Sylvia Lecce: runs the kitchen of the orphanage in Italy along with her husband Rosario

Cardinal John Moretti: One of the top Vatican officials, the Pope's close friend, and head of the Brotherhood of the Labor of the Sun

Other Members of the Inner Circle of the Brotherhood: Cardinal Paul Tegano, Cardinal Antonio Ribraldi, Cardinal Luke Park, and Cardinal Francisco

Father Ezekiel- lower level member of the Brotherhood

The McAdams Family

Mary Jane: widowed mother, nurse

Joe:16

Shaun:15

Molly, 13, nephilim

Susie-2, kidnapped in *The Belial Plan*

Billy- deceased father and Fallen

* This list is not a complete list.

ABOUT THE AUTHOR

R.D. Brady is an American writer who grew up on Long Island, NY but has made her home in both the South and Midwest before settling in upstate New York. On her way to becoming a full-time writer, R.D. received a Ph.D. in Criminology and taught for ten years at a small liberal arts college.

R.D. left the glamorous life of grading papers behind in 2013 with the publication of her first novel, the supernatural action adventure, *The Belial Stone*. Over ten novels later and hundreds of thousands of books sold, and she hasn't looked back. Her novels tap into her criminological background, her years spent studying martial arts, and the unexplained aspects of our history. Join her on her next adventure!

To learn about her upcoming publications, sign up for her newsletter here or her website (rdbradybooks.com).

BOOKS BY R.D. BRADY

The Belial Series (in order)
The Belial Stone
The Belial Library
The Belial Ring
Recruit: A Belial Series Novella
The Belial Children
The Belial Origins
The Belial Search
The Belial Guard
The Belial Warrior
The Belial Plan
The Belial Witches
The Belial War
The Belial Fall
The Belial Sacrifice

Stand-Alone Books
Runs Deep
Hominid

BOOKS BY R.D. BRADY

The A.L.I.V.E. Series
    B.E.G.I.N.
    A.L.I.V.E.
    D.E.A.D.

The Unwelcome Series
    Protect
    Seek
    Proxy

Be sure to sign up for R.D.'s mailing list to be the first to hear when she has a new release!

Copyright © 2018 by R.D. Brady

The Belial Fall

Published by Scottish Seoul Publishing, LLC, Dewitt, NY

All Rights Reserved. No part of this book may be reproduced or transmitted in any form or by any means, electronic or mechanical, including photocopying, recording, or by any information storage and retrieval system without the written permission of the author, except where permitted by law.

Printed in the United States of America.

Made in United States
North Haven, CT
28 December 2023